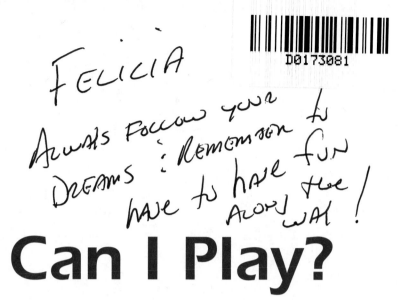

FELICIA
ALWAYS FOLLOW YOUR
DREAMS & REMEMBER to
HAVE to HAVE FUN
ALONG the
WAY !

Can I Play?

J. Dillard

7/3/07

StickyRocks Publishing

Tacoma, Washington
www.stickyrocks.com

This is a work of fiction. Names, characters, places, and incidents are either the product of the author's imagination or are used fictitiously. And any resemblance to actual persons, living or dead, business establishments, events, or locales is entirely coincidental.

StickyRocks Publishing
Tacoma, Washington

First trade publication May 2005
Third print February 20074
ISBN: 0-9768954-0-4

Printed in the United States of America

This book is dedicated to my wife Jodi
and all my children who have supported
me from the start.
Without your support this would still be
just a dream, today it's real...
Thank you!

Acknowledgements

Many people share in the credit for this book. Without them, Can I Play would not have been told.

First to Ted Wilson, my real mentor. I never got a chance to thank him for all he did for me so many years ago. Thank you, Coach. And I would like to thank all the hundreds of young people who have allowed me to coach them over the years. You are all a part of my story.

I would also like to thank Jerry and Connie Isgro for all they have done for me and my family. I hope one day to find a way to repay you. Your friendship, trust, and generosity are things I carry with me every day.

To my grandfather. I wish you were here to celebrate this with me. Many years ago, I watched you write a book about our family. I wish you could read mine. You are still my hero.

Thank you to my children Taylor, Megan, Allison, Trevor, Kaitlin, and Courtney for listening to my story over and over. And a special thanks to Sherri Canaday for allowing me to learn the game of volleyball from you over the years and for reading this book and giving me suggestions at a critical time.

Last to my wife Jodi. You figured out how to find the resources to make my dream come true. I adore you always.

I know I have forgotten many others. Thank you all. One last thanks and that is to God. You have blessed my life.

Peace be with you all...Thank you.

CHAPTER 1

A DOOR OPENS

"Excuse me. Aren't you Keli Stennes from Falls City?"

Keli turned around to the booth behind her. She studied the dark, curly-haired woman smiling at her. "Yes, I am," she said.

"I'm sorry I couldn't help but overhear you and your mom talking about signing up for the Dragon volleyball camp this summer. I'm Breanne Lindsay. I'm the head volleyball coach at Dallas High. I generally run the camp, but this year my head assistant Jim Edwards will be in charge. I can't attend this year."

Keli knew Lindsay had been a star player in college and had taken Dallas to the state tournament every year she could remember. "Yes, I'm thinking about going."

The coach stuck out her hand to Keli, "I hear you're quite the player."

Keli grinned as she grabbed the coach's hand to shake it. "Thanks, but I will never be the player you were."

Lindsay frowned slightly. "What makes you think you won't do the same thing?"

Shrugging her shoulders, Keli answered, "Not too many college recruiters make it out to Falls City."

Keli's mom reached her hand across the table. "Hi, I'm Cindy Stennes, Keli's mom."

The coach smiled, "It's really nice to meet you both." Then she reached across and gently tapped Keli's shoulder. "It would be fun to have you come to our camp this year and show some of my girls how it is done. Think about it, Keli. It would be good for your game to play against some strong competition." She smiled again and began turning away.

Keli turned back towards her mom and took a sip of her soda. She mouthed, "Mom, that's Coach Lindsay!"

Cindy laughed out loud. "Yes, I figured that out." Her look got serious. "It's a lot of money, but I think we can swing it if it's something you're really serious about. Wouldn't it be nice to see how you stack up against the kids from the bigger schools? Maybe now's the time to find out."

Keli Stennes lives in Falls City, a tiny town in the foothills of the Cascade Mountains. It's a tight-knit community of 800. Many of the families have lived there for generations. The little town's short main street nestles up to the Little Luckimutte River, and a hill runs up each side of town. On the upper end of town is its namesake, a beautiful 40-foot water fall that is the summer-time hangout for the locals.

The town's pride is its schools, and the school sports teams are the bonds that truly unite this little community. The triumphs, the what-ifs, the rivalries, the individual legends have given the town its identity although each year the townspeople have to fight and scrape to keep the school and their own history alive. With each graduating class, they wonder if it will be the last.

The thought of their kids going to school in Dallas, the nearby "big" city, would be a hard pill to swallow. It would mean an end to Friday nights on the playing field, an end to the caravans of cars following the buses to away games, and eventually all the old stories of greatness would fall silent.

Keli's father was a big part of this town's history. Even though Butch Stennes died in a logging accident when Keli was 3, he is still a huge icon in the tiny town. Butch led the Falls City Mountaineers to back-to-back state titles in both football and basketball in his junior and senior years. Keli has grown up hearing story after story about her dad.

Now Keli's generation has a chance to do the same for the school and the town in the coming two years in volleyball and basketball. Both the boys' and girls' teams are full of kids whose parents are from the legendary generation of athletes like Butch Stennes that the town is still talking about. The whole town is beaming about the possibilities.

Keli has grown up with a special group of friends. Sticky, the skinny, floppy-haired boy next door, is her best friend; and Charlee is her closest girlfriend and teammate.

Charlee's parents went to school with Keli's parents back in the 1970's and were the same best of friends as the kids are today. Along with Sticky and Charlee, a handful of others have all gone through school together. It's been a tight group of kids, at least until now.

For the rest of that afternoon, Keli sat at the desk in her cozy attic bedroom. Volleyball camp was the only thing she could think about. She picked up the summer camp flyer again and reread it even though she had memorized it. The last thing she wanted to do right now was study for another test, but tomorrow was her last day of finals and she knew she needed to focus on her studies.

Her bedroom window was wide open and when Sticky started the lawnmower, she was distracted again from the math book. She tried to refocus, but her mind wandered back to the camp and her conversation with Coach Lindsay. She glanced at the flyer again. "Okay, enough of this," she thought. She put the flyer down, got up, walked over to her door, and yelled down the stairs, "Hey, Mom! If you think we can afford it, I really would like to go to the camp."

Cindy was all curled up in her favorite chair reading. "Okay, sweetie, that's great. I'll get the money part worked out. Now, stop thinking about it and start studying. No camp if you don't do well tomorrow!"

Finals consumed the last day of school. Keli didn't have much of a chance to think about the camp. Sticky was the first one done with the last final, and he waited for everyone outside on the lawn. He was the tallest boy in the high school, and for a long time he had been one of the skinniest. Over the past year, he had been secretly working out trying to fill out the thin frame that had given him his charming nickname. Keli and the others had been oblivious to the emerging young hunk. He was still just her old friend, Sticky.

Charlee and Keli walked out a few minutes later. Their sophomore year was officially over! One by one, the rest of the group joined them on the lawn in front of the old ivy-covered brick building.

Grunts was the last of the gang to make his way out. Only a couple of years before he had been the undisputed leader of their tight group, but now he was barely hanging on. He had developed a new group of friends who had been making poor choices, and he had followed them into a lifestyle that took him away from his old friends.

Today, however, they were all together to celebrate the end of the school year, just as they had been for each of the past nine years. Charlee and Sticky truly are siblings for Keli. She thinks of their parents as her own, she never thinks about knocking when she goes to their houses, and she sleeps over at Charlee's without being invited. They are her extended family. The other kids in the group are tighter than most siblings.

Dan looked around at the bunch strewn about the lawn. "Hey! Let's go up to the falls!" he said suddenly. He could see the soon-to-be seniors all heading for their cars. Dan pointed at them, "If we want the high rocks, let's go!"

Charlee and Rachel piled in the front, and the rest jumped in the back of Dan's old pickup for the short ride up to the falls. As he drove down the small main street, Dan laid on the horn announcing the official end of their sophomore year. Right behind them were two cars of the new senior class trying to figure out how to get to the falls first.

Keli and Grunts were the first to jump out of the truck and they raced to the prized spot, the high rocks above the falls.

The sophomore class was proving to be a great class, academically and athletically. Beating the seniors to the rocks was another way to show the upperclassmen who was the best. Keli loved the rivalry. She made it to the high rocks at the top of the falls first, yelling to claim victory. And just as she was the first one to reach the rocks, she had subtly become the leader of the group over the past couple of years as Grunts fell away from them.

After about ten minutes, the bantering between the two classes finally died down. They all sat there, each on their own special rock, watching the water tumble down into the cove below the falls.

Keli looked around at her classmates and said, "So what is everyone doing this summer?"

No one answered. So she pointed at Tracie, "So, girl, what is on your calendar this summer?" Tracie was the historian of the class; she even looked the part with her small gold-rimmed glasses. She could remember everything that happened between their groups. She and Dan had been going out since the start of freshman year.

Tracie shook her head a little. "Not sure. We might go down to San Diego to see my dad's brother. Other than that trip, most likely hanging out up here. I wish I could find a job, but I don't have any way to get into town to get one."

Sticky looked towards Grunts, whose family called him Duane. "Hey man, do you remember when we used to hike up into Black Rock, spend the night, and hike back when our food ran out? Maybe we should do some camping again."

Grunts paused. He knew his answer wasn't going to be a hit with his friends. "Well, I think I am heading for Idaho with Blaine and Justin. Justin has a brother..."

Sticky had heard enough. "Damn, Grunts! When are you going to drop those dudes? They're bad news from the get-go. Neither is going to make it through school and if you hang with them..."

Grunts stood up. "What, Sticky...then *what*?"

Sticky stood up too. Then he picked up a rock and threw it down into the water. As it splashed Sticky looked around at the rest of the group, then back at Grunts. "Grunts, they're dragging you down the path to nowhere with them. Man, we had dreams. You have way too much going for you just to hand over your dreams to a couple of losers. That's what you're doing. You're just saying, 'Hey, you drive my life and wherever we end up, I guess that's what it's supposed to be.'"

He paused. Sticky was the conscience of the group. "Grunts, you should stay here, work out, and get ready for football next year." The two friends stood there staring at each other.

Charlee grabbed Grunts' hand and pulled him back down. He just sat there staring down at the water for a few seconds. "The truth is my grades suck and I am tired of school... I know I ain't going to college so what's the big deal? We are all just going to work in the woods or at the mill in town. I love you guys, but things for me are different." Then he directed the focus to Keli. "So Kels, what are you doing this summer?"

"Let me see," she thought for a few seconds. "Well, I'm going to volleyball camp in a couple of weeks. That is probably the highlight of my summer."

It was Charlee's turn to get upset. "Dang, Kels, what's this about volleyball camp? Why didn't you ask me to go?" Charlee never liked it if Keli planned something; they had grown up with Charlee in control, partly because Keli could rarely afford to do things and Charlee would at times use that on her. Actually it was how Charlee got control over most of the poorer kids in the community. She was quick to let Keli and others know how generous she was when she wasn't getting her way. Keli mostly ignored that and loved her anyway.

"I just decided to do it yesterday," Keli said matter-of-factly. "I was going to tell you today and see if you wanted to go too." She smiled at Charlee. "Chill, girlfriend, we can go together."

Charlee smiled back. Keli's answer was just what she wanted to hear. "I will ask my mom tonight when I get home." Then she frowned, "That will probably be my highlight too. I don't think we are going anywhere this summer. My dad's business is hurting pretty bad right now."

Sticky tossed another rock into the water. "I get to stay home and work at the store." His parents owned the local general store, Rodewald's Market. "From the sound of everyone's exciting descriptions, we are all totally lame."

Keli stood up and said, "Oh yeah, for those of you who have forgotten, tomorrow is my birthday. I emailed each one of you a list of things that I want. It would be cool if you would pick two or three things off the list and coordinate with everyone else so I don't get any duplicates. And as for a party, I think you guys could skip that and just take me into town for pizza and a movie or bowling."

Sticky quickly answered back. "How about we all throw in ten bucks so you have enough money to bribe the driver's license instructor tomorrow? You're going to need it."

That drew the loudest laugh of the day. Keli pushed out her lower lip in a pout and sat back down.

She looked around to see who hadn't answered the summer question yet. "Rachel, you haven't said what you're doing this summer."

Rachel looked at Charlee. She was the shyest one of the group. She had always used Charlee to help in the social arena. "I told you last night, remember?" She was still looking at Charlee.

"Yeah, but you haven't told anyone else," her friend said. Then just like she had for years, Charlee answered for her. "Get this! Rachel's grandparents are taking her to Europe for six weeks!"

Keli's mouth dropped open and Dan pleaded to go with her.

Sticky repeated, "And I have to stay here and work all summer."

Rachel spoke quietly, "I really hope that I can go over there and study after high school. My grandpa told me that they would pay if I want to go."

Keli was shocked. "I didn't know your grandparents were rich."

Rachel looked a little embarrassed. "Well, they aren't very rich, but they told me they are getting old and they would rather spend it then just give it to all their whiney kids."

Sticky busted up laughing. "Did they really say that?"

Rachel grinned and nodded her head.

Keli was still in shock. "Well, I'm going to have to get a scholarship to pay for school or go way into debt to do it. My goal is to get a scholarship playing volley-ball, but either way I am going."

Charlee sighed, "Keli, be realistic. You're good and all, but no one from here gets scholarships, you know that."

Keli stared at Charlee. "Well maybe not, but I'll do whatever it takes. I don't want to sound cocky, but I am going to do it. I am going to dedicate these next two years to making it happen somehow."

CHAPTER 2

KELI'S BIRTHDAY!

Keli hopped out of bed and started heading for the shower. Her appointment at the DMV was at 11:30. She could hear her mom singing "Happy Birthday." This was a tradition her mom had started when she was young. As soon as she heard Keli get up, she would start singing. When she was finished Keli yelled down, "Thanks, Mom. You're awesome!"

Cindy yelled back up, "Hurry up or we are going to be late!"

It didn't take Keli long to get ready. She rarely wore makeup and her thick shoulder-length brown hair was perfect for a quick ponytail.

The drive into Dallas was 12 miles of rolling hills and farmland. Keli had been on this road a thousand times but today was different. Today she was nervous as she drove the car towards town. She was ready, but still the nerves were doing cartwheels in her stomach. The last thing she wanted to do was fail her test and have to tell everyone. She was the last of her group to take the driving exam and everyone else had passed on their first try.

Cindy broke the silence. "I have a couple of things I want you to know."

Keli looked over at her mom, who quickly said, "I'll do the talking. You watch the road. Keli, I want you to know how proud I am of you. I want you to know I wouldn't let you have a driver's license if I didn't feel you were mature enough to handle it. For a while, I know each time you take the car, I'll be nervous and anxious until you get home. But I trust you and I know you will handle this huge responsibility properly."

She paused. "Also make no mistake. If you abuse this privilege in any way, you'll lose it 'til you're 18. That might sound harsh, but those are my rules."

Keli drove into the DMV and turned off the car; she reached across the seat and grabbed her mom very tight. "Mom, I love you. Thanks for being my mom."

A little over an hour later, Keli come racing through the front of the door of the DMV with a huge grin on her face. She didn't need to say anymore. Cindy gave her a simple nod as if to say, "I knew you would."

As they walked back to the car, Keli handed the keys to her mom. "I have been driving us around for the last year. Why don't you drive?" They both laughed.

"So, where do you want to go for your birthday lunch?" asked Cindy.

Without hesitation Keli said, "I want to go to the Pit."

"Wow! That surprises me!" said Cindy. "You generally avoid the Pit." Her mom smiled to herself as she drove towards the popular Dallas hangout.

The Pit was a 1950's-style burger place that was the local favorite for ice cream and shakes. Inside, it was packed with kids. They scanned the noisy restaurant and spotted a booth on the far side. As they ate lunch, Keli was focused on a table of girls. They all looked like athletes. She was startled when she looked over at Cindy, who had tears in her eyes. "I am so proud of you, young lady..."

Keli's eyes darted around to see who was watching their table. "Don't go there, Mom. This is the last place I want to get all teary-eyed." She glanced back at the table with the group of girls.

Cindy looked over too. "Do you know any of them?" she asked.

Keli shook her head. "Nope. I was just wondering how different their world is from mine."

Her mom stuck out her hands, inviting Keli to grab them. "Different for sure, but who is to say better? Things always look better from the other side of the window."

On their way back to Falls City, Cindy asked, "So what are you going to do with the rest of your day, birthday girl?"

Keli thought for a moment. "I'm guessing I'll get together with the gang. Maybe we can go to the movies or something. Usually by now we have something planned."

Cindy pulled the car into the driveway. "Go over and get Sticky moving. You two can get it figured out."

Keli jumped out of the car and headed straight for Sticky's house with her brand-new driver's license in hand. Janet, Sticky's mom, was going out the front door as Keli was coming in. Janet greeted her with a big hug. "Happy birthday, sweetie! By the looks of it, you got your driver's license. Sticky is up in his room. Knock on the door and make sure he is decent in there."

Keli wandered down the hall to the last door of the Rodewald's huge house. Instead of knocking, she burst right in and caught Sticky by surprise. He was just covering his easel.

Sticky quickly turned around, standing in front of the covered easel. "Hey, ever heard of knocking first? So what's up, anyways?"

"What's up?" Keli raised her voice. "What's up," you asked?" She held out her license. "This is up. No bribery needed!" as she waved it in Sticky's face. He laughed and gave her a high five.

Keli loved Sticky's room. He loved to draw and paint, and he had drawings everywhere, even ones from when he was very little. She loved to look at his work. Some were nature scenes of places they had hiked many times, some were cartoons, and some were of their gang.

It had been a while since she had been in his room. She noticed a couple of new ones. Keli eyed the one under cover. "So, can I look at this one?" She walked toward the covered easel.

Sticky stopped her in the middle of the room. "When it's done, you can see it."

He stood between her and the easel.

Keli respected his wishes and backed off towards his bed. "Hey, no worries, Stick! Your picture is safe. I'll wait 'til you're ready to show me, but you have to promise I get to be the first one to see it."

He smiled. "I promise." He changed the subject. "So, what do you want to do tonight?"

Keli flopped down on his bed and shook her head. "That's why I'm here. It's your job to figure it out for me."

Sticky laughed. "Right, it's always been my job, but today is your birthday, so you pick!"

"Nope," said Keli. "Call me when you have my birthday planned out." She gave him a quick smile and a wink and headed for the stairs. Her thoughts went to Charlee. She turned and sprinted through the small Christmas tree field between their two houses. "Mom, can I take the car to Charlee's house? I want to show her my license and get my present."

Keli grabbed the keys and raced out the door. A few minutes later, she walked back in.

Cindy had a puzzled look on her face. "That was quick. What did you get from Charlee for your birthday?"

Flopping on the couch, Keli said, "Well, I guess Charlee is hanging out with Rachel and Tracie." For the first time in a long time, she felt rejected. Charlee always called her first to do things. "Mom, were there any messages for me when we got home?"

Cindy poked her head out from the kitchen, "No, sweetie."

Keli pulled herself up and went into the kitchen. "So why do you have to work today?"

Cindy frowned, "It's supposed to be my day off but Jack called. Lucille can't work. Hank got hurt at work and she needs to be home to baby him."

Just then, the phone rang. It was Charlee on the other end. "I hear the roads aren't safe any more, is that true?"

"Very funny. Where were you? I stopped by your house a little while ago and you weren't there. What's up with that? It's my birthday and you don't invite me to hang out with you?"

"Hey, sorry I wasn't here. Mom said you stopped by. Tracie and Rachel came over and wanted me to go into town with them. We should have called you to see if you wanted to go."

"Oh, don't worry about it. I didn't get back from the DMV until an hour or so ago."

The jealousy of not being invited quickly faded from Keli's thoughts. "Sticky is figuring everything out for tonight. You should call him and help him out."

"I already did. He told me pizza first, then the movies," answered Charlee.

Keli heard the back door open. Sticky's voice rang out. "Hey! How am I supposed to call you if you're on the phone?"

Charlee could hear Sticky yelling in the background, "Okay, girl, sounds like Sticky is barking...see ya in a while."

Keli put down the phone. "Sorry, it was Charlee. Do I need to say anymore?"

Sticky smiled. "Are you ready to go?"

"Uh, how 'bout no?" answered Keli. "I need to get ready. Come back in a half hour or watch some TV." She didn't wait for his answer but raced up the stairs.

Sticky yelled up the stairs as she shut the bedroom door. "I'll be back in 15 minutes. Be ready!"

She looked at the clock. "Okay, 15 minutes!"

When she heard Sticky's noisy car start up, she jumped up and added the final touch to her jeans and pale green tank top, a green-and-yellow University of Oregon Duck hat. Then she raced down the stairs and met him in the driveway.

As he pulled up, he didn't miss the opportunity to comment on her clothes. "It's great to see you get dressed up for the big night out."

Keli didn't respond. She had dressed this way forever and he always teased her. As they pulled up in front of Charlee's, Sticky didn't shut off the engine. "You go get her. I bet you she's not ready yet."

"No way dude, shut it off. You're coming with me. It will take two of us to get her away from the mirror."

They both ran inside without knocking. "So Mother Kay, where is she?" asked Keli.

Kay, Charlee's mother, was at the computer. She smiled and pointed upstairs. "Where do you think she is?"

Sticky yelled from the bottom of the stairs, "Hey Charlee! Let's go!"

"Come on up. I'm not ready yet", was the reply.

Keli ran up the stairs and opened the bedroom door to an explosion. The whole room erupted into "SURPRISE!" The bedroom was full of what seemed like the entire school, all singing "Happy Birthday."

As they all walked down the stairs, Charlee was laughing and saying, "We really didn't go into town. We were here the whole time. We were in the backyard putting up decorations."

Keli looked over at Kay, who was smiling broadly. The plan had worked perfectly.

Charlee pushed Keli towards the backyard. When they made it to the back deck, Keli ran into the second wave of "SURPRISE!" There were as many people waiting in the back yard as had been piled into the bedroom.

The first to greet her on the back porch was her mother. "Mom, I thought you were at work."

Cindy winked at her "I don't have to go in 'til later."

Sitting over by the food was her grandpa Tom. She went over and gave him a hug.

Keli looked around. There must have been a hundred people. For a town the size of Falls City, a crowd that size said quite a bit. The music started to blare and people were filling up plates of food and looking for places to sit.

Keli was in a happy shock. It was the first time she had ever had a surprise party. Charlee whispered in her ear, "Did we get you? Did you have any idea?"

Keli punched Charlee's arm in embarrassment, and her friend she knew she had gotten her.

Over by the cake was a small table with a few presents on it. Charlee yelled to all to gather around to watch Keli cut the cake and open up her gifts. The last present she opened was a new volleyball from Charlee. Keli's eyes brightened. Her ball was worn out.

"Hey, let's play a little!"

Charlee interrupted her. "Just a minute," she said as she looked over at Sticky. "It's your turn."

Keli spun around to see Sticky standing behind her. Keli noticed Sticky was standing in front of his easel. He seemed nervous as he looked over at Keli and then at the rest of the group. Keli's eyes went from the easel to Sticky and back to the easel again. Keli started to walk over a bit closer.

Sticky was really nervous and he stuttered a bit. "I...I...thought I'd draw you a picture of your two favorite things together." He stared back at Keli for a second and then with his other hand slowly dropped the cover off his drawing.

The whole crowd went silent as they stared at his drawing. When he turned back to Keli to see her response, his friend had tears running down her cheeks. Someone in the crowd called out, "My God, how pretty is that?"

The drawing was of Keli standing on her favorite rock above the falls dressed pretty much like she was right then. She was looking down at the water with a volleyball under each arm. There she was as big as life.

Keli walked straight to Sticky and gave him a hug like none he'd ever had before. She whispered in his ear, "Thank you so much. It is truly beautiful."

The party dwindled down over the next hour. It was time to say goodbye one more time to Charlee. "Words can't express how awesome you are," said Keli, with a hug of thanks.

Charlee smiled, "You're worth it!"

Sticky helped her gather up all the presents. Keli took the drawing and Sticky had the rest. It was late and they were both tired. There wasn't much said between them.

When they got everything into the house, Keli was glad to see her mom home from work. She realized that her mom hadn't seen the picture that Sticky had drawn. When she unveiled it for her, she too cried and gave Sticky a motherly hug.

As they walked back to the car, Keli gave him another hug. Sticky was a bit embarrassed; he was used to getting high five's. As he got into the car, she asked, "If you're not doing anything this weekend, it would be cool if you could work out with me to help get me ready for camp."

Sticky was still thinking about the hugs. "Yeah, sure, call me and we will get it figured out."

When she got back inside, Cindy was looking at the picture. She looked at Keli and said, "I can't believe how gifted an artist he is. That looks just like you."

They were both amazed at the colors and how well he had captured the falls. And he had made Keli look almost superhuman as she stood there on her rock.

Cindy looked at Keli and asked quietly, "Do you realize that is the image he has of you?"

"I don't understand," said Keli.

"Look at the picture," her mother replied. "He sees you as strong, confident, bold, and most of all, beautiful."

Keli stared at the picture. She was almost embarrassed by it now. She looked back at her mom. "Do you really think so?"

Cindy gave a little smile. "Yes, I do."

Leaning over, Keli kissed her mom. "Thank you for everything." She headed for the stairs.

"Hey, do you want one more present? I wanted to give it to you earlier, but we ran out of time." She was holding a black satin pouch.

Keli walked over and took it from her. Cindy looked her daughter in the eye. "Before you open it, I want to say I wish I could give you everything you ever wanted in life but with the way things are, sometimes the best I can do is share with you what I have."

Opening the pouch, Keli pulled out a set of car keys.

Her mom's eyes softened and her voice cracked at bit. "As of today, the car is yours as much as it is mine. I want to share it with you. I wish I could give you your own, but I can't. You can call it your car and I'll come to you as you'd come to me to ask to use it. As of today we share it."

Keli was overwhelmed, "I love you, Mom." As she gave her another hug, she whispered, "You're the best!"

She grabbed the keys, the satin pouch, and her picture and headed to her room. She leaned the picture against the wall, laid her satin pouch down on her desk with her keys on top of it, and fell into bed. She had just had the best day of her life.

CHAPTER 3

A BREAKFAST OF NERVES

Keli spent the next three days running the local hills and doing crunches by the hundreds. She had only a few days to prepare for volleyball camp. Charlee was a no-show for the workouts; she had to help her parents with their struggling logging business.

By the second day, Sticky was afraid to go outside or to answer the phone because he knew it would be Keli asking him to go with her one more time down and up the hill.

Monday finally came. The hardest decision was choosing which shirt to wear. She went back and forth between a Mountaineer shirt and a plain old tank top. Finally the Mountaineer shirt won out.

When Cindy came into the kitchen, she started laughing. Watching Keli frantically making her lunch and mumbling to herself, she asked, "You need some help?"

Keli nodded. "How 'bout some breakfast? That would be a huge help."

"You know Keli, it's just a volleyball camp. It's not the state championship. You should try and relax and just have some fun." Her mother stood at the counter calmly buttering toast. "What time do you have to be there?"

"About 9," answered Keli, chewing through a piece of toast.

Her mom shook her head. The clock read 7:30. "Slow down, girl, you've got plenty of time. You don't have to be there for an hour and a half."

Keli took another huge bite. "I don't know if I've ever been this nervous before, Mom."

"You are going to do just fine, sweetie." Cindy sat down across from her. "Are you more nervous driving by yourself or going to play volleyball against the other girls?"

Keli reached for a box of cereal, "I don't know for sure, probably playing against the other girls."

Cindy looked at her. "Well, I remember when your dad used to play, and your grandpa would tell him the only way to get over the nerves was to keep talking about it and not let it build up inside you. Then when it's time, just play your butt off!" Cindy started to laugh. "I can remember Tom telling Butch that before every big game." Her eyes wandered off into the past. Then she forced a grin. "He would be very proud of you. I know his spirit burns inside of you. You remind me of him nearly every day."

A half-hour later, Keli grabbed her bag and headed for the door. Keli started the Honda and looked in the rearview mirror as she'd been taught. She was startled by a shadow flashing across the rear window. Sticky was standing there out of breath.

"Dang dude, you should work out more if you're breathing that hard." She laughed as she rolled down the window.

Sticky nodded. "I just wanted to come over and say..." he paused for a second.

"I just came over here to tell you not to kill anyone on your way into town." He gave a huge grin.

Keli couldn't help but laugh again. "Right! I'll do my best. Let's talk tonight." As she backed up, she yelled out the window, "Hey, did I tell you how much I really like my picture?"

As she drove through downtown Falls CityKeli realized that she was all alone. She scanned the sidewalks and driveways hoping to see someone she could show off her driving to. She drove by the high school and took a long look at the gym, the gym she thought of as her own. She realized as the car left town that she was heading for a new gym, but what she didn't realize yet was that she was embarking on an adventure that was going to change her life.

CHAPTER 4

CHARLEE STARTS—AND QUITS

The 12-mile drive into Dallas was uneventful, but as Keli approached the high school, all her nervousness came back. She brought the car to a stop in the gym parking lot and sat there frozen in her seat staring out the window.

Finally, she turned off the car. She could hear other girls' voices as she watched them head towards the gym entrance. Something came over her and she sat up straight and said out loud, "Okay, it's time to be me."

With her backpack over her shoulder, Keli headed into the gym and over to the registration table. The coach not even glancing up just said, "Name, please?"

"Keli Stennes."

The coach scanned the list, found her name, checked it off, and without looking up asked her T-shirt size.

"Medium."

The coach reached over, grabbed a medium, and for the first time made eye contact with her. "You're the kid from Falls City Coach Lindsay was telling me about."

"I am."

He stuck out his hand and said, "You can call me Jim. I'm one of Coach Lindsay's assistants and I am pleased to meet you."

Keli gave a big grin and shook his hand. "Pleased to meet you, sir."

"Okay, go into the gym and soon as you go through the doors, turn right. They're going to measure you and put you through a couple of jumping drills just to get an idea of some initial stats before the camp starts."

Opening the door was like walking into a whole new world. There were at least a hundred girls walking around, standing in groups talking, all waiting for the camp to start. Keli walked over to the next station.

Again, "Name please?" That in itself was foreign as she was used to everyone knowing her name. Another assistant had her stand next to the height chart. "5'11"," he called out.

Keli looked back at the chart; she didn't realize that she had grown an inch and a half since last season. "Are you sure?" she asked.

The assistant smiled and said, "Yep, I am looking right at it." Then sitting down, he said, "Over here you'll see a series of pegs. I want you to try to jump up and touch the highest one you can reach."

The nerves came back again because she hadn't even started to warm up. The coach sensed her apprehension and said, "Don't worry. None of the girls got to warm up. We're just trying to get a base on how well you jump."

Keli stared up at the staggered pegs, crouched down, took a deep breath, and exploded off the floor, barely flicking the top peg. The coach stood up. "Do that again," he said.

Keli again crouched and jumped, this time missing the top peg but getting the next peg down. The two assistant coaches looked at each other. Then the first one said, "Very good, Stennes. Go over and start stretching. Coach Jim will be ready to start here in a few minutes."

Keli walked over towards the middle of the gym wondering how well the other girls had done in the jumping. As she scanned the room, she noticed that the girls ranged from really young all the way through seniors. As she sat on the gym floor, stretching her calves, she scanned the floor looking for Charlee. A loud whistle echoed through the whole gym.

All the girls jumped up as Coach Jim came into the gym. He asked everybody to sit down on the bleachers. As she sat down, Keli made another quick scan for Charlee and noticed a few girls were staring back at her.

Coach Jim divided the girls by ages, asking the juniors and seniors to go to the far end of the gym and the freshman and sophomores to stay where they were.

As Keli walked towards the far end of the gym, she noticed that girls from as many as ten different area high schools were wearing their school colors. She looked down at her yellow T-shirt with FC Volleyball printed in purple, wondering if there were any players from her league. She was also amazed by the fact that there were four volleyball courts set up. In Falls City they had room for just one. She scanned the group again hoping to recognize anyone, but no luck. She looked back at the entrance wondering what had happened to Charlee.

The whistle blew. It was time for the first drill. Keli moved up the line ready to make her first pass. As the ball came towards her, she could feel eyes watching her. It was critical to make a good pass on the first try. She got down low and made a good platform and passed the ball perfectly back to the girl across from her.

Her mind was only partly on what she was doing and the rest of it was wondering where Charlee was. For the next 15 minutes or so, they continued this drill. The line seemed to move quicker and quicker, and each time it was Keli's turn she made a good pass. At the end of the first drill, most of the nerves Keli had been feeling at the start were gone. She was just playing volleyball, which she loved.

As they moved into the next passing drill, she saw Charlee across the gym talking to one of the other coaches. Her heart started to race as she realized that she finally had a friend there.

The next drill was significantly harder. The coaches were hitting down balls instead of easy free-ball passes at the players, and they were yelling to call for the ball.

Keli's mind was still distracted. She kept looking for Charlee, and this time her lack of concentration caught up to her. She shanked the ball to the right for her first error of the day.

The error snapped her out of her lack of focus. She made eye contact with the coach, who just nodded at her as if to say, "Come on. Get into what you are supposed to be doing."

Keli got her concentration back. She realized this wasn't about Charlee and put her out of her mind. She zoned in on the drills the coaches were running them through, and her next three passes were excellent. It seemed that the coach was hitting the ball harder and harder at Keli to see what she had.

This excited her, and she couldn't wait for her next opportunity. Over the next hour, Keli seemed to handle the drills perfectly. At the same time, when it wasn't her turn, she watched closely comparing herself to some of the other players. As the morning drills went on, Keli got more and more excited because she knew that she had the ability to play with these girls.

Finally, after about an hour and a half, they had their first break. Charlee was still standing by the entrance, and Keli bee-lined her way over to her with her palms in the air. "Where were you? Why were you late?"

Charlee looked around to see who might be listening to the conversation before answering. She even looked a little embarrassed. She stammered and then said, "I had a flat tire and had to wait for Dad to come and fix it. Why are you yelling at me anyways? You know, Keli, sometimes..." she didn't finish what she was going to say.

Keli toweled off her sweaty face and asked, "So are you ready to play some? Our coach had us moving pretty fast and hard. They don't mess around and all the girls are really awesome players. It's amazing"

Charlee looked around the gym. "Well, I think it's a bad idea just being here. These girls are better than both of us. All we are going to do is embarrass ourselves." She dropped her bag on the floor. "This is what happens when I let you plan things." She picked up her backpack again and looked at Keli.

Keli stood there stunned at Charlee's suggestion. Then she looked back at the floor. The coaches were walking towards the stations. She looked back at Charlee and said, "Leave if you want, but I want to be here."

Charlee glared, turned, and walked out of the gym.

The rest of the morning was filled with drills and as each one was completed, Keli felt stronger and stronger. By lunchtime, she was sky-high. She knew that she was as good or better than most of the players on her court.

For most of the lunch hour, Keli sat by herself and ate her lunch. She could see the kids had bunched together mainly by school. When she finished her lunch, she walked over to the trash can to throw the empty bag away. Two Dallas Dragon players met her there.

The blonde had the whitest teeth Keli had ever seen. She introduced herself as Ashley and her friend as Greta. Keli thought that Ashley could be a model; her features were that perfect.

Keli smiled back and wiped her hand off on her shirt before she stuck it out for Ashley and Greta to shake. "Hi. My name is Keli, Keli Stennes." Her voice cracked a little from nerves.

Greta was taller than Keli by a couple of inches. Her long black hair was pulled back into a ponytail. Her dark hair contrasted against her milky white skin.

Keli's eyes got stuck on Greta's exposed belly button. It was pierced and had a dangly silver chain hanging down about an inch.

Ashley noticed Keli staring. "It's ugly, isn't it?" She laughed, "I think it's ugly!"

Keli frantically tried to come up with the right answer. The last thing she wanted was to say the wrong thing right now. "Uh no, it's kinda cool." She looked back up at Greta. "Did it hurt to get it done?"

Greta grabbed the silver chain and gave it a little tug. "A little when I first got it, but it was worth it...the guys love it."

Ashley looked almost disgusted. "The wrong guys, that is."

Keli started to laugh. "You two fight like sisters, but you don't look anything alike. It's nice to meet you both. Who do you play for?"

"Dragons," answered Greta, who started to brag. "Ashley here has been on the Varsity since she was a freshman, and she is the best setter in the state! I play middle and have to beg her to set me."

Keli looked back at Ashley and her bright white teeth. "I'd love a chance to play some. I have never really gotten to hit off a real setter before."

"Do you play out in Falls City?" Ashley was pointing at Keli's T-shirt.

"Yeah, I have been out there my whole life."

"Very cool," answered Ashley. "Well, hey, I am going to stretch and get ready for this afternoon. It was nice to meet you."

The afternoon was filled with team-oriented drills. It didn't take long for Keli to forget the troubles she'd had earlier with Charlee. At the mid-afternoon break, the coaches announced that they would be putting together scrimmage teams for a mini "league" competition. Friday would be the championship game; the winning team would receive water bottles. Coach Jim added that the staff would be picking camp all-stars after the final scrimmage game. That put Keli right over the top on the excitement meter.

When the scrimmage came, Keli was put on a team with Ashley. The day just kept getting better, Keli thought.

Ashley did everything she could to get the ball to Keli whenever she could throughout the scrimmage. She was amazed how high Keli could jump, and she was equally surprised how much work her approach needed. After each play, Ashley would whisper pointers to her.

Keli was soaking it up. She loved the level of competition and was completely in awe of Ashley's abilities.

When the match was over, they had won both games. Keli was grinning ear to ear as she congratulated each of her teammates.

During the ride back to Falls City, Keli thought about the scrimmage and what it was like playing with Ashley.

Keli pulled in front of the Falls City restaurant. She could see her mom was having a slow night. There was only one customer sitting at a table.

She burst through the front door almost walking on air. Her mom could tell that she had had a great day. "Hey honey," she said. "It looks like some young lady went in and showed the big girls what it was all about today."

Keli grinned. "Not exactly, but it was the best day ever! I met a couple of girls from Dallas, and one of them was the most amazing player I've ever seen. Mom, you have to watch her play...she is awesome! And there were at least a hundred girls from ten different schools. All of them were good players too."

Then Keli paused. "Mom, did you see Charlee this afternoon?"

Cindy grimaced. "Kay called me and told me that she didn't even try to play. What happened?"

"Well, she was late getting there. I guess she had a flat tire on the way in. We were taking our first break when she got there. She immediately got all mad; you know how she can be sometimes. Well, the next thing I know she is telling me to leave with her. She got all hot, saying we weren't good enough and told me we should just go." She leaned up against the counter, "I think she is mad at me now because I stayed, but Mom, it was total fun and I learned a lot. I can't wait for tomorrow!"

She grinned. "I think I played pretty good, Mom. My team won our scrimmage games and even some of the players from Dallas came up to me and told me how well I did. I don't care if Charlee is mad at me. I like playing with them."

Cindy smiled, "Well, I guess you're glad that you made the decision to go then?"

Keli grinned, "I sure am. Okay, I'm going home and calling Charlee. I know she is going to be mad, but you know Mom...I'm getting kind of tired of her acting like that. She has this idea that if it's not good for her, then it's not good for any of us."

"Okay sweetie, try not to get into a fight with her about it," said Cindy. "And don't worry about picking me up after work...Kay is going to take me home. We are going to the coast this weekend and we want to make plans. I talked to your gramps about you staying with him. Are you okay with that?"

"Sure, Mom. I love it when I stay there. He spoils me."

"Oh really? Is this coming from a young lady who left the kitchen a mess this morning, didn't make her bed, forgot it was trash day, and..."

Keli ended the barrage waving a napkin like a white flag. "Do I need to call Gramps or anything?"

"Actually, I asked him if he could give you a ride to volleyball the rest of the week. I am working double shifts this week so I can have some spending money for the weekend. Do you mind?"

"No worries. I'll call him and confirm." Keli struggled off the stool. Her legs had tightened. "I understand about the car. It's cool that Gramps can take me."

When she walked into the house, the phone was ringing. She knew it would be Charlee.

Charlee started right in on her. "So how did it go? I want you to know I thought you were wrong for not supporting me today."

Keli couldn't believe what she just heard. "What 'support' you? I was the one who wanted to go to this in the first place, remember? Come on Charlee, you didn't even give it a chance. You walked in there mad and left without even trying. What's up with that?"

Keli started to speak again, but Charlee wasn't going to let her. "Listen Keli, it's different for you. I would rather hang out at the falls and not waste my time with some pipe dream that has no value. We are fine where we are. Sometimes I don't think you get it. I have already told my dad that I'm not going back. He agrees with me."

She knew Charlee well enough to know there was no changing her mind. "Okay, maybe we can hook up this weekend, I am going to be at Gramps house. I heard our moms are going out of town."

Charlee was short. "I guess we'll talk then."

Keli felt sad when she hung up the phone. Then she shook it off and thought about her day and the new kids she'd met. It was one of the best sports days of her life. The taste of that level of competition intoxicated her.

CHAPTER 5

SUMMER CAMP CAMARADERIE

The second day of camp was even better than the first. The thought of Charlee didn't even come up, and with each drill Keli's confidence and ability grew. The gym was loud, the kids all worked hard, and the enthusiasm was everywhere. The coaches all knew her name. Keli loved every minute of it; it was a new level that she hadn't even known existed.

The day seemed to fly by ending with her favorite part, the scrimmage games. Just like the first day, Ashley and Keli made for a formidable combination. Ashley continued to lead the team and coach Keli on the fly. There seemed to be a bond between the two, a chemistry that sometimes just happens between players. They easily won both games and now were the team to beat.

Greta's team also had won both of their games, too. She yelled across the gym, "Hey Stennes. Your team doesn't have a chance against us come Friday when we play you."

Keli looked at Ashley, and then yelled back…"Get serious. I have her on my team," pointing at Ashley and laughing."

Ashley bowed to Keli, then gave her a high five. She whispered quietly to Keli, "Careful. She has Trish Gammons on her team who is like all-world or something. We don't want to get too cocky with them."

The camaraderie was building between them. Keli loved it…the bantering, the competition, and most of all, the acknowledgement from her new peers.

Tom hobbled over towards them. Ashley asked, "So is that your dad?"

Keli grinned, "No, it's my grandpa."

"Dang, the old dude is tall," came from Greta.

"Yeah," answered Keli, "he's like 6'5" or something." When Tom got to them, Keli made the introductions to her new friends. They chatted a bit and headed out.

The ride back to Falls City was filled with Keli's chatter, telling her gramps all about the past couple of days. "Gramps, it's amazing playing with all these really good players. The games are so much more fun. I am learning so much…I never realized how little I really knew about the game."

Tom waited for Keli to take a breath and quickly asked, "So what happened with Charlee?"

Keli looked at him. "You know Gramps, I am really getting tired of the way she treats me. She decided to quit even before she tried it and got mad when I didn't quit with her."

He adjusted his cap and pondered both what Keli said and how she said it. "Well, sounds like maybe you two are starting to separate a little…it's kind of a natural thing at your age. Maybe sports isn't as high on her list as it is on yours."

Keli stared out the window, watching the sheep grazing in the field. She had never given any thought to the possibility that she and Charlee might move in different directions. Her mind slipped back to earlier in the day and how much fun it was playing.

Tom broke her daydreaming. "So are you ready for a weekend with your old Gramps?"

She turned back towards him. "Yep. Are you going to make a big pot of chili like you normally do?"

He smiled and nodded as they entered into Falls City.

As they drove by Rodewald's Market, Sticky was standing outside talking to Dan. Keli said quickly, "Gramps, can you just drop me off here. I'll see you in the morning same time, okay?"

Keli hopped out of the old Jeep and ran across the street. "So, looks like you're working hard as usual. Your parents actually pay you?"

Sticky ignored the teasing. "I hear you dumped Charlee the other day. She said it sucked over there and you wouldn't leave with her."

"What?" Keli was ready to blow up. "That sounds like something she would say. Forget it. I am not going to talk about it. Charlee is..." she paused and didn't finish what she wanted to say. "Hey, I'm going home."

She took off towards the pedestrian bridge that crossed the river. "Sticky, if you're not too tired after work, give me a call and let's watch a movie or something." She turned around smiling. "Oh yeah, Dan, it was nice talking to you too."

CHAPTER 6

COME PLAY WITH US!

The sun was shining through the window when Keli woke up. She lay there for a second. All she could think about was playing. Then she stared across the room at the picture Sticky had drawn for her birthday, as the sun was shining directly on it. That seemed a happy omen.

She received a warm welcome at the gym. Coach Jeff, a short Asian coach and a favorite with the girls, greeted her first. "Hey, everyone, we can start. Keli is here!"

Ashley and Greta walked in behind her. "Hey, everybody," echoed Ashley. "I hear Keli is transferring to Dallas this fall and playing with us."

Everyone within earshot looked at her. Keli blushed

Ashley winked at her as she walked by. "Some of us have been talking, and we think it's a good idea. So tonight when you go home, tell your mom and dad the news."

The morning drills were the same. The girls were all getting more comfortable with each other, and there was a little more bantering between them. Just before lunch, Coach Jim, Lindsay's top assistant, called over Keli and a few other hitters who were having trouble with their approaches and timing to work with him. Jim stood out, nearly 6'6" and very large. There was nothing skinny about him. His dark eyes and beard added to his intimidating look—until you heard him talk. His voice was very soft; it definitely didn't fit the rest of him.

After about 20 minutes of the help-session, he sent them back to rejoin the drills. Keli waited until the others left. "Coach, can I ask you a question?"

He looked over at the drills going on, then answered, "Why don't you save your question until lunch? I really think you should go work on what we just talked about."

"Sure thing, Coach," she started to jog towards her court.

Jim called out, "Hey, Stennes."

Keli stopped and turned around, "You really need to get your approach down. There is a tremendous attacker inside that body of yours. Your brain just needs to teach your body what to do."

Keli smiled at the compliment.

When the morning drills ended, Keli quickly grabbed her lunch and headed for Coach Jim.

The soft-spoken giant smiled at her eagerness. "So, what's on your mind?"

Keli was nervous, "Well, first, I've never really played on the outside. I generally play in the middle for my school."

Jim picked a piece of sandwich out of his dark beard. "How about for your club team? Do you play middle for them too?"

Keli looked confused. "'Club team'? We don't have a club for volleyball in Falls City."

Jim looked over at Jeff, who was listening to the conversation. "Anyways, about your question."

Keli sat down on the bleachers just below where the coaches were sitting and looked up at them. "Well, I think I get what you're saying about the steps, but the part I don't understand is how do I figure out when to start. The setter is all over the place. I can't seem to figure out how long it's going to take for the ball to get into the hitting zone you coaches have been talking about all week. I am really trying but I seem to be either early or late and it's driving me crazy." She dropped her head. "I don't get it...some of these girls make it look so easy."

Jim looked at her, "First off Keli, have patience with yourself. It's a whole new world out there. Give yourself some time to learn it. I think the best thing you can do is watch every set while you're waiting in line for your chance. Pretend like you're the hitter every time. Remember what I said earlier about your brain teaching your body what to do. This is what I am talking about. When you're in line you need to work on visualizing the set coming towards you, tell yourself mentally what to do and picture yourself going through the whole process each time. Just keep working at it. One of these days you will make it look easy too."

"Keep your head up. It will come in time," added Jeff. "You jump better than anyone here. It's going to be scary when you get it all figured it."

Keli's face darkened. "I hope so...but I only have a couple more days to learn it. When I get back home, it's not something that I will get much of a chance to work on."

She walked across the gym. Most of the girls were outside lying in the sun. It wasn't the answer she had been looking for. She sat on the floor and stared around the gym at the many banners hanging from the rafters. She marveled at the run of league championships Dallas had had in volleyball over the past half-dozen years. Her mind went to Ashley's comments at the start of the day.

She played with the idea of changing schools for a few seconds until the thought of Sticky and Charlee overran the idea. She sat up trying to put it all out of her mind. Sounds of the players coming back into the gym helped her snap out of it.

The whistle blew and the afternoon session kicked in. So did Keli. The only thing on her mind was playing well. Coach Jim's comment was planted right in the middle of her thoughts, and she watched everything. She started to understand a little about what he was saying. She could see and quickly tell when other players were too slow or too quick. She started to get a feel for the timing.

The last drill before the scrimmage session was a 3-on-3 Queen of the Court with setters. Beside the scrimmage, it was Keli's favorite drill as it was for most of the others. Ashley and Trish were the setters. Keli's group was the last to rotate in; she came in on Ashley's side of the net.

Ashley looked at Keli as if to say, "Be ready." Sure enough, Ashley took the pass and lofted a perfect set. Keli saw it perfectly and for the first time really did everything correctly. Her approach and timing were right on, and she exploded off the floor and zinged the ball cross-court for a winner!

"Yes," yelled Ashley, "nice play!"

Keli glanced over at Coach Jim as she ran under the net and got ready to play from the queen side.

Jim gave her a small grin, and Coach Jeff yelled like always, "Great play, Stennes!"

Her mind was racing. It was like her first taste of chocolate cake, and she wanted more.

When the drill ended, all the girls were sweating. It was hot in the gym, and Keli went straight for her water bottle. Ashley went straight for Keli, "So have you thought about what I said this morning?" She looked around to see if anyone was listening. "Why don't you come to Dallas in the fall? It would be great! Keli, you're really becoming an awesome player and..." Ashley hesitated.

A grin was cemented to Keli's face. "And what?"

Ashley's face turned a bit red with embarrassment. "Okay, okay," she answered. "I really like the way our friendship has grown these past few days. It would be great to have you around. Besides all that, Coach Lindsay is the best coach in the state. She could really help your game. I can tell you really want to become a better player. I'm not knocking Falls City, but I don't think you can get much better out there."

The whistle blew, saving Keli for the moment. Ashley quickly said, "I want to talk about this more later. Think about it, okay?"

Keli nodded as they both ran to their court. Greta yelled at them from the next court over. "You guys had better win. I want you to be perfect when we destroy you on Friday."

Ashley and Keli both ignored the comment. And just like the first two days, they cruised through their games, as did Greta and Trish's team. It was looking like a showdown on Friday afternoon.

Keli's gramps had slipped in during the match to watch. Keli didn't see him until it was all over, and so she was surprised when he brought up her game on the way home.

"Why are you hesitating on your blocks? I think you are jumping just to jump. You can't become a good blocker until you go up right on the hitting arm and your eyes are wide open, not closed like they were today."

Her mouth dropped open, "Gramps, when did you become such a volleyball expert?" The most she had ever gotten from him before was, "Good game." She stared at him, waiting for an answer.

He smiled but didn't answer her question. "So, tomorrow try keeping your eyes open." He chuckled. "It's tough to block when you can't see the ball."

Keli's mind wandered back to Ashley's comments about her going to Dallas. She wanted to tell Tom about the conversation she had had with Ashley, but she chickened out all the while wondering where his knowledge of volleyball came from.

CHAPTER 7

ASHLEY PUTS THE PRESSURE ON!

Tom was right on time to take Keli to camp the next morning. Keli didn't wait for the Jeep to pull out of the driveway before she asked, "How do you know so much about volleyball?" She stared right at him waiting for an answer.

Again he changed the subject. "Do you think it would be okay if I watch more of the camp today? I really don't have much to do, and I would like to watch you."

Keli leaned up against the door staring right at him. "Gramps, I have asked you twice now about you and volleyball, and twice you ignored my question. What's up with that?"

He scratched his ear; Keli could tell he was thinking about what to say. "Well, I tell you what. It's a long story, but I promise when we have time, I will tell you all about it."

Keli had to content herself with that.

Keli and Gramps walked into the gym to find Ashley and Greta blocking the entrance. They were holding a small sign that said, *"Keli Stennes, please come to Dallas."* Keli stopped dead in her tracks and laughed.

Tom put his hand on Keli's shoulder. "Interesting thought, isn't it?"

"Right, Gramps, like I could really leave Falls City and come here to school next year."

Greta answered, "Yes, that is exactly what you could do. Why not, Kels? It would be great for your game."

Keli walked by them. "Come on, we need to get ready."

Gramps smiled at them as he walked by. He said under his breath so they could hear but Keli couldn't. "I think she likes the idea."

The coaches really picked up the pace, barking at every mistake and pushing the girls to stay focused on the drills. They kept reminding them that it was Thursday and that they only had that day and the next. Coach Jim also seemed to be picking on even the smallest details of Keli's game, critiquing every time she touched the ball.

At lunch Keli looked for her gramps, but he had slipped out. Instead, she saw Ashley and Greta waving her over to where they were sitting.

Keli looked around one more time, hoping she would find Tom to bail her out. No such luck, so she walked over and sat down with them. "Can I ask you guys a question?"

"Sure," answered Ashley as she filled her mouth with a huge piece of orange.

"So why does Coach Jim hate me? He never let up the entire morning. I could not do anything right and he let me know it."

Greta giggled, "He doesn't hate you. Actually it's his way of saying he likes you. Ashley's dad says he is an old school coach; he doesn't waste his time when kids don't listen to him. He likes to coach kids who respond. He always tells us in practice that he can tell the kids that love it and want it by how they respond to coaching."

Ashley got into the conversation. "Yeah, he says he isn't going to waste his time on kids that are quick to make excuses or shut out the coach thinking they know more. You watch. He is great at reading kids."

It was Greta's turn again. "That is another reason to come here. He sees something in you, too."

Keli sat there listening to all they were saying. Finally she opened up on the subject. "You know it's awesome, everything you've said, and a part of me would love to try playing for a bigger school. This week has been the absolute best experience I have ever had." There was a long pause. "But it's not that easy. I have grown up my whole life in Falls City. Some of my friends would never, never understand, and I would be letting down my whole school."

Keli's face saddened. "I like you two a lot and it would be awesome, but it's just not possible."

Ashley looked at Greta and then back at Keli. "Okay, I understand some of what you're saying. Just think about it. Your grandpa thinks it's a good idea; maybe you should talk to him about it."

The afternoon drills picked up right where they left off, and Coach Jim was still making it a point to direct a lot of his attention at Keli. She kept replaying what Ashley and Greta had told her at lunch. Especially the part about staying focused on what he was saying and trying to make the changes he was suggesting. Then it started to click between the coach and player. By the end of the drills, Keli began to look for him and his instructions after each play, nodding and sometimes asking questions. She was no longer thinking he was picking on her; she knew he was really there trying to help her with her game.

Finally, the best part of the day. Keli yelled out to Ashley, "It's scrimmage time!"

Immediately the bantering began, with Greta proclaiming that their team was going to be camp champs. Both teams did their part again winning their matches. Now the whole camp was starting to talk about the big game the next day matching Ashley and Keli's team against Greta and Trish's team. As Keli walked towards her gramps, she overheard one of the girls predicting to another that Ashley and Keli's team would win the next day. She smiled, very pleased to be noticed.

Just like the day before, Tom had slipped back in during the scrimmage and was waiting for her by the exit. A huge grin was on her face. "Hey Gramps, did you see us win again today?"

She didn't wait for his answer; she couldn't wait to get him alone. Instead of stopping when she got to him, she kept going, pushing him in the direction of the car. As soon as the Jeep pulled out of the parking lot, Keli looked at him, "Gramps, can I ask you a serious question and you have to promise not to talk to anyone about it?"

He looked over at her. "Are you talking about going to Dallas this fall?"

Her mouth fell open. "Yes, how did you know what I was going to ask you about?"

He took his hat off and scratched his head before putting it back on his bald head. "Well, let's just say I could see it coming all week, and the sign this morning was kind of a give away, don't you think?" He scratched his head again before answering. "Before I answer this, I need to say that I am only able to give you my opinions and thoughts on the subject. It will really come down to what you think is most important and what you're willing to give up. Do you know why you would even consider making this change? It's a huge decision." He looked over at her.

Keli was staring straight ahead. He could tell she was trying to organize her thoughts.

His voice turned serious. "Why don't you think about it? And when you come over next weekend, we can really dissect it."

Keli nodded with some relief. Gramps was right, she thought. It was a huge decision, if not an impossible one. "You're right", she answered. "We can talk about it next weekend."

CHAPTER 8

THE FINAL DAY OF CAMP

Coach Jeff greeted Keli when she walked into the gym. "Here is your camp T-shirt," he said, holding it out to her. It was white with black and red lettering that said *Dragon Volleyball Camp.* "We want to take a picture around lunch time with everyone, so make sure to wear it for the picture."

"Sure thing, Coach," answered Keli. She was one of the first few campers to show up for the final day. She sat in the middle of the court and stared around at the gym. It was twice as large as the one back home. She looked up again at the banners and noticed that Dallas had won state championships the same year Falls City did back when her dad played.

She thought about Ashley telling her how great Lindsay was as a coach. Her mind wandered to the time she met Lindsay before she signed up and how she encouraged her to come to camp.

Greta's bag came crashing down on her. "What's up, chick?"

Keli looked up at the dangling belly-button chain that was right in front of her. She grabbed Greta's bag and shoved it back at her. She stood up, pointing her finger at Greta. "You startled me," she teased. "Now you're going to really pay this afternoon. So where is Ashley?"

"Don't worry! She'll be here in time to play this afternoon. She had something to do this morning, but she told me to tell you she would be here after noon."

During the midmorning break, Coach Jim walked over to where Keli was sitting and sat down next to her. "Hi, Keli."

Keli looked at him curiously, "Hi, Coach."

"I want to tell you what a pleasure it's been to have you at our camp this summer. I really have enjoyed your attitude and passion for the game."

She smiled, not knowing what to say.

"Keli, do you play volleyball year around or do you play other sports?"

"I play all of them. In Falls City, we all need to play them all to have enough for teams. It's kinda fun, going from sport to sport."

"So you don't play club ball?"

"No," answered Keli, who had heard all about club ball from Ashley, "we're too small to have a team. It would be fun to play. Volleyball is my favorite sport." She paused for a second, then continued. "Deep down I have always dreamed of being able to play volleyball in college, but I know it's kind of a silly dream since I play in the middle of nowhere." She lowered her head and stared down at the bleacher below her feet.

"Well, I wouldn't rule that out. You should sit down with your mom and talk to her about playing on a club this winter—you have the tools to be an excellent college player. You're right when you say that where you're playing is a problem, but really it's during the club season when most kids get their foot in the door with the colleges. Most college coaches recruit during the club season, not during the high school season."

Jim set his clipboard down on the bleacher next to him. "Don't give up on your dream. You have the right attitude and tool base, Keli. You really do. You just need to play more and against better competition."

He stood up. "Good luck with everything...it's been a joy to have you here this week."

Keli looked up at him. "Thanks, Coach. I will talk to my mom about the club thing."

When the coach got back down to the gym floor, he looked back up at her. "Hey, Stennes, this afternoon I hope you guys kick the pants off of Greta's team." He smiled and winked at her.

Keli smiled back.

By the afternoon, some of the campers' parents were starting to show up to see the progress their kids had made during the week. Keli scanned the stands a few times not recognizing anyone.

Two o'clock and it was time for Queen of the Court and the scrimmage. The coaches called everyone together for the group photo. Keli ran over and pulled her new camp T-shirt out of her bag and pulled it on over her own sweaty shirt. Then she took a seat on the end of a row about halfway up in the group. She stared down at the shirt and for the first time in her life it said "Dragon" on it. She giggled to herself about how ridiculous it seemed. She had grown up almost thinking of the Dragons as the archenemy. Even though they didn't play each other, there was an unspoken rivalry.

"Scoot over so I can sit down."

She looked up to see Ashley standing there. "It's about time you showed up," said Keli. "Where have you been?"

Ashley sat down, "You know, here and there. Sometimes you just have to take care of business." She looked over at Keli and grinned. "So you ready to kick Greta's butt. I am sick and tired of listening to her."

"Taking care of business, huh?" answered Keli.

Queen of the Court was a hit with all the campers; even the parents were getting into it, calling balls in or out and cheering on their kids and friends. Keli was sky-high playing, but she kept scanning the small crowd just hoping to recognize anyone to show off her game.

Finally with a few minutes left to play, she saw her gramps and her mom walk through the door. Her heart almost exploded with excitement. As she stood in line waiting her turn, her eyes followed them all the way to their seats. She waved at them just as they sat down. Her mom waved back excitedly.

It was perfect. Keli was paired with Greta and Trish. They served to the queens, who included Ashley. On the return ball over the net, Greta made a perfect pass to Trish, who returned the set to Greta. Greta then hammered the ball right at Ashley, who passed the ball to a teammate. Keli could see she was setting the ball to her side; she picked up the hitter and the ball perfectly and met them over the net. This time her eyes were wide open blocking the ball straight down. It was perfect. Greta and Trish both gave her a high five, and they all hurried to the queen side of the net.

They ended up staying there to the end of the drill, and Keli was all smiles when the final whistle blew. She looked up at her mom, who was standing clapping. Tom smiled and pointed at his eye to acknowledge that she was playing the net with her eyes open.

It was now time for the big scrimmage. Ashley whispered in Keli's ear, "Okay, watch me. If I put my right arm in the air early, that means I am setting you, so be ready. Also, Trish is going to set Greta every chance she can, so you really need to forget the back set and concentrate on the middle, and force Trish to set it some place else."

Keli looked at Ashley with admiration and then nodded.

Coach Jim yelled out, "Okay, ladies, one game to 25." He tossed the ball to Trish and the match was on.

The teams battled back and forth all the way to 22-22; neither team was able to break away from the other. With the score knotted at 22, it was Ashley's turn to serve. She bounced the ball a couple of times, then winked at Keli and backed up about ten feet. She tossed the ball high in the air and took off, jumping just before the end line and meeting the ball perfectly with a laser with so much top spin that when the ball got past the net it just dove straight for the floor, almost hitting the 10-foot line.

Keli ran to meet her. "Where did that come from? That was amazing."

Ashley grinned. "I have been working on it for a while now." She laughed. "Watch out! The next one could hit you!"

Greta was yelling at her teammates to be ready, trying to put them in the right spots for the next serve, but it did no good. Ashley hit almost the exact same ball. Trish got her hand on it but not nearly enough to do anything with it.

Keli was jumping up and down, clapping. "One more, come on, one more," while Greta was again barking orders on positioning.

Ashley crossed them up and hit a floater in the deep left corner. Greta's team was able to play the ball. Trish and Greta called for a slide to get Keli out of position, and it worked perfectly. As Keli moved to the middle to help block, Greta faked the middle and slid to the outside. Trish made a good set, and Greta easily finished it off, bringing the score to 24-23.

Ashley calmed her team down. "Okay, we need one good pass and we can finish this thing."

Keli rotated back to cover deep left. Greta bounced the ball twice and served a rocket right at her. As the ball got to her, it started to move sharply to her left. She had to lunge at it and had just enough time to get it up. The ball floated to the middle of the court very high, so Keli regrouped and made her way to the outside.

Ashley had her right hand in the air almost immediately. Keli was excited and nervous at the same time. Sure enough, the ball headed right for the pole. She paused just for a split second, then exploded towards the net and leaped high off the floor meeting the ball well above the net. Greta and Trish were both there and ready to block. Keli's hang time gave her just the extra moment needed to see an open space vacated by Greta in the middle, and instead of trying to power the ball through their block, she dropped the ball gently into the vacant spot on the floor. Game over!

She threw her arms in the air, and Ashley ran over and gave her a hug. "Thank you! Now I won't have to listen to her anymore this summer."

Keli laughed. She looked up in the stands, and again her mom was standing clapping.

Camp was over. Keli looked around at some of the kids who were already heading for the doors. She realized that for most of them it was just a small part of their volleyball world. For her it was like the Olympics or the World Championships. She saw the coaches taking down the nets, others packing their bags. She didn't want it to be over, but it was.

Keli headed for Ashley and Greta. "Hey, I want to thank you both for everything this week. It was awesome to play with you. You're both amazing players."

Greta grinned and winked at her. "We know."

Ashley shook her head. "And humble too, right? Actually, Keli, thank you for coming and playing with us. It was you who gave me back the passion for the game. Sometimes I forget how fun it is, and you gave that back to me this week." She stuck out her hand. "That is why I really would like you to come to Dallas and play with us."

Keli smiled, then frowned. "I wish I could, but it's not possible. We should stay in touch though. It would be fun to watch you play this fall."

Ashley reached in her bag and scratched her phone number on a piece of paper. "Call me when you can." She reached over and gave Keli another hug and headed for the door.

Keli stood there and watched them walk out the door.

"So, young lady, you ready to get out of here?" Her mom put her arm around Keli's shoulders.

Keli picked up her bag and shrugged. "Not really," she said.

Cindy put her arm around her. "You played great today. I am amazed how much you improved this week."

Keli answered. "Yes, I did. The competition really made me stretch. I only wish..." She paused. "Oh, never mind."

CHAPTER 9

GUESS WHO?

Keli sat up in bed, startled by Magic, her golden retriever, who was barking out the bedroom window. She could see an unfamiliar car in the driveway. She grabbed an old Mountaineer sweatshirt and said, "I betcha somebody is lost. What do you think, Magic?"

A loud knocking at the front door sent Magic flying down the stairs.

"Just a minute!" she yelled as she put on sweat pants. As she made her way to the door, she could see that there was more than one lost person standing on the porch. In fact, Ashley, Greta, and Gretchen, another girl from camp, all had their noses pressed against the glass.

Ashley started to bang on the door when she saw Keli coming. "Hurry up and let us in before the bears or something gets us," she yelled at Keli.

Keli opened the door and they all piled into her small living room. Before Keli could say a word, Greta said, "Let's go get some breakfast down at that restaurant we saw down by the river. Didn't you say your mom works there? Maybe she can get us a deal!"

Keli looked at them like they were crazy. "What are you all doing out here anyways?"

Ashley answered with a laugh. "Dang! Is that the way you show love in the morning?"

Gretchen and Greta both laughed. "We came to say hey. I can't believe how hard it was to find your place," said Greta. "We've been wandering around knocking on doors."

Gretchen jumped in. "Hey, we knocked on your neighbor's door," pointing towards Sticky's house. "Did you know the hottest guy on the planet lives right next door to you?"

"Yeah, let's invite him to breakfast too," pleaded Greta.

Ashley sat down in her mom's chair. "We all thought it would fun to hunt you down and buy you some oatmeal, eggs, or whatever you eat for breakfast. Are you up for it?"

Keli stuttered, "Uh, yeah, I guess. Sure! Give me a minute to get ready."

Gretchen said, "Girl, we are all starving. You look great. Let's go!"

"Right," answered Keli. "Just give me five minutes. Let me put on some clothes that I haven't slept in and get some flops for my feet." She ran upstairs to her room.

"So can we come up and look at your room?" asked Ashley.

"Sure," yelled Keli. "Come on up!"

They all quickly made their way into Keli's small attic room. Gretchen and Ashley both flopped on her bed. Greta went for the window. "Great view," she laughed, pointing at Sticky's house.

As they made their way down the stairs, Greta pleaded, "If you get the hot guy to come, I'll buy your breakfast!"

"There is no way Sticky would come," Keli answered, "I'm sure he's already gone back to bed."

Greta's eyes glazed over. "Sticky? How cool a name is that!" Ashley and Gretchen grabbed Greta by the arms, pulling her towards the door.

A couple minutes later, Keli led her new friends into the nearly empty restaurant.

"Hi sweetie," her mom said as she studied the girls that trailed behind her.

"Hi, Mom. Look who showed up on our doorstep." Keli started to introduce them, but Greta interrupted her. "Hey, let's order and then we can do the chitty chat thing...I'm starving."

Cindy laughed, "Well then, have a seat here." She plopped down a handful of menus on the big booth in the back corner. "Hi, my name is Cindy. I'm Keli's mom. You must all be from Keli's summer camp."

The girls all nodded. Ashley spoke first, "It's nice to meet you, Keli's mom!" Her face turned into a big grin as she stuck out her hand for Cindy to shake. "Hey, we want you to know how excited we all are that Keli is coming to Dallas and play with us this fall!"

Keli blushed. "Hey, I never said that!"

"Well, she did mention that some of you had asked her to," answered Cindy.

The two other tables of patrons in the restaurant were now listening intently to the conversation and whispering about it.

Cindy and Keli looked at each other. They knew that by the afternoon the whole town would have heard the rumor. The other girls didn't notice and just started ordering.

Keli was the last to order. Ashley said, "Put hers on my tab, please!"

"Hey, you don't have to do that, Ashley. Mom, I'll buy my own."

Ashley shook her head. "There is a big tip in it if you put hers on my bill." Giggling, she gently pushed Keli. "I invited you to breakfast. You can invite me next time."

Cindy took their orders and headed toward the kitchen window.

Greta leaned across the table. "So, Keli, you got a thing for Sticky?"

Gretchen answered. "Of course she does. He's hot and he lives next door!"

Keli answered for herself. "Nah, we're just friends. We have known each other since we were 3 years old. Actually he's my best friend. We hike a lot together and stuff, but we aren't boyfriend and girlfriend."

"Wow! So give up his phone number then!" shrieked Greta.

Gretchen asked, "Does he have a girlfriend?"

"Nope, I don't think so," answered Keli. "Actually I don't think he ever really has had one." The food came and saved her from more questions about Sticky.

As everyone finished eating, Keli pushed her half-eaten pancakes away. "What are you all up to for the rest of the day?"

Ashley answered with an evil grin. "Well, as soon as you tell us you're coming to play for us, we will leave you alone."

Keli's mouth opened but nothing came out. She looked over at her mom, who stared back wondering what she was going to say to Ashley's comment. She looked back at Ashley, "Well, nothing's changed since we talked about it this last week."

Ashley smiled. "Okay. But actually the real reason for coming out here today was to ask you to come to my birthday party. I should've asked you last week. Anyway it would be great if you could come! Bring some of your friends if you want. Tell them to bring swimming suits. We have a pool."

Keli grinned. "I'll talk with my mom. It sounds like fun. But my mom is going out of town, and I am supposed to stay with my grandpa this weekend. I'll call you and let you know."

Ashley smiled. "I'm counting on it. It was nice to see you again. Come on, ladies. Let's get home. I told my dad I would work this afternoon at the store."

"Don't we need to give Kels a ride home?" asked Greta.

"Actually you saved me from having to walk down here and get the car from my mom, so it works out great." Keli stuck up her hand. "Thanks for breakfast. I guess I owe you one now."

As the Dallas girls walked out, Keli went over and sat down on her favorite stool by the cash register. Behind her, she heard the bells clang as the restaurant door opened. She turned around thinking it was one of the girls coming back in for something, but it was her grandpa.

He pointed to the car pulling away from the restaurant. "Aren't those your teammates from summer camp?"

Jack, the cook, yelled from the back of the kitchen. "Yeah, they're here recruiting Keli to go to school in Dallas next year!"

Tom let out a little grunt as he sat down besides Keli. As he reached for the menu, Keli teased him. "You know what you're gonna order so why do you look at the menu?"

He chuckled and said, "I keep hoping that one day I'll open it and find something new."

Cindy came over to them. "Now that I have you both here, it's a good time to go over this weekend."

Keli quickly interrupted, "I was just invited to a party at Ashley's house tomorrow night, and I was wondering if I could go."

Cindy gave a quick glance at Tom for a reaction, who said, "I think it's a great idea."

Cindy poured him some coffee. "Keli, you need to make sure your grandpa knows exactly what is going on, and you need to be home no later than 9:00!"

"How 'bout 10?" negotiated Keli.

"Okay, 10 and that doesn't mean 10:15 either, right?"

Keli beamed. "Right, Mom. Thank you, thank you!" She stood up. "Mom, when do you get off work? I'm going to take the car home and wash it. Call me and I will come pick you up."

Cindy leaned across the counter and kissed her forehead. "Okay, I should be ready in a couple of hours."

As Keli drove off, Tom watched Cindy stare out the restaurant window. "She's growing up before our eyes," he said quietly.

Cindy poured a coffee and sat down next to him. "Yes she is, and I'm not ready! Actually Tom, I am a little afraid of being alone, and I know in a couple of years that's going to be the reality."

Tom put his hand on Cindy's arm. "While she is growing up quick, two years is a long time, and you don't know how things will be then. Things like this seem to work themselves out."

Cindy leaned over and put her head on Tom's shoulder. "You're a good man. Thank you." Then she straightened up and took a sip of her coffee. "So what do you think of these kids coming around asking Keli to switch schools? You know last Friday morning, that Ashley came out here and talked to me about that very thing. I was impressed with her. She is mature and very convincing. She thinks Keli can be very good, and she seemed to really like her."

Tom looked at her. "Keli brought it up with me last week. I told her to think about it and we would talk some this weekend. It's a pretty appealing thought. I know Butch used to think about it, and I am sure Keli is thinking about it now."

Cindy looked at Jack in the back. "And I know the townspeople would scream if she changed."

Tom shrugged. "I don't think that is what's most important."

CHAPTER 10

THE SMART CHAIR

Saturday morning Keli made her way downstairs, yawning and scratching her head.

"Do you know where my green sweatshirt and hiking boots are?" Cindy looked frantic.

"Uh, your boots are in the garage and I have no idea where your sweatshirt is. Do you want to use one of mine?"

At her mother's nod, Keli made her way upstairs and grabbed her favorite, a gray hooded one. She used it a lot when she hiked. Keli proudly bounded down stairs.

"Here, Mom. This is my favorite. It will be great when you're hiking on the beach."

Keli's mom packed it in her bag and announced she was ready. Keli grabbed her mom and gave her a big bear hug and said, "Mommie, I am going to miss you," in her 10-year-old voice.

Cindy saw through her act. "Right, let me see. You have a big party to go to and a grandpa ready to spoil you to death. I'll bet you'll miss me."

A loud honk came from the driveway. "There's Kay right now! I'm out of here. Oh, one last thing. Do you have money for the weekend?"

"Uh, actually I don't," answered Keli.

"Okay. In my room in my tip box, you can take $20 out of there."

"Wow! Are you sure I can take that much? "

"Yes, you will need to buy Ashley a present and get gas. Don't worry. I'll have a list of things I will want you to do to pay me back with."

As Cindy closed the front door behind her, the phone rang.

"Where is your mom going?" the familiar voice said.

"Hey Stick, so you spying on us again?" teased Keli.

"Yeah, I have my cameras running 24/7 on you guys. So what are you doing right now? Do you want to do something?"

"Actually I am going to spend the weekend with my grandpa, and tonight I am going to a birthday party for Ashley from my summer camp."

"Oh, so now you're hanging out with your new friends and us ol' country kids are left in the dust?"

"Stick, that's not fair. I was just going to ask you to come with me. She has a swimming pool and it sounds like fun. Come with me?"

There was a pause. "Well, I guess I should go so I can make sure you don't get into trouble."

Keli's voice perked up. "We'll have a good time. And the girls are going to be all over you."

"Sure they will...I'm quite the catch."

"Yes you are." As she spoke, Keli realized what she had said. She immediately wondered if that had come across right. "Can you pick me up at my gramps' around four?"

"Sure, I'll see you then," answered Sticky.

Keli jumped off the couch and raced upstairs to pack for the weekend. A few minutes later with a huge bag that rivaled her mom's, she yelled for Magic.

Keli honked as she pulled into her grandpa's half-circle driveway in the front of his old two-story log cabin. Gramps was rocking in his chair and Zack, his old yellow Lab, was standing at the edge of the steps wagging his tail and barking. Magic was excited too. His head was out the window, and his tail was wagging and banging against the back of the seat.

As soon as Keli opened Magic's door, the two dogs were immediately rolling in the dirt growling and wrestling. Keli grabbed her bag and headed towards the porch where Gramps was reading in his rocking chair.

"Hi, Gramps, I talked Sticky into going to the party tonight with me. I hope that's okay."

Tom nodded. "Sure," he said and turned back to his book.

Keli opened the screen door to the smell of something good coming from the kitchen.

As she wandered through the small living room, she glanced over at a picture of her father's graduation day and another of her grandmother that sat on the mantle on top of the rock fireplace. Keli never walked through the room without catching a glimpse of her dad's picture. Her only memories of him were stories and pictures. Being in this room somehow made her feel closer to him.

She made a pit stop in the kitchen to see what her grandpa was cooking. She grabbed a potholder that her grandmother had made hanging by the old black stove. Everything in the kitchen had a story behind it. Actually everything in the house had a story. All she had to do was ask her grandfather or mention she liked something and a half hour of story went by. She loved his stories. As she lifted the lid on the pot to see what was in there, she wondered what the stories were going to be this weekend.

The pot was full of chili, and the smell was divine. Keli loved his chili. She quickly put the cover back on the pot and bolted for the front porch.

"Gramps, you did make chili!"

"Yeah, sweetie. It should be ready in an hour or so. Maybe you can have some before you leave."

"Did you make corn bread too?" answered Keli.

"I'll make some tomorrow. Tonight you only get a taste. My guess is you'll have plenty to eat at the party. So whose party is this anyways?"

"Do you remember Ashley from my summer camp?"

Tom smiled and said, "Was she the setter or the tall one with the thing hanging off her belly?"

Keli laughed, "She was the setter on my team. Hey, where did that chair come from?"

"Funny you should ask," said Tom.

Keli laughed to herself. She knew here came story number one!

"Pull it over here closer. And while you're at it, look at the back of it."

Keli walked around and stood behind the chair. She stared at the headrest with a puzzled look. "So what does that mean, Gramps?" Whittled in the back of the headrest was "Butch's Smart Chair."

"Sit down and let me tell you."

"Gramps, what time is it?"

"3:00."

Keli grinned, "Do you think you can tell me the story in an hour? Sticky will be here at 4:00."

Tom laughed. "I'll do my best. Let me see. About 30 years ago, no, it must be going on 35 years now, your dad and I had a great idea that we thought was going to make us rich."

Keli, intrigued, sat up a little straighter in the old chair.

"We were going to make office furniture and sell it to rich lawyer types. Well, we made about 15 chairs in our first batch. We thought we could sell those and with that money make 30 more and maybe some tables or desks next. Well, we sold a grand total of 14 chairs." He laughed. "Some get-rich scheme, huh?"

Keli looked down at the armrest. "Let me guess. This is number 15."

"Yep. It made its way to the porch and the chair became kind of the lecture chair. Your dad was a good kid, but he got into his share of mischief and then of course, there were the post-game conversations. He was a lot like you. He asked a lot of questions. After one of those conversations, he whittled that phrase on the chair."

He paused for a second, and Keli could tell he was remembering one of those conversations. Then he said, "He would always razz me about it. 'So, Dad, should I go sit in the smart chair?'"

Keli smiled as she wiggled around in the chair somehow hoping to feel something of her father's presence. "Gramps, why have I never seen the chair before? Where has it been for all these years?"

"Well, I kinda forgot about it until a day or so ago. I put it in the attic after your dad moved out on his own. I thought back then that once he settled down and had a place of his own, I would give it to him."

Again he paused, his face softening with sadness.

Keli's heart melted. "You miss him a lot, don't you?"

Tom leaned back in his chair and very clearly answered. "Yes, Keli, I do. Your dad was my best friend and there isn't a day that goes by where I don't think of him. Do you remember him?"

Can I Play...

It was Keli's turn to pause. She desperately wanted to say yes, but she couldn't. "Not really. I wish I could. Sometimes I lie in bed and try as hard as I can to remember but I can't."

Sensing that tears were close, Tom quickly got back to the original story. "Your dad claimed that he got all his smarts from sitting in the chair."

Keli smiled. "You know, I feel kinda smarter right now too," winking at her grandpa. She leaned back in the chair, still feeling a little emotional. "Hey, Gramps, do you think the chili is ready?"

Later, between bites, Keli asked, "Gramps, I have been giving a lot of thought to whether I should change schools. Do you think we can have that conversation now?"

Tom looked at the clock above the stove and then shook his head, his mouth full of chili.

"Not enough time."

"Hmm...how about at breakfast tomorrow?"

Gramps swallowed. "That sounds a lot better. You and Sticky go have some fun tonight, and we can talk tomorrow when we aren't rushed."

Keli looked right into his eyes. "I love you!"

Tom's heart swelled. "I love you too, special one!"

CHAPTER 11

ASHLEY'S PARTY

Keli and Sticky drove down Main Street on the way to Dallas. Charlee and Rachel were coming out of Rodewald's Market, and Keli stuck her hand out the window and waved.

Charlee looked at her curiously and slowly raised her hand and waved back.

"So I'm guessing you didn't ask Charlee to come with us?" asked Sticky. "You know she is going to freak out when she hears about this."

"No I didn't. I thought about it, but I know her and she would have tried to talk me out of going. You know Charlee, she wouldn't have let up either until I agreed with her." Keli leaned back in her seat. "I'm getting tired of her expecting me to do everything she says, and just because I made some new friends. It's no big deal."

Sticky quickly glanced over at Keli, then back to the road. "Hey, just so you know, she has been calling me the past few days pretty upset. She thinks you're too overboard on this volleyball. She even said she thinks you're going to go to Dallas next year!" Sticky again quickly glanced her way to see her expression.

Keli stared straight ahead and then boldly denied it. "No way, Sticky." Her brain was fighting, part wanting to tell the truth and the other side in complete lie mode. "No way. I have gone to Falls City all my life. All my friends are here."

Sticky didn't challenge her anymore on the subject. Keli had a couple more minutes to listen to her own thoughts. She battled the rest of the way with how to tell Sticky that it was at least something she was thinking about.

"Hey, isn't this a birthday party? Where's your gift?" asked Sticky.

"I made her a card and told her I'm buying her breakfast like she did for me."

"So, when did she buy you breakfast?"

Keli didn't really want to answer this question, but she knew it was something she had to do. She had already lied to Sticky today for the first time in her life, and she didn't want to do it again. "Actually, Ashley and a few of the other players took me to breakfast yesterday."

"So that's what they were all doing at your house yesterday morning?"

"Can you just drive? We're going to be late."

Sticky laughed. "Hey, I was just kidding with you. Don't take this so seriously. We're going to a party, so loosen up!"

Keli stared straight ahead. Then her conscience started to talk to her. She looked over at Sticky. "You're right. I'm being a dork. I'm just nervous going over to this party. Actually, right now I am even second-guessing myself whether we really should go."

Sticky pulled up to the stoplight and looked at Keli. "Hey, we're here now. It's just a party. Let's go. Keli, you're a person who has always done what you said you were gonna do, so don't freak out. Besides, you've got me all built-up thinking I am going to have a bunch of girls after me. Don't let me down on this. So what street am I looking for again?"

Keli grabbed the paper sitting between them. "Hilltop Lane."

"Jeez," whined Sticky. "The rich folks live up there!"

As they got to the top of the hill, it wasn't hard to figure out which house it was. There must have been more than 100 people milling around. Sticky and Keli looked at each other.

"Sticky, you sure you're still up for this?"

"Of course, let's go see how the other half lives. It's going to be great!"

Keli grabbed the card and they headed up the hill, admiring each house on the way. As they approached Ashley's house, they ran into Greta, who was crossing the street.

"Hey, Keli," yelled Greta. "Ashley is going to freak. She didn't think you'd come." Greta's eyes locked on Sticky, who was watching the people going in and out of the house and didn't notice Greta's trance.

Keli did notice, and she elbowed him to get his attention and made introductions. Greta froze for a second as Sticky said, "Hey, Greta."

Greta led the way in and Sticky quickly whispered in Keli's ear, "I hope she's one of the bunch you were talking about. She is totally tight!"

Keli smiled. "Wipe the slobber from your chin before someone notices! Greta, this is a birthday party? There are more people here than in all of Falls City!"

"Wait 'til you go in the backyard," Greta answered with a smile. "Everyone loves Ashley."

"KELI!" boomed from the top of the stairs. Ashley was leaning over the banister. "I can't believe it. You came, Keli! That is so very cool!"

Ashley ran down the stairs to greet her with a hug. She looked at Sticky. "So Keli, who is your friend?" Ashley winked.

Keli yelled loud enough to get over the crowd. "This is Sticky, the friend I was telling you about, remember?"

Ashley repeated, "I'm so freaked that you came. I really didn't think you would!"

"Well, to be honest, I did have second thoughts, but I am glad I came. Ashley, your family has the most amazing house I have ever seen!"

"Thanks, my dad's a workaholic. He's the one you need to compliment! So are you guys hungry? Did you bring your swimsuits?"

Keli looked at Sticky. "We forgot the suits in the car."

"Well, maybe later," said Ashley. "I think the pool is pretty full right now anyways. Let's go outside, Keli. I want you to meet my dad."

Sticky and Greta were walking behind them, almost in a contest to see who could catch more glimpses of the other without getting caught.

They finally made their way through the enormous house to the backyard where there was a huge pool and a hot tub that was standing-room-only with people. Ashley, still with Keli in tow, headed for the BBQ, where a dozen people waited for the next burger to come off the grill.

"Dad, I want you to meet the new friend I've been telling you about from Falls City!"

Ashley's dad flipped a burger and turned around with a big smile. "Hi Keli, it's nice to meet you!" Keli was impressed that he knew her name.

He stuck out his hand and said, "You can call me Frank."

Ashley added, "Actually, everyone calls him Big Frank."

Keli thought that was easy to understand. Big Frank must have been 6'6" and nearly 300 pounds. His big beard was turning gray. Keli shook his hand and then introduced Sticky to Frank. "So are you hungry? I have some burgers ready."

Sticky and Keli looked at each other to see who would be first to say yes. Keli took the lead. "Maybe later. By the look of the line, we might start a riot if we were to cut in."

Big Frank laughed. "Well, when you're ready, you come straight to the front of the line. Some of these kids have already eaten half a cow."

Greta broke back into the conversation, inviting Sticky to get something to drink. As they walked away, Ashley laughed and said, "Greta will not let go for the rest of the night."

Keli watched them disappear into the crowd. "I hope she doesn't hurt him." They both laughed.

As the two girls made the rounds around the crowd, Keli was introduced to dozens of people. Then Ashley walked up to three boys standing by the basketball hoop. Keli could tell by just looking at them that they were stud athletes, especially the tallest one...real model quality.

Ashley said, "Hey, guys, meet my new friend from Falls City. Keli is a stud volleyball player." Ashley gestured towards the shortest one and introduced him as Ryan, then Carter. "And this one," she said, "who can't play a lick of football, is Steen."

Steen smiled, and they all said "Hi" to Keli, who tried to make eye contact with each one even though she didn't want to take her eyes off Steen.

Ashley then promptly announced that Keli was thinking about transferring to Dallas in the fall. Keli looked at Ashley, then back at the boys, especially Steen to see what their reaction was. They all chorused together, "Right on! Very cool! Tight!" Keli stammered and said she was thinking about it.

Keli looked at Steen and thought to herself that he was perfect—tall, blue eyes, muscles everywhere, pretty smile, and an athlete.

Steen bounced the basketball once, then said, "That would be awesome. We have a great volleyball team and it's a pretty good school."

Keli wanted to say, "Okay; I'm in right now" after Steen spoke to her, but she held her composure and just smiled.

As she walked by him, she grabbed the ball and shot it in the hoop from about 15 feet away, then looked at all of them. "Why don't you all practice some and maybe we can play later?"

When the girls got far enough away...Ashley busted up laughing. "Girl, that was a gutsy move. Isn't he like the hottest thing alive!"

Keli answered, "Did I just do that? Really, did I just take the basketball from him and tell that god to practice?"

Ashley busted up. "You are way too funny, Kels! Let's get a burger or something. I'm starving."

Keli scanned the crowd for Sticky. The line had died down, and Big Frank plopped a bun and burger down on her paper plate. "So pull up a chair you two, and Keli, tell me about yourself. Ashley says you live in Falls City."

"Yep, all my life actually. Well, I was born here in Dallas, but that doesn't count."

Big Frank smiled. "So you live out there with your folks?"

Keli looked over at Ashley, then back to her dad. "I live with my mom...my dad died when I was 3."

Big Frank's smile softened to a sad look. "That's right. I'm real sorry. I knew your dad. He was the best basketball player around and a real good guy!"

Keli brightened up. "Really, you knew my dad?"

"I did. Your mom never remarried?"

"Nope. Me and Mom have done great."

"Well, tell your mom Frank said hello. I met her once with your dad at a 4th of July celebration."

Ashley broke in. "Dad, I'm trying to get Keli to come to Dallas go to school next year."

Big Frank looked at Keli. "Is Ashley stiff-arming you?"

Keli shook her head. "No, but she is spreading a pretty big rumor."

"Well, Keli, I'm sure you will do what is best for you. You really should talk with your mom and anyone else who really knows you to get the best advice you can. It's a big decision."

"Yeah, I know." Keli finished off her last bite of her burger and said, "So you know you own the coolest store in the whole town. I love to come into your store and just wander around and look at everything."

Frank laughed, "Well, thank you. Maybe that's why you look familiar."

Ashley elbowed Keli to get her attention. "Here comes Greta and Sticky."

Sticky was carrying their swimming suits. Ashley stood up. "Let's go swimming."

Keli stood up too and thanked Frank for the burger, and they moved off to the pool.

The pool became a frenzy when they joined in. The music was blaring, and Ashley turned the pool into a line dancing session; Big Frank caught it all on video.

Finally, after a couple of hours of water line dancing, volleyball, and Marco Polo, Ashley jumped out of the pool and shouted, "I'm ready for some cake!"

Frank lit all the candles, and everyone gathered around singing "Happy Birthday." Sticky and Keli sat and watched her open present after present. Sticky quietly said, "It's like being in a whole different world from back at home."

Greta jumped back in the pool when the last present was opened. Sticky started after her but Keli called him back.

"I told my grandpa I would be home by 10. I guess we'd better get going."

Ashley and Sticky begged her to stay longer, but Big Frank helped Keli out. "Yep, you'd better get on your way. No need to get yourself in hot water at home. But you have to promise to come back."

Keli smiled and promised.

But Sticky wasn't ready to go. "Kels, call your grandpa and see if we can stay longer." Sticky wore the full "please, please puppy dog look," and Ashley was mimicking that look. A few seconds later, Keli was on the phone praying that she wasn't waking him up.

"Gramps?"

"Hi Keli, I was wondering when I might be getting this call."

"Gramps, she said, "Sticky and I were wondering if we could stay a bit longer. Everyone wants to go swim..."

Tom cut her off. "Anyone drinking at this party?"

"Drinking?" said Keli, confused.

"You know what I mean."

"No, Gramps. I haven't seen anything but soda. I promise."

There was a pause. "Then I think it would be all right if you stayed a bit longer. But be home no later than midnight."

Keli was shocked. "Thanks, Gramps!"

"Okay, be careful on your way home and make sure Sticky calls his parents so they aren't worried."

"Okay, Gramps, will do. Good night."

After an hour of playing more volleyball in the pool, the group was hungry again. Keli yelled over to Sticky, "Hey, after we eat, we need to get going, okay?" Sticky nodded as he toweled off.

As they sat around the table eating cold burgers, Ashley looked over to Sticky and asked the question. Keli could see it coming but couldn't stop it. "Hey Sticky, don't you think Keli should come to Dallas and play volleyball with us next year?"

Greta and Gretchen both said, "Yeah, you should come here too!"

Sticky nearly choked on his burger. "Ah you guys are great, but I don't think so. We have an awesome school."

Ashley took a quick peek at Keli. Keli was petrified; she wanted nothing to do with this conversation.

Sticky went on. "We'll get over here to watch you play...and maybe you all can come out to the sticks and watch Kels dominate our league. She is easily the best player!" He looked over at Keli, who was staring down at her plate, trying to be invisible.

After a pause, Sticky said, "Kels, Falls City is a great school, right?"

All eyes turned to Keli whose brain raced for the perfect middle-of-the-road answer. "What? I'm sorry. I'm getting tired. I didn't hear what you said."

Sticky said, "Tell them that we are Falls City through and through."

Keli couldn't look Ashley in the eyes, so she used Greta. "Yeah...we are Falls City kids." She felt miserable, but Sticky grinned and finished off his last bite.

Ashley didn't say anything after that, and Keli knew it was time to leave. "Ashley, hey...I can't even begin to tell you how great a time I had tonight. Thank you so much for inviting me."

Ashley mustered a smile and said it was fun. Keli could tell that she was upset. Keli grabbed Sticky by the arm and they headed for the open gate beside the house.

As they walked to the car, neither talked. They were both in their own worlds. Sticky was dreaming about being the center of attention, and Keli was worried about losing her new friend.

As they drove home, Sticky broke the silence. "What do you think about me asking Greta out on a date?"

"Well," said Keli, "would that be your first real date since you went bowling with Rachel back in the 8th grade?"

"I guess. If you didn't take up all my time, I would go on lots of dates," answered Sticky.

"Me taking your time?" Keli responded. "Whoa, now I've heard it all. Yes, I think you should date her! And I'll make sure not to take up your time in the future."

Sticky stammered out a response. "I, I was kidding. Don't get mad!" But Keli didn't answer.

As they pulled into the driveway, Sticky said, "So are we going hiking tomorrow?"

Keli chuckled sarcastically and said no. Then she closed the door and headed into the house. Tom met her in the living room. "How was your night?"

Keli sighed. "It was really awesome 'til the end."

He headed for his chair. "What happened at the end?"

"Oh, nothing... just Sticky!"

He smiled and walked over and kissed her on the cheek. She watched him slowly walk back to his bedroom. Keli looked over at the picture of her dad. She walked over and picked it up and stared at it. Tears came. "Dad, I miss you," she whispered. "What would you do if you were me?"

Instead of putting the picture back on the mantle, she took it into the bedroom with her and placed it on the nightstand. As she lay there, the tears kept coming. It had been a long time since she had felt the loss of her dad. She fell asleep before the tears dried.

CHAPTER 12

KELI'S DAD

Morning came quickly, and Keli woke to the smell of bacon cooking. She rolled over to see the picture of her dad still there. This time she smiled back at the smiling picture. "Morning, Dad!"

Keli pulled herself out of the warm bed and headed for the bathroom, then made her way into the kitchen in her sweatshirt and shorts.

Gramps set a plate of eggs, bacon, and toast in front of her. Keli stared down at the full plate of food.

"Dang, Gramps, I generally don't eat this much in the morning."

Tom sat down in front of his own plate. "Well, what you don't eat, I'm sure Zack and Magic will be more than happy to help you finish."

Keli grabbed a piece of bacon. "So how did you sleep, Gramps?"

"Pretty good after I knew you were home safe."

"Thank you again for letting me stay longer!"

"Sure, you're a good girl and deserve to be able to stretch things once in a while. You've shown a good deal of responsibility. I called your mom and told her after you called me, and she was okay with it too. So, tell me about the party."

Keli sipped her coffee, then answered. "Gramps, you can't believe how nice their house is. It must have cost a million dollars! I am not kidding. I've never seen anything like it. There were probably 200 people there. It was really amazing! You should have seen Sticky. All the girls were gaga over him, especially one from my camp named Greta. I think Sticky is going to ask her out on a date."

Tom smiled.

"I met Ashley's dad. He's a really nice person. He knew my dad too. He said Dad was the best basketball player around!"

"What's his name?

"Uh. Big Frank."

Tom looked at her. "You mean Frank Webb?"

"Yep, you know him?"

"I know of him. He was quite an athlete when he was younger. Your dad and he were the local icons back when they were in school. They never got a chance to play one another, but there was an article written in the *Gazette* when they were seniors about how both had led their football and basketball teams to State championships."

"Wow! I wish I could have read that article," Keli said wistfully.

Tom rubbed his chin. "Maybe later today we can get into the attic. I have a box of stuff I kept of your dad's old clippings"

Keli stood straight up "What? You have newspaper clippings from when my dad played?"

"I think I might still have them."

Keli screamed "Yes" as loud as she could. "Come on, Gramps, let's find them right now!"

Tom motioned for Keli to sit back down. "Later. Let's finish our conversation."

"So who was the better player?" she asked.

Tom thought for a second. "You know, it depends on who you ask. Personally I thought your dad was better at basketball, but the scouts all picked the Webb kid. He ended up playing football for the Ducks."

Keli's shoulders sunk a couple of inches. "What happened to Dad? Why didn't he play if he was that good?"

Again Tom paused. "It was a long time ago. Most of the colleges that gave scholarships gave them to kids who went to the bigger schools. A couple of scouts came and watched, but in the end no one offered him a scholarship. He was very disappointed. He planned on making enough money to go walk on and make a team." Tom took a drink of his coffee, then added, "Then one thing led to another and his dream faded away."

Keli frowned. "That is so sad."

Tom took his glasses off and squinted a little as he looked at Keli. "Well, sweetie, things changed for your dad. He fell in love with your mom and they made plans. They were working hard on a new set of goals. Your mom was going to school, your dad was making good money working in the woods, and then you came along! It was a great little happy family. I was so proud!"

Most of this she had heard many times from her mom. "So, Gramps, what happened with Big Frank?"

"He played at Oregon like I said; then he played a couple of years in the NFL for the 49ers before he injured his knee and retired."

Keli's eyes almost bulged out of their sockets. "He played pro football?"

"Yep, I'm pretty sure it was two years. I think he did a good thing by saving his money and opening up the sporting goods store."

Keli began thinking out loud. "If Dad was as good as Frank, then he might have played in the pros too."

"Well, we spent many a night talking about the what-ifs."

Keli slumped down in her chair. "Gramps, can we talk about my situation?"

"Okay. Why don't we go set out on the porch and catch some sun?"

Keli grabbed their plates and quickly rinsed them off and followed her grandfather out to the porch. She dragged her dad's old smart chair over close to his and sat down. Tom sat there with his arms folded and gently rocked, waiting for Keli to start. Keli stared down at the porch trying to figure out her words.

A few seconds later without raising her head, Keli threw the bomb. "Gramps, I have been thinking a lot about this... I really want to change schools!" She waited for a response and when it didn't come quickly, she raised her head to see if he had heard her.

Tom still had his arms crossed as he continued to rock in his chair. He cleared his throat and said simply, "Why?"

"I want to become a good player, not just for a small school. I want to become a good player no matter what size school. I want to get a scholarship and be able to see more than just Falls City when I grow up. When I played in that camp, I really got a chance to feel what it is like to play against really good players. Here in Falls City, most teams might have one or two kinda good players. This summer everyone was good. Heck, I was not even close to being the best. Here in Falls City I am easily the best. How would I ever get good enough for some college to give me a scholarship? I'm the best player in my whole league as a sophomore yet in a summer camp I was an average player, and some of the best players from the schools didn't play. If there are that many good players out there, I am doomed if I stay here. My only chance is to go play against them and prove myself."

She paused. "You just told me Dad was good and his dream died. I don't want that to happen to me too! Besides I really like the kids that I played with and the coach at Dallas...she is supposed to be amazing."

Tom rubbed his forehead as he thought how to answer her. "How do you know that the only way to your dreams is changing schools? I think times have changed and if you're good enough, colleges will offer you a scholarship even if you come from a small school."

Keli shook her head. "The problem is I don't think I can get better here. I improved more in one week than I ever have, because I got to play with better players and had better coaching."

Tom stopped rocking and leaned forward in the old chair. "Have you talked with your mom about this yet?"

Keli shook her head again. "I just came to this conclusion last night. I think I am as far as I can go here in Falls City from a sports standpoint."

A couple of minutes went by as they stared off into their own thoughts. Tom broke the silence. "What about your friends? You know how difficult it would be to leave them after all these years."

"Well, if they're my real friends, they would want me to better myself, wouldn't they?

Tom looked over his glasses at Keli. "Do you really believe that? These kids adore you. You're the leader, a sister to many of them. You going to a different school would be extremely hard for most everyone in this town to accept. You know the rivalry this town feels for Dallas. For your friends and your town to lose one of their best would be a tough pill to swallow."

Keli closed her eyes. She knew her grandfather was right. She could feel the tears start to seep out and run down her cheeks. Her hands quickly covered her eyes to hide what her grandfather could already see.

Tom said softly, "Keli, it really is your decision."

Keli shook her head as she wiped away her tears. "You're right. Everyone would hate me."

Tom turned the subject completely upside down. "Let me paint a scenario for you to think about. Let's say you do change schools, become this elite player, and get a scholarship to a Pac-10 school. You graduate from college and maybe find some place to play volleyball or teach it. But to have all this, you have to give up your friends here and 10 years from now you have no idea how their lives are going. Here's another one to think about. What if you change schools, lose your friends, and you don't get a scholarship?"

Keli again closed her eyes. She didn't really know how to answer these questions.

Tom stood up. "I am behind whatever decision you make. And I really think you should talk about this with your mom; she knows you best. Do this for you, not for your dad or for anyone else. If you want it bad enough, then go for it. That's my only advice."

"Gramps? What would you do if you were me?"

Tom grinned. "I'm not sure. I'm not you." He disappeared into the house.

CHAPTER 13

FATHER AND DAUGHTER GOALS

"Magic! Let's go, buddy!"

Magic's ears perked up and he headed for the trail. Keli loved the hike that started from behind Tom's house and wiggled its way about two miles to a nice flat deep part of the upper Luckimutte. As Keli walked, she could hear Magic crashing through the brush. Keli smiled. They loved being out in the woods. Her thoughts went back to her conversation with her grandfather. She thought about the lie she had told Sticky and wondered how it would affect their relationship. Finally she made it to the river. Magic had already swam to the other side and was lying on Keli's favorite rock.

Keli wasn't in the mood to sit still, so she whistled for Magic and headed back up the trail. Her hike back was filled with pro and con scenarios to her dilemma. As she got closer to the house, she remembered the newspaper clippings and she broke into a full sprint leaving her problem for the moment behind her.

As she climbed up the porch steps, Gramps was reading in his rocking chair. "Any chance we can go up into the attic and find the clippings about my dad?"

He smiled. "While you were gone, I found them and put them on your bed. Enjoy them...they're yours now!"

Keli gave her gramps the biggest hug and kiss. She raced into the house and straight to her room. There sitting on the bed was a small box and a picture album. She spent the rest of the afternoon reading and rereading each clipping. She stared at each picture trying to imagine being there. She was rereading the article Tom had told her about at breakfast for the third time when the phone rang.

It was her mom on the other end. "Hey sweetie, how are things going? How was the party last night?"

Keli gave the same glowing report she'd given her grandpa at breakfast. After she hung up, she didn't let go of the receiver. Instead she dialed Ashley's number. Ashley answered.

"Hey Ashley, it's me, Keli. I just wanted to call and thank you again for inviting me. It was the best party I've ever been to."

Ashley paused for a minute and said, "It was fun having you here."

Keli said quickly, "The other reason for my call is that I just want you to know that how the party ended really put a downer on things. Sorry."

"Don't worry about it."

"But that's just it. I am worried about it. I really feel caught on this deal. If I come to Dallas next year, I will probably lose a lot of my friends and disappoint a lot of people, but on the other hand it's really what I want to do!"

"Hey, I understand. I know I'm being selfish trying to pressure you into this. I hope you decide to do it, but I will understand and hope we can stay friends no matter what!"

It was exactly what Keli was hoping to hear, and she felt better when she hung up. Her mind went back to the box in her bedroom. She sat down on the bed and picked up the photo album. As she turned the pictures, she stared at an 8x10 portrait of her dad running across the goal line scoring a touchdown. He had the ball in one hand and his other hand raised in a fist above his head. Keli smiled proudly. She gently rubbed his number 10 and something from under the picture slipped out just enough to peek out from the bottom of the picture.

Keli moved her finger down and gently guided the piece of paper out from behind the picture. It was a piece of notebook paper folded in quarters. It had yellowed some over the years. She quickly unfolded the paper. It had "1985 Goals" handwritten at the top of the page, a page written by her dad. Keli's hands started to tremble as she read it.

1984/85 Goals
Goal sheets must be turned in by August 15
to be able to start practice!

Name: Butch Stennes   Year: Senior   Date: 7/19/84

Get a least a 3.75 GPA.
Get my assignments turned in on time.
Get to school on time—at least better than last year!
Be nicer to Lloyd Isham.
Join the Drama Club.
Win the State Championship in football and basketball again!
Get a date with Kay.
Be all state in both sports.
Get a scholarship to play either football or basketball.
Not get hurt.

If you could change one thing, what would it be?
I would not be afraid to change schools and go play for Dallas.
Or Falls City could become a bigger school!
Oh well... Go Mountaineers!

Keli's mouth fell open. She started towards the door to show her grandpa, then stopped short of the doorway. Keli went back to the bed and sat down and stared at the paper. He didn't turn this in, she thought. She wondered if she changed it before he turned it in.

Keli looked over at her dad's picture. She realized she was in the same position he had been nearly 20 years before. Keli really wished her mom were there. She lay back on the bed and whispered, "Mom, I need you!"

Tom called up the stairs. "Are you ready for dinner?"

Keli grabbed her father's goals and headed for the kitchen. "Gramps, any idea what this is?" She proudly held up the old piece of paper.

Tom was concentrating on moving two full bowls of chili to the table. "So what did you find in that old box?"

"It's not what I found in the box. It's what I found in the album."

"What did you find, an old love letter or something?"

"Not even close, Gramps!" Keli held it out.

Tom sat there quietly and read it. Then he looked up at Keli. "I wondered whatever happened to Lloyd. Your dad did treat him terrible. The kid wasn't an athlete and your dad teased him mercilessly."

Keli was shocked that he didn't comment about the last part of the paper. "Gramps, look at the last part! Look what Dad wrote about changing schools!"

Tom raised his eyebrows as he read.

"Did he ever ask you if he could change schools?"

"Well, I think the subject came up a few times, but it was more like an envy thing. He didn't ever ask to go to school there. More like he wished our school was bigger or he wished they could play teams like Dallas."

"So what would you have said if he had asked?"

Tom smiled. "Well now, I guess it's time for me to answer your question from earlier. When it comes to your future, honey, you need to talk with your mom."

Keli was impatient. "Gramps, you're stalling. What would you have done if Dad had come to you and asked to change schools?"

Tom stared across the table at Keli and said, "I would have encouraged him to go for it. But I get to answer this question now and not back then."

Keli was confused.

"Knowing what I know now, I would encourage him to do it. I can't honestly say how I would have answered it back then. I was younger and time does bring wisdom. I have hindsight today. I can see that he didn't get a chance at a dream he had back then. As I have grown, and to be perfectly honest I probably didn't learn this until I became a grandfather, as parents first and foremost, we are to raise you the best we can and part of that is to encourage dreams, not deny or limit them. Had he asked and I had said no, I would have been controlling a part of his life that was his and not mine to choose."

"Do you think he would have been successful?"

Tom shrugged. "My guess is yes. The most successful part would have been him trying. Every time someone sets a goal and honestly tries their best to achieve it, the easier it is the next time to try."

Trying not to get too philosophical, Tom looked at Keli and said. "I think your dad had a real chance and staying here limited him. But Keli, this decision does not lie between you and me. It's something you and your mother need to decide. Also, while I would have encouraged your father, I would have made sure that he was truly committed to his decision. In order to achieve what he—or you—would be attempting means giving up a lot. My best advice for you is to make darn sure you have completely thought this through."

Keli broke into a smile. "I will, Gramps. I promise."

Tom nodded. "If your mom asks how I feel about it, tell her to give me a call."

Keli stood up.

"So, young lady, you get my answer and now you're leaving me?"

"Nope, I am going to get you a beer and me a soda, and then I am going to kick your butt at Yahtzee. When I am done, I am going to go home," she said with a huge grin.

CHAPTER 14

KELI HAS A DREAM

Keli was hoping her mom had somehow beat her home, but no luck. She took her bag and the box of clippings up to her room. Keli looked out her window to see if she could see Sticky. But again, no luck.

She wandered downstairs and hit the message button. It was Charlee's voice. "Keli, call me." The next message was Charlee again. "Kels, where are you? I came by and you haven't been home all weekend. What's up?"

Keli hit the erase button and sat down by the phone. She realized that this was probably the first weekend that she hadn't talked with Charlee when they both were in town. But all Keli wanted right now was for her mom to get home. After a few minutes she stretched out on the couch and fell asleep. She went straight into a dream.

She was sitting in the Falls City gym watching a game. She wondered why she wasn't playing, but for some reason she didn't care. Charlee, Rachel, and Morgan were all playing, and Keli was cheering them on. As she jumped up and screamed "Great swing, Charlee," she heard a deep voice from behind her say, "Why aren't you playing?" She turned around to see it was a teenage boy, he looked strangely familiar to her. Even his voice was one she had heard before. Keli stared but said nothing, she was trying to remember how she knew him. Again the boy said, "Why aren't you playing?" Keli looked around in her dream to see if anyone else could see what she was seeing, but now they were the only two in the gym. Keli started yelled out, but as she did, she woke up. She lay there for a moment, shaking.

The front door opening startled her even more. Keli jumped up and ran over almost knocking both of them to the floor. "Mom, I missed you so much. We need to talk, Mom. Right now, okay? Please?"

"I tell you what. Let's get something to drink and go sit out on the deck. It's nice outside."

Keli nodded. She went to the kitchen and poured two glasses of juice and headed for the deck. Her mom followed behind her.

Keli was nervous. "I don't know where to begin."

Cindy smiled. "Tell me about the party."

Keli repeated the same story she had told her grandfather.

"It sounds like you had a great time," said Cindy. "I think I remember meeting Frank Webb years ago. I remember he was the star of Dallas like your dad was here in Falls City when we were all in school."

Keli took a big drink of juice and sat back in her chair. "Mom, before you answer, please listen to me and promise to think about it before you answer, okay?"

Her mom grinned, and Keli took that as a yes.

"Mom, I think I want to change schools and go to Dallas next year! I know this sounds crazy and maybe it is, but I have been giving it a lot of thought and I think it's my chance to really become a good player and get a scholarship. There are lots of kids in Dallas that keep asking me to come to their school."

Her mom started to respond.

"Wait, Mom, let me tell you a few more things before you say anything, please. This weekend while I was talking with Gramps, he told me he would..." Keli stopped mid-sentence. "Wait. I'll be right back."

She sprinted into the house and a few seconds later she flew back onto the deck with the clippings box.

"Mom, Gramps gave me all these old clippings of Dad when he played. And when I was browsing through everything, I found this behind a picture in this old album."

Keli opened the album and pulled out her father's goals. "Look at the last part of what he wrote, Mom. He said he wished he could have changed schools too. I swear I had already been talking to Gramps about all this before I found it. Mom, don't you see? I am kinda stuck the way Dad felt he was back then."

Her mom stared at the paper as she gently folded it and then looked back at Keli.

Keli said, "Wait. One more thing, then I'll be done, I promise. Right before you got home, I fell asleep on the couch and dreamed that I was watching Falls City girls playing and you won't believe this...Dad was like my age and he asked me why I wasn't playing in the game! It freaked me out so much, I woke up, and then you walked in the door. Mom...please let me do this. I know it will be hard to leave my friends."

She paused. "Please, Mom?" She sighed heavily and leaned back in her chair.

Her mom looked down at the folded paper she was still holding. "You know, Keli, this is a lot to swallow. It's a very big thing you're asking. What did your grandpa say when you asked him?"

"He said I should talk with you, but he also said that he thinks it's a good idea and if you want to call him on the subject, you can. What do you say, Mom?"

"What do you say we talk about this more tomorrow?"

Keli tried to hide her disappointment in not getting the answer she wanted right then.

"Please, Mom. I really want to do this."

Magic lifted his head and wagged his tail. Sticky was heading towards them.

"Okay. Tomorrow then?" Keli nodded. Her mom bent over and kissed Keli and headed back into the house to unpack. Keli waited for Sticky.

As Sticky stepped onto the deck, Keli said, "Hey, hottie boy, what's up?"

Sticky threw back his shoulders and said, "I'm just taking a break from my posse."

Keli laughed, "Sit down, stud!"

Sticky remained standing. "So what are you doing tonight?"

"Not sure. I haven't been home at all. Mom just got home too. Why?"

"Well, a bunch of the gang is going down to the Falls and build a fire and hang out tonight for a while. I tried calling but no answer. So I thought I'd walk over and find out if you want to go with us."

"I guess so. I need to ask, but I am sure I can."

"Cool. I'll pick you up in an hour!"

"You got it, hottie!" said Keli.

Sticky played the game with her, pretending to style his hair as he walked back towards his house.

Keli went inside, "Mom, I'm going up to the Falls with Sticky for a while. Is that okay?"

"Not for too long" came from her mom's bedroom.

Keli grabbed the phone and called Charlee.

Charlee picked up in her room. "Where've you been all weekend? I've been trying to reach you."

"I was up at Gramps'. You should have figured that out. My mom was with your mom, remember?"

"Yeah, duh! So are you going up to the Falls tonight?"

CHAPTER 15

PARTY AT THE FALLS

Keli and Sticky pulled up into the field above the falls; there were six other cars sprawled out with room for a dozen more. They ran down the steep, well-worn path to the rock walls that lined the deep channel that ran from the cascading water. There were about 20 kids standing or sitting on the rocks talking. Grunts and Dan were getting the fire pit ready to torch the fire. Music was blaring. When Charlee spotted Keli, she dropped the conversation she was in and raced over for a hug.

Suddenly, Grunts yelled, "Stand back! Let there be fire!" as he threw the match into the pit and flames shot six or seven feet into the air. Everyone cheered and laughed. The pit was a safe rocked hole in a wide-open area 20 feet or more from the cliff walls where the kids dove and jumped into the channel. It had been there for generations.

As the fire settled down some, the kids pooled their money and sent Grunts for hotdogs and marshmallows. Sticky and Keli looked at each other across the fire. They seemed to read each other's minds on how different this party was from the one the night before. Both smiled and pointed at each other.

As they finished eating, Charlee climbed up the highest rock and stood there with her hands raised above her head. "Attention, everyone. Hey! Shut up and listen! Falls City rocks! State champions this year! Awesome friends! Nobody has it better than we do!" She worked the group into a small frenzy, giving each other high fives and hugs. Keli was right in the middle of it as she climbed to the top of the rock and gave Charlee a high five.

As the evening wound down, Charlee asked Keli about the party the night before. "Sticky was bragging that he had all the Dallas girls hanging all over him!"

"Yeah," said Keli, "but I had to spend every penny I had to get them to do it!"

The other kids busted up, all teasing Sticky in their own way.

Charlee pressed Keli for details. Keli was reluctant to go into too much detail, almost wanting to keep it for herself. "It was cool. It was at Ashley Webb's house. Her dad owns Webb Sporting Goods. Did you know he played in the NFL?"

"Well, I'm glad you didn't call me. There's no way I would have gone. They are all snobs." Charlee was just getting going on the subject.

Grunts broke in. "Webb was a huge star back when my dad played. My dad said Webb was a wimp and Butch Stennes was a lot better."

Keli asked herself, "How many wimps get to play pro football?"

Sticky stood up then, "I am outta here." He looked at Keli. "You ready to go?"

As they walked up the now dark trail to the car, Sticky asked, "Whose party was the best?"

Keli lied, "Ours was better!"

"Right...especially the heated falls," answered Sticky.

Keli laughed.

As they drove home, Sticky said, "Do you realize that three weeks from tomorrow we are back in school? And in one week football and volleyball practice starts!"

Keli's mind froze. She hadn't thought about how close the time was for making a decision. A lot would have to be done if her mom agreed to let her switch schools.

CHAPTER 16

STEEN CALLS

Keli woke up to the sound of the phone, but she made no attempt to get to it before the answering machine. She managed to open her eyes long enough to see it was nearly 11:00. She knew she had to get up. If her mom were calling, she'd be in for a day of chores for sleeping so long.

Keli threw on her running clothes and headed down the long gravel road, then down through the shady forest and finally to Main Street. She waved at each car as they drove by. Keli thought how out of shape she had gotten in the past week since camp. She panted heavily as she made her way into the restaurant.

The restaurant was full for a Monday. Keli heard the usual chorus of, "Hey Keli, how are things? You girls ready for this year? Do you think we can win the championship?"

She shrugged and smiled like usual as she sat on her stool at the counter. Her mom whizzed by carrying nearly a half-dozen plates at once. Now wasn't going to be the time to talk to her.

Keli yelled back to the cook, "Hey, Jack! The Dowels are missing their dog. You wouldn't know where it is, would you?" Jack glared at her and Keli winked back. Jack shook his head and smiled.

Keli waved at her mom and headed for home. The run was considerably tougher since it was uphill all the way back. As she jogged into her driveway, Sticky shut off the lawn mower and yelled, "Hey! Why didn't you call so I could go with you?"

Keli could see Sticky was only teasing. "I knew you wouldn't be able to keep up so I didn't ask."

As she passed the answering machine in the kitchen, she hit the play button to see who had called and headed for the bathroom to get a towel to dry off.

"Hello, Keli, this is Steen from the party the other night. I got your number from Ashley. I hope you don't mind. I was calling to see what you were up to and maybe..." There was a pause. "I was wondering if maybe you and I could hit a movie or something. Well, let's see, I guess that's it."

Keli could tell he was very nervous. "Give me a call if you want," and he rattled off his number. Keli looked around for a pen with no luck. She kept repeating the number in her head over and over as she raced to her room to get a pen and write it down.

The message machine started the second message before she finished writing Steen's number down. "Hey, Keli, it's Ash. Just a heads up that the hottest kid at Dallas High called me and asked for your number, so don't be surprised if he calls. Oh, yeah, I want all the details after he calls. Damn, girl, do you know how many girls are after him? Anyways, call me. Oh, yeah, one more thing. Do you realize that next Monday tryouts begin? Hint, hint!"

Message three. It was Tom. "Hi, Cindy, I am returning your call. I'm not sure of your schedule but I will either see you at the restaurant around one for lunch or give me a call later."

Keli looked at the clock. It was 1:30 and she knew Gramps was now at the restaurant discussing what they were playing phone tag over. It had to be her changing schools.

The phone rang. Keli said out loud, "Please be Mom, please be Mom... Hello?"

"What do you mean 'keep up'?"

Keli didn't miss a beat. "I knew you wouldn't have enough energy to run and mow the lawn."

Sticky changed the subject. "So what else are you doing today?" You could always tell who won the battle of words between them. The loser was the one to change the subject.

"Not sure," answered Keli, "maybe going on a date with Steen." She wondered if Sticky would bite. But Sticky was smooth and didn't even begin to touch it.

"Well, if you don't," he said matter-of-factly, "some of us are going down to the football field and goof around."

Keli was disappointed that Sticky didn't say anything about the Steen date. "Well, if you see me, you see me," she said.

Sticky knew he had gotten her back. He tried not to laugh. "Okay, see you later maybe."

Keli hung up the phone frustrated. She looked out the window at Sticky's house hoping to see him running over to get the details about the date with Steen, but no Sticky.

Keli lay down on the couch and dialed Charlee to tell her about the date proposal. "Hey, you'll never guess who just called me?"

"It'd better not have been Derrick." Keli knew Charlee had had a crush on Derrick since the 8th grade.

"No, you know Derrick loves you, and as soon as he learns to talk to girls, I'm sure he will ask you out."

Charlee laughed. "Well I hope someone teaches him soon. I am not going my whole high school years without a boyfriend."

Keli brought the subject back around. "Sooo, do you want to guess or not?"

Charlee sighed. "No, Kels, just tell me. Oh, yeah, before you do, I'm coming over to spend the night. My parents are going out and I'm staying with you."

"Okay, but bring your own pillows 'cause you're not hogging mine this time! Hey, while you're at it, rent a movie or two." Keli knew that Charlee hated it when she bossed her around like this. "So Chuck, when are you going to be here?"

There was silence from the other end. Keli silently laughed. She knew Charlee was steaming on the other end.

Finally Charlee answered. "I changed my mind. I'm going to Rachel's instead."

Keli busted up laughing. "Right you are... so really when are you going to be here? You know I am only kidding with ya!" She paused. "I was going to tell you who asked me out."

Charlee stopped her. "Hey, I'd like to hear all about it, but I have too many errands to run. I will be there around 7 or so. Gotta go!" Click.

Keli looked at the phone in disappointment.

CHAPTER 17

IT'S YOUR DECISION

Keli could hear Sticky's truck start up. She knew he was heading down to the football field. Her mind wandered back to changing schools, and a cold chill came over her. She looked at the drawing he had done of her for her birthday and she could feel herself tighten a little more.

The box of her dad's stuff was sitting on her desk. She went over and grabbed the piece of paper hoping to gain some strength from it.

The Honda pulled into the driveway. Keli looked at the clock. Why was her mom home at such an odd hour of the day? She put the piece of paper back in the box and thought that maybe she was there to talk about changing schools.

She raced downstairs just as Cindy walked in. "Mom, what are you doing home?"

"It was slow. I have to go back in a little while. I thought we should talk about you and school." Cindy looked serious.

Keli wasn't used to seeing that. She immediately thought the worst, that she wasn't going to be able to switch schools.

Magic sensed the tension and snuggled up next to Cindy when she sat in her chair.

Keli sat on the edge of the couch, staring at her mom.

She smiled at Keli. "You know this is crazy..."

Keli started to speak, but Cindy held up her hand cutting her off. "Keli, this whole idea is pretty crazy. I just talked to your grandfather about it." She leaned back in her chair. "I really don't know what the right answer is. All I know is we have lived here our whole lives, and your dad and I went to school here, and your friends are here."

She paused for a second. "Are you really sure this is what you want to do? Have you really thought this through? Do you understand how completely different your life will be?"

Her face turned serious again as she waited for Keli's answer.

Keli folded her hands together and talked slowly. "Mom, you're right. It is crazy. I am scared to death, but I really do want this. It's hard to explain. The week I spent at camp was a whole new world, and I want that world, Mom. I dream about it all the time. I have made some new friends that I know will support me."

She slipped off the couch onto her knees in front of her mom and looked up at her, "It's my chance. I don't know if I will get another one."

Cindy's eyes filled with tears, "Okay, honey. It's your decision and I'll support it." Cindy leaned down and kissed Keli's forehead.

There was silence for a minute or so, both contemplating what this meant. Then Keli sat back and crossed her legs. "Mom, if you think this is a bad idea, please tell me."

Cindy smiled. "I think most of my concern is that my baby is growing up. I never really have thought about the fact that one day you'll actually be gone. I know this is the first step and I have to let you take it."

She smiled again. "A week or so ago your friend Ashley skipped out of camp and came and saw me about this. She sat at the restaurant for a couple of hours trying to convince me this was the right thing for you. You do have a good friend; I know she will be there for you. At the same time, the hardest part of all of this are your friends back here. They really are your family, and I am pretty sure they won't understand this or accept it. If you're going to do this, then you need to be straight with all of them, and you need to do it as soon as possible."

Keli looked down and nodded. She knew that she needed to start telling her friends about changing schools. "You're right," she looked back up. "I'm petrified about it. I think I am going to get a group of them together and tell them at the same time instead of going through the speech over and over."

Cindy patted Magic on the head and nodded. Then she stood up. "I need to get back to the restaurant before Jack has a coronary. I think he has figured out what is going on...I think if we get slow later, I am going to tell him."

She looked down at Keli. "Just so you know...as of right now, I am not hiding this, and if I am asked by anyone, I am telling them what's going on."

Keli looked up at her. "I understand." She stood up and hugged her mom.

CHAPTER 18

MAKING THE SECOND DECISION

Keli had only six more days until both schools started fall tryouts. As much as she desperately wanted to play for the Dragons, she was terrified at how her teammates and friends would take the news.

She played different scenarios in her head. She thought she could call them on the phone, or tell Sticky and have him break the news, or wait until she knew they wouldn't be home and leave a message on their machines.

As she sat there staring out her bedroom window, the feeling that she wasn't going to be able to tell them became stronger and stronger, and panic started to set in. She jumped up from her chair and put on her running shoes. As she started down the gravel road towards town, Sticky rounded the corner, driving straight for her. The last thing Keli wanted to do right then was talk to him; she thought he'd be able to see right through her.

As Sticky slowed down, she could see him cranking down his window. Reluctantly Keli stopped, she could see he was all sweaty..."So what have you been up to?"

"Grunts, Don, and a bunch of us have been working out with some of the dads."

Keli was still nervous but mustered a smile. "From the looks of it, they really made you guys work."

Sticky sighed. Keli could tell he was really tired. She quickly played on this. "Well, hey, you need to get into the shower. I'll talk to you later."

Sticky nodded. "What are you doing tonight? The guys were thinking we would get a group and head into Dallas for pizza and a movie. You want to go?"

Keli's heart pounded a little faster. "Sorry I can't...no money. You guys have a good time without me."

Sticky smiled and said, "I'll cover you. Come on, it'll be fun. Maybe we can run into a few of the Dallas spanks and have a little rumble." Sticky always talked big. A rumble to him was yelling out the window and speeding off.

Keli shook her head. "I don't want you to always have to buy. You guys go without me."

Sticky wanted nothing to do with that. "Hey, it's no biggie on the money. Really. It's worth it to have you come along ...please?" He pulled his long face.

Keli had no good comeback, so they settled on a time. Then Sticky asked where she was headed.

Keli stammered. She didn't want to answer him. "Uh, I feel like going for a run."

Sticky nodded, "I'll call everyone and get everything set up."

Keli headed down the road. As she jogged across the bridge and through town, she was feeling sick to her stomach. After all these years, she and Sticky had a relationship that didn't even have the word "lie" in it. Now twice in the past couple of weeks she had lied to him, and she knew he was soon going to know that.

She ran up in front of Tom's house. As usual, he was sitting in his rocking chair reading. He could see by her face that she wasn't doing very well. "How are things?"

Keli walked up the couple of steps and pulled over the smart chair and sat down. "Gramps, I'm really in a bad spot. Mom agreed to let me change schools." She paused. "I have no idea how to tell everyone. I am lying to Sticky, my gut hurts," she leaned towards him, "and I have no idea what to say or how to do it. Next week practice starts and I know I need to tell everyone what I am going to do. I am ready to just give up on it. It is so hard."

Keli started to cry. Then she stood up. "That's my answer. I'll just give up on my goals." She started to wipe her eyes.

Tom's voice deepened as he spoke. "Keli, why don't you sit back down?"

Keli finished wiping her eyes. "That's okay, Gramps. I have my answer." She leaned over and gave her grandfather a kiss and headed towards the steps. This time his voice was a little sharp. "Keli, sit down. We need to talk about this!"

She turned to find a look on his face that she hardly ever saw. She sat down.

Tom set his book down, leaned back in his rocking chair, and gave her a big smile. "Well, we have a lot to talk about, young lady. Fear is no reason to run from your goals." He leaned forward and looked right into her eyes. "Keli, you're on the edge of becoming an adult. This kind of decision will shape you for the rest of your life. It's true you really must decide what is more important to you. And I think there is a more important question to ask yourself. Do you see yourself living in Falls City, working and raising a family here?"

Keli thought for a second, then shook her head. "I hope I don't. I've always dreamed of living in a big city or in a resort-like place. I want to travel and see the world before I get too old. The thought of marriage, kids, and working never enters my mind."

"Then let me ask you another question. Do you think Sticky, Charlee, and the others will always be your close friends?"

Keli quickly answered. "If I don't go to Dallas, they will."

Tom smiled again. "Well, I don't think so...most kids growing up make friend-ships with their schoolmates, but once they get out of school generally everyone goes different directions because of jobs, interests, and a lot of reasons. You hap-pen to live in a small town where those who choose to continue to live here stay friends, but for those who leave..."

He paused. "Those bonds they built with the high school friends generally die off into memories. They do, Keli, they really do. Ask your mom how many people she is a still close friend with who have moved away from here? Even if they only moved 10 miles away. As we grow up, our lives get caught up in our own worlds, and if these friends of yours right now aren't still in your world, they will slowly fade away. Again not from a lack of friendship, but from a lack of keeping up with them. The interests you share with them in high school won't be the interests you will have when you're an adult. Please believe me. I have been through it myself and have watched many generations go through it. It's just life." Tom could see that Keli was thinking hard.

"Keli, if you do decide to leave, then you will have to face your friends and community being mad and sad. This community has a lot of pride. Don't kid yourself. They will feel abandoned, and their pride will be hurt by you going to a town that they have always felt second to. That sounds harsh, but it's true. But equally true, while this community loves you, they can't help you with your dream either. So it boils down to what is really more important to you. If this dream is the most important thing in your life, then follow it. You will need to step out and face it head on."

He paused again. "I have a feeling that some will eventually come around and support you. Know one thing. If you choose to leave, you have two people for sure who will support you no matter what!" Keli knew he was talking about himself and her mother.

Tom leaned over and reached out both of his hands. Keli grabbed them tightly, tears again beginning to flow. "I'm scared, Gramps."

"You should be," he answered. "But you can do it, if you want. I have watched you grow up and I see this young lady growing and getting stronger year after year."

Keli looked up at her grandfather to see tears in his eyes too. Her heart melted.

"Keli, I wish I could have had this conversation with your dad. You remind me so much of him. My last bit of advice: Dive right to the middle of your heart and whatever is there, do it! Don't look back. No regrets, head tall, and don't stop 'til you get wherever you're going."

Both wiped their tears. Keli smiled at her grandfather. "I love you so much, Gramps! I just wish it was easier."

Tom nodded in agreement.

Keli stood up and said, "I guess tonight is the night."

He gave her an inquisitive look.

"Sticky and some of the gang are going into Dallas for pizza and a movie. Sticky invited me to go along. Since I will have most of them together, maybe it's the right time to tell them."

His eyes twinkled. "You can do this! Tonight would be the right time to tell them."

CHAPTER 19

I HAVE SOMETHING TO TELL YOU

Sticky honked the horn as he pulled into the driveway. Keli checked her eyes one more time to making sure the red swelling was gone, then grabbed her Mountaineer sweatshirt and headed for the car.

As they pulled out of the driveway, Keli realized she hadn't even talked to her mom about going out or her conversation with Gramps. "Sticky," she said, "who else are you picking up?"

"Charlee and Rachel."

"I need you to drop me off at the restaurant. I haven't even asked Mom if I could go. You go pick them up and then come back and get me, okay?"

Sticky nodded as he turned onto the paved road and headed down the hill towards town.

After Sticky dropped her off, Keli scanned the restaurant through the windows to see how busy it was and how easy it would be to tell her mom about what was going on. Good, she thought to herself, only the Dunaways and Bathkes were there having dinner.

Everyone acknowledged Keli as she made her way through the clanging door. "Hey Kels, you ready for a run at the state championship?" came from Mr. Dunaway.

Keli smiled and ignored the question. "Mom, do you have a minute? I need to talk with you."

Cindy took a look around to see if everything was okay for a quick timeout, then nodded and headed to the back room. Keli walked in first and started talking before her mom even got the door shut.

"Mom, first can I go into Dallas with the gang for pizza and a movie?"

"Sweetie, I don't have any extra money."

"I don't need money. Sticky invited me. I told him I couldn't afford it, and he said he would buy."

"Sure, I guess. When will you be home?"

"Well, that brings me to the next thing I want to talk with you about. I just got back from talking with Gramps, and I am going to tell everyone at pizza that I am going to Dallas next year."

Cindy frowned. "Are you okay? You positive you want to do this?"

Keli nodded. "Practice starts next Monday and the longer I wait, the harder it will be."

Her mom's eyes teared up.

"Mom, are you okay? I won't go if you don't want me to...be honest!"

Cindy shook her head, fighting back the tears. "No, I want you to follow your dreams. I am just struggling with you growing up is all."

A muffled clanging sound came from the front of the restaurant. Keli knew it would be the gang looking for her. "I need to go now."

"You go and take care of it, sweetie. I'm very proud of you."

Keli headed for the door but her mom called her back. "I know your dad would be proud of you too!"

Not wanting the tears to turn back on, Keli hurried to meet her friends.

Charlee was standing over by the Dunaways and Bathkes. She saw Keli reach for the passenger front door of Sticky's car. "Hey, sorry, girl. I already called shot-gun. Ask Sticky."

Sticky shrugged his shoulders and grinned as Keli got into the back. "Hey Rach...how are you?" Keli asked.

Rachel smiled. "Glad to be out of the house. My parents are fighting again." None of the kids wanted to touch that subject.

Keli looked around the car at her friends. She had known them all her life. Her heart started to beat faster, knowing in a few minutes all their lives would be turned upside down.

Charlee started to put in a CD, but Keli broke the silence. "Hey, when we get to the restaurant, I have something to tell all of you guys."

Charlee stopped and turned around. "Dang, girl, now we're curious. Just tell us now!"

"No. I'll tell you when we get there." Sticky caught Keli's eye in the mirror, trying to figure out what she had to say by the look on her face.

Keli quickly moved on. "Hey, what CD are you putting in? Let's have some music."

Charlee said slowly, "It's Matchbox 20."

Sticky said, "I'm tired of that one. Just turn it on. I have the All American Rejects in there." Keli and Rachel both vetoed Sticky, and Charlee started her CD.

As they pulled into the restaurant, Keli's heart felt like it was going to explode. It didn't calm down any as they found a table and got drinks. She finished filling up her cup with soda and started to walk towards the table. She looked around to see if she knew anyone in the place. Before she could even set down, Sticky was already sensing bad news. "So, what's up, Kels?"

Charlee and Rachel were focused waiting to hear.

Keli took a drink of her soda and then a deep breath. Again she quickly searched the restaurant for anyone she knew. Charlee said, "Quit stalling and tell us."

Keli thought of her gramps, which gave her a boost of confidence. "Okay. First, I want you all to know that you are my very best friends in the whole world and nothing will ever change that." Her heart was beating so hard she thought she was going to faint.

Charlee said, "Yeah, so?"

Keli took another deep breath and said, "I know you all are going to probably hate me, but, but..." Keli hesitated, trying to find the right words. Then her mind went back to Tom. "Okay, here it is. I'm not going to Falls City this year. I am going to..."

Charlee exploded. "What? What do you mean you're not going to Falls City this year?"

Keli looked around to see if they were making a scene. A few people were staring. Keli tried to talk in a lower voice. "Let me explain."

She looked over at Sticky who wouldn't look back at her. "I'm changing schools because I want to play volleyball against better competition. I want to get a scholarship and I don't..."

Charlee interrupted again. "Jeez, girl, we all would like to get a damn scholarship, but we aren't good enough and neither are you!" Charlee stood up. She was practically shouting, "So where are you going this year?" She was glaring at Keli waiting for an answer.

Again Keli glanced at Sticky hoping for support, but Sticky was just staring off into space. Keli looked back at Charlee. "I am going to Dallas."

Charlee laughed sarcastically. "I should have guessed. You've been hanging onto those girls ever since camp."

Keli wanted to fire back at Charlee. Instead she said, "Charlee, sit down and let me explain everything. You guys have been my friends since we started school. I was hoping you would support me. It's not like I'm moving. We can still hang out. I will just be going to a different school."

Charlee finished her sentence by adding "...and playing for another team! What about our goal this year of winning the state championship? So you dump us to go play on a better team, with kids you don't know and leave your friends behind."

The server interrupted the conversation by bringing over the pizza. It just sat there. Nobody had any appetite. Keli looked at Rachel, who was staring at Charlee. Rachel never was one to stir up anything.

Keli leaned back into her chair and said, "Sticky, are you going to say anything?"

Sticky shook his head without looking at her. Charlee grabbed a piece of pizza and before taking a bite, she threw Keli one last shot. "Well, I am kinda glad you're going. I'm a little sick and tired of you always thinking you're better than the rest of us. You'll fit in good with the Dallas arrogance. I hope you fall flat on your face!"

Keli's mouth flew open. She had never imagined Charlee acting this way. She looked over at Sticky, who was refusing to get involved in the conversation. Keli blurted out, "STICKY, say something!"

Sticky looked at her for the first time. His eyes were sharp and so was his tone. "I really have nothing to say to someone who lies to me." He took a piece of pizza and Keli knew that she was sitting at a table where no one wanted her. She sat there for a moment sick at heart and wondered what to do next. She glanced up at the clock to see that it was close to 7:00. Her mom was about to get off work.

Keli stood up and, without saying a word, walked out. As she walked along the sidewalk looking for a phone, she was numb from what had just happened. Her two best friends in the whole world hadn't even given her a chance to really explain. They had dumped her just like that. Keli thought about what her grandfather told her about how people change and go their separate ways.

Back at the pizza parlor, Keli's friends were as shocked as Keli. Rachel was the first to open up. "Did I hear what I just heard?"

Sticky threw his pizza back onto the tray. "Damn it! Twice she lied to me about this. I asked her and she promised me that this wasn't going to happen."

Charlee slapped the table. "I spent the night over there last night and she didn't say one thing about it. She acted like everything was just peachy."

Rachel looked at Sticky. "Should we go get her? She can't walk home from here."

Charlee angrily answered, "Let her walk or let one of her new friends give her a ride."

Sticky was falling into a deep sadness. "I can't believe it." He scratched his head for a few seconds. "Keli has made a choice and I am not going to go chasing her."

Charlee's anger and revenge meter was rising by the second.

Just then, Ashley, Greta, and a few other kids walked in. Sticky almost fell off his chair. He turned to Rachel and Charlee. "You are not going to believe this. Guess who just walked in?"

Without even turning around, Charlee said, "I don't care what she has to say. I am over her," thinking it was Keli.

Sticky shook his head and said, "It's Ashley and Greta, the two girls from Keli's summer camp."

Charlee turned around to see if she recognized them. "Of course, she probably invited them here, thinking we were going to dump her after she told us. I am going to talk with them and let them know what I think!"

Sticky reached for Charlee, "Hey, they didn't force her to switch."

Charlee shrugged her shoulders, "I don't care," and headed towards their table.

Ashley noticed Charlee heading towards them. She smiled at her. "Hey, you're Keli's friend."

Charlee glared at them. "We aren't friends anymore. I just came over here to tell you that Keli going to your school is a good thing. You can have her. She is full of herself and you guys will get sick of her too! Oh yeah, all you Dallas people think you're so cool. I am here to tell you you're not...you all suck!"

Greta had had enough. "Hey, I'm not sure who you are or where you're coming from, but I have had all I am going to take from you. Go back wherever you came from. If this is what Keli had to deal with, then if she is coming to Dallas this year, you're the reason. Now get away from our table." Greta yelled at the server, "Hey, Justin, can you ask this person to leave us alone?"

Charlee glared and walked back to her table without saying any more.

Sticky made eye contact with Greta. She raised her arms as if to say what was that? Sticky felt completely awkward. He and Greta had become friends, and his interest in her made him feel caught in the middle. He shrugged his shoulders, hoping that would be good enough.

Rachel looked at both of them. "Hey, can we go? This is a nightmare!"

As they walked by Greta's table, Sticky told Charlee and Rachel he would catch up in a minute. Charlee glared at Sticky with a how-could-you-talk-to-them expression.

Sticky mustered a smile and said, "Hey, I want to apologize for my friend's outburst."

Greta smiled and said, "What was that all about anyways?"

Sticky wrinkled his nose and mouth, "Well, it's a long story. I'll call you and tell you, okay?" That was good enough for Greta.

Ashley said, "If I understood that crazy chick, Keli is coming to Dallas this year?"

Sticky looked puzzled. "Yeah, didn't you know she was coming?"

Ashley looked at Sticky. "Well, we talked about it but until just a minute ago, I didn't know for sure. I know that she was really confused about what to do."

Sticky didn't know what to say. "Well, hey, both of you have been really cool to me and this is pretty much a shock. I feel like I am losing my best friend, and our school is really going to be upset that she is leaving."

Ashley and Greta almost simultaneously said, "Why are you losing your best friend? She is just changing schools."

"I think she needs her best friend to support her," Ashley added, "assuming she really is your best friend."

Charlee opened the door and yelled in, "Hey, Stick, let's go!"

Sticky gave them a sad bit of smile and said, "Hey, I gotta go." He looked at Greta as he walked away.

CHAPTER 20

WHAT DO I DO NOW?

Keli found a phone booth and dialed the restaurant. As it rang, tears again began to flow. Her mom could tell things weren't right. "Mom, can you come get me...please? I just told Charlee, Sticky, and Rachel and it didn't go very well and I left the pizza parlor."

"Where are you?"

"In front of the Safeway."

"Where are the others?" Cindy was worried. "Are you okay?"

"I guess they're still at the pizza place. Mom, they were being so mean. I couldn't take it anymore so I left."

Cindy was getting mad. "How were they being mean to you?"

"Well, it was mainly Charlee and she was yelling and saying a lot of mean things. I'll tell you all about it when you pick me up."

"Sweetie, I don't get off 'til 8:00 and there is no one here to relieve me."

"It's fine, Mom. I'll just hang out here until you get here. I'll be fine."

Just as she sat down at the coffee shop next to Safeway, Sticky's car pulled out of the pizza parking lot. Her eyes followed it until it disappeared. She could tell that they didn't notice her sitting there. From the direction they were heading, she knew they weren't going to the movies but were headed back to Falls City.

By the time the evening was over, the whole town would know that she was changing schools, and from the way Charlee had acted in the restaurant, she knew that she wasn't going to be welcome anywhere.

The thought of "what have I done?" started to settle into her consciousness. She knew she couldn't take it back.

The hour dragged by but finally the old blue Honda pulled into the parking lot. She could tell that there were two people in the car, and she was relieved to see it was her grandpa.

She raced to meet the car and tried to jump in almost before it had come to a complete stop.

Both her mom and gramps turned around and looked at her. Tom asked, "Have you eaten? Why don't we get a pizza?"

Cindy kept glancing at Keli through the rearview mirror. "I want to know everything that was said when we get there."

Keli looked back at her in the mirror and nodded slowly.

One more time Keli entered the pizza place, only this time almost running into Ashley as she and Greta were leaving. "Keli!" exclaimed Ashley. "Wow, you aren't going to believe what just happened here!"

Inwardly, Keli groaned and slowly said, "I have a pretty good idea." Ashley's eyes brightened. "Hey, we are stoked that you're coming to Dallas this year! It's going to be great. Have you told Coach Lindsay that you're coming?"

"No, I just really came to the decision yesterday, and I wanted to tell my friends first before I did anything else."

"Well, your friends are pretty pissed," Greta blurted out. "Ooops, sorry!" as she realized that wasn't the best way to put it in front of Keli's mom and grandpa.

Ashley grabbed Keli's arm. "Girl, give your friends some time. They'll get over it."

Keli tried to smile. "I hope so!"

"I am going to find a table and I'll order," interrupted Cindy. She looked back at Ashley and Greta. "It's nice to see both of you again."

A moment later Keli sat down at the table and slouched in her chair.

"Ashley is right. Give them time. What happened was a complete shock to them and it's natural for them to be mad and hurt." Cindy reached across the table and patted her hand. "Don't make it worse by saying something you can't take back. Remember you are the one who chose this path. You talked to me and Gramps many times, going back and forth. You felt it was worth the risk of losing your friends to follow this path."

I did make this decision, Keli thought, staring at Tom balancing a tray of drinks. He put the drinks on the table and sat down. "Keli I'm sure you don't want to go into the nitty-gritty details, but what is going on in that head of yours right now?"

"I'm in shock, I guess. I knew they weren't going to take it very well, but I guess I was naïve as to how bad it would be. Charlee was really mean, and Sticky wouldn't even look at me. He said he couldn't be friends with a liar. That is all he would say. Rachel, well, you know Rachel, she is too quiet and polite to say anything, but she will go along with whatever Charlee says."

She paused. "I think the thing that hurts the most right now is how Sticky thinks of me. I have to admit there have been a couple of times in the past couple of weeks when the subject came up, and I led him to believe that I wasn't going to change schools. I was confused, and I really didn't know for sure that I was going to do it. Now he hates me and thinks I'm a liar. It is going to be so awkward to see my friends now, and it will be impossible not to."

Keli looked at her mom. "Mom, what do you think of moving to Dallas?"

Cindy laughed. "Sure! Let's hurry up and eat and then go pack!"

Tom thumped the table to get their attention. "Keli, these next few months are going to be awkward. There is no getting around it. You need to be as close to the same old Keli as you have always been. It's really your only chance to have both worlds. When do tryouts at Dallas start?"

"Next Monday," answered Keli.

"Well then, you have a lot to do, young lady. You still have a few people to talk to like your old coach and the rest of your friends. And you can't just show up for tryouts next Monday without getting enrolled in school. You need to get a hold of your new coach too."

"You're right, Gramps. I will talk to both coaches tomorrow, As for the rest of my friends, well, they all probably know by now. Mom, I am going to need your help getting enrolled."

Can I Play...

Cindy winked at her and looked at Tom. She was grateful that he had taken over the conversation and had Keli working on the solution and away from the train wreck that had just happened.

CHAPTER 21

SHE'S NOT GOOD ENOUGH!

The next six days were torture to both Keli and her mom. While they were making the arrangements for the school switch on Cindy's days off, the town was building up a head of outrage. How could Butch's daughter, the king sports figure for the past couple of generations, do this to their town?

Thursday morning when Cindy returned to work, the restaurant was full of people waiting to hear what she had to say. As she walked towards the front door, she could hear the group clamoring, but as the front door clanged with her entrance, the place went silent.

All eyes were on her as she made her way behind the counter to get her apron. Jack, back by the grill, called for her. Cindy scanned the room of groups whispering now.

"Hi Jack," she said. "Busy this morning, huh?" She knew why they were all there.

Jack motioned for her to come closer. "The lynch mob has been brewing the past couple days while you were off. Now make sure that whatever you say, you remember these people pay our wages, and we can't let them allow their anger over this stop them from coming in here."

Cindy nodded, but Jack wasn't through. "Cindy, you have worked for me for a good number of years, but I have a business to run, and if I don't have any customers because of your family decision, well, hopefully you understand what I am trying to say."

Cindy, shocked by the threat, started to respond.

Jack interrupted her. "Cindy, this isn't about what I think. As far as I am concerned, Keli should do what you and her think is best. But this is about my business and what is best for it." He softened his tone a bit and said, "Hey, let's just try and work through this, okay?"

Cindy knew Jack was right. It wasn't his fault and he shouldn't be penalized for their decisions. "I understand, Jack. I'll try to make this sure this doesn't affect your business and if it does, I'll find other work." Cindy gave him a tight smile and went to address the crowd.

Cindy made her way back behind the counter and scanned the room again. She put both her hands down on the counter and asked, "Before we go any farther, is there anyone in here that wants me to serve them some food before we talk about Keli?"

About half the room responded with yes and the other half started firing questions. Cindy raised her hand in the air and her voice rose above everyone else's. "Okay, first, this is Jack's place, and the people who want food, I will take care of first. Once everyone gets what they want, I will talk about Keli. Until then out of respect for Jack and me, let me do my job."

The restaurant went mostly quiet. Cindy made her way around the room taking orders and filling up coffee cups.

As Cindy made her way back to the ticket spindle, she caught Jack's eye. He winked and smiled at her. Cindy smiled back. So far so good, she thought.

About 45 minutes later, she had accomplished the first task. They all had full stomachs. She made her way back to her original spot again with both hands leaning on the counter.

"Okay, now that we have got everyone fed, let me start. I understand that Keli's friends would be mad at her for her decision, but frankly I am a little surprised by your reactions.

I have known most of you all my life. A lot of us went through school here; so did our parents and so did their parents. That is all well and good. For us going to school here, choosing to raise our families here was our choice. I am pretty sure most of us at one time or two and for some a zillion times thought or dreamed about leaving here. We have all wished for a better job or to live in a big city or on a golf course somewhere." A few folks smiled at that.

Cindy looked straight at Charlee's parents and said, "I know for myself, when I was Keli and Charlee's age, I thought about going off to college. Butch dreamed about that all the way through school and then kicked himself 'til the day he died for not changing schools where some college recruiter might have given him a scholarship." She paused to let Butch's name sink in.

"I don't know about the rest of you, but I can't afford to help Keli with college. If her dream is to go off and see the world and never come back to this town, that is her choice. I look around this room and see all of you thinking somehow that Keli is the property of this town, and she should have to live by the choices we have made. I am here to tell you that's not right, and I support her completely, and you all should too. Keli is a great kid and who knows? Maybe with the right coaching and playing against better kids, she can get good enough to get a scholarship somewhere." She looked around the room, making eye contact with those who would look at her.

"Keli hasn't done anything wrong; all she wants is a chance. I have to agree with her. Here she doesn't have much of a chance. Now if any of you have anything you want to add, you let me know. I am proud of my girl and I know Butch would be too."

Charlee's dad responded. "Cindy, everything you say may be true, but our kids are really hurt by this, and just like you, we want to support them. Some of our kids' dreams are being shattered by Keli's decision. I can only speak for Charlee, but she came home and hasn't been able to stop crying. Not only does she think she has lost her best friend, but she had dreams just like the rest of the school of the girls winning State. They have been talking about it since they started playing sports. We parents have traveled all over the state supporting and helping them build this thing, and right now when it's ready to happen, Keli decides to pull the plug. It's pretty hard for all of us."

Cindy nodded. "I understand...I really do. Believe me, Keli and I have spent many hours going over this. Keli has spent many hours going over it with Tom also. Until three days ago she was still up in the air. She agonized over this and the only reason she did was because of how it was going to affect everyone else."

Charlee's dad looked around the room, checking for support, then finished with the same theme that Charlee had used on Keli in the pizza parlor. "You know, Cindy, Keli is a heck of a player here in our Casco league. She is probably the best player in the whole league and maybe in the whole state in our class of school. But I have to be frank. At best, she would be an average player up in the 4A schools. Here she is a star, and there she might not even get off the bench. I love Keli, we all love her, but she isn't *that good* a player. She belongs here playing and helping Falls City win a championship."

Cindy clenched her teeth. "Well, you know maybe she isn't good enough to make it, but she has made a choice to try. I guess we will all have to make our own decision on whether we are going to support her or not."

Then she changed the subject back to restaurant business. "Anyone here need a fill-up on their coffees?" A few raised their cups. As she made her way around the room, only a few would say anything.

When it was time to fill the Poes' cups, Charlee's dad held up his. "Now, Cindy, please don't take what I said wrong. I just wanted to tell you my opinion."

Cindy smiled, remembering her conversation with Jack. "Bill, I understand. We have known each other for over 30 years. You might be right. I am just not going to limit Keli's dreams. Out of respect for me, please understand that."

Cindy glanced at Kay, Charlee's mom, who quickly looked back over to Bill.

As the crowd broke up, Cindy was relieved. She went back to the grill to get a read on how Jack thought things had gone. He was busy scrapping down the grill and without looking up said, "Well, my hat's off to you, Cindy. You handled that as good as anyone could have done."

Cindy sighed. "Thanks, Jack. I really needed to hear that!"

CHAPTER 22

THE NIGHT BEFORE TRYOUTS

The final few days dragged by. Keli had somehow managed to avoid contact with any of the kids in Falls City. Mostly she had taken care of all the requirements to enroll in Dallas High and had told her old coach, who had sincerely wished her luck.

Keli sat at her desk and looked out towards Sticky's house. The past few days, she wasn't sure if she had done a better job of hiding from him or he from her.

She heard a knock at the front door. She half-hoped it was Sticky and Charlee. She sat there frozen until there was a second knock and made her way down the stairs. Her heart was thumping. She exhaled in relief when she saw that it was Ashley and Greta.

The girls didn't wait for Keli to open the door; they did it themselves. Ashley stepped in first. "Go get your things," she said laughing. "We are kidnapping you on the eve of tryouts. We figured we'd better or you would be out partying all night and wouldn't be able to make it."

"I can't just leave," said Keli. "My mom..."

Ashley finished her sentence. "...said it was just fine. We stopped at the restaurant on the way up here. So go get your stuff!"

Keli smiled. "Really? You stopped and talked with my mom?"

"Yep," answered Greta. "Call her if you want, but hurry; let's get going. We told your mom we would bring you back after tryouts tomorrow."

In a flash Keli was up the stairs and shouting down to ask about a sleeping bag. A few seconds later they were in the car pulling out of the driveway.

Keli looked over at Sticky's house. "Greta, are you still talking with Sticky?"

Greta gave a glance over at the house. "No, I tried calling him a couple of times, but he never returned my calls." Greta turned to Keli. "Have you talked with him?"

Keli shook her head. "I haven't seen him or talked with him since last week."

"Wow, really? They aren't still pissed about you changing schools, are they?"

"Oh yeah, they are. Their parents even went down to the restaurant and gave my mom a hard time about me leaving."

They drove past the high school. Keli glanced at the reader board. "Football and Volleyball Tryouts Aug 16." She stared at the sign. Even before she got to high school, she couldn't wait for that date. She never liked summer. She would show up and watch the whole practice. Now, for the first time, it didn't have the same meaning.

Keli tried to block out these memories by getting her mind on what was in front of her. "Hey, so what's up for tonight? And tell me a little about how the tryouts work."

Ashley made eye contact with Keli through the rearview mirror. "Well, tonight we are just having dinner with my dad, and maybe we can swim a little. I think there will be a few people over but I'm not sure. As for tryouts, we'll make sure you get your rest. Girl, you're in for a trip through hell. Coach will spend the first day trying to see who really wants to play. That means running and more running. Hopefully we will touch a volleyball tomorrow."

"We tease Coach after tryouts are over that she should be a football coach or a drill sergeant," said Greta.

"So is she like that the whole season?" asked Keli.

Greta turned around and faced her. "No, she does it to see who really wants to play. It weeds out a handful of players who are probably good enough to make the team but don't have the desire or attitude to play hard."

Keli thought about how Falls City's tryouts were more of a formality. The biggest part was to see if there were any new kids and if they could play. Other than that, it was really just a practice. The freshmen and a few of the non-athletic sophomores were going to make up the JV team, and the Varsity was everyone else. Once in a while, the big news would be incoming freshmen who had made Varsity.

Keli snapped out of her reverie as Ashley drove into her driveway. Big Frank was in the driveway washing his new Hummer. "Hey girls, grab a hose or a rag and help me finish this and I will take you out for dinner."

Ashley did the negotiating. "Hey, how 'bout you hurry up and then you can take us out for dinner?"

"Okay, but if you want to be back here by the time your friends show up, then you should grab a rag!"

Ashley looked at Keli and Greta. Keli quickly said, "Hey, let's help."

Greta laughed. "Dang, you don't need to suck up now. Save that for tomorrow!"

By the time they got back from dinner, cars were already starting to dot the street, but there wasn't anyone in the cars or hanging out. "So where is everyone?" asked Keli.

Greta answered. "Swimming. They think it's a public pool."

Frank looked at his watch. "Okay, remember, 10:00 is the limit. You girls have a big day tomorrow."

"No problem, Dad," said Ashley. "I will get everyone out of here by 10:00!"

The girls quickly dressed and joined the others at the pool. When they entered the backyard from the kitchen, there were balloons and a big sign welcoming Keli to the Dallas Dragons.

Keli's mouth dropped. She immediately turned red, and everyone was calling her name. Keli looked at Ashley and Greta. They were both laughing. Ashley stuck her finger right at Keli and yelled, "Gotcha!"

After a brief moment of embarrassment, Keli followed Ashley into the pool with Greta close behind. Keli's head popped out of the water only two feet in front of Steen.

Steen splashed her and said, "Do you always ignore people when they call you?"

Keli splashed him back. "Only when I feel like it." She smiled at him. "So how've you been?"

"Well, I've been good. Bummed summer is almost over and we have daily double tryouts starting tomorrow. I am glad you're coming to Dallas this year." He splashed her again. "By the way, I've made it one of my goals this year to get you to return one of my calls."

Keli laughed. "You only called twice!"

Steen smiled at her, "Hey, good luck tomorrow. I hope you make the Varsity!" He pulled himself up out of the pool. "Gotta run. We have a team meeting in half an hour. I just wanted to stop by quick and wish you good luck."

She had been startled by his comment. Was he kidding? She had never given any thought to the fact that she might not make the Varsity.

The next thing she knew she was under the water. A couple of girls from summer camp had dunked her. She came to the surface gasping for air. The next two hours they played rag tag, and Keli had put Steen's comment out of her mind for the moment. But as the party wound down, his comment came back and a cold chill of fear came over her.

Keli was anxious for the three of them to get upstairs to Ashley's room so she could ask them about it. As soon as they all got into their pajamas, Keli just blurted it out, "So do you think I will make the Varsity team?"

Ashley looked over at Greta, then back to Keli. "Yeah! Just get in there and bang. I have never seen anyone jump as well as you! As soon as the coach sees that, you're a lock."

Keli welcomed her answer but it wasn't quite what she was hoping to hear. She had always been the best until this summer.

Big Frank yelled through the door. "Lights off and get some sleep. 8:00 is going to come early."

Ashley answered loud enough only for the girls to hear. "Yeah, especially since I haven't gotten up before 11:00 since summer break started."

Greta laughed and Keli wondered if she was serious. Within minutes the room was quiet.

CHAPTER 23

TRYOUTS—DAY 1

Keli stopped at the doorway and looked around the gym. It seemed different somehow from summer camp. While it was the same gym, today she felt strangely out of place.

Ashley yelled, "Hey, are you coming?"

Keli smiled and yelled back, "Yeah, I was just checking it all out."

Keli walked over to the sign-in table. Coach Lindsay looked up. "It's nice to see you here, Keli. I was surprised and excited when I heard you decided to come and play with us this year." Lindsay looked back down at her clipboard, then back at Keli. "What position did you play in Falls City?"

She shrugged her shoulders. "A little of everything, depending on what the coach told me to do. Mostly I played in the middle."

The coach looked her up and down and said, "Rumor has it you can really jump. Is that true?"

Keli felt embarrassed. She knew there were other girls standing behind waiting to sign in.

"Yeah, I guess I can jump pretty good."

"Well, today I want you to work with the outside hitters and let's see how you do, okay?"

Keli nodded. The coach stuck out her hand and Keli shook it. "Keli, we're glad you're with us. Good luck today!"

Keli smiled and felt a little more comfortable. Outside hitter...she knew she wasn't very good on the outside. Falls City never really had a good enough setter to get the ball out there. Most of their points came from the middle or back row hitting. As she walked over to the net labeled "Outside Hitters," she glanced back. Ashley was already barking orders over with the setters and Greta was stretching with the middles.

"Hey, what's your name?" Keli looked around and saw two girls. She didn't recognize them from summer camp. Keli stuck out her hand and before she could get out her name, another player she vaguely recognized from camp interrupted her "Her name is Keli Stennes. She's from Falls City and she's here to play on our JV team."

Keli froze. Her eyes went back and forth between the first two and the girl who had just blasted her.

One of the two girls quickly jumped in and yelled, "Oh, Alix, why don't you go over and get ready!"

Alix gave Keli a smirk and then looked back at the other two. "Well, she is. I've seen her play."

They all watched Alix walk away. Keli stuck out her hand. "Well, I guess you know my name."

The tall brown-haired girl smiled and shook Keli's hand. "I'm Jesse and this is Libby. So you came to the summer camp? You must be the one Ashley has told us about."

"Don't worry about her," answered the taller of the two. "Ashley says you can jump right out of the gym."

Keli shyly smiled.

"Well, Keli, welcome to the team. And don't mind Alix. She's hard on everyone. Good luck on making the team!" This time Jesse stuck up her hand for a high five and Libby followed.

Keli now was officially panicked. She watched the group of outside hitters, and there must have been 25 of them warming up or stretching. For the first time she really was nervous about her chances. Every muscle in her body was stiff and heavy. She could hear Alix laughing above all the normal gym noise, and she was sure she was still making fun of her.

A loud whistle snapped her out of her petrified state. Keli turned to see Coach Jim in his crisp new T-shirt with "Dragon Volleyball" printed across his chest and a clipboard in his hand. Keli smiled and sighed. She felt a little more comfortable just seeing him.

Coach Jim motioned for everyone at the outside hitters' net to come over to him. He quickly announced that Jessie would lead the warm-up calisthenics and running lines. After half an hour, girls were whining, cussing, and already threatening to quit. All Keli could think about was water. She was less discouraged. The drills were hard, but she was in as good a shape as anyone there.

Each girl's height and reach was measured, and then she was weighed. Keli was in line behind Jessie and Libby. She could hear the assistant calling out "Jessie 5'11, 7'8" reach, 149 pounds. Libby 6', 7'9" reach, 160 pounds."

Keli stepped up. Coach Jim said, "Keli 5'11, 7'9" reach, 148 pounds." Jim motioned to Keli. "Go over by the others and start stretching and get ready for the jump and speed tests." He winked and whispered, "I think the girls are going to be in for a little surprise."

Keli looked at him and smiled, not sure what he meant.

In a few minutes when he finished the last of the girls' stats, he blew his whistle again to get their attention. "Okay, when I call your name, I want you to stand here. Jesse, let's do you first."

Jesse bent down one more time to stretch her legs. She got to the spot the coach had pointed out. He blew his whistle, and she made a three-step block move and jumped as high as she could with both arms reaching for every last inch. Once she hit the floor, she made a three-step block move back to her left again jumping with both arms and hoping for a little more. Once back on the ground from a stationary start, she jumped straight up with both arms like a middle would do to block.

Keli watched with great curiosity. She had never done a drill like this. She was also impressed with the measuring device, which had wooden slats. The highest one you could move was your measurement. Keli quickly started to understand the competition the girls had about this drill. Everyone was whispering and bantering about who would be the Queen of the Jumps.

Coach Jim called out Jesse's numbers: Right slide block 9'2", left slide 9'1", middle block 8'10".

Keli could hear the "oh's" and "ah's" and a few "That's nothing, I got that." Libby was the best by two inches until it was Keli's turn. Coach Jim saved Keli for last. He looked down at his clipboard, then back up at Keli. Then he pulled on the cord that reset all the wooden slats.

Coach Jim blew his whistle, and Keli was off to her right and exploded off the floor. She came back down to her left, and then she strained as high as she could to reach. Then she finished with the middle. Keli stepped back and turned around to see all the other girls staring up at her marks in awe.

Coach Jim said, "Well, I think we have the Queen of the Jumps, ladies. Keli's scores: right block 9'6", left block 9'5", middle 9'4"." Keli had won the competition easily.

He blew the whistle again. "Ten-minute break. Get some water and be back on court 3 at 11:15."

Keli headed for her bag. She was excited to see Ashley and Greta standing where they had all left their bags. Greta saw her coming and said, "So...?"

Keli shrugged her shoulders. "Okay, I guess," and she reached for her towel to wipe off the sweat. "You guys never told me this was boot camp."

They both laughed, and Ashley pushed Keli and said, "Hey, you're in the big time now...get used to it."

Greta was more interested in the Queen of the Jumps. "Hey, so what did you score in the jumps contest? We're next and I want to know what to beat!"

Keli played it cool. "I did okay. I should have done better." Greta knew Keli was messing with her, but let it go. Ashley yelled over to Libby, "Hey, who won the jumps for you guys?"

Libby looked at Keli and pointed. "She killed us!"

This time they both pushed Keli. Keli struggled not to go crashing on her butt. "Hey, I thought this was the big time." She winked as she laughed and ran back towards court 3. Greta and Ashley could hear Keli yell over her shoulder, "Good luck!"

Keli was the first one back to the net. Jessie and Libby were next to make it back.

"Hey, Keli," Jesse smiled. "Great job on the jumps. How's your hitting?"

Keli could feel her face getting warm. "Actually, I've never played much on the outside, so I'm guessing I suck."

Libby chuckled. "As good as you jump, when you learn, you'll be a monster out there."

"I played with her this summer, I don't think there is much chance of that," smirked Alix. "She might have been a star out in Falls Wherever, but she is just an average JV player."

All the girls were back now and listening to the conversation. Jesse looked at Alix. "Hey, regardless of who is on what team, we are just that." Jesse looked over to Libby for support. "If my memory serves me, weren't you JV last year?"

Can I Play...

Alix's eyes got beady. "Hey, I'm just telling you what I saw this summer."

Libby jumped in this time. "Listen. We are a team. We're here to support each other no matter what. If anyone here isn't up for that...there's the door." She pointed to the entrance. Keli could see very clearly who the team leaders were.

Alix snickered and turned away.

Keli was taken aback. Competition to make teams was not something that she was used to, nor was she used to people like Alix.

Jesse patted Keli on the shoulder. "Regardless of what happens the rest of the tryouts, you are the Queen of Jumps!"

The whistle blew. Coach Jim had set up a setting machine. Keli stared at the machine; she'd never seen one before.

"Okay, girls. Line up on the outside. We'll start with hitting 4s. You will get 12 hits each. Shag your own ball and hustle back to the line. I want everyone clapping hands and encouraging your teammates."

Keli's hands began to sweat.

"Hey, don't choke" came a whisper from behind her. Keli didn't have to look to know who it was. She tried to ignore the comment, trying to focus on how this was going to work. Each girl started at the net. Coach said "Go" and the hitter worked herself back and to the outside, calling for the ball.

Fling! The machine threw the ball perfectly to the out line. Jesse and Libby were at the head of the line. Each hit the ball harder and better than Keli had ever seen before. She watched each girl go through their steps and each hit the ball in, none nearly as well as Jesse and Libby, but nonetheless all were good hits. It was her turn, and she still wasn't clear how to do the drill. She stepped to the net more nervous than she had ever been in her whole life. Coach Jim yelled "Go" but Keli turned the wrong way, and before she knew it, the ball was in the air. She quickly tried to get to the ball, but she was too late. All she could do was pass the ball back over the net.

She ducked under the net to retrieve her ball, but she wanted to keep running right out of the gym. She could hear some encouragement, but none of the comments helped. As she ran back to the ball cart, she kept telling herself not to look at Alix, but she couldn't help it.

Alix pointed at her and nodded her head. Keli knew she was saying, "Yep, I told you all she sucked."

The entire drill was pretty much the same. Her first 11 tries she never even got a hit on the ball that went over the net. Keli approached the net for her final try. She looked at Coach Jim, who had the ball ready to go. He looked at her and said, "Come on, Keli, you can do this. Get this one! Come on! GO!"

Again she worked her way off the net and this time was ready. The ball was coming perfectly. Her approach was awkward, but she exploded off the floor and caught the ball perfectly and punished it, hammering it just beyond the 10-foot line.

The hit was impressive, and all the girls applauded and gave Keli high fives. Keli knew it was only a sympathetic gesture. She knew she had been the worst at the drill. Her thoughts were fixed on the fact that she was in over her head and didn't belong.

Coach Jim yelled, "Ten minutes. Be back here ready at 12:30."

Keli started for her bag but the coach beckoned her back. "Help me move this ball cart out of the way, okay?"

Keli grabbed one end, but she could see it was a one-person job. "So, Keli, that drill was pretty tough on you. I'm guessing you've never hit off of a setting machine before."

"No," she grumbled. "Actually I've never really hit from the outside before either. Coach Lindsay asked me to play there. I played in the middle mostly last year."

"Well, hey, don't get all worried about it. You'll get this drill. By the start of the season, you will love this contraption."

Keli said, "Yeah, while I'm playing on the JV team."

Coach Jim fired back, "You just come to these three days of tryouts. Play your guts out and let the chips fall where they will."

He looked her in the eye. "Keli, you have more untapped talent then anyone on this team, but to be honest, you're behind because you have played out of position and you haven't had the resources of the others. You came here for a reason. I suggest you stay focused on your goals. It's been a couple of hours and your head is in the toilet. Am I to guess this is what you're made of?"

He looked at her seriously. "If it is, these girls will chew you up and spit you out. Look around, Keli. Most of these girls have played all their lives against the very best and are hardened to this kind of competition. They know what it's like to have to really compete for a position."

The coach pointed to Jesse. "She's the best player on this team. She's been playing competitive volleyball since she was 10. She has set the bar, so to speak, and works very hard to challenge people around her to play to her level. Next year she is going to Washington and will be just where you are right now, at the bottom looking at the ladder wondering how to climb it."

Keli's mouth dropped open. Coach Jim nodded. "Yes, University of Washington, and I assure you she is going to find herself feeling exactly how you're feeling right now. It will be up to her to figure out how to climb the ladder. I can also promise you that if she demonstrates the attitude that she can't do it, she will sit at the end of the bench for four years."

The coach put his hand on Keli's shoulder. "My best advice right now is to set your sights as high as you can and start working your rear off until you can at least see them. Keli, you have the tools to be a great player if you really want it. But you'll have to work for it. If not, go back to Falls City and just have fun with the game."

The afternoon drills continued to show Keli how much she was behind most of the others. It was a real nightmare. She wanted to hide when it was over, but she knew Ashley and Greta would want full details from the Queen of Jumps. Keli had been pretty cocky earlier in the day, and now she was on the brink of complete defeat despite Coach Jim's words.

When the final whistle blew, every girl was ready to crawl out of the gym. Ashley and Greta were too tired to ask many questions. As they made their way out the door, Keli's grandpa was waiting by Ashley's car.

"Hey, Gramps, what are you doing here?"

"I had to do some shopping, and I was going to stop by and watch for a minute, but when I got here, everyone was walking out."

Keli jumped on the opportunity to have him give her a ride home. The last thing she wanted right now was a lot of questions from the girls on how things had gone.

CHAPTER 24

YOU HAVE TO BE KIDDING!

"So how was it?" asked Tom.

Keli stared straight ahead, trying to find words to describe her day.

He tried to help. "Let me guess. They were better than you thought and you're not sure what to think."

Keli's head whipped around towards her grandfather. "Were you there watching?"

He smiled. "No, I wasn't there, but you know I know a little about all this stuff too."

"How so?"

He quickly took his eyes off the road and glanced at her. "It's a long story. But you will have to trust me on this. I have a pretty good idea what happened today. So, young lady, what are you going to do about it?"

Keli shook her head. "Not so fast. What is a long story and what do you mean what am I going to do about it? Gramps, you're kinda freaking me out here. What do you know?"

Gramps slowed down a little so he could look at her for a second. "How 'bout you and me pick up some dinner and have a little talk?"

"Gramps, I'm really tired. Is there a short version?"

Gramps chuckled. "Nope...But it can wait if you want."

Keli sighed, "Okay, I need anything right now that can help me."

The rest of the ride Keli sat wondering how he might have known about her struggles. When they entered Falls City, she snapped out of her trance. As they passed the high school, she was fixed on the gym wondering how the day had gone, if anyone had missed her, or if anyone had talked about her. Her mind went to the last thing Coach Jim had said to her: "If you just want to have some fun, go back to Falls City and play." She slumped down in the seat tired, defeated, lonely, and most of all confused.

The old Jeep pulled up in front of the restaurant. Keli gave her grandpa quite the look. "Are you crazy? Do you think I am going in there?"

"Yep, let's grab some dinner."

"Gramps, I'm not..."

Tom interrupted her. "Keli, you're not going to hide from this. Listen to me, young lady. Hold your head up, go in there, and be yourself. If you can't do this, then there is no need for all this."

Too tired to argue, Keli sighed and muscled the door open. "Come on, Gramps, let's go."

The door made its usual clang as it opened, and everyone in the place looked to see. Keli's nightmare had just climbed to new heights, for at the big table in the back was the whole gang. She should have remembered it was pretty much a routine for everyone to gather for shakes. Keli's eyes quickly went in search of her mom. Her stomach was in her throat. Tom nudged her, and she beelined to her favorite stool

She buried her nose in the menu even though she had memorized it when she was 8. Tom put his hand on her back, leaned over, and whispered in her ear, "Be yourself."

Keli didn't want any part of his advice. What she really wanted was to get out of there as quickly as possible and without any contact with the table that was only 20 feet from where she was sitting.

Cindy was back by the grill and yelled out to them. "How did it go today, Keli?"

The whole restaurant got silent waiting for her answer. Keli couldn't believe what was happening. She knew everyone in the place was looking at her and waiting to hear her answer. She looked at her mom, shrugged her shoulders, and quietly said, "It went okay, I guess." She wanted to look around the room to see what kind of response everyone had, but she couldn't.

Her mom smiled. "Okay sweetie, you can fill me in on the details later."

Tom yelled back to the kitchen. "How 'bout a couple of Mountaineer burgers to go? I'm going to take Keli up to my place. Can you pick her up after work?"

Cindy looked at Tom, sensing something was wrong. "Sure, but I'll be a couple of hours."

"Hey Keli, so really how was it today?" She was relieved that the voice didn't come from the table in the corner with all her old friends. She turned to look at her old coach and his wife. He pulled out an empty chair at their table to invite her over. She paused for a second, then sat down with them. "I hear they have a handful of really good players. Who is that one, Jesse somebody? Didn't she get an offer to play at Washington or somewhere?"

Keli nodded. This conversation was saving her from the awkwardness of sitting on the stool trying to ignore her old friends. "Yeah," she answered, "Jesse is amazing."

"So how do you think you stacked up against them today?"

"I, I did okay in some areas and not so good in others. I was pretty nervous, I guess."

Coach Edwards gently smiled and said, "Well, that seems pretty normal. You hang in there, you hear me?"

Keli forced out a smile. "So how was practice here today?" Again she wanted to scan the room but forced herself to stayed fixed on the table where she was.

"Pretty good. We have two new girls who transferred in. They are sisters from up in the Portland area. They should help us. One is pretty good and the other one is only a freshman, but I think she is going to be really good one of these days."

A twinge of jealousy engulfed her.

Keli could hear in the background that their burgers were ready. "Well, I guess I need to be going."

Coach Edwards stood up and shook her hand. "Good luck tomorrow, Keli. Remember you take it right at them, okay?"

Keli gave a faint smile and nodded. She didn't look over to the table of her old friends as she left the restaurant.

As they pulled away from the restaurant, Keli hit the proverbial wall. She was completely wiped from the day. She wanted to hear Tom's story, but she wanted sleep more. "Hey, Gramps, any chance I can take a rain check on our talk? I am so wiped. I need a shower and sleep if I am going to make it through tomorrow."

He just nodded and turned the Jeep towards Keli's house. She tried to reassure her grandfather that she was still interested in the story.

Keli was stiffening up as she wobbled into the house. She took her bag and burger up to her room. As she finished the sandwich, she could see Sticky's car turn into his driveway. Sticky got out, and Keli moved closer to the window watching him. He grabbed his huge bag of football gear and started for his front door. Keli whispered to herself, "Look over here, Sticky. Please look over here."

But Sticky staggered into his house without looking over at Keli's. She moved back into the chair and crumpled up the burger wrap.

A few seconds later the phone rang. Keli knew it was Sticky and raced down the stairs as though she hadn't done anything all day. But it was her mother. "Hi, honey, I was just calling to check on you. Gramps called and said you were too tired to go over to his place. It must have been a long day, huh?"

"Mom, it was unquestionably the absolute worst day of my entire life. Especially walking into the restaurant and seeing everyone in there. I couldn't believe it. My life completely sucks."

"Tom said tryouts didn't go all that well. Are you sure you're up for this? There is no shame in coming back to Falls City..."

Keli interrupted her abruptly. "Yes, Mom, there is, and I am not coming back. I am going to do this! Do we have to talk about this right now? I'm tired and want to take a shower."

"Sure, sweetie, I am just worried, that's all."

Keli said goodbye and hung up the phone and made her way back up the stairs nearly on all fours.

The next thing she knew her alarm was going off. She sat straight up and looked around the room. She was still wearing the clothes from yesterday. Every muscle in her body ached.

CHAPTER 25

ANOTHER TALK WITH GRAMPS

"Mom! MOM! Why did you let me sleep like this?" Keli looked at her bag. It was still full of her sweaty clothes

"What, Keli? Come down here. Breakfast is ready." Keli strained to lift her smelly bag. Her arms hurt almost as much as her legs. Making her way down the stairs was a challenge, her legs screaming at her. Keli entered the kitchen to the smell of pancakes.

"Hi, young lady." Keli was a little surprised to see Tom at the kitchen table with a cup of coffee.

"Hey Gramps. Mom, why did you let me sleep? I didn't get a chance to take care of my workout clothes or take a shower."

Cindy poured pancake batter onto the griddle. "Sweetie, I called your name about 20 times and even shook you. There was no waking you up, so I let you sleep. You have other workout clothes. Wear them today. Eat now and then take a shower. Gramps is taking you in today."

Keli looked over to her grandpa, who stood up and waved his coffee cup at Keli. "Do you want some?

"Please and how about some ibuprofen too?"

"Sure. I am at your service."

Keli was in no mood for his banter this morning.

"Here you go, Kels. Eat up. You're going to need it today."

Keli frowned. "What does that mean?"

Cindy whipped around. "Hey, young lady. It means that you have a long day ahead of you, and you will need food in you to make it. Get rid of the attitude right now!"

Keli knew it was time to chill. "Sorry, Mom. I'm just tired and sore."

An hour later they were headed for Dallas. Keli had loosened up some. Her muscles still ached but not nearly as bad as when she first got up.

Tom turned off his talk radio show. Keli knew that meant he was going to start up the pre-game talk. "First, before I say anything, tell me again why you are doing this."

Keli looked at him. "What do you mean?"

"You know what I mean. Why are you changing schools and playing for a new team this year?"

Keli paused, trying to figure out what her grandpa was trying to get out of her. "You know, Gramps. I want to become a good player and get a scholarship."

Tom held silence for a moment and let that statement sink in. Then slowly he said, "So you want to become a good player?"

Keli nodded.

"You want to become a good player so you can get a scholarship, right?"

Again Keli nodded. "Yes, Gramps, that is what I want."

Gramps paused again. Then he said, "So I guess then you have two years to get this done?"

Keli was confused. "Yeah, I guess, but I'm not sure what you mean."

"What I mean is that becoming a good or great player isn't going to happen in one day or even one week. If you went there thinking you were going to stroll in and be all that, you're being a little naïve, don't you think?"

Keli now knew what he was saying. It was similar to what Coach Jim had said to her the day before. "So," he startled her when he snapped his fingers, "just like that, you walked into the gym and you were suddenly just going to be at the top of the heap?"

She could tell he was serious.

"Keli, I am as old as dirt and have been around this stuff all my life. I can tell you, yesterday was just the start...the first day on a journey to see if you can make it. Lots of kids start that first day, and most don't make it. Some because they just don't have the talent, but they work their butts off anyway. For a coach, those are the kids it's the hardest to watch, 'cuz you know. Then there are kids who let other things become more important than their goal. For these, it's sad because they just didn't see it coming, and one day it's over and they will think about the what-ifs the rest of their lives. Then there are some who have the talent and give up too soon...they make excuses, they sell themselves short, and eventually they convince themselves that they weren't good enough. And after all these kids fall by the wayside, the ones left are the ones who make it. They put in their time. I mean lots and lots of time...they sacrifice, they keep their priorities straight, and when the smoke clears, they are sitting on their dream cloud."

He glanced over at her. "There are those four groups, Keli. The only thing I know for positive sure is that you're not in the first group. You have the God-given talents inside of you. It's up to you to decide which of the other groups you're going to fall into. It's completely silly to think that just because you decide to try that it's like going to the store and picking your dream off some shelf and buying it. It doesn't work that way. The door of this store doesn't open for everyone, and it only opens when the customer has earned it."

The Jeep bumped into the parking lot of the Dragons' gym. Keli looked at the clock—9:40. She undid her seat belt and lurched across the vehicle and squeezed her grandpa as hard as she could. "Thank you...I needed to hear that."

Tom responded, "Know this, girl. There are no guarantees in life, but if you really truly work for it, it will be worth it when you're done regardless of the outcome. I promise you that."

Keli grinned from ear to ear. "I haven't forgotten you owe me a story."

He chuckled, "Yep, I do...now go in there and play."

Keli opened the door and jumped out of the truck. He called her name one more time. "Watch everything in there...sometimes watching others will teach you more than when you're playing."

Keli's face crumpled in confusion. Up until then, she had understood everything he had said.

He waved her towards the gym. "I'll explain that later."

CHAPTER 26

TRYOUTS—DAY 2

Everything looked the same that second day except the players. They were all moving slower, and most weren't doing much talking. They were all as sore and tired as Keli. She made her way over to Ashley and Greta, who were putting on their socks and shoes. Neither said a word as Keli set down beside them.

"Hey, ladies, are you ready for today?" Keli asked.

Greta said, "Quiet, I need all my focus to get these damn shoes on."

Keli laughed. "And you, Ashley? How in the heck are you?"

Ashley whined as she tried to put her hair up in a ponytail. "Even my hair hurts. Let me guess. You're not even sore, right?"

Keli laughed again. "I was crawling only an hour ago and I slept in my clothes on top of my bed all night."

Right at 10:00 sharp, Coach Lindsay blew her whistle. The coaching staff today was all in black and red, the Dragon colors. Coach Jim yelled for everyone to take a seat in the bleachers.

Lindsay greeted the players. "Good morning, Lady Dragons!" The group of 60 girls yelled back, "Good morning, Coach!"

"Okay, day two. I'm sure none of you are sore." This brought a laugh from nearly everyone. She launched into advice about stretching and drinking lots of water. Then she said, "Today is a critical day. This morning will be more conditioning and drills. After lunch, we will do a lot of 2-on-2, 3-on-3, and 6-on-6 drills. This will be very important. At the end of today, we will be announcing initial squads for Varsity, JV, and C team."

Keli looked at Ashley, who was still fixed on Coach Lindsay.

"Tomorrow will be final cuts. What that means is if there are 20 girls tomorrow in the JV pool, for example, there will only be spots for 12 of them. Same with the Varsity. All seniors will be put into the Varsity pool; this is the only team you can make. Girls, take these next two days very seriously. We coaches will be, I can guarantee you that. As a team, we have very lofty goals. I expect this team to compete for a state championship, and I am looking for only the very best attitudes and work ethics. Anything short of that and you'll be watching this team from the stands this fall."

She scanned her gaze over the 60 girls. "For those of you who aren't asked to play on the Varsity squad today, I will expect the same intensity from you. Our goal here is to build a program so that when it's your turn to compete at the Varsity level, you're ready to take their place, and the Dragons can be known as the team to beat. This comes from team attitude...all championship teams have it, and I demand it here."

She paused. "C-team, most of you will be freshman or someone we feel deserves to still be a Lady Dragon. Learn from the older kids. Your turn will come quick enough. Remember, girls, no one with less than a champion's attitude will be on this team! We will break into the same groups as yesterday for this morning. Work hard, and if you're not going to, please leave now!"

Lindsay climbed the bleachers with her clipboard into the crow's nest as the other coaches blew whistles and yelled for girls to get to their stations.

Keli was awestruck by what the coach had just said and how everything was happening. Back in Falls City everyone was loose and ready to have some fun. Here she could feel the pressure in the air. When she got to court 3, Keli could tell that five or six girls hadn't shown up.

Coach Jim stood tall by the net. "Jesse, lead them in calisthenics and, let's see, how 'bout a dozen lines in four minutes?" There were a few groans as Jesse circled them up.

The morning drills weren't much different from the day before, except Keli's attitude was much better. She took a peek at the crow's nest every chance she could to see what Coach Lindsay was up to. By the end of the morning drill, Keli had survived without any complete blunders.

Ashley and Greta were already waiting in the bleachers eating lunch. Greta reached into Keli's bag snooping.

"How did it go?" asked Ashley.

"I think it went pretty well," said Keli. "I'm pretty sure that I am not going to make the Varsity team though. There are a lot of girls who are just better than me."

Ashley was chugging on her water bottle and almost choked. "What? No way, girl! All this stuff so far was to weed out the wannabes. This afternoon is where it's at. You just play your game. I think the coach will play you right side. The way you jump and with Jesse and Libby out taking 4s and Greta in the middle, you're perfect for the right side this year. Then next year it will be us three dominating the whole show."

Greta pumped her fist and gave the whoop-whoop call! For a few minutes, Keli's spirits were lifted with her friend's idea of how things could be. Keli polished off her peanut butter and jelly sandwiches. Her mind worked double-time thinking about what Coach Lindsay and her gramps had both said this morning. She looked around still in astonishment at where she was. It still wasn't completely real to her.

The coaching staff reappeared from the coach's room all looking down at their clipboards. The whistle blew and all the players gathered back onto the bleachers

Lindsay settled them all down. "Okay, girls, listen up! First, great job this morning! I am excited by everyone's efforts. This afternoon we will do some scrimmaging. Each of you will be put with players with different skills. If you're a senior and you're put with a couple of freshmen, so be it. Play hard and be a leader. We have put together these different groups for a reason. Do not forget attitude and effort this afternoon. Play to win, of course, but more importantly, play as a team. Make the others around you better. Those of you who have played for me in the past know what I mean and those of you who haven't, watch the veterans and do what they do!"

She looked around the group. "We will start with 2-on-2 scrimmages using half nets, and all games this afternoon will be to 7 with rally scoring and win by one. Good luck, ladies!" Lindsay then repeated her climb to the crow's nest above the bleachers. Coach Jim and Coach Jeff started calling names.

Keli and a girl named Christine were asked to report to court 2. Keli made her way over, trying to figure out who Christine was. Coming to join her was a smallish girl with red wristbands that denoted she was an incoming freshman.

Great! thought Keli a bit sarcastically, but she smiled at her. "I'm Keli and you must be Christine."

The girl nodded shyly. "You can call me Chris if you want."

"Cool," answered Keli. "What position do you normally play?"

"Well, at my middle school, we really didn't play positions, but so far I have been playing outside."

Keli thought to herself again, Great, I'm stuck with a 5'3" freshman outside hitter, but Keli did her best to pump her up. "Okay. What do you say we kick a little butt?"

Chris smiled. "How tall are you?"

Keli smiled back. "5'11"."

Chris face's saddened. "I wish I could be that tall."

Keli's mind went to Tom's four groups. Then she put both hands in the air and Chris slapped them. Coach Jeff blew the whistle at court 2. Keli looked across the net only to see Ashley and Libby on the other side. Keli almost peed her pants, but Ashley winked. Keli quickly glanced up to the crow's nest hoping the coach was focused on another net.

The two teams met at the net and wished each other luck. As they turned away, Ashley said, "Hey, Keli?"

Keli turned and went back. Ashley grabbed her arm under the net and said, "This game was set up for you. The coaches want to test you. You're the only one who matters in this game. We are supposed to win. They just want to see what you're made of."

Keli smiled, relieved, and made her way back to Chris. "Do you want front or back to start?" she asked the younger girl. Chris shrugged.

"Okay," Keli said, "then you take front. When I pass to you, all I want you do to do is set or pass the ball high, and I will do the rest. Be ready. These two girls are awesome and we have to just try to survive!"

Keli's instincts took over. She forgot about Falls City, her failure at the setting machine, everything. She waited with her arms extended for the serve from Ashley. A split second later the ball was ripping towards her. Keli leaped to her left only to have the ball glance off her arms and out. Keli looked at Ashley, who wasn't letting up an inch. "Okay, Chris," she said, "let's get this one!"

Again the ball rocketed towards her. This time Keli was able to dig it up and Chris put the ball high in the air all right but way too far outside for Keli to do anything with it other than to free ball it back over the net. Libby made a great pass to Ashley, who put the ball right where Libby wanted it and wham! Point: Ashley and Libby.

Keli lined up again, arms ready. This time she handled Ashley's serve. Chris made a high bump set, and Keli got a read on the ball and went high in the air and hammered the ball hard. Libby was in position to block. There was a quick explosion as the ball met Libby's arms and the ball flew out of bounds. Point: Keli and Chris.

Libby quickly reached under the net to congratulate Keli on a great kill. It was the first and only point Keli and Chris would get in the game, which ended 7-1.

Most of the rest of the 2-on-2 games went the same way, until the last one. Keli and Chris were matched up with Alix and Anna, another girl who threw shots about Keli to some of the others. They met at the net, and Alix looked at Keli. "Well, how does it feel to get pounded every game, JV girl?"

Keli stared back fiercely. "Let's play," answered Keli and she turned back to Chris. "This game we win..." she pointed right at Chris. "This game we win. Do you understand?" Chris didn't know whether to be more scared of Keli or their opponents. Chris nodded. Then Keli stuck up both her hands and Chris slapped them.

They started the game the same way, with Keli receiving. Anna served what should have been an ace, but Keli dove and pancaked the ball straight up in the air. Chris, who had resigned to bump setting by the second game, bumped the ball high in the air. Keli jumped to her feet and exploded in the air and pounded the ball right at Alix as hard as she could. The ball ricocheted off of Alix's shoulder. Alix stared at Keli, then said, "Come on, Anna, let's go."

Keli grabbed the ball to serve. "Chris, after I serve this, I want you to move back to take the pass if there is one."

Keli served the ball back to Alix, who made a great pass to Anna. Then Anna made a great set for Alix, who met the ball and hammered it. Keli was right there and blocked the ball straight down in front of Alix for point two.

Keli grinned and grabbed the ball from Alix. "That's 2-zip. Chris, same play!"

Chris smiled.

Keli served the ball to the same spot. Alix tipped the ball over Keli's out-stretched arms. Chris was there to make the pass, and Keli set the ball to the out-side, and Chris jumped and hit a weak ball. Anna was there to block it, but it went slightly out. Chris jumped in the air.

When the dust cleared, Keli and Chris had won their only match, 7-5. Keli hugged Chris. "Great job!" Keli wished her luck with the rest of the tryouts.

Most of the other games were over, and when Keli headed for her water bottle, she could see many girls had been watching their match. Keli realized she had completely forgotten everything around her. She hadn't looked up to the crow's nest since the first game. The last hour she had been in a zone just playing. For the first time since tryouts began, Keli was Keli.

Ashley walked over to meet her. "Damn girl, awesome game. Everyone was watching. Do you realize how amazing some of that was? Nobody can jump the way you can. How do you do it?"

"Well, getting good and pissed helps. I can't stand Alix or Anna, to be real honest."

Ashley laughed. "So what's new? Even their parents don't like them!"

Keli was in the middle of taking a big drink of water and laughed so hard she snorted water out her nose.

Greta looked disgusted. "Okay, that's nasty! Get it together, Keli. Come on."

Keli had just enough time to change her sweaty shirt and socks before the next round began.

The rest of the afternoon Keli found herself up against teams that she couldn't beat, playing mostly with freshmen and JV players. Even during the 6-on-6, Keli wondered if she was doomed for the JV squad. There wasn't a for-sure Varsity player on her team. But she didn't give any of this much thought when the games were going on. She played hard the rest of the day.

Coach Lindsay blew her whistle and everyone came running. "Okay, listen up. Change of plans. We are not going to announce the first cuts 'til first thing in the morning. Go home and get some rest. See all of you at 10:00. Good job, ladies... well done!"

Day two was over. It was like a blur. Keli had no idea how to rate things. She hadn't really gotten to watch others play, and her teams had lost most of their matches.

Keli put on her last dry shirt and her flip-flops and noticed her grandpa by the front door.

Just then Ashley asked if she wanted to come over and swim, but Keli frowned and said no, pointing to Tom.

On her way, her path intersected Coach Lindsay, who was reviewing her clipboard. "Good job, Keli. I liked your attitude today!"

Keli smiled. "Thanks, Coach!" That was just what she needed to hear. She had a grin on her face all the way over to her grandpa.

"So, how was day two?"

"Better than the first day for sure. I still don't know if I will make the Varsity."

Out in the parking lot, Gramps had parked next to Alix, who was standing with Anna and a couple of other girls Keli hadn't met yet. As she got closer, they all giggled and turned away, ignoring her. That was fine with Keli. The brightest part of her day was winning the game against Alix and Anna.

Keli threw her bag in the back of the Jeep, the girls still giggling. She started to get into the Jeep, then stopped. "Hey, Alix..."

Alix and the group stopped laughing and looked over at Keli, who looked right at Alix as she put on her sunglasses and said, "Good job today!" Then without waiting for an answer, she climbed into the Jeep and closed the door.

As Tom backed out of the space, Keli focused in on Alix as if to say, "I got you today and you know it!"

The ride home was quiet. Keli tried to relax and her grandfather didn't interrupt. There was no stopping at the restaurant today. As they drove by, Keli could see Sticky's and Charlee's cars out front. Today she felt stronger about the whole thing.

Once home Keli got organized for the next day. While her clothes were washing, she was up in her room playing Ben Jelen as loud as her stereo could go. She thought her mom would be surprised that she had cleaned her room without any threats on her life.

As Keli folded some clothes that were strewn on the floor, she looked at the picture Sticky had drawn of her standing by the Falls. She grinned, set the folded clothes on the bed, and decided it was time to hang the picture. It had been leaning against the wall on the floor since her birthday party.

She cleaned off the top of her dresser and leaned it up against the wall. Again she stood back and admired it for a minute or so. She glanced out the window towards Sticky's house, even though she knew he wasn't home. She missed him the most.

The phone rang, and she hurried down the stairs cursing. "I wish I had a phone in my room. This is crazy!"

Her hello was met by, "Hey! We are on our way out there to get you. Pack a bag. We are hanging out at my place tonight."

Keli smiled. "Ashley?"

Ashley picked up her voice a little. "Do we have a bad connection? Pack a bag. We will be there in 20 minutes to get you." Click!

Keli looked at the phone. Okay, pack a bag. She stopped and headed back to the phone and called her mom at the restaurant only to find out Ashley had already called before she called Keli.

Twenty minutes later on the nose, Ashley's horn blared all the way down Estelle Road and into her driveway.

"Hey, Greta, you got shotgun last time. Now it's my turn," whined Keli.

Ashley laughed. "You go, girl!"

Greta fought back. "No way, chick. I am already here."

Keli opened Greta's door. "Rock, paper, scissors. Let's go." Greta rock, Keli paper. Greta lamely tried to negotiate for two out of three with no luck.

They drove past the restaurant as Keli's old friends were leaving. Keli looked at Sticky, who was looking at her. Keli smiled and Sticky smiled back. Her heart melted. It was only a smile but it was nice.

Greta sat up and leaned forward. "Hey, Sticky just smiled at me when I waved."

Keli was a little embarrassed but didn't say anything.

Ashley said, "I got a call after practice from Tina."

Keli turned to Greta. "Who's Tina?"

"She is probably going to be the libero..."

Ashley interrupted Greta's profile. "So anyways Tina called me and told me something very interesting. Anyone interested?"

Keli laughed and, "Nah...what are we doing for dinner?"

Greta busted up laughing.

Ashley frowned and slumped down behind the wheel. Keli said, "Okay. Go ahead. We don't want you to pout all night. What did libero Tina have to say?"

Ashley sat back up. She looked over at Keli and said, "Everyone on the team knows Alix and Anna have been flicking you crap. Well, today when your team won, they were really pissed and really started talking trash about you. I guess there was a bunch of them standing by her car after practice when you walked up to your car."

Keli knew what was coming.

"Tina really doesn't like Alix and only hangs around her to pick up the dirt to tell the rest of us. Well, you really, really pissed Alix off when you, as Tina says, coolly put on your shades and called her name and said, 'Good job today'."

Greta lost it laughing, grabbing Keli's shoulders and shaking her. "Did you really do that?"

Keli grinned sheepishly. Ashley and Greta were both waiting for her answer. Keli yelled out in excitement. "It was great. First I kicked her butt in the game. Then it was perfect. They were giggling at me and making it obvious. I yelled her name and got all their attention, then put my sunglasses on and said it. Then I got in my Gramps' Jeep and we drove off. It was perfect."

CHAPTER 27

DAY 3—FINAL CUTS

As they entered the gym, most of the girls were already waiting in the bleachers for the coaches. They found their usual spots and waited. Keli started to feel anxious and her chest tightened. She looked around at the 50 girls still there. What if she didn't make the Varsity? She knew Alix and her gang would be relentless with their teasing, and she knew her old friends back in Falls City would be saying it serves her right. But worst of all it would be the end of her dream of getting a scholarship to play in college.

A whistle startled her. The coaching staff was making their way over to the bleachers.

"Good morning, ladies," Coach Lindsay said. "Before we begin, I want you to know we have struggled with our decisions. These past couple of days were the best tryouts I have ever experienced. If we can bring that to our daily practice and games this year, we will truly have a shot at the big prize."

Lindsay looked down at her clipboard. "I will read off the names of each team. Varsity players, report to court 1, and I will meet you over there when I am finished. JV, report to court 2 with Coach Jim and C-Team, report to court 3 with Coach Jeff. All the girls who don't get selected, please stay here for a minute. I would like to have a word with you."

"Okay, for the Varsity," Coach Lindsay cleared her throat and read off the list: "Jesse...Libby...Morgan...Teresa...Megan...Taylor...Alison...Kaitlin...Greta...Ashley... Alix...and..." Coach Lindsay paused for a second after losing her place, "Becca."

Keli's heart was instantly broken. She had to do everything in her power not to cry. She didn't want to look at anyone so she stared straight down at her feet.

"Okay...JVs," announced Coach Lindsay. It was a blur. Keli didn't want to listen, but the third name the coach called was hers. She felt like her butt was stuck to the bleachers; she couldn't believe it. She finally made her way up and grabbed her bag. "I failed," kept echoing in her head as she slowly walked over to court 2.

Coach Jim was waiting for them. Keli looked around and saw Anna not far from her trying not to look at anyone either. "Okay, girls. Keli, lead them in calisthenics and six lines. Let's go. Same today as yesterday, drills in the morning and scrimmages this afternoon. Do not forget that there are 18 of you here, and when the day is over, only 12 can make the team."

Keli cleared her throat trying to remember the workout Jesse had put them through the past couple of days. "Okay," she said, "let's circle up."

As the morning went on, Keli kept telling herself not to give up. Play hard...just play hard. The JVs took their turn using the setting machine when the Varsity finished with it. Keli hated the machine. Two days in a row she had been embarrassed by it. But when Coach Jim asked who was going first, she said, "I'll go, Coach."

"Good, Keli. Move quicker to the outside and take a strong first step with your left foot." Coach Jim paused before putting the ball into the machine. "As soon as you get your steps down, you will kill this thing."

Keli was ready to kill something. Keli bounced off the net, worked herself to the outside...she stepped quickly with her left foot, then exploded off the floor and punished the ball right down on the 10-foot line. All of her teammates clapped and cheered, even Anna.

As they worked the drill, Keli continued to punish the ball, hammering it with every opportunity. Coach Jim used her as an example to the others, saying, "Watch how she is reaching for the top of the ball."

The morning was finally over. Keli sat right there on the court and dug into her bag for her lunch. Ashley and Greta were on the bleachers and knew she needed her space. After she finished eating, she lay flat on the floor staring up to the ceiling asking herself if she had the guts and maturity to handle the demotion.

The hour break went quickly. Coach Jim called them back together and broke them up into two-person teams for 2-on-2. The afternoon session went better. Keli loved to play, and once the competition started, she was truly herself, diving for everything, screaming everything she saw, trying to help whoever she was playing with. The 2-on-2 session ended with Keli's team beating Anna's team 7-0. Keli went to all the girls giving high fives.

Coach Jim called for a 10-minute break. Ashley was hanging out by court 2, waiting to talk with Keli. Keli went to her bag for water, ignoring Ashley out of embarrassment.

Ashley came over anyway. "Hey girl. I am so sorry. I can't believe you didn't make the team. You're better..."

Keli cut her off. "No worries, Ash. I'm cool. I'm just going to have to work harder, that's all." Keli smiled and gave Ashley a hug. "Don't forget your lowly buddies though, okay?"

"Not a chance. One of these days we will all be trying to keep up with you." Ashley grabbed Keli's arms. "Hey! Promise me you won't give up." Keli smiled. Ashley squeezed a little tighter. "Promise me!"

Keli said, "I promise. We still have to get our parents hooked up, don't we?"

Ashley jumped off the floor. "You're right, Sis. You are absolutely right!"

The whistle blew for Ashley. Keli pushed Ashley towards court 1. "Get going before you have to run laps."

Ashley looked at her. "Are you okay?"

"Yep, I'm okay." Keli gave her a weak grin.

Keli went over to Coach Jim. "So who do I have next round, Coach?"

"Who do you want?"

"Give me the two you have down on the bubble you need to look at."

Coach Jim looked up from his clipboard at Keli. He stared at her for a second, then just nodded his head.

When the afternoon finally ended, Keli was exhausted. She had buried herself into practice to hide herself from the devastating blow her pride had taken. She sat on the bleachers, changing her shirt. Ashley said, "Hey, are you up for staying another night? I already called your mom, and she said it was okay."

Keli looked at her and Ashley winked.

"Come on," pleaded Ashley. "We don't have practice 'til 2:00 tomorrow."

Keli sat there exhausted. "Can I borrow your cell phone? I need to call my mom and tell her about today if I am going to hang out here." She slowly dialed the number to the restaurant, really not looking forward to what she had to say.

"Hi sweetie, how did it go today?"

At the sound of her mom's voice, Keli felt herself starting to choke up. "Not so good, Mom. I didn't make the Varsity team."

"Oh, honey, I'm so sorry. What are you going to do now?"

"Well, Gramps says I need to just play harder. That is what everyone is telling me, and I am trying my best. The tears were streaming down her face.

"Sweetie, I am sorry. Do you want me to come get you?"

Keli wiped her face. "No, I am going to stay in here again tonight if you're okay with it."

"Are you sure, Keli? I can come get you right now."

"No, Mom. Really, I'm okay. I'm pretty down, but to be honest, Mom, the coaches here have already made me a better player. I believe in my heart that I can do this. I am not giving up. I have really grown to like Ashley, Greta, and some of the others. Ashley and I have a lot in common. Did you know her mom died when she was only 7?"

"No sweetie, I didn't know that. It does sound like you have found a good friend to talk with."

Keli paused for a second. "Mom, do you think my old friends will ever come around? I really miss Sticky and the rest of them."

Cindy quickly answered, "Yes, sweetheart, just give them some time. I can tell when they come into the restaurant that there is a hole. Especially Sticky. His eyes are always sad when he looks at me. Just give them a little more time."

"Okay, I'll be home right after practice tomorrow. Mom? I love you!"

"Bye, Kels. Have fun tonight, and Keli? I am so very proud of what you're doing!"

Tears welled back into Keli's eyes. "Thanks, Mom. You're my hero."

Keli found Ashley and Greta over by Coach Lindsay and Coach Jim.

Coach Lindsay broke from her and looked at Keli, "I want you to know we have high expectations for you here. We coaches are excited that you're a part of the program."

Ashley pushed Keli. "Coach, I think you should cut her. You know she is really lazy and can't jump!"

Coach Jim chuckled and said, "You three leave right now or we will have you sweep the floors."

On the way to the car, Ashley announced, "We need to run by the store. I got a message from my dad saying we needed to stop by."

Keli knew the subject of her making the JV team was going to come up. She took a big breath and sighed. Her gramps' voice kept popping into her head. "Keli, just be you."

When they walked into the store Big Frank was talking with a man who was even bigger than he was.

"Stand back, girls!" Ashley put out her arms to stop them. "Frank is closing a big sale."

Greta chuckled, "So what do you think he is selling the guy?"

"Who knows?" answered Ashley. "Come on. I don't want to wait. He can call us. Let's get home and hit the pool."

Once there, the girls quickly dumped their bags and changed. Keli was the first one in the pool. "Dang! This feels good. Hurry up, you two!" They both jumped in and buried Keli in their wake.

Ashley looked at Greta and Keli. "So do we want company tonight or the pool to ourselves?"

Keli quickly answered, "How 'bout just us? To be honest, I'm really not feeling like a lot of people."

Greta agreed. "Let's just watch a movie or something."

Keli looked over at Greta. "Can I ask you a question?"

Greta said, "Sure. Ask away."

"Do you live here or what?"

Greta said, "Well, actually I do."

"Really?"

"Yep, Ashley is my cousin. I have lived here for about three years."

Keli looked at Ashley and then back to Greta. "Really? Why didn't I know that?"

"Because you never asked," laughed Ashley.

"Well, why, how, what's the story?"

Greta looked at Ashley. "It's a long one."

Not wanting to pry, Keli quickly said, "Hey, it's cool. We don't have to talk about it."

"It's okay," said Greta. "To tell you the truth, my dad is in prison and my mom is well...actually I don't know where my mom is. A few years ago, they got heavy into drugs, and my dad was convicted of robbery and my mom was supposed to go into treatment. She couldn't handle it and took off, and I haven't seen her since. Frank came and got me."

Keli was silent a moment. "So Big Frank is your uncle?"

"Yeah, he's my mom's brother."

"Wow! Do you ever talk with your dad?"

"Only one time. He sent me a letter."

"When does he get out?"

"It depends, but I think in about a year if he does all the right things."

"Where did you live before this all happened?"

"Up in Tacoma, Washington."

The conversation was interrupted when Big Frank came through the French doors with a pizza box in his hand. "Guess who I found banging on the front door?"

Greta answered, "The Avon lady?"

Frank shook his head, "Anyone else want to try?"

Keli was the first one out of the pool and took the box out of his hands. "Hey! Let me help you with that."

Greta and Ashley weren't far behind. "So, Dad, did you make the sale?"

A big laugh filled the backyard. "Yep, sure did," proudly came from Frank. "I sold him a bass boat with all the bells and whistles."

"Dad, bad news," said Ashley. "Coaches put Keli on the JV team."

Big Frank had his mouth full but answered anyway. "I heard. Sorry, Keli...I also heard that once you refine some of your skills, you're going to be the best damn player on the team."

Ashley said, "Who did you hear that from?"

Big Frank grinned. "I have my sources...so the rest of you'd better watch your back. There is a new kid on the block. And I hear she is coming for anyone who gets in her way."

Keli smiled. "Well, I'm not sure about your sources or your prediction."

Big Frank snatched the last piece in the box. "Anyone want this?" as he took a bite. "Hey, do you three want to make a few bucks tomorrow?"

Ashley shook her head and said, "Nope! Work is overrated."

Keli quickly answered, "Sure, I can use the money."

Frank said, "Good, I've got a bunch of things that need doing at the store. How about you all be there about 9:00, and I'll figure you will be done by 1:00 or so. Your practice starts at 2:00, right?" Frank did a sweep to see if there were any objections. "So what's up for the rest of the night?"

Greta suggested renting a movie.

Ashley said, "Not if we have to be at work at 9:00. I want to get some sleep."

Keli nodded. "Hey, anyone have some clothes I can wear tomorrow?"

Greta laughed, "You'd better borrow some of my stuff. Ash's taste is really lame."

CHAPTER 28

WHEN THE STUDENT IS READY...

The work at the sporting goods store was as much play as it was work, and the four hours went by quickly. When they were finished, they went over to Frank with their hands out waiting to be paid. Frank pointed to Scotty, who reached in the register and handed them each $40.

At the gym, a few girls were already milling around. Jesse saw them coming towards her. "Hey, Keli. Coach said she wants to see you in her office."

Keli looked at the other girls and they shrugged their shoulders. On her way there, she had to go by Alix and Anna, who were passing back and forth. Keli tried to ignore them, but Alix didn't pass up the opportunity to say in a snotty voice, "Good morning, superstar!"

Keli smiled at Anna and said good morning. Anna smiled back but didn't say anything.

When she opened the door to the coaches' room, she found Coach Lindsay at her desk. "Have a seat, Keli. How are things with you? This has been a big change. I thought it would be good for us to have a little talk."

Keli became a little more nervous. "No, Coach, things are pretty good."

Lindsay put her elbows on the desk. "What do you mean 'pretty good'?"

Keli didn't want to answer. She didn't want to make the coach think she had a bad attitude. "It's really nothing that I can't handle, Coach, really."

Coach Lindsay sat back in her chair and pointed to the closed door. "First thing you need to learn is when that door is closed, this becomes a player and a coach. The team is out there."

Keli gathered all the strength she could find and then slowly responded. "I am really pretty good. I'm bummed I didn't make Varsity, but I am dealing with it the best I can." She looked up at the coach. "Can I ask you a question?"

Lindsay folded her arms and nodded.

Keli looked at the floor and then looked up at Lindsay. "My gramps keeps telling me to be me. So here goes. I came to this school for one reason, to become a player who would get a scholarship to a college. It's really the only thing that is important to me. I don't have a boyfriend, I get good grades, and the only thing that matters to me for the next two years is to become a college volleyball player. I came here hoping to achieve this." Keli looked away.

"You're a legend as a coach and a player. I figured that playing for you would give me the best chance for this to happen. I have alienated all my childhood friends with this choice, but still I'm okay with it. If you tell me, I'm now not good enough to play on the Varsity team...while it hurts and is to a certain degree embarrassing, I have accepted it. I have grown up a little these past few days."

"Yesterday when I was walking out, you made a comment to me. You said that you have high expectations for me here. You also said the coaches are excited that

I am a part of this program. I need to know a couple of things. Did you say it just to make me feel better or did you mean it? Coach, I have really high expectations and if you meant it, then I want you to teach me how to achieve my goals. If that means playing JV, so be it."

"Coach, I will do exactly what you ask of me. I will come in early, stay late, or whatever it takes. My gramps says to always stick with the winners and he says when the student is ready, the teacher will appear. Well, Coach, I'm ready." Keli looked back at the floor, wondering what was going to happen next.

"Keli, I'm not sure I have ever heard such honesty and courage from a young lady before." Lindsay smiled. "I called you in here to tell you that I had a conversation with Coach Jim after yesterday's practice. He told me you walked up to him during your practice and offered to help him with the kids on the bubble, even though you had just been put into maybe the hardest moment of your life—when you didn't make the team. We were astounded by that. As a coach, you dream of finding a kid with that kind of make-up. As for your grandfather, he is a wise man and you're very lucky to have such a person in your life. Never take that for granted!"

"You have passed every test I could put you through. Now it's my turn to be honest with you. We decided to put you on the JV team for two reasons: to test your attitude and to refine your hitting skills. That might sound a little tough, but a lot of these girls have been working hard for many years and they are at a point where bringing in a new player could upset the apple cart, so to speak. Your skills are not as refined as most of the others on the Varsity team, but their natural skills, like jumping, are not as good as yours."

"It's a long season. Coach Jim is the best hitters' coach I know. He played the position in college. He can refine your skills, and I promise as soon as he says it's time, then I will make a spot for you on my team."

Coach Lindsay leaned forward, "To be real honest with you, I knew why you came here. An old friend of mine told me. This is the reason I put you on the JV team. You need Coach Jim right now. You have to trust me on this. He is the best teacher for you right now."

Just then Coach Jim walked in. "Hey, Keli, how're things this morning?"

Keli looked over at Coach Lindsay and smiled. "Do I have to start at the beginning again?"

Lindsay laughed. "No, why don't you go warm up, and I'll give Coach Jim the short version."

Keli stuck out her hand and Coach Lindsay shook it. "Thanks for the time, Coach." Keli smiled at Coach Jim as she made her way back on to the gym floor.

As she pulled up her kneepads, her head was replaying the conversation. A ball glanced off her head to snap her out of her wonderful thoughts. Standing in front of her were Ashley, Greta, Jesse, and Libby. Jesse raised her hands in the air. "So what happened? Did they move you up?"

Keli shook her head. "Nope, I'm just a lowly JV player."

Libby looked around, then said, "You know you're getting screwed here. You're better than at least four players who made it."

Keli pulled up her second kneepad. "Thanks, but Coach explained it to me. She wants me to refine my skills with Coach Jim, and when I'm ready, then she will move me up."

Keli realized that maybe the statement should have stayed in the coaches' room. "Hey, please don't tell anyone I told you that. Some of the girls around here make life hard enough for me as it is."

Jesse, being a true leader, looked at the other three and said, "If this gets out, I'll kick each one of your butts. We understand each other, right?"

Keli thought her face was going to break, she was smiling so hard.

Right now it didn't matter to Keli that she was on the JV squad. Her new friends all genuinely respected her. Her coaches believed in her. She was ready for anything, even Alix, who walked by and couldn't pass up the opportunity to add another dig. "So I hear you were in the coaches' room crying and begging. Is that how mountain kids get their way?"

Keli didn't feel a need to say anything back. She was over Alix and her petty acts of meanness. Keli took a big drink of water as Alix waited for a comeback. Instead she bounded down off the bleachers, and as she walked by Alix, she patted her on the butt and said, "Have a good practice today." She didn't look back to see Alix's reaction.

Coach Jim blew his whistle and the team raced over. Keli was impatient to get going and wanted to prove right then that she was ready, but the practice was mostly about conditioning and fundamentals. Coach Jim was a stickler for details; he would not tolerate mistakes. "Do it over! Come on, do it over right this time," rang through their ears for the next couple of hours.

As practice ended, Tom was waiting by the entrance like magic. Keli started towards him, and Ashley ran over and asked about her plans for the weekend.

Greta shyly asked, "If we have a little party, would you be mad if I asked Sticky to go?"

Keli stopped dead in her tracks and turned around. "Tell you what. If you can get Sticky to go, I will be there even if I have to walk into town from Falls City."

He waited until they pulled out of the parking lot before quizzing her. "How are you feeling with not making the Varsity?"

She told him about her conversation with Coach Lindsay. "To be honest, I'm a little confused about it, but I think she has a plan for me. It's weird, but mostly I am okay with it. At this point I really don't have much of a choice, do I?"

"You know, you're going to have to handle people who are going to second-guess your decision. The kids back home are going to talk about how you messed up. How are you going to handle them?"

Keli looked out the window. "I'm not sure, Gramps. Right now I'm hanging on by my fingernails to just be me, and since I really am not sure who I am, I am just going to go it alone right now. People who are with me are with me and those who aren't just won't have a place in my life. I know I can't handle it any other way."

Tom broke into a grin. "Good for you, young lady. That is probably the wisest thing I have ever heard anyone say, no matter what their age."

As they passed the high school, Keli glanced at the gym. "Gramps, have you heard anything about the two girls who moved into town?"

Gramps glanced over to the gym. "Rumor has it that the older one is pretty good, and the young one will be pretty good down the road. I'm guessing they're hoping that Tanya will be able to take your place."

"Tanya? Is that her name?" Keli's mind raced. "I've been gone for less than a week, and I have already been replaced and to boot I'm now a JV player! Gramps, if you don't mind why don't you drop me off here? I'll wait for Mom."

Tom pulled the Jeep over in front of the restaurant.

The dinner crowd was just arriving. Today Keli didn't seem to care as she had a few days before. Almost everyone in town knew the story by now.

Keli made her way to her stool.

"So how did it go today?" asked Cindy.

Keli could sense again that most people there were waiting for her answer. "It was a good day. I'm excited to tell you about it when we get home. And hey, Mom, I made 40 bucks this morning at Webb's helping Big Frank get ready for some sidewalk sale."

Cindy was busy taking an order...and nodded her head.

Keli decided to sleep in the car until Cindy got off work, and she was startled awake when Cindy opened the car door.

Keli asked the usual first question, "Was it a good tip day?"

"I think so...I haven't counted it yet. People are so cruel. You know I am starting to think some of your old friends aren't as good kids as I thought. Especially that Charlee..." Then she realized that this might not be the right time to discuss it and she quickly tried to change the subject. "Let's not talk about that. Tell me about practice today."

Keli looked at her mom as she drove up the hill. "Wait, Mom. You can't just say that, then change the subject. I really don't care what they're saying right now, but you shouldn't try to hide it from me either! I understand where things are. And to be honest Mom, I have come to the conclusion that I'm right where I am supposed to be, and if they don't like or can't accept me for doing it, then that's fine. I don't need the distractions. It's too bad, but I am not going to live my life according to anyone's rules anymore."

"It's my life, and if I don't start doing something for myself then when am I? It's weird, Mom. A week ago I was so confused...I was ready to throw in the towel because of what others thought. I have done that all my life. Whenever the group wanted things a certain way, I would always give in. Well, Mom, you have not raised me to be that way. Being away quite a bit these past couple of weeks has helped me understand a lot of what you and Grandpa have been trying to tell me."

They pulled into the driveway, and Cindy broke in, "Let's go inside and finish this, okay?" As she got out of the car, Magic was so excited to see her he almost knocked her over. She gave him a big hug. "How're you doing, buddy?"

Cindy made her way straight to the kitchen to make some macaroni and cheese. In a few minutes they were both at the kitchen table eating it right out of the pan.

"Keli, I want you to know the things you told me on the way home make me so proud of you. You sound a lot like your grandpa, you know that?"

Keli smiled and continued telling her mom about her day, about her friendships with the new girls, and about her conversation with Coach Lindsay. Then she thought for a moment and added, "I think what I'm most worried about now is starting classes next week. Do you realize Dallas High has almost 1500 students?"

Cindy smiled. "That is quite a change from the 90 kids here, huh? Hey, this weekend we need to hit the sales and see what we can find. I have about $80 and with your $40, we can get some things for you."

Keli scraped the last bite out of the bottom of the pan. "I really don't need much, but we can go look."

"Last thing, with you using the car, it is going to be hard on me...so we are going to have to really talk to make sure we can make this work. I have been thinking we should get you a cell phone."

Keli's eyes widened. "A cell phone...that is awesome, Mom! Can we look for one this weekend?"

CHAPTER 29

FIRST DAY AT THE NEW SCHOOL

Sunday night finally came. Keli went over all the details, making sure her back-pack and volleyball bag were ready. She looked over at her desk at her new prized possession. It was past 7:00 and she could make unlimited calls, so at 7:01 she dialed Ashley, but no answer. Keli waited for the beep. "Hey, just wanted to give you my new cell number and see what was up for tomorrow...give me a call when you get this."

Keli hit the end button and looked out the window towards Sticky's house. She felt like calling Sticky to give him her new number, but she was really not into rejection right then.

The alarm clock went off at 5:30. Keli was already lying there waiting for the buzzer to go off. Forty-five minutes later she was ready to go. As she passed the high school reader board, it said, "Welcome back, Mountaineers!" Keli smiled and whispered under her breath, "Good luck, guys." Then she picked up speed and headed for Dallas.

She pulled into the parking lot and was amazed by the number of cars, hun-dreds of them. It took a few minutes to find a spot. There were kids everywhere, but she didn't recognize any of them. There were no hellos or smiles; every little group seemed to be in its own world. Back in Falls City everyone greeted each other. You already knew them.

Keli worked her way into the school to find wall-to-wall kids. She was now on overload. She pulled her class schedule out of her pack back. History first period, Room 213. She thought about Falls City having only eight classrooms.

Keli was startled when someone pulled her class schedule right out of her hand. She turned around expecting her first confrontation only to see Steen read-ing it. "Cool, we have the same lunch and 5th period together."

She grabbed it back. "So how do I get to Room 213?"

Steen smiled and said, "Well, good morning to you too."

Keli took a deep breath and said, "Good morning, Steen. I guess you can see I am a little stressed this morning. So how 'bout Room 213? Can you help a poor girl from the sticks find her way?"

"I'll show you where your class is if you will eat lunch with me today."

Keli scratched her forehead as her stress level took another jump.

Keli looked at her watch. "Okay. You show me where all my classes are..." she waved her schedule in front of him..."and I will have lunch with you today. Deal?"

Steen quickly upped the ante. "All your classes? That will cost you two lunches!"

Keli rubbed her forehead again, then looked at her watch. "Okay, sure, two lunches and you show me where all these classes are. Let's go!"

Each class was a completely foreign experience for Keli. The teachers didn't know any of their names, and some of the kids showed no interest at all, reading magazines or sending text messages on their phones while the teachers talked. It wasn't until 3rd period before she knew anyone in her classes, but since it was Alix, it would have been better if all of them had been strangers. When they made eye contact, Alix leaned forward and whispered something to a huge football-looking guy in a letterman's jacket. He gave Keli a glance and a wink.

She made a point of not looking over in that direction for the rest of the class. Finally it was lunchtime, but she had forgotten her deal and almost walked right past Steen, who was leaning against the wall across from the classroom. Steen stuck out his arm to slow her down. "Aren't you forgetting something?"

"Steen, wow, yes! I did forget. Sorry, not on purpose, but I am pretty much still in shock here. Falls City has fewer kids in the whole school than I can see in this hall right now."

"Don't worry about it. I remember when I first came here. It was the same for me."

Keli stopped right in the middle of the hall. "What do you mean, when you came here?"

Steen put his hand on her shoulder and gave her a gentle nudge to get her moving again. "Let's find a place to eat and I'll tell you all about it."

Steen led her outside to the quad; they scanned the area for an open spot. Ashley yelled from across the quad, "Over here!"

Steen looked at Keli with a slight frown. Keli grabbed his hand, "Come on, we can still talk." Keli's spirits were lifted when she saw Greta, Jesse, Libby, and most of the others from the team. "So are we having a meeting or something?"

Ashley made some room on the table for Keli and said, "We all get together for lunch. Coach calls it 'bonding'."

Jesse looked up at Steen and said, "Thanks for bringing her over to us."

Steen held his hands in the air. "She owes me lunch."

Libby threw a grape at him and said. "Shoo, boy jock, this is our table."

Keli raised her eyebrows. "I'll see you next period, okay?"

Steen put his hands in the air again and said, "Just so you all know. She owes me two lunches. Just ask her!"

After Steen walked away, Keli explained how she and he had met that morning.

Libby yelled down the table, "Steen is stalking Keli."

Keli blushed.

Jesse looked around at some of the other players. "We will vote on what days you can be excused from having lunch with the team."

Keli looked around the table and said, "So do we really get together for lunch everyday?"

Greta answered. "Yep. I have to eat lunch with these people for the next two and a half boring months. By the time this is over, all the really hot guys will already be taken."

Ashley threw a chip across the table at Greta. "Damn, girl...it's volleyball season. What does the coach say about dating?"

All the girls chimed in together. "Dating is a winter sport!"

Keli looked at Ashley. "Does she really say that?"

Jesse nodded. "I have heard it now for three years. So we hang out here, go to the dances together, the football games together, the movies together, until the season is over."

"Speaking of that, Friday night is the first football game. We should all get together for pizza or something, then go over together." Ashley mumbled through a mouth stuffed full of cookie.

Keli quickly answered, "Before I can commit, I need to check with my mom. I don't think I will be able to afford it and I have a transportation..."

Ashley interrupted. "Why don't you spend the night in town on Friday?"

Keli finished the last bite of her sandwich and then swiped Ashley's water bottle and finished that too. "I'll see what I can do. It sounds like fun, but really don't forget, it's just my mom and me, and we have just the one car and no money, so don't count on it."

Ashley was quick. "Why don't you have her drop you off at school on Friday and I will bring you home Saturday? Don't worry about the money. My dad wants to know if you want to work again this Saturday. He says you are better than me and Greta put together."

Keli opened up her chips and said, "That doesn't surprise me. All you two did was argue. If I was your dad, I would fire you both and hire me!"

Keli found Steen in the biology classroom pouting. She started laughing when he turned away when she walked into the classroom. "You're not serious. You know I had to have lunch with the team. But I really wanted to hear your story." Keli sat at the desk across from Steen and wrote her new cell number and email address on a piece of paper and handed it to him. "Call me tonight and we can talk."

Steen turned towards her and smiled.

The rest of the day was like the morning, no volleyball players in her classes. By her last class, she was starting to have a feel for what it was going to be like. She liked being faceless in her classes in comparison with how it was in Falls City. It made concentrating easier. She wasn't going to get into as much trouble joking around as she had in the years past.

CHAPTER 30

DO YOU KNOW HOW TO PRACTICE?

After school that first day, practice was intense, and there was no let up. At Falls City, there was a natural slip in how everyone practiced. After a couple of weeks, the newness wore off, and it got a little loose. At Dallas, everyone wore the same practice uniforms, and the two hours were all business. The coaches demanded it. Anyone who was cutting corners, not hustling, not paying attention during meetings got lines to do before and after practice. The seniors also put the clamps down. It was their year, and they expected everyone to go all out.

Keli loved it. To her, there was nothing better than really grinding it out every day. Coach Jim had already started counting on Keli as the JV leader. It was an easy decision; most of the girls were already following her lead.

But when practice was over, he asked her to meet him in the coaches' room. Keli hurried to dress and then made her way over

"Keli, we need to fix something right now," said Jim.

Keli looked at him confused.

"Well, I guess the first lesson I would like you to learn, actually that I would like everyone to learn, is that practice is a hard thing to learn to do. Most athletes never really learn how to practice."

Keli smirked. "What do you mean, Coach? We all do or at least try to do what you tell us. Isn't that practicing?"

"Yes, that is a part of practicing. Hear me out. What I am going to tell you might be hard to understand." He paused for a second. "Let me start with a question. Did you know that most kids only practice about 30 minutes at most during a 2-hour practice?"

Keli really looked confused now. "Coach, I don't get it...I was there the whole time and did everything you told me to do. I'm not sure what you're talking about."

The coach raised his hands in the air. "First, don't get all worked up. I just want you to think about what I am going to tell you, and then tomorrow and each day after think about this conversation and you will start to understand what I am talking about."

Keli shifted in her chair, getting ready for what the coach was about to tell her.

"We have all heard the words 'concentration' or 'focus' so many times that they've lost their importance. Generally, after a coach uses either word, within seconds the player has lost it. It's a very hard thing to do. Concentrating is the key to most everything, especially in the world of sports."

He paused again, trying to put his words together right. "Let's start with playing in a game. That might be easier, and it's important to what I have to say. When a game starts, you put all your effort into being completely ready, right?"

Keli nodded.

"Okay. What happens in games and in practice is that kids lose their concentration. Here's an example in a game: You serve the ball into the net...side out. You start kicking yourself and you spend the next few seconds thinking about the mistake. You just gave up valuable time to get ready for the next point, and now you're going into that next point unprepared. The same thing can happen after a good play. Those seconds are very critical; a lot needs to be done."

He looked at her intently. "You're not the only one on the floor. You have a responsibility to make sure everyone is where they are supposed to be, to read what the other team is doing, to look for a play from the setter or coach. When you spend that time on something else, your chance of making a mental error and costing your team a point is very good. It takes discipline to not let yourself fall into this trap."

"It's even harder to concentrate during practice. But it's where you learn to play the game, and it should be where you learn to discipline yourself on how to stay focused at all times. Players think if it's not their turn, then they are free to think or focus on other things. An example might be you waiting your turn in line. Like today, I noticed a handful of times you were staring off watching the Varsity or just looking around. Your focus was broken; at that point, you are no longer practicing. Then by the time practice is over, you have lost a lot of valuable time."

He paused to let this sink in. "And the most critical part is that you didn't work on the most important thing: how to concentrate for long periods of time. Every time you have a thought about school, a boy, dinner, a movie, or anything like that, you have left practice. When you are in line, you still should be at practice; you can learn a lot by watching everything and listening to everything. When I am instructing someone else, you should be listening, you should be visualizing your next opportunity, you should be watching for weaknesses, studying your setters for tendencies. These are just some of the things you should be concentrating on while you're waiting for your next turn. Keli, if you are truly serious about what you and the Coach talked about last week, you will learn to do this. Practice will become a full two hours, not this in-and-out deal."

"I'm not picking on you. I 'm giving you something I think you're ready for. Most players aren't nor will they ever be; they will just never grasp the true meaning and depth of concentrating. The great players in any sport all have this in common. Watch their eyes. They have this extreme ability to focus. I promise you. Learn to stay completely on the task, and your game will go to a level you might not believe is possible."

Keli smiled slowly. She thanked him and stood up to leave.

Coach Jim looked at her. "One more thing, Keli. This is not an easy thing to do. It will take you quite some time to master it. Don't expect to get it completely right...and to be honest, no one ever perfects it...there is always room to improve. Even the greatest will tell you that. Keep digging deeper and you will find more and more of your ability! But if you just stand in line, your game just stands there with you!"

When she got to the car, there was a note on the windshield. Keli pulled it out from under the wiper and unfolded it. "Answer your phone tonight!" She smiled, then thought about working on Saturday. Suddenly she dialed 411 and got the number for Webb Sports. As the phone rang, her hands got sweaty. Frank answered.

After greeting him, Keli stuttered, "I was wondering, uh, I was wondering if you ever needed someone to work on a part-time basis. I would love the chance to work for you. I really liked it last weekend. It was fun. I would do a great job, I promise."

Frank cut her off. "Did Ashley ask you to come in on Saturday for a while?"

"Yes, she did."

"Okay. After we're done with the back room, let's talk and see what we can work out."

Keli's heart almost leapt out of her chest. "Sure thing, Frank. Thank you, thank you!"

Keli set the phone down and screamed as loud as she could. If she could get a job at the store, maybe she could make enough money for her own car. She spent the rest of the ride planning the whole thing out even though she still didn't have the job.

CHAPTER 31

THE JOB

Cindy barely made it in the door before Keli bombarded her. "Mom, I need to talk to you. Today on my way home I called Frank and asked him about a part-time job. He..."

"Keli it's too much. There's no way." Cindy put her things down on the kitchen table. "You change schools, play tougher volleyball, and now you want to get a job? How are you going to fit it all in? I don't think it's a good idea." She stopped in the middle of the room and looked at her daughter.

"Wait, Mom, here is my thought. What if I only worked on the weekends? I thought if I could work, I could get my own car so we don't have to struggle to make it work. I know it would be hard, but it would make things easier in some ways."

She looked intently back at her mom. "I can do it. Give me a chance and at any time if you think I am slipping on school or volleyball, you can pull the plug and I promise no whining."

Cindy sat down thinking, realizing it might be a good idea. "Keli, I am a little apprehensive, but if it's only on the weekends and not too many hours, we can try it. If it gets to be too much, you'll have to quit."

Keli jumped to her feet, "Yes, thanks, Mom...you'll see it'll work."

Keli barely made it back to her room after dinner before her cell rang. The caller ID flashed Steen's name. She jumped on the bed and got comfortable before she answered.

She didn't even say hello. "Are you ready to tell me your story?"

Steen played it down. "Ah, it's pretty boring stuff. Let's talk about..."

"Come on, Steen. Tell me, I really want to know. It's been real tough on me making this move and I want to know your story. Please?"

"Okay, but before I tell all of this to you, promise me it's completely between you and me. Some things people know, but over all, I really don't want to become some party topic."

She quickly agreed.

"Okay then. In the middle of 8th grade, my dad's company started to fail. It was weird. The whole time I was growing up, it was never really something that any of us ever thought or worried about. But in a period of six months, he closed it down. My parents almost divorced over it. I think that scared me the most. Anyway, right before the start of my freshman year, I mean right before, like a week, my parents sat us down and said we were moving. My older sister almost had a mental breakdown and my little sister practically did the same thing. For me, I had always dreamed of playing football, and I really wanted to play for the coach at my old school. I grew up thinking he was the best coach in the world. He used to let me hang around when I was younger, and I really idolized him. So for all of us kids, it was pretty tough. It was so hard on my older sister that I thought for a couple days she was not going to handle it. She still hates it here, and when she graduates, she is going back for sure."

Keli had the phone tight against her head so she wouldn't miss a word. "So where did you guys come from anyways?"

"Cheney, Washington."

"Where's that?"

"Not too far from Spokane. It's kind of like Falls City is to Dallas. Cheney is a little bigger, but still here we all were in a new town and we didn't know anyone. Football practice had already started, and if not for a no-cut freshmen policy, I wouldn't have been able to play football my freshman year."

He paused for a second, putting together the next part of the story. "My sister still fights with my parents. Jill, my little sister, and I have pretty much adapted to Dallas. My dad now works for a company that used to be one of his customers. It's worked out although I know he still feels bad about it. My mom is adjusting. She grew up back in Cheney, went to college there, and taught school there. She teaches at Dallas High. So I see her every day. That can be good and bad sometimes."

Keli laughed. "You'll have to introduce her to me. So what was it like when you got here, as far as school and sports were concerned?"

"It was really hard both ways. Football, no one really wanted to talk with me. Most of the good players all went through middle school together and they didn't want a new quarterback to come in and play. So they called me names and wouldn't try hard when it was my turn for a while. It took nearly half the year before I started to fit in. Really it wasn't until last year before I was liked by most of the team. It really sucked. I thought about quitting many times, but the coaches kept telling me to stick it out."

"As for school, it was a lot like football until last Christmas. I didn't really have any friends except Carter, who was a new kid too. Looking back, some of it was my fault too; I really had a chip on my shoulder and didn't go out of my way to be nice. During Christmas break, Ashley threw a little party and invited Carter and me. It wasn't nearly like the big ones now, but it was good. Everyone was in a good mood with the holiday season and all. So when school started back up, I had a new group of friends and it's gotten better ever since."

Keli heard Sticky go down his driveway. "Steen, do you still keep in touch with your old friends back in wherever you said?"

"Cheney. A little bit. In the beginning I did a lot, but the past year I really haven't. It's sort of weird. After all those years of growing up with them, time kind of changes things. I went back this summer for a few days, and it wasn't the same. Some of the closeness was gone. It was good to see them and all, but I was happy to get back here."

Steen changed the subject around. "So tell me. What has been the hardest part of you leaving Falls City?"

Keli wasn't prepared to answer his question. "Hey, this is your story, remember?"

"I just told you my story. It's your turn. What are you struggling with the most?"

Keli sighed. She knew she needed to tell him. "Well, my friends here in Falls City hate me, my two best friends especially, and it really sucks that I did this and ended up on the JV team. To tell you the truth, I'm not sure which thing I hate the most."

"They hate you? Why?"

She thought it was easy to understand. "They didn't want me to change schools. From where I come from, there is this unspoken thing that Dallas is like the devil or something, and we have this ongoing ego thing where everyone there is stuck up and full of themselves. So then here I go and say, 'Guess what? I am leaving to go play with them.' They just exploded and haven't talked to me since. I think maybe that is the hardest part."

She paused. She could hear Cindy calling her name. "Steen, I need to go. My mom is yelling for me and I need to do some homework."

"Hey, before we get off the phone, what do you think about going to a movie sometime?"

Keli's eyes got big. "Steen, you know it's great to make a friend like you, but right now with everything going on, it's pretty hard for me to add in anything else. Please understand. I really think you're great, but right now with trying to move up in volleyball, getting a job, and homework, it would be rough to fit any more in."

Steen was quiet for a few seconds. "Sure, I understand...actually I need to focus on football. What do you say after the seasons are over, we try it?"

Keli grinned at the phone in her hand. "That sounds awesome."

She hung up as her mom walked into her room. "Didn't you hear me calling you? Who was that on the phone?"

"His name is Steen. I have a class with him and he plays quarterback in the football team."

"Steen? Keli, you amaze me...every time I talk to you, there is another thing happening. Are you sure you know what you're doing?"

She was quick to answer, "Yes, Mom, I have everything under control. Even though he might be the best looking guy in Oregon, we are really just friends. He is kinda new to Dallas too. We were just comparing stories."

"Really? So get your homework done or your only friend will be Magic!"

"I am starting it now." Keli realized this wasn't a topic she wanted to debate with her mother. "Mom, as far as Steen is concerned, it's not going to be a routine. I know I really need to concentrate on school and volleyball. Give me a couple of days to adjust, you'll see. Right now things are really crazy and I will adjust."

Cindy sat on the end of her bed. "I know I am being pretty strict and controlling, but this move scares me. The last thing I want is for it to backfire on you and school to take a back seat to all this. Remember, maintaining your grades is the most important thing, no matter what happens with volleyball. If you have the right grades when you graduate, you can go to school even if we have to borrow money to make it work."

Keli finished spreading her books out on her bed and then answered. "You're right, Mom. I will make sure nothing gets in the way. Thank you for everything."

Cindy smiled. "You know how crazy this is?"

They both laughed. "Well, it's about time we did something crazy, Mom. And if Ashley and I have anything to do with the craziness, it's going to get even worse."

Cindy raised her eyebrows. "What do you mean by that?"

"Well, let's just say we have a plan. But I can't tell you anymore than that!" Keli turned an imaginary key on her lips to tell her mom she wasn't getting anymore information.

"Well, how 'bout putting 'crazy' in its cage for the night and getting your homework done?"

CHAPTER 32

VOLLEYBALL 101

The next day after school, Keli quickly dressed for practice. She still felt a little uncomfortable wearing the black and red gear; all she had ever known was purple and gold. After warming up for a few minutes, she watched Coach Lindsay and Coach Jim go into the coaches' room.

Keli jumped to her feet, raced over, and knocked on the door. "Coach, you have a minute?"

"Sure, Keli, come on in," said Lindsay. "What's on your mind?"

Keli looked over to Jim. "Yesterday we talked about this practicing thing. Well, I thought a lot about it last night. How exactly do I learn it?" She paused for a second "...and the other thing," as she turned to Coach Lindsay, "I need a lot of work on understanding defense positioning. We never really worked on that kind of stuff before. So I am wondering if I show up here a little early before practice, if you're free, could you give me some ideas on these things?"

Both coaches looked at each other. Coach Jim answered, "Sure, Keli. Practice begins at 3:30, and we are generally around an hour or so before practice. Stop by any time."

Coach Lindsay stood up and went to the grease board. "Have a seat, Keli. Let me give you your first lesson of the day, and this ties in to what you and Jim talked about yesterday. The first thing you need to know is how to understand what the other team is trying to do on any given play and then what your responsibilities are against that particular play."

"The more you learn to concentrate in practice, the easier it will be to pick up quickly in games how people like to play, their timing, tendencies, weaknesses, strengths, and things like that."

The coach turned around. "Don't worry, Keli. I am giving you a lot right now, but if you want to learn to play at the highest level, you will need to learn all of this in time. Today let's talk about defense a little. You play on a team. All six of you need to work as a unit. Depending on where the ball is coming from, you need to cover certain areas on the floor and at the same time read the hit to know your responsibilities to cover it. A lot of times kids will do one or the other. Too many times kids get so caught up in watching the ball fly around that they freeze. You need to always be in motion; that doesn't mean running all over the court, like you sometimes do."

Keli looked over to Jim, who was nodding in agreement.

"A player needs to be in motion moving and flexing trying to get in the optimum position on the floor. Achieving this is most of the battle. Then it's having your body set for the type of hit."

Lindsay turned back to Keli from the grease board. "Lots of kids get to the right spot, then make a poor pass because they didn't get their body set right to make a good pass. It might be that you're standing too tall, your arms are too far apart, or in a lot of cases they're too high or low. Remember that given where the ball is coming from, any team is going to rotate so that all angles are covered. The key part once you rotate is reading the hitter and her swing plane. What I mean by that is that her motion towards the ball is the first key. You need to be right in the path. And second, unless the hitter is truly elite, which most aren't, they have a swing plane, meaning the direction their arm is heading. It's the most likely place the ball will go. A good defender will take away this spot and has the best chance to make a good pass or dig."

Lindsay put the marker down and turned around. "We're out of time. If you stop in again, we can go over more."

Keli grinned. "What do you mean 'if'? I'll be here tomorrow and the next day," and as she shut the door, she yelled, "and the next day too!"

Coach Jim walked out behind her. "Hey, Keli, I want to add one more thing."

She walked back to him. He put his hand on top of her head and said, "Today, pay close attention to the setter. Watch how she handles the different kind of passes she gets. The more you understand, pretty soon you will just know where the ball is going to be. When there is nothing going on, envision yourself getting into the right spot and making a perfect approach. Do it over and over again whenever you can."

The coach took a step back and looked right at her. "Keli, I wish we could bottle your desire. It's something a coach really appreciates. Keep working...every time you feel yourself slipping away, jump up and down a couple times to get the juices flowing again. When you're focused on this stuff, think of yourself as a coach. What would you tell the player to do next?" He smiled and walked off.

CHAPTER 33

GRETA HAS A MIND OF HER OWN

The week flew by. Between school, volleyball, and studying, it was a blur, but finally Friday came. Keli pulled three bags down the stairs that morning instead of the usual two. She needed the third one for clothes for the game that night and for work on Saturday.

Keli left her bags at the bottom of the stairs and headed for the kitchen where she found her mom pouring coffee. "Hey Mom, don't forget I'm staying in town tonight. The Dragons have their first game and I'm working for Frank tomorrow." Keli filled a bowl of cereal and sat down. "So, what are you doing tonight?"

Cindy looked over to her, wondering why she was asking a silly question. Keli looked back oblivious. "So are you going to tell me?"

Cindy turned back to her coffee. "I'm going to the football game tonight."

Keli cringed. "Oops, I forgot. They should kill Eddyville. I think next week the Dragons play away, so I will go to that game with you." She thought a moment. "The girls have their first volleyball game this afternoon too."

Cindy nodded.

"Wow, it's strange, Mom. It's like I've been completely consumed with everything going on in my world and have forgotten what's going on here. Is that wrong, Mom? Am I being selfish?"

Cindy put her hand on Keli's. "No, sweetie. Your life has taken a different turn and that isn't bad. You need to be thinking about your school and team. These kids here have the same thing going on. I 'm sure they haven't given much thought to your world."

"Well, I hope they win, and it will be fun to watch them next week. Hey, we gotta go or I'll be late. Wish me luck on getting the job tomorrow."

Cindy stood up to pour another cup of coffee for the road. "It would be a help to get another car. I just hope it's not too much of a burden."

For the first time, as they drove by the high school, most of her old gang and a few new faces she didn't recognize were hanging out at the picnic tables. They all watched as Keli and her mom drove by. It was surreal. Keli stared back but made no attempt to wave or smile. A few seconds later they were clear of the school and the town.

By the time biology rolled around, Keli was starting to get into the spirit of her first Dragon event, and the last two periods of the day were taken up by a pep rally. Keli met up with most of her volleyball team high up in the bleachers to watch. Keli was in awe as she scanned the gym. There wasn't an empty seat, and the teachers lined the walls.

Jesse nudged Keli. "So I hear you're getting the coaches' room workout over with now?"

Keli turned to look at her in the row behind. "Yeah, it's amazing how little I knew about the game."

Alix overheard the conversation and added, "Well, the real question is how much sucking up will a girl do to get to play?"

A handful of girls laughed under their breaths. Keli stood up and edged her way over to Alix. She was ready to have it out right there. Ashley jumped up as did a few other girls and ended the confrontation. Keli sat through the rest of the rally waiting for it to end. She wasn't finished with Alix. She stared up her way a couple of times just to remind her that it wasn't over.

When the rally ended, the girls needed to report for practice. When they got to the practice gym, there was a note posted canceling practice for today. Ashley led the cheer, and Greta grabbed Keli's arm. "Quick! Let's get out of here before someone changes their minds."

All the girls scattered, yelling, "Flying Pie at six."

On the way to Ashley's house, they passed Alix and her group. Ashley looked at Keli. "Sorry, I should have just let you pummel her right there today."

Keli's jaw tightened. "You know, I have always gotten along with everyone. I'm not sure what's up with this chick, but tonight I'm going to find out."

Greta took off her seat belt and leaned towards the front seat. "Keli, you can't just go get into a fight. You'll get kicked off the team."

Keli shook her head. "I'm not going to fight but I am going to get into her face. She'd better hope she can get through this, or when the season is over, so is she."

Ashley yelled, "You go, girl! Kick some tail!"

Greta and Keli laughed. Keli slumped into her seat. "You know, if it weren't for Alix, everything would be great. I don't get people like that."

Greta leaned back and put her seat belt back on. "You know why you don't?"

Keli turned her head to look at Greta. "I wish I did."

"Duh, girl...she thinks you're going to take her spot. The last year or so she has used intimidation to keep her place. She isn't getting any better, and now here comes this freak who can jump out of the gym. She's smart enough to know that once you get our system down, she is gonzo. She sees you go into the coaches' room everyday and come out a little closer to her, and it's driving her crazy."

Keli looked over at Ashley, who quickly glanced at her. "Greta is right on, Kels. Keep your nose clean on this. The day will come when you will get the last word. Hang in there and don't do anything stupid."

After they changed their clothes, they moved on to the pizza parlor. Anna and Alix were standing at the door collecting $3 a head so the group could pay for pizza and soda. Greta and Ashley looked at each other and were ready to break up World War III just in case. Keli handed Anna her money and said, "Alix, we need to talk right now."

Greta started to reach for Keli. Keli backed away just a little. "It's okay, I really just want to talk with her for a minute."

Alix glared at them and said, "Hey, I don't have anything I want to talk about."

Keli said, "Well, we can do it right here, or we can go over to that table over there." She pointed to a table over in the corner. "Take your pick, but make no mistake. We are going to talk and we are going to do it right now."

Alix looked around at the dozen or so girls who had already shown up. All of them just stared back. It was a showdown of sorts. Keli stood there waiting to see what Alix wanted to do. Finally Alix sighed heavily and stormed over to the table. Keli crinkled her nose at Ashley and followed Alix to the table.

All the girls watched closely ready to pounce on the two if there was the slightest sign of a fight. Alix and Keli jarred back and forth for nearly 10 minutes. Their teammates strained to hear what they were talking about, but no one could make out anything for sure over the loud music. In the end, Keli stuck out her hand across the table at Alix, hoping she would shake it. Alix peeked over to see who was watching, then looked back and quickly shook Keli's hand. Alix abruptly got up and headed back towards Anna, who was still manning the door.

Keli slowly got up and made her way over to the others. She plopped down at the big table. "Well, we'll see if that makes it better or worse."

Jesse leaned across the table. "So what did you guys say to each other?"

Keli shook her head, "It's between me and Alix. Call it an air-clearing conversation. Let's just see if it works, okay?"

After the pizza was nearly gone, Ashley and Keli finally gave into to Greta, who was long finished. "Come on, let's go."

Ashley bumped Keli to get her attention. "Betcha she wants to meet a guy there. She is sick unless she has at least two on the hook at all times. They need to name a disease after her or something."

Keli looked over at Greta, who was looking back up to the clock on the wall.

Ashley was right. As soon as they got to the field, Greta announced she would catch up later.

Keli busted up laughing, but Ashley yelled, "I'm leaving right after the game is over with or without you!"

As they walked across the track towards the home-team stand, Keli had her first twinge of homesickness. She looked out on the field and up into the stands to see all red and black. Ever since she was old enough to remember, it had been purple and gold. The stands had been filled with familiar faces. Now as she walked behind Ashley up into the bleachers, it seemed strange. Gone was the comradeship she had grown up with.

Nevertheless, the game was exciting. Watching Steen barking out the signals, Keli was impressed with his talents. He was a true leader on the field. Keli smiled broadly when it seemed Steen was looking in her direction. Her mind went to their long conversation a week ago. Keli spent the rest of the game with one eye on him and the other on the game. When it was over, Dallas had won mainly due to Steen's last-second heroics. He threw a perfect pass as he was being tackled for a touchdown.

On the way back to the car, they ran into Big Frank. "Hey girls, how about some ice cream?"

Keli looked to Ashley to answer, who nodded. Frank noticed Greta's absence. "So let me guess. She was going to catch up with somebody, right?"

Ashley looked at Keli with an I-told-you-so on her face.

"Well, I guess she will be getting up early to pull weeds or something. I'll meet you two over at Hal's. We'd better hurry before it gets too crowded."

Greta was waiting by the Jeep. Ashley yelled, "Too late...we just ran in to Dad."

Greta's head dropped. "Damn it...what did he say?"

Keli started giggling, "He said something about getting up early and pulling weeds. So what's this guy's name anyways?"

Greta slammed the door. "Austin."

"Austin 'the loser' Skaw?" Ashley blew up. "Not that guy! Please tell me you were with anyone but him."

Greta tried to defend him. "He's cute and he has an awesome..."

Ashley put her hand up. "Please don't say 'car' or I'll puke! Jeez, Sis, come on. If you keep hanging around dudes like that, you're going to end up with a guy like that. Think about it. He isn't going to college. At best he is going to struggle to find a decent job and then will probably spend every day after work stopping with his buddies at the local tavern in his really cool car. Sounds like a great life to me." Her voice dripped with sarcasm.

Greta didn't say a word. Keli wisely kept her mouth shut too.

Hal's parking lot was already full. It was the chief hangout after football games. Inside Frank and some of the other boosters were already discussing the game. Frank waved them over; he had saved them a little booth behind his table.

"Hey everyone, do you all know Keli Stennes? Remember back when we played a guy named Butch Stennes from Falls City? This is his daughter. She is going to be the next star of the Dragon volleyball team."

Ashley punched her dad on the shoulder. "Hey! One of the stars!"

Keli politely said, "Nice to meet all of you."

"Not only is she going to be a star, she works for me and so the rest of you, hands off!"

Keli's eyes got big and she looked at Big Frank, who winked back.

When Steen and his family walked in, Keli was staring so hard that when she went for her straw, her mouth missed and it hit her in the nose.

Greta noticed and laughed, "Dang, girl, where is your mind? Oh, let me guess. Who just walked in?" Then, acting like an announcer in a little louder than normal voice, she said, "Number 4, quarterback for the Dallas..."

Keli reached across the table to cover Greta's mouth.

Steen made eye contact with Keli and waved. Keli gave him a thumbs-up. Steen smiled and then was inundated with friends.

Keli tried to sell the table that they were just friends. Ashley said, "Right...just friends with the hottest dude in the whole school. Yeah, Keli, we believe that!"

"So, Kels, it sounds like you have a job at the store!" Greta said.

Keli bounced up and down in the booth. "It sounds like it. Do you know how cool that is? My mom and I struggle most of the time with money and this is going to be huge for us."

Ashley smiled. She loved how genuine Keli was. She always seemed secure talking about things that most kids would try to cover up.

CHAPTER 34

MOVING UP

The next morning, Keli came into the kitchen dressed in jeans and a T-shirt. "So what should I wear today?"

Frank looked over his newspaper. "That's fine. We'll get you a Webb Sports shirt when we get there."

On the way to the store, Frank threw a bunch of questions at her. "What does your mom think about you having a job? Is this going to interfere with your studies?"

Keli seemed to give all the right answers.

"Well, then, welcome to Webb Sports. Your hours will be noon to closing, which is 8:00 on Saturdays." As Big Frank pulled the keys out of the ignition, he looked over at Keli. "I just want you to know that I think you're a great kid, and if you ever need anything, you come and talk with me, okay?"

Keli smiled and nodded.

As they walked towards the entrance, Keli stopped. "Can I meet you inside? I would like to call my mom."

"Sure, be late on your first day."

Keli didn't catch his humor right away and said, "I can do it later."

Frank chuckled. "Just kidding...of course call your mom. I'll see you inside."

Keli told her mom about the job and her new schedule and just before she hung up, she asked about the Falls City games.

"We won both games," said her mom.

"That's awesome. How did Charlee and Sticky do?"

"They both played well. It was different though without you there. I see in the paper your boyfriend was the hero in the game last night."

"He isn't my boyfriend. We're just friends. Mom, I've got to go."

Keli loved her first day on the job. She couldn't believe that she was getting paid for putting away and selling sporting goods. The rest of the weekend she buried herself in her homework; she wasn't going to give her mom any reason to think she couldn't handle her new job.

Monday finally came. She was anxious for school and to get back on the volleyball court, especially since the coach had cancelled practice on such short notice on Friday. Just like the past couple of weeks, Keli promptly made her way to the coach's office right after school.

As the door swung open, Lindsay didn't even look up from her paperwork. "Good afternoon, Keli. How was your weekend?"

Keli sat in her usual chair. "Good, Coach. So why did you cancel practice Friday?"

"I had an unexpected meeting that I needed to attend. I'm guessing the team liked the break." Lindsay looked up for the answer.

"Yeah, we all ended up eating pizza before the football game."

Coach looked back down at her paperwork. "I hear we won."

"Yep, we came back at the end to win. It was pretty exciting."

The coach finished her paperwork and closed the folder. "Good. I see in the paper Falls City won without you Friday, too."

Keli nodded, not really wanting to talk about Falls City.

"Well, let's get started."

Just then Jim walked in "Sorry I'm late." He sat down over at his desk facing Keli.

Both of the coaches were just staring at her. "Okay, you guys are making me a little nervous here...what's up?"

"We are moving you up to the Varsity team," answered Lindsay. "Today Becca had to quit because of family reasons."

"Wow! Can I ask what happened? Why can't she play?" Keli was stunned and excited as the news sunk in.

Lindsay looked over at Jim. "Well, we can't go into that...but because she can't play, Jim and I think as far as you have come these past few weeks, you're the person to fill her spot."

Keli looked a little nervous. She had already become comfortable with being on the JV with its lesser pressure. She leaned back in her chair. "Are you sure I'm ready? When I watch the Varsity practice, I can see where I need to improve."

The coaches both smiled. "We think you're ready. You just keep working as hard as you are now, and it won't take you long to convince yourself that you can play with them."

Coach Jim stood up and stuck out his hand. "Congratulations, Keli! In the short time I had you on my team, it was amazing to me to coach someone with your desire. Don't lose that! And just know that since our talk, you've shown me that kids your age can learn to practice the whole time. Thanks for proving that to me." He looked over to Coach Lindsay. "If she starts messing up, send her back to me!"

They both watched Jim shut the door behind him.

"Okay, next item of business. I know you and Alix have been struggling for whatever reasons. Make sure you understand this. Under no circumstances will I tolerate any negative things going on. This team will stay united or both of you can go play on the JV team and battle it out. Are we clear on this?"

Keli looked shocked. She'd had no idea the coach even knew about the conflicts. "Yes, Coach, I understand."

"You need to get out there and stretch and play some pepper. I have a little meeting with your new friend here in a minute. As for hitting 5s, you are going to get thrown into the fire on this, so as with Coach Jim, I expect you to be at practice 100% of the time and when you're not directly involved, then you should be watching and studying everything. It's critical for you to pick this up. Ask questions of me or the captains. I don't want a lot of 'I didn't know.'"

"One more thing...don't forget what I said about your situation with Alix. There is zero tolerance on this issue." The coach was lasered in on Keli. There was no doubt in Keli's mind that she meant business.

"Thanks, Coach. I'll do my best...I really appreciate the chance."

Keli closed the office door slowly behind her in shock. She looked around the gym; most of the girls were going through their normal routines. Alix was headed her way. Keli waited for her by the door. Alix was trying to avoid eye contact, but she couldn't. Keli was right in her path to the door.

"Alix, I just want you to know that like I said on Friday, I am willing to try and become friends and teammates. We need to try to get past what's happened. Think about it." Keli raised her hand to give Alix a high five.

Alix looked at Keli with her usual smirk. "Nice try, Mountain Girl." Then she walked by Keli without giving her a five back.

Keli stood there for a second while her blood pressure started to rise. The coach's words were still ringing in her ears, and she wasn't about to mess things up. All of a sudden it hit her: I am on the Varsity team now! She sprinted over to the bleachers and dropped off her bag and backpack. Instead of stopping at court 2, she walked right by giving Coach Jim a double high five as she made her way to court 1.

Jesse and Libby had the rest of the team warming up. They all stopped and looked at her. Jesse asked, "So what's up? Did we steal one of your balls or something?"

Some of the other girls laughed.

Keli smiled and looked at Ashley and Greta, then back to Jesse. "Can I play with you guys?"

For a moment everyone just stared. Then Ashley and Jesse pumped their fists in the air followed by the rest of the team clapping and cheering. Keli looked back over to court 2. Coach Jim pointed at her and the rest of the JV team was clapping too.

It was a tradition that when a player moved up from the JV team, she was greeted by each of the Varsity players. As she walked down the line getting a high five from each player, Keli was in heaven. This was the best moment in her life. As they finished the welcome line, Coach Lindsay and Alix walked out of her office and headed towards them. Jesse under her breath said, "Okay, two laps. Let's go."

Everyone headed off around the court.

Coach Lindsay blew her whistle and motioned them back to the net. All the players gathered around the coach. "As you all know, we lost one of our teammates. Becca won't be with us anymore, and Keli is joining our team. We have been working hard all year, and this is a tough day. I know Becca was an important part of this team, but we need to move on and work towards our goals."

Lindsay looked serious. "The season starts tomorrow. We have a lot of work to do today; we are a day behind because of Friday, so I want everyone working double hard today if you want to play tomorrow."

It was easy to see one of the differences between the two coaches. Coach Lindsay was no nonsense and very serious. She demanded full-out effort and when she didn't get it, you got it from her. The next two hours were the toughest practice Keli had ever experienced. When it was over, she was exhausted.

Coach Lindsay gave them her final instructions: "Everyone in bed by 10:30. All Varsity players must be dressed in full warm-ups by the start of the JV match. We meet in the prep room at 6:15 sharp. For those of you who are new to being a Lady Dragon, two other rules. Under no circumstances are you to watch the game with boys or other friends; we are a team. Second, be sure you have your body ready to play. It's your responsibility to hydrate and eat properly. Do not spend all your time on a game day goofing around and then show up at the last minute without having eaten or having kept yourself hydrated. It is very selfish. If these rules are broken, expect a two-game suspension...no exceptions. Last thing, this is a great team. I have only one expectation and that is to play for the state championship. Anything less will be a disappointment! Tomorrow we start this journey. Everyone, be ready to do your part. Again for those of you who think you might get a second chance, ask the veterans. Any questions?"

The coached scanned the team. "Okay, then see you all tomorrow." She put her fist in the air, and all the players joined her. "On the three...Dragons!"

Keli and the rest of her teammates made it over to the bleachers. Most were quiet after the long hard practice. As the girls pulled off their sweaty socks, Keli asked Libby, "Are all the practices like this one?"

Libby quietly said, "No..."

Keli said, "Good!"

Libby smiled and said, "They are generally harder, but today was the day before a game."

Keli's mouth fell open. "No way!"

She looked over to Ashley, who was nodding. "Why do you think we aren't laughing and talking after practice? The coach takes everything we have every day. She says the only way to know what you've got is to use it all up to see. Believe me, every day she tries. Get used to it!"

The varsity team manager was an old man named JoJo. He had worked with the sports teams for nearly 50 years. JoJo slowly walked over to Keli with a Lady Dragon bag with her warm-ups and uniforms inside. "I hear you're the new girl on the team."

Keli's eyes were fixed on the leather bag. "That's me."

His posture had slipped over the years and he stood slightly bent over. He nodded at her and said, "Wear it proudly." He straightened up a bit and looked right at her, "I remember your dad. You remind me of him." As he walked away, he said, "I'm sure he is very proud right now."

Keli watched as the old man walked back into the equipment room.

Jesse grabbed the bag out of her hand and pulled out the warm-up jacket. "We all wear our jackets to school the day of the game. Oh yeah, and we all wear black sweatbands on our left arms between our elbow and shoulder pointing to the spot. Do you have any?"

Keli shook her head.

"I have extras," Jesse said. "I'll bring you an autographed one tomorrow. It will be a collector's item one of these days."

Keli grinned. "Sure, I'll sell it on eBay to help with my retirement."

Jesse stuffed the jacket back in to the bag. "You know it, girl." Keli really liked Jesse's attitude and confidence.

As Keli drove home, she kept glancing over to the passenger seat to see the Lady Dragon bag. It was like a prize. This past six weeks, her life had turned upside down, the setbacks, the lost friends, and now she had her first vision of what she had set out to do.

When she pulled up in front of the restaurant, her first thought was to bring the bag in with her, but she realized it would cause a scene and she left it in the car. Keli looked in the windows to see who was there, hoping to see some of her old friends. She opened the clanging door to find the restaurant mostly empty except for a couple she didn't recognize.

Keli looked at her mom, who was filling up the saltshakers. "Hi Mom! Any chance I can have a burger? I'm starving."

Cindy looked up at her. "Sure, sweetie, you have a job now, and I am sure you won't mind spending some of your own money on a burger. Come to think of it, how 'bout buying your poor old mama a burger too?" Cindy stood there smiling at Keli as she sat down on her stool.

Keli grinned. "Hey Jack! How about two Mountaineer burgers for me and my mama!"

Jack yelled back out to Keli. "Your mom says you have your first game tomorrow."

Keli nodded. "Are you coming?"

Jack poked his head back in the opening. "Sorry, I'll be here working for your mom. What time is the game?"

Keli took a quick peek over to her mom, who was still filling the shakers. "It's at 7:00."

Jack yelled over to Cindy. "Hey, you told me the game was at 5:00 and you needed to be out of here at 4:30."

Cindy put down the salt. "It is at 5:00." She walked over to the schedule she had on the wall.

Keli beamed. "That was before today."

Cindy looked at her puzzled.

"I got moved up today. I am now officially a Lady Dragon!"

"Wow!" said Cindy. "You should have called and told me!"

"It happened so fast, I didn't learn until right before practice."

Cindy yelled back to Jack. "Okay, I can stay longer tomorrow. We need to call your grandpa and let him know."

CHAPTER 35

NUMBER 21

When Keli and her mom got home, she couldn't wait to dig through the new bag. She wasn't used to this kind of gear. The bag was a very cool heavy black leather with a red lady dragon spiking a ball over a net. It had "Lady Dragons" printed underneath it.

She pulled out her white-and-black uniform tops. She was number 21. The black spandex bottoms had Dallas on one leg and Dragons on the other in bold white. The warm-ups were heavy stretch cotton, black with red and white stripes down the sides. The back of the warm-up top had the same red lady dragon hitting the ball as the bag. There was also a red long-sleeved T-shirt with Dragon Volleyball on the front and her number on the back.

There was a small notebook with a daily workout schedule, a suggested eating plan, all the team rules, and a history of Dragon Volleyball. Pinned to the front of the notebook were shoe and kneepad requirements. Keli was in awe. She tried on the white uniform including the warm-up gear and headed downstairs to show her mom.

Her mom smiled and handed the phone to Keli. "Gramps wants to talk with you."

"So I hear you have cleared another hurdle."

Keli could hear the pride in Tom's voice. "Congratulations! You've worked hard, and I'm proud of you. So your mom says the game is at 7:00?"

"Yep, though you could come at 6:30 to watch warm ups too."

Tom laughed. "Well, we'll see about that, but you can sure expect us by game time. Just in case, though, you never know what things come up. So if we aren't there by game time, you play as if we were. A lot of kids get rubber-necking around, looking for their parents or friends like that is the most important part."

Keli giggled. "Gramps, you're sounding more and more like a coach...do you know that?"

"Just remember what I said, okay?"

Keli grinned at her mom. "Yes, Gramps, I'll remember. See you tomorrow."

Cindy stood admiring the uniform. "That is quite the get-up. Take off the warm-ups and show me the uniform."

Keli took off the jacket and said, "Look, Mom" as she tore away her warm-up pants. To Keli this was better than Christmas. Her mom stared at the uniform. Keli got a little self-conscious. "What, Mom? Is there something wrong?"

Cindy shook her head and looked back into Keli's eyes. "No, sweetie, nothing is wrong."

Keli was confused. "Then what? I can always tell when something isn't right."

Cindy grabbed her hand and pulled her down next to her on the couch. "Number 21 was your dad's number. Did you know that?"

Keli looked a little confused. "Wasn't his number 10?"

"Yes, in football it was, but for basketball and baseball, it was 21."

Keli frowned. "Is it wrong to wear his number?"

Cindy squeezed her hand, "No, of course not. I think your dad would be proud that you are wearing the number he wore. Sometimes," Cindy bit her lower lip, "sometimes little things like that bring back memories. Your dad was a good man. It's a shame he isn't getting to watch you grow up."

Keli squeezed her mom's hand back. "Yeah, for me too. It's weird not having a dad."

Keli remembered the note about shoes and kneepads. "Mom, I need a certain pair of shoes and different knee pads."

Cindy looked annoyed. "What are we going to do about this now? They give this to you today and tomorrow you have a game? Great!"

"Wait," said Keli. "I can call Ashley."

Big Frank answered and congratulated her. "I hear the coach finally came to her senses and just in time I might add."

"Thanks, Frank. Are Ashley or Greta home? I was going to see if they might have black knee pads and..."

Frank interrupted. "And you need the Nike shoes too, don't you?"

"Yep...I got a note in my bag and since I got it just today...well, I guess I am going to have to make do."

Frank said, "Remember when I told you if you ever needed anything to call? Well, this is obviously one of those times. Stop over at lunch tomorrow. I'll have what you need waiting for you. What size shoe do you wear?"

"I wear a 10-1/2."

"Okay. I'll put them on account for you and you can take $10 a week out of your check to pay for them. How does that sound?"

"Perfect! Thank you, Frank!"

"No problem, just remember your old friends when you make it big, okay?"

Keli laughed, "Sure, I won't forget...what did you say your name was again?"

Keli hung up the phone and told her mother the good news.

Cindy threw the rest of Keli's sweaty clothes in the washer. "Frank seems like a good man," she called from the laundry room.

Keli didn't miss an opportunity to plug him. "Mom, he is a great guy and he is a hunka hottie, too! After the game I'll introduce you to him."

"We'll see. It'll be late and you have school the next day."

CHAPTER 36

RODEWALD'S MARKET

Keli could hardly sleep for thinking about the game. She got up early and packed her bags. Her proudest moment came when she put on the Dragon warm-up jacket with her jeans. She looked in the mirror every direction she could, then hurried down to show her mom. She walked into the kitchen to pick up her lunch, and her mom did a double take. "Well, that red and black is going to be hard to get used to after all these years."

Keli giggled, "We'll get used to it. Mom, I need a double lunch because I need to eat before the game. One of Coach's rules is to be fueled and hydrated. She is pretty strict on a lot of things actually. She looks nice on the outside but the girls on her team know she really is evil."

Cindy looked up and said, "She sounds like a good coach then. Hey, sweetie, you're going to have to stop at Rodewald's or some place. I don't have anything to put in your lunch other than a sandwich."

On her way to school, Keli pulled up in front of Rodewald's Market to pick up some fruit. Parked right next to her was Charlee's car. She thought about putting the car into reverse, but she didn't. Okay, here goes, she said to herself, grabbing her wallet.

Charlee, Tracie, and two other girls were standing at the checkout counter. Charlee immediately saw Keli walk in in her Dragon warm-ups. Tracie waved at Keli unconsciously, and Keli felt a strong wave of confidence come over her, "Hey, Tracie!"

Keli nodded at Charlee. She smiled at the two girls she didn't know. She figured they must be the new transfers.

"Congratulations on your game on Friday. I hear you killed Eddyville." Keli was looking at Tracie.

Tracie smiled and said, "It was Charlee and Tanya...you know me, I just take up space out there."

Keli laughed politely. She looked again over to the new girls and then stuck out her hand. "Hi, I'm Keli. I'm guessing one of you is Tanya." Her eyes darted back and forth at the two, waiting for Tanya to acknowledge herself. The taller, older one said, "Thank you, and this is my sister Tess."

Keli then looked at Charlee. "How're you doing?"

Charlee picked up her bag off the counter, glanced at the others, then said, "I'm doing great," although there was no warmth in her voice. Then she smirked as she stared at the Dragon logo and wished Keli luck in the game.

She smiled and started to say "Thanks" when she heard Charlee say, "JV game, that is." Then Charlee started to quietly giggle as she and the other girls walked out of the store.

She wanted to chase after them and rub in the fact that she was now on the Varsity team, but she restrained herself and went to get the fruit.

When she got back to the checkout, Sticky's mom Janet was behind the counter. "Hi there, honey," she said with a sad look on her face. "How's it going? Things been pretty tough for you lately?"

Keli mustered a grin. "Thanks, Janet...I'm doing pretty good." Keli looked at her. "So how is Sticky?"

Janet's face softened. "He misses you as much as I think you miss him."

Keli nodded, "I really wish we could get past this."

Janet put Keli's orange and banana in a bag and said, "I think things will get better real soon. He told me he saw you last week. I can tell he is coming around."

Keli's face brightened up. "Please tell him 'hey' for me."

"Ok, sweetie...I will." Janet looked down at the big Dragon. "Looks like you have a game today, huh? I heard that you didn't make the Varsity, but hang in there. I am sure that will change one of these days."

Keli picked up her bag and said, "Actually, I was moved up to Varsity yesterday."

Janet smiled warmly. "Way to go! I knew you would."

Keli put the bag back down on the counter and went around to the other side and gave Janet a quick hug.

As she started back around to the front of the counter, she stumbled into a box on the floor. She looked in the box and saw flyers that read, "Don't forget to vote "Yes" for our Schools!" She looked at Janet, "It's that time of year again, huh?"

"Yes," Janet handed a green flyer to Keli. "This year I am a little worried what with logging way down and all. I'm a little afraid that we might have a bigger fight than we've had in the past. They want to raise our property taxes quite a bit, and I think it has a lot of people thinking."

Keli shrugged. "Well, every year it works out. This year won't be any different." She grabbed her bag and headed out to her car.

CHAPTER 37

GAME DAY TRADITION

Jesse stood up and said, "Tradition time!"

All the girls around the table yelled it loud enough for all the kids in the area to hear. A crowd quickly gathered around the table. Jesse jumped on top of the picnic table and did a slow 360 turn, saying, "Can I have everyone's attention? Every year before our first game, tradition says that the newest member of the team must stand and sing the Dragon Fight Song. This year our newest member," Jesse looked down at Keli, who was pretending not to be listening, "is Keli Stennes."

Everyone cheered. Keli looked up at Jesse, who was laughing and holding out a piece of paper. Ashley and Libby each grabbed an arm and hoisted her upwards. Keli, smiling but reluctant, got up on top of the table. Jesse handed her the paper with the fight song printed on it.

Keli chuckled. "You mean I have to sing this in front of everyone?" scanning the crowd around the table.

Greta was laughing so hard she was gasping to get enough air. The crowd started chanting her name "Keli...Keli...Keli." She stared at the paper knowing there was no way out of it although she'd only first heard the melody at the football game. As she started to sing, Jesse waved her hands to quiet everyone, which even made it worse.

Keli's face was redder than the dragon on her warm-up, but she finally finished and did a few bows to get the crowd chanting her name one more time. She punched Jesse in the arm and then jumped off the table and buried herself back in her lunch. Ashley threw a piece of cookie at her to get her attention. "If it's any consolation, I had to do it as a scared little freshman. Now that was bad!"

After lunch, Steen met Keli at her locker. "Hey, congrats! I heard you're taking Becca's place."

Keli took it wrong, thinking somehow she was unworthy of her advancement. She slammed her locker door and didn't say a word as she busted towards the biology room. Steen chased after her. "Hey, what did I say?"

Keli didn't slow down and went straight for her seat. Steen sat across from her like he always did. "Hey, if I said something wrong, I'm sorry. I was just trying to say 'good job'."

Keli finally talked. "I know most people are thinking I don't deserve to be here, and I am like the token player."

Steen broke in, "I didn't say that, and I surely didn't mean it. Keli, I'm your friend...friends don't do that to their friends." He sat back in his seat a little upset himself now.

Keli realized that she was taking out some of her own frustrations on him. She reached across the aisle and touched him on the arm to get his attention. "Sorry... I'm way wrong for how I acted." She gave him a little smile.

Steen smiled back. "No worries. Good luck today, okay?"

Keli nodded. "Thanks...I hope I get to play." She realized that was where the frustration was coming from. She was worrying that she might sit on the bench the whole game. She was used to playing.

Steen picked up on the source of her real problem. "I'm not sure if you need any advice, but I was exactly where you are last year."

Keli turned to him. "Hey, I'll take anything right now."

Steen leaned a little closer to her. "Okay, you just need to be ready to play whenever that is. Encourage your teammates...when you're on the bench, be the vocal leader...it helps you stay into the game and most of all, be patient. You'll get your chance." Steen was staring at her, and Keli was staring back at him. It was exactly what she needed to hear, and Steen was the perfect person to tell her.

The next three hours dragged by, but finally it was nearly 5:00. Keli did her share of cheerleading from high up in the bleachers during the JV game. She felt part of the team; a lot of the girls had already started to count on her. Almost on every play she was barking directions or encouragement. Some of the other Varsity players were making fun of her...calling her "Coach."

Jesse stood up and called to the rest of the players, "It's time, ladies," and they all paraded around the end of the court during a timeout.

Coach Lindsay was waiting for them in the prep room. The blackboard was full of diagrams. The starting line up was posted on the far left board. Greta and Taylor middles, Jesse and Libby outside hitters, Ashley setter and Alix right side. It wasn't a surprise, but still Keli was a bit disappointed. She had never not started a game before in any sport.

Coach was extremely serious. She pointed to the top of the blackboard. She read it out loud "State Champs 2004...if **we** want it bad enough. For the past few weeks, you have worked like state champions...tonight you get a chance to show off your hard work. I'm proud of the tradition we have built here over the years."

She looked at Jesse and Libby and some of the other seniors. "This is your year to leave a piece of history. This team is as talented as any team I have ever coached. We need to go out there tonight and dominate...no matter what the score, I expect complete concentration and teamwork. If I see anyone letting up or not into the game, expect to be watching. There are girls on the bench very capable of playing, and believe me they will be too. Okay, let's go play!"

The coach stuck her fist in the air, and the team broke into a roar, jumping up and down yelling, "Dragons... Dragons... Dragons." They ran out of the room and through the hall and out onto the floor. Keli was amazed at how many people were there. She tried not to scan the crowd, but she couldn't help it. She spotted her mom and grandpa. Also Big Frank and some of his buddies that she had met before. As they started to warm up, her eyes wandered back to the stands and found her old coach, Coach Edwards, smiling at her.

When the warm-ups were over, the announcer started the introductions. His voice boomed throughout the gym. Keli thought she was at an NBA game or something; it was so different from what she was used to at Falls City where they didn't have introductions. When he finished introducing the starters for the McMinnville Grizzles, the announcer's voice went up a few notches. The lights went dark and the music picked up again and, "Now, here are your Lady Dragons!" echoed through the gym.

Keli felt goose bumps all over her body. A spotlight appeared on the court and as each player's name was called, she bolted to the spotlight clapping for the next player to join her. Keli wasn't expecting to hear her name called, but since it was the first game of the year, they announced the whole team. It finally came, second to the last person..."A junior, 5'll" and Queen of the Jumps, number 21 Keli Stennes." Keli ran out onto the floor in complete astonishment. She had never felt like this before in her whole life. She was immediately addicted to the feeling. At this point it didn't even matter if she played that night or not.

When the lights came back on, all the players gathered around the coach, who was repeating a bit of what she had said in the prep room. As they broke the huddle, Keli grabbed Ashley's arm, "Good luck!"

Ashley grinned, "Is this cool or what?"

Keli quickly answered with a high five, and a few seconds later the game was on.

The game was close for the first half dozen points, both teams nervous and pressing too hard. Keli was yelling, as were most of the other players on the bench. With the score tied at 7-7, Alix dug the ball and made a textbook pass to Ashley, who laid the ball perfectly outside and Jesse hammered a cross-court kill. The Dragons didn't look back and ran off 11 unanswered points. When the first game was over, it was Dragons 25 Grizzlies 14.

Game two was a carbon copy of the first game. The Grizzlies didn't have an answer for the power and blocking of the Dragons. Even the score was a repeat 25-14.

Coach Lindsay had pretty much used the same rotation the first two games. Keli and Alison were the only two players who didn't play. That changed in game three, when the coach started Alison for Taylor in the middle and Keli for Alix on the right side. Keli's hands were sweating and her heart was pounding so hard that she didn't think she could even play. As they walked onto the court, Jesse told Ashley, "Let's see what the mountain girl has."

Keli looked at them both, nodding "That's right. Give me the ball." She was so nervous she really didn't mean it, but she knew she needed to say it. The last thing she wanted right now was to screw up and make mistakes. So far, the first two games had been practically flawless. Keli wanted to peek up in the stands to see her mom and grandpa, but she forced herself to concentrate on the game.

It didn't take long for Keli to get involved. The first serve by the Grizzlies came zipping right at her. Keli handled it and made a good pass to Ashley. Ashley made a quick set to Greta, who found an opening to her right for the point. Keli's nerves settled down a little as the game went on; her instincts took over and her nervousness went away. With the score Dallas 9 Mac 5, Keli set up on their outside hitter and made her first solid block for a point. Keli pumped her fist high in the air. On the next play, McMinnville ran the same set, and Keli was there for another block. This time her teammates mobbed her. When the game ended, Keli sighed in relief that she hadn't messed up. Others were more impressed with her jumping ability and the plays she made. The Dragons made it short, winning three games to zip.

Can I Play...

Keli waited by the bleachers for her mom and grandpa. She could tell her mom was all excited by the way she hurriedly tried to make it down the bleachers. Cindy couldn't wait and yelled out, "Great game, honey. You played great!"

Tom had that look on his face that said 'we'll talk about it later.' Keli was in heaven.

Just then Ashley and Big Frank walked up. "Great game, Keli...I loved those blocks."

Keli smiled and said. "Thanks. Frank, I'd like to introduce you to my mom and grandpa."

Cindy stuck out her hand. "Actually my name is Cindy."

Frank laughed, "You've raised an amazing young lady."

Cindy had "proud" written all over her face.

Frank and Tom shook hands. Then Frank looked at his watch, "I know it's a school night, but it would be great if you all would join us down at Hal's for some ice cream."

Keli looked at Ashley; both were thinking the same thing. Cindy looked at her watch, then frowned. "It's late. How 'bout after a Friday game or something?"

Frank stuck his hand back out towards Cindy. "Okay, I'll hold you all to that!"

Cindy smiled, "I want to thank you for giving Keli a job. It really helps us out."

Frank patted Keli on the shoulder. "She's a great little worker. I wish I could get my two to work as hard as Keli."

Ashley caught Keli smirking, so she stuck her tongue out...to say "Suck-up!"

The ride home quickly turned quiet. When they got home, Keli went straight to her bedroom, and when she got to the top of the stairs, she paused. "Thanks, Mom, for coming...you being there was the best part."

"I wouldn't have missed it, and Keli, you made the right decision to change schools."

Keli looked back downstairs at her, "I think so too, Mom."

Keli closed her door and headed for her desk to finish her math homework. Her eyes were drawn across the way to Sticky's house. She could see his light still on and his silhouette behind his curtain. She grabbed her cell phone and dialed his number...then froze and hung up. She started to dial the number again, but this time she didn't even finish with the numbers before she folded the phone shut and laid it back down on the desk. She stared out the window and whispered quietly, "Sticky, I miss you. Please call me."

CHAPTER 38

ATTITUDE

When Keli walked into Lindsay's office, the coach had a couple of things on the board that were specific to Keli's game. Keli sat there quietly trying to understand the diagrams. The coach looked up from her paperwork. "So do you understand what's up there?"

"Most of it, Coach," answered Keli.

Lindsay looked up at the board, then back to Keli. "You've gotten caught a few times watching the hitter and not recognizing the tip down the line quick enough. First off, you were playing a little too deep. Close the gap towards the net, make the hitter try to hit it over your head. You don't have deep corner."

"On offense, if the back set is a good one, you need to be ready to attack. Generally the sets are going to be flatter and quicker than if you were playing on the left side. You don't have much time. What's happening is that you're waiting too long and you're settling for a weak attack or a free ball. The last thing you want to do is waste a good set."

Keli leaned back into the chair and stared at the board. The coach stood up and erased it. "Keli, you need to keep working hard to change your attitude."

Keli's mouth dropped open. "What do you mean, Coach? I try to always have a good attitude."

Lindsay finished erasing the board. "There is more to attitude than positive or negative."

Keli's head turned tilted to one side. "Huh?"

Coach smiled. "You think about it, and we will talk about it tomorrow." She looked at the clock. "You should get out there and warm up. I think Jim has the setting machine up...you should get some extra swings in."

"You know, Coach, I hate it when you do this to me."

"Good. I will look forward to your answer tomorrow."

There were a handful of girls, mostly freshmen and sophomores, listening to Coach Jim explain approaches. Keli quietly slipped into the group. "Okay, chase your own ball."

All the other girls backed up and let Keli go first. She laughed. "Hey, I'm still trying to figure out this stupid machine too."

The coach showed her the ball and dropped it into the machine and the ball shot out. Keli gauged it perfectly and made a nice cross-court hit. The other girls all complimented her, although Keli knew it was only a fair hit in comparison to the Jesse's of the world.

When she got back to the coach with her ball, Jim looked at her, "Why are you holding back?"

"I'm not, Coach," answered Keli.

When it came around again for Keli to hit again, Jim paused, "If you want to continue, I need to see you go all out on this ball. Don't leave anything on this side of the net."

Keli bent over and did a quick deep knee bend to stretch her legs. The coach again showed her the ball...this time Keli exploded to the net and swung as hard as she could. The ball screamed straight down just on the other side of the 10-foot line. This time the other girls were silent...they all knew there was no way they could hit the ball like that.

When Keli got back this time to the coach, he said, "See? You really can hit the ball if you want to. When you get sets like that, then hit it like that."

Keli nodded. She could tell the difference.

"You don't have to be mad to make a swing like that," said Jim. "It's an attitude."

Keli immediately glanced over to the coach's room. She got back in line and for the next 15 minutes she continued to punish the ball. She could start to feel an inner strength building with each hit.

The next couple days of practice were consistently brutal. The coach never let up. She kept the focus on Friday's game and what they were working on at that moment. When a player broke from the team's focus, she was running lines. The trainer would start the scoreboard clock. If the lines weren't done in the given time, she would do it over until she got it right.

Keli managed to stay out of Alix's way, and Alix did the same. The other players could smell the competition between them rising. It was the only starting position where there was true competition; for all the other spots, there was a clear drop off in talent from the starters and their backups.

Friday finally came. The football team was on the road playing their archrival Central. Keli and Steen met at their usual time in front of Keli's locker before the start of 5th period and walked to class together. Both were dressed in Dragon gear. Steen still got all the attention as they walked down the hall, and Keli got evil stares from the girls who had their eye on Steen.

The game routine was the same. When they met with the coach in the prep room, Keli's eyes went straight to the starters' list, only to see the same lineup as Tuesday night's game. She took the same seat as she had the last game and immediately looked down at the floor to gather her thoughts.

Coach Lindsay was intense. She even looked a little nervous. All the girls started to look around at each other, wondering when the coach was going to start. Finally the coach stopped staring at her clipboard and let it drop straight down onto the desk, making a loud clattering sound that startled the girls.

"Okay, I have just a couple of things to say about Stayton. They believe they are a good team. Teams that really believe that are dangerous. They are in the room across the way," pointing at the wall to her right. "They are talking about winning tonight. They have dreams and high goals for this season too. They aren't going to be intimidated by us. You are going to win this game because you're better than they are."

"Our communication and teamwork has to be better than last game. We beat a JV caliber team on Tuesday. This team is for real and they know it!" Then she immediately went to the various drawings on the blackboards, making sure everyone understood the game plan.

When she was done, she looked around the room, "Ladies, this is a real game tonight. Do not take it lightly." Then she motioned to Jesse and Libby and said, "Lead them out of here."

The rest of the team jumped to their feet and made their way onto the court. Keli noticed that there weren't nearly as many people in the stands as they ran out onto the floor. It dawned on Keli that the crowd was in Independence, watching the football game.

It didn't take long to find her mom and grandpa. They were sitting in the same spot, and sitting next to them was Frank. She looked at Ashley, who was staring back at her smiling. Ashley clapped her hands a couple of times, both cheering for what she saw in the stands and also to get Keli and herself back into the warm ups.

The Stayton girls were tall and seemed very focused as they went through their own warm ups. Dallas didn't seem to be as sharp as they had been on Tuesday. When the warm ups were over, everyone gathered around Coach Lindsay. She looked into most of the girls' eyes, then tapped her clipboard with her finger, "You aren't ready to play...I can see it in your eyes. Do not fall behind and let them think they have a chance to win."

The game started and just as the coach had predicted, Stayton ran off the first five points. When Dallas finally called a timeout, Stayton led 9-2. The coach set the starters down on the bench and crouched in front of them with the rest of the team huddled behind her. "Okay, who wants to play? I have six other girls right behind me who are ready."

Jesse's eyes grew intense. "This kind of play is not acceptable. No one is moving their feet. We aren't talking, and the worst part of it is that we don't seem like we care."

The coach took back the conversation. "We start playing now. Back row, read the play quicker and make a good pass. Win the first point right now." The coach stuck out her hand for the others to grab. "Ladies, we can only get back into this game one point at a time. Do not make mistakes. Take what they give us, be patient, and remember: one point at a time."

Dallas broke out of the huddle. Keli was right in Alix's path to the court. Keli instinctively stuck her hand in the air, "Kick butt, Alix." Alix tried to look the other way, but she couldn't. That didn't stop her from ignoring Keli as she brushed by her without acknowledging the gesture.

Keli's eyes caught both Lindsay and Jim's eyes right after it happened. The coach slammed her clipboard down on the table next to her seat. Keli immediately went to the end of the sub line to cheer the team. The last thing she wanted was to be labeled as a snitch.

Dallas came out and won the next two points, but the rally died after that. The entire game was a nightmare. Dallas seemed to be a step slow on the block and their passing never allowed for a good set. They were sending over way too many free balls, and Stayton made them pay. Finally they were put out of their misery 25-17.

The teams switched ends. Jesse was clapping her hands and yelling encouragement to each girl as they crossed under the net.

The coach called Keli over. "You're in for Alix this game. I need a lot of energy out of you right from the start. Do you understand? There is no time to be nervous."

Keli nodded as she stared right back at the coach.

"Okay, listen up. Keli is in this game. And Alison, you're in for Greta."

Keli quickly glanced at Greta, who was staring at the floor to hide her disappointment.

Alix went to the bench and sat down. Coach Jim yelled over to her, "Get up and stay in the game." Alix rolled her eyes and stood up in the back of the group.

Dallas had the serve first in game two. Ashley started the game off with a couple of aces. The substitutions seem to change the energy level of the Dragons. Keli had an immediate impact with two blocks in the first six points. They didn't let up and blew out the Lions 25-15 in game two.

Game three was a repeat of game two. Lindsay stayed with the same group on the floor, and Greta and Alix tried to hide their disappointment. The Lady Dragons didn't let up and won the next two games with ease. Ashley went straight for Keli after the final point hugging her, "You played great."

After they congratulated the Lions, they all grouped up with the coaches. Lindsay was not in a celebratory mood. "We got lucky tonight," she grumbled. "We need to prepare better before games. We'll meet 45 minutes early tomorrow before practice in the prep room."

CHAPTER 39

GRETA TAKES OFF

Keli couldn't wait to hear what her mom and grandpa had to say. A handful of people walked by her as she waited for her mom to make it down the bleachers and congratulate her. Just like last game, her mom couldn't wait, and she yelled from a half dozen rows up. Tom stopped and clapped his hands and dipped his head slightly. Frank was bringing up the rear, patiently waiting for Tom to make it down.

When they all met at the bottom of the bleachers, Frank asked, "So how 'bout some pizza and ice cream tonight?"

Cindy smiled and said, "I'm game."

Keli looked at her and thought 'I'm game'...how lame was that?

"Where's Greta?" asked Frank as he looked around the gym.

Ashley cringed and let out a big sigh. "She told me to call her on her cell with where we were going and she would catch up." She looked at her dad. "Don't get mad at me."

There was silence. Everyone could tell Frank was upset with the news. Cindy quickly said, "We can do this another time, Frank, if this isn't a good time."

He shook his head. "Ash, call her and tell her to be at Flying Pie in 20 minutes or else."

"Why don't you call her, Dad? She listens to you better."

Frank thought for a second and then nodded. "You two meet us there. I'll give her a call."

Ashley and Keli headed towards the door. Right in their path was Alix, Anna, and their parents. They could see Alix saying something to the group, and then everyone stared at them as they approached. Keli smiled at all of them as they walked by. As they passed, Alix's mother said under her breath but loud enough for Keli and Ashley to hear, "She'd better not get used to playing. Lindsay will have her back on the bench next game where she belongs."

Keli started to turn around, but Ashley grabbed her by the arm. "Let it go," she leaned closer, "they're all jerks."

When they got into the car, Ashley started to put the keys into the ignition, then stopped. She adjusted herself so she was facing Keli more straight on. "Keli, I want you to know how awesome I think you are. I'm not just talking about your volleyball, which is starting to become amazing...but it's everything else. Your confidence and desire...not too many kids could go through everything you're going through. You are about the only person besides my dad that I can really count on. My dad and I talk about it a lot. I just wanted you to know how much I appreciate you and our friendship."

Keli felt like crying. Instead she giggled nervously, then said, "I'm not sure I would have or could have if it weren't for you, Ashley. So I guess we are in this together."

Then Keli asked, "So what's up with Greta? Between you and me, it looked like she didn't even want to play tonight."

Ashley nodded. "Get this...she told me after school she is thinking about quitting!"

"WHAT? No way! She didn't really tell you that, did she?"

Ashley looked over at Keli. It was easy to see that she was sad and worried. "That isn't all either...for the past week or so, she has been sneaking out after Dad goes to bed and she isn't getting home until like 3 or 4 in the morning."

Keli was shocked. "Have you talked to her about all this?"

Ashley nodded as she pulled into the parking lot. "She tells me to mind my own business."

Keli had her questions all lined up: "Have you talked to your dad about this? What is she doing when she goes out? Is she still hanging out with that Austin kid?"

Ashley sighed. "I told her I was going to talk with Dad about it, and she told me that would be the end of our relationship if I broke the trust. Yeah, she is still hanging out with that spank...he is such a complete loser."

"What do you think we should do about it? I will help you any way I can...I can talk to Frank."

Ashley shook her head. "No, you can't. Greta will know I told you. If it gets any worse..." She paused. "DAMN IT. She is starting to remind me of my Aunt Renee."

Keli gave her a quizzical look. "Who is Aunt Renee?"

"That's Greta's mom. My dad has told me stories about her when they were growing up. Greta is starting to act just like her. My aunt ended up marrying the creep...and you know most of the rest of the story...I don't know what to do. If she quits volleyball, my dad will go completely ballistic. He keeps telling me that Greta is going to escape all the hell that she saw her mom go through. Not only will he go ballistic, it will break his heart."

Just then Austin's silver Eclipse pulled into the parking lot. Keli saw them first. Then Ashley turned and saw both Austin and Greta getting out of his car.

"Shit...he isn't coming in too, is he?"

They caught up to Greta and Austin at the door. "Hey, Sis, what's up?" said Ashley, ignoring Austin.

Greta had her attitude on. "Dad called me and said I needed to get over here. It's Friday night...and I have to hang out with the family. That is completely lame."

Frank was up at the counter ordering and waved them over...Keli sensed that this might be a private conversation and headed towards her mom and grandpa.

Keli greeted them both with a kiss on the cheek. "Hey, how did you like the game tonight? What do you think of Frank? Isn't he great?"

"You played as good as I have ever seen you play. Actually to be honest, I really never thought you could ever be that good," answered her mom, who was talking to her but watching Frank at the same time.

Keli looked over to her grandpa for his comments.

"Well, young lady, you've come a long ways since this summer. Your concentration seems to be a lot better and so is your floor game. The coaches have finally taught you how to play your position."

Once again she was impressed by her grandfather's knowledge of the game. "Gramps, you still owe me that story." Keli looked over to the counter. Frank and the girls had moved away a bit. She could see Frank was getting into Greta's face. Greta wasn't backing down one bit and was throwing words back at Frank as fast as he was to her.

Suddenly, Greta and Austin headed for the door and Frank and Ashley were coming towards them.

He sat down a pitcher of soda. "Sorry about the interruption. I am having a little challenge with Greta right now. She is dating this guy who is feeding her a lot of bad advice." He sat down scratching his head and added, "She has been sneaking out at night."

Ashley's mouth dropped wide open; her eyes darted at Keli, who was also shocked. He knew this whole time.

Cindy put her hand on Frank's arm. "We really understand if..."

"Thanks, Cindy, but we're all hungry and we have two young ladies who played some very good volleyball tonight. Let's focus on them for a while." Frank looked over at Keli. "Well, you had everyone in the stands talking tonight. You know you really messed things up...the coach is now in a pickle. Alix isn't going to take to coming off the bench. Her parents are going to scream pretty loud." Frank scanned the area around them, then said, "Her parents own the *Polk Bulletin*."

Keli choked on her soda. "They own the newspaper?"

Ashley nodded. "Yeah, and they have been known to use it too."

"Great," frowned Keli, "one more chapter in my life's saga!"

Tom put his arm around her. "Hey, you just keep being you and everything will work out."

Frank slapped the table. "Your grandpa is a wise man. That is exactly the right thing to do."

The pizza came and as they ate, Ashley suggested Keli stay over again and ride to work with Frank. That seemed a good idea to everybody.

As the meal ended, Cindy looked over at Frank. "I think we are going to pass on the ice cream tonight. I work the early shift and I should get going."

"Sure, of course. It was nice tonight, thank you." Frank was looking right at Cindy.

The girls both noticed and tried to kick each other under the table, only they missed. Ashley kicked Gramps and Keli kicked Frank. Both yelped. Frank said, "Hey, all I said was it was a nice night." The whole table erupted into laughter.

Back at the Webbs', the girls disappeared upstairs. Almost immediately Ashley's cell phone rang. It was Greta. "How pissed is Dad?"

"Plenty," answered Ashley. "If I were you, I would get my butt home pretty soon."

Greta didn't pause. "Don't wait up for me...we're going to hit a late movie."

Ashley yelled over the phone, "Greta, are you just plain stupid? Where is your head?"

Greta hung up instead of answering.

"I need to tell Dad," said Ashley. "I am not covering for her anymore. She is not being fair."

Both girls went back downstairs. They found Frank in his office.

"Dad, I just got a call from Greta." Ashley paused for a second. "She told me that she wasn't going to be home 'til late, that they were going to a late movie."

Frank picked up the remote and turned off the TV. "Both of you sit down. We need to have a talk."

CHAPTER 40

WHERE ARE WE GOING, GRAMPS?

The next day at the end of Keli's work shift, Cindy walked into the store. Frank saw her from the other end and left a customer trying on shoes to greet her. Keli shook her head. "Dang, Frank, you got it bad," she thought.

Frank greeted Cindy warmly. "Thanks for letting Keli stay over. It meant a lot to Ashley. She needed a friend last night."

Cindy's eyes softened. "Is everything okay with Greta?"

Frank shook his head. "She didn't get home 'til going on 4 this morning."

Keli looked at Frank. Cindy sighed, "If there is anything I can do, please don't hesitate to ask, okay?"

"Thank you...that's very kind. I just might take you up on it one of these days. I don't have a woman's perspective on all this."

"Call any time." Cindy put her hand on his arm. "Let's hope she pulls out of it."

When they were out of Frank's range, Cindy asked Keli, "So really what is going on? Do you think she is into drugs?"

Keli got a little defensive. "I don't know, Mom."

"Okay then, let's talk about you. What's your homework situation?"

"I have a few hours, nothing I can't handle."

"Okay, you need to try and get it done tonight. Tom called and has a little trip planned for you two tomorrow."

The next morning, Keli was awakened up by the sound of her grandpa's Jeep in the driveway. He purposely revved up the engine a couple of times. He knew she was probably still sleeping.

She threw off her covers and struggled to her feet. When she got downstairs, he'd made toast and coffee, which she inhaled. Finally he stood up and said, "Are you ready?"

Keli chuckled. "Ready for what exactly? Mom says we are going on a road trip."

Tom smiled but ignored the question as he poured the rest of the coffee into a couple of travel mugs and said, "Let's go."

She could tell he was in one of those moods and she wasn't going to find out until they got there. Generally this meant something good. She followed him to the Jeep. As they pulled out of the driveway, Keli saw Sticky raking leaves. She could tell he was looking over her way...she waved her arm out the window at him. She was surprised when he waved back.

She wanted to stop the car and run over there, but it was too late. Tom turned up the road and the moment was over. It didn't matter about the rest of the day. Sticky waving at her had already made it a great day.

About 45 minutes later, Keli watched the Corvallis city limits sign pass by them. Keli was so confused she wasn't even going to try and figure out what he was up to. A few minutes later he pulled into the parking lot of Gill Coliseum on the Oregon State campus. Keli looked up at the reader board. "Oregon vs. Oregon State - Volleyball 1:30 pm."

Keli yelled, "Yes! Gramps, you are so awesome!" She had never watched a college volleyball game before. She couldn't wait to get inside. There was a small crowd gathered by the entrance, most dressed in orange and black for the OSU Beavers and the rest in green and gold for the Oregon Ducks. Keli had always been kind of a Duck fan and luckily had worn her Duck hat today. She adjusted it proudly and followed her grandfather.

When they got to the ticket window, he said, "You should have two tickets for Tom Stennes."

The young woman on the other side of the window smiled, went to a little box, and pulled out an envelope with his name on it. Keli stared curiously at what had just happened.

When they made their way inside, Keli was in awe...it was so big. The teams were just starting their warm ups.

Tom elbowed her. "Do you want something to drink?" Keli mustered a nod, but her eyes were fixed on the players. She didn't see him get up and leave. A few minutes later, he showed up with a program and sodas. Keli broke away from the warm ups to look at the program.

"Look," Keli was pointing at a name on the Oregon roster. Tom leaned over to see what she was pointing at. "Look where she went to high school." His eyes followed her finger across the columns to high school...Dallas High.

Keli shook the program. "She played for the Dragons." Her eyes went back to the other statistics and read them out loud. "Her name is Katie Berger. She is a senior this year, 5'11", and she plays outside hitter just like me. Number 10."

Keli quickly looked up and scanned the Duck players. She found the ex-Lady Dragon in line getting ready to hit. Keli watched very closely. Katie, like each of the players before her, hit a nearly flawless ball.

Keli grabbed Tom's arm and hugged it. "Thank you so much for bringing me here."

"I thought you should see what the next level looks like. Their biggest difference is speed. The game is much faster. Just think about how much quicker the game is played at Dallas than at Falls City. When you watch the game today, pay attention to how the players react and their concentration. Listen to how they talk to each other...most of all, watch their eyes. If your game is going to continue to improve, it will come from quickness. I don't mean physical quickness, but mental quickness."

Keli stared at him impressed with his knowledge of the game. As she sat there thinking about what he had just told her, an older woman wearing a green-and-gold Duck sweater approached them smiling. "Hello, Tom, it's good to see you."

Tom stood up and gave the woman a hug. Keli couldn't help but stare. "Judy, let me introduce you to my granddaughter, Keli."

He looked at Keli and said, "Judy was the coach at Oregon for quite a long time."

"Hi Keli." The woman held out her hand. "Your grandfather tells me you're a heck of a player."

Keli looked back at the woman, smiled, and politely said thank you.

"Well Tom, I need to get back to my seat... it's really great to see you again." She looked at Keli. "Keep working on the game and maybe one of these days this might be the next stop for you."

Keli just smiled and nodded at her.

When she got far enough away, Keli grabbed his shoulder. "Okay, Gramps, what was that all about? Who is the woman and how does she know you? Does this have anything to do with you knowing so much about volleyball?"

The game was about to begin. Tom smiled, "I'll tell you the story when the match is over."

It didn't take long for the game to take over Keli's thoughts...she was amazed at how good they all were. At the end of the first game, she asked, "Gramps, they are so awesome! Do you think I can get that good?"

He rolled his program and gently popped her on the head with it. "Most of these girls don't hit the ball much better than you or jump any better...they just know how to play quicker than you! I told you to watch that part of the game. Start thinking ahead of the play. Don't wait until the ball starts coming at you before you start playing. Any good player can make a good pass or a kill if they are in the right spot. It's getting there...plays are made because they play ahead of the ball."

Keli's eyes went back to the court. She didn't quite understand what he was saying, but she was starting to.

The match lasted the full five games with the Ducks pulling out the match with a two-point win in the deciding game. When it was over, Keli noticed Katie was staring up at her. Keli smiled and waved at her. Katie smiled back and waved her down. She froze, "Gramps, the girl from Dallas is waving at me to come down there."

Gramps lightly pushed her and said, "Well, I guess you better go see what she wants."

Keli made her way to the edge of the court. Katie stuck out her hand. "You play for the Dragons, don't you?"

Keli was surprised. "Yes, how did you know?"

"Well, your sweatshirt caught my eye at first and then I recognized you from the game last Friday."

"You were there?"

Katie nodded. "Yes, I went home after classes on Friday for my little brother's birthday party on Saturday and caught most of the match. You played pretty good...you're a junior, right? You guys have a really good team again this year. I am guessing 'nothing-is-good-enough' Lindsay has got you all working your butts off."

Keli laughed. She knew exactly what Katie meant by "nothing is good enough."

Keli turned the conversation to Katie. "You played great today. For a while there, I didn't think you guys were going to win."

Katie grinned. "I didn't either. Well, I need to get in there and get changed or I will miss the bus." Keli stuck out her hand and Katie shook it. "Here, let me give you my email address" as she reached over to the scorers table and grabbed a pen. "If you ever have any questions about this silly game or want to come down to Eugene to catch a game, let me know."

Keli handed her program to Katie and watched as she scribbled on it. She smiled as she handed it back to Keli and said, "Good luck with the rest of the season. It sounds like you made a good choice changing schools."

Tom was making it down the bleachers and over to Keli. "What do you say we head to one more place before we go home?"

As soon as they got into the car, Keli was all over him. "So, Gramps, I want the whole story right now. How did you know that lady and why do you know so much about volleyball?"

"Well, before I moved to Falls City with your grandma, I used to work for Judy. It started when I was a senior in college. I got a job through the school to be the manager-trainer for the volleyball team. Back then, you didn't need any kind of training or degree. In the beginning, I mostly washed uniforms and towels. As time went on, I started taping ankles and I would tell the players things that I saw while they played. Over time, they started to come to me when they messed up, wanting my advice on how to change things...by the end of the season, Coach Wilson asked me to work at her camp over the summer."

"Then for the next five years, I stayed there and worked for her as an assistant. Actually that is where I met your grandma. She was a junior when I was a senior. I started to notice that she came around a lot more often than most of the others looking for advice. By the start of the next year, it started to be a frequent thing and we would talk volleyball for hours. During her senior year, we both kind of knew that our friendship was growing past just volleyball. The summer after she graduated, we didn't have the coach and player worries. I was 23 and she was 22. We spent the whole summer falling in love. We both got jobs teaching in Eugene, and I coached for another four years as an assistant. When your grandma got pregnant with your dad, we decided we would like to find a small town and raise a family. We applied for a lot of jobs in small towns all over."

"One day I got a call to teach in Falls City. Your grandma had complications delivering Butch and never was quite the same. She had various health problems. So I needed to be home as much as possible to help her with the house and Butch. So I never really got a chance to get back into coaching."

Keli looked very sad. "Why didn't you ever tell me about all this? Does Mom know?"

Gramps shook his head, "No one really knows. Your grandma always felt extremely guilty about it, and I didn't want to make it worse so I never really talked about it. It was a very long time ago. But after you started to take the game seriously, those years really came back to me. Last week, I called the school and they got me in touch with Judy and she set us up with the tickets. I didn't know she would be here. She was an excellent coach and a great mentor. Your grandma was a pretty good player too. You and your dad got your athletic ability from her."

Keli shook her head, "Grandma was a college volleyball player and you were a coach. This is weird, Gramps, very, very weird."

CHAPTER 41

THE CAR!

Keli really wasn't paying attention to where her grandfather was driving until the Jeep came to a stop. She looked up to see that they were in the middle of a used car dealership. "What are we doing here?" she asked.

"Well, I think it's time for you to have something of your own to drive. Your mom and you can't keep sharing one car. I have talked with your mom and here is my proposition. I will buy the car, and you will pay me back a little every month out of your paycheck. You will need to pay for your own insurance and gas." He took off his glasses. "What do you think? Do we have a deal?"

Keli's eyes filled with tears, and all she could do was nod.

A couple of hours later, the salesperson handed Keli the keys to a red 1997 Jetta.

Tom walked her over to her new car. "Okay, you follow me home. I don't want you speeding the first day and getting a ticket."

"I don't think I would know how to get home anyways," giggled Keli.

When they finally got back to Falls City, Keli drove very slowly through town hoping to see anyone to show off her new car to, but no luck. Her grandpa made the turn to go to Keli's house. When they arrived, Cindy met them outside.

Cindy gave Tom a huge hug. "Thank you...you're a blessing."

On the way into the house, Keli stopped and gave Gramps the biggest hug.

Keli spent nearly as much time staring out the window at the shiny red car in the driveway as she spent finishing her homework. Ashley and Greta popped into her head when she closed her biology book.

She dialed the number while staring at her car. Frank answered, "Well, hello Miss Keli...I hear you had quite the day today."

"How do you know about my day?"

There was a pause. "Well, let's just say a birdie told me that you were down in Corvallis today."

Keli laughed. As she waited for Ashley, she could see Sticky standing by his window looking towards the house. She knew he was looking at the car.

Ashley interrupted her thoughts about Sticky and her car. "So Dad says you got a new car today. What did you get?"

Keli almost choked on air. "Jeez, is he in the CIA or something? It's a really cool red Jetta. How can he...?"

Ashley broke in. "Don't you know Big Frank knows all...at least that's what he claims. Let me guess. A little birdie told him."

"So how did your father hear?"

Ashley's voice got all giddy. "He talked to your mom today. Can you believe it! He drove out there to the restaurant and ate lunch. He said it was no big deal; he just felt like a drive." Ashley was laughing so hard. "He was acting just like a teen-ager trying to lie his way out of it."

"I've got to go and talk to my mom!" Ashley was laughing when Keli hung up the phone and yelled, "Oh Mother, we need to talk!"

Cindy was in her chair reading.

"So I hear you had a special guest at the restaurant today."

Cindy marked her page and tried to hide a smile. "Do you mean Frank Webb?"

Keli put her index finger on her cheek and nodded.

Cindy thumped her book against her knee. "It wasn't a big deal. It wasn't like a date or anything. He said he was just out for a drive and decided to stop in for lunch."

Keli busted up laughing. "Well, I think Frank is a good guy, and if you two want to date, I am all for it."

CHAPTER 42

GRETA IS SICK

Keli piled her bags and lunch into the car. She was so excited to drive her new car to school. She made two extra trips back to the house hoping Sticky was looking out the window and saw her. Finally she gave up on the idea that she was going to run into him.

She headed down the hill in a Dragon T-shirt and her special baseball cap on backwards. She loved to wear a baseball hat backwards to school. Some of the kids picked up on it and started doing the same to mock her. Within a couple of weeks, the fad really started to catch on.

She made a point of stopping at Rodewald's Market when she saw Charlee's car in front. As she got out of the car, Charlee and the rest of the group were all coming out of the store.

"Hey ladies..." Keli was smiling at them.

Charlee looked at the car and back to Keli. "Did you and your mom get a new car?"

It was just what Keli was hoping for. "No, this is my car. Mom still has the Honda. Gramps is helping me. I am paying him each month from the money I make working at Webb Sporting Goods."

"Tracie, we'd better get going or we will be late for class," Charlee really didn't want any more to do with the conversation.

Tracie ignored her. "I saw your name in the paper on Saturday...congrats on making it up to the Varsity team."

Keli gave her a big grin and quickly glanced at Charlee. "You know it would be cool if you could come watch a game some time." Tracie looked at Charlee knowing what her answer should be, but she threw Charlee a curve. "I will try and make it over."

"That would be awesome." Keli glanced at both of them, "I checked my schedule and I think in two weeks, I am going to be able to come watch you guys play."

Charlee interrupted, "Tracie, I am leaving..." She had to get in one more dig as they walked away, "Hey, Keli, don't bother showing up to our game. You're not welcome there."

Keli laughed. She was done being talked to like that. "You know, Charlee, the last time I checked, you aren't the person who decides things like that. You just play the game and I will watch it if I want to. I look forward to seeing how your game is coming along."

Keli didn't wait for a response and headed into Rodewald's. As she walked through the door, she realized she'd started all this. She really didn't have a reason to stop. Keli looked around and bought a pack of gum. She was a little relieved that Janet wasn't there.

On her way out of town, Keli glanced at the school feeling a little guilty for stopping and flaunting her new car. Her cell phone rang to break up her guilty thoughts; she could see it was Ashley. "Hey Ash, what's up?"

There was nothing on the other end. "Ashley, are you there?"

"Sorry..." She could tell Ashley was crying. "It's Greta."

"I will be there in 10 minutes." Keli hung up the phone and hurried to school. She pulled into the parking lot scanning for Ashley. Finally she found her standing in a vacant spot that she was saving for her.

Ashley smiled and did the thumbs up in approval of Keli's new car. Ashley jumped into the passenger side..."I really like your car."

Keli threw her a quick grin. "So, what's up with Greta?" She could tell Ashley had been crying for a while. Her eyes were hollow and her mascara had run.

It took a couple of seconds for the words to come out. "She didn't come home at all on Saturday. Dad found her at a friend of Austin's on Sunday. She had been drinking..."

"How 'bout drugs? Was she using drugs too?"

Ashley shrugged. "I don't know...she said she hadn't, but I don't know if I believe her."

"What did your dad do?"

Ashley started crying again. "He told her that if she wanted to live with us, she couldn't see Austin anymore. An hour later, she left and we haven't seen her since. My dad is completely devastated. I know he thinks that she is doing exactly what his sister did back when they were kids."

Keli looked around the parking lot for Austin's car. "Have you seen her at school today?"

Ashley shook her head. "Come on. Let's get inside and see if anyone knows what is going on."

The morning came and went without any news...Keli raced to the team table. Ashley wasn't there either. Keli went over to Jesse and Libby and whispered in their ears. "I need to talk to you right now."

The three moved away from the others. Her eyes darted around the immediate area. "Do you have any idea where Ashley or Greta are right now?"

Both Libby and Jesse shook their heads. Libby answered for both of them. "No, what's going on?"

"Well, I can't tell you much, but Greta is really messing up. The past couple of days she has hardly been at home and today she didn't show up for school. We were looking for her this morning and planned on meeting up at lunch... now Ashley is nowhere. I'm afraid she is out looking for her when she should be at school."

Libby tapped Jesse on the hand. "I told you Greta was starting to stray." She looked at Keli. "We've been hearing rumors for a while now."

Keli put a hand on each of her teammates. "Promise me you won't say anything to anyone until we have had a chance to talk with Ashley."

Jesse and Libby looked at each other and then nodded.

As Keli walked towards her next class, her phone beeped. She reached into her backpack as fast as she could. The caller ID told her it was Ashley. "Where are you? Is everything okay?"

At first, Ashley was pretty matter-of-fact as she talked to Keli. "I just wanted to tell you that Greta is with me and Dad. We are taking her to a treatment center. She broke down and told us what has been going on. I can't tell you any more right now, but I will call you tonight. Please don't tell anyone."

Keli didn't quite know what to say. Then she asked, "What about practice to-day? The coach and everyone is going to ask where you guys are."

"Dad called the coach a little while ago and as far as the team goes, they're just going to have to wonder for now."

"Okay, Ashley, I understand. Please tell Greta that I think what she is doing is awesome. If either one of you needs anything, call me. I don't care what time it is!"

"Dad wants to know if you can work the store tonight and tomorrow. He said if you have too much homework, he will find someone else."

"Tell him I'll be there!"

Keli could tell Ashley was crying now. She could hear Greta in the background crying too. Ashley hung up the phone. Keli looked up and down the empty hall. It was almost unbelievable, she thought. How could this happen to Greta who seemed so normal?

When Keli walked into class, everyone stared at her. She wasn't able to hide her feelings. Mr. Lippon stopped her by his desk. "Is everything okay, Ms Stennes?"

"A family emergency. I'm sorry for being late."

CHAPTER 43

GRETA IS OUT

After school Keli avoided the coach's room before practice for the first time in weeks. Jesse and Libby came straight over and whispered, "Where are they?"

Keli stammered, "I'm not sure exactly."

Fortunately, Coach Lindsay blew her whistle and pointed towards the prep room.

In the front of the room was a TV and on the blackboard were notes on Friday's game.

None of the comments were positive. When all the players were seated, Lindsay walked to the front of the room. "Girls, before we get going, I need to tell you we will be missing Ashley and Greta today and perhaps for tomorrow's game."

Various small conversations picked up between the players. Lindsay raised her hand to quiet them. "Listen up, ladies, we need to focus on the video and then practice today. The game tomorrow is our first away game, and it's not an easy place to play."

Lindsay spent the next 30 minutes doing a play-by-play of the video. It was the first time Keli had seen herself play. The coach caught every detail and didn't miss an opportunity to explain what went wrong.

Her voice boomed through the room. "Desire is attitude, plain and simple. There were times in the game when attitudes got on the floor that were ego and self-centered. Those attitudes will destroy a team. We need to start to come together as a true team. Egos and self-centeredness are not wanted here."

"One last thing. As for Greta and Ashley, I want you all to stay focused on what we need to do. If they aren't able to play tomorrow, that means we are going to need others to step up. Practice hard today." She turned away and started to erase the blackboard.

The girls filed out onto the court. The last thing Keli wanted right now was to be cornered on the Ashley/Greta deal. But sure enough, Jesse and Libby were right there, wanting to know what was going on. Keli begged off, saying she'd promised Ashley. They could tell she was in a hard spot.

Jesse looked at Libby and then back at Keli. "Let us know as soon as you can, okay?"

Keli answered, "I will. I promise and thanks for not pushing it right now."

Practice was terrible. As much as the players tried to get into it, they just weren't able to get going. Teresa filled in at setter and Alison took over for Greta in the middle. Keli hoped to hear her name called for the first unit, but Lindsay stayed with Alix.

When practice was over, the whole team looked like they'd had the wind kicked out of them. It wasn't the same team without Ashley and Greta, and everyone knew it.

Keli saw Lindsay was standing over by her office door looking in her direction, but she pretended not to see her. Tonight she wanted to go home. The last thing she wanted to do was show the coach her frustrations.

On the way to the car, Alix was talking to Taylor and Morgan by the entrance. There was no way for Keli to avoid them. She tried to quickly pass by, but Alix was ready. Just as Keli passed, she said, "Maybe you should try out for setter or middle. I hear we are going to need one of each."

Keli turned around and walked nearly nose to nose with Alix. "You know, one of these days, you're going to get yours. I'm not sure if I have ever known anyone as evil as you."

Keli turned and started to walk away; then she paused and pointed her finger at Alix. "One day, you're mine! Make no mistake of that." She smiled at the other two and then added, "You know, hanging out with the devil is never a good idea."

Even sitting in her new car didn't relieve the anger and frustration that she felt. She tried calling Ashley but it went straight to voice mail. Work popped into her head. She had forgotten that she was supposed to take Greta's shift. When she got to the store, it was busier than she thought. After an hour she finally got a chance to call her mom and fill her in on everything.

Cindy was waiting for her when she finally walked in the house. Keli looked beat. "You've had quite the day, sweetie."

Keli plopped down on the couch and kicked her bags away from her feet. "Mom, how does a person who is smart and seems to have things figured out just do an about face and go in a completely different direction with their life? A month ago Greta was a completely different person."

Cindy shook her head. "I'm not sure."

"Do they know how long she'll be gone?"

"Frank thought she could be there for a month."

Keli stood up almost yelling, "A month?" Keli blew up. It was the last piece of news she could handle. "Mom, I need to take a shower and get my homework done. Are you coming to my game tomorrow?"

Cindy looked sad. "Sorry, sweetie, I have to work. Where is the game?"

Keli was halfway up the stairs. "Okay, I understand. Don't worry about it."

CHAPTER 44

SIT WITH ME

Keli slept as long as possible before getting up. It was pouring outside, and the beautiful Indian summer was over.

Her mom was ready for her in the kitchen. "Here's your lunch. I packed your gear, and there's a second lunch in your volleyball bag for the trip. Good luck today. I wish I could come up there and watch, but Falls City plays at home today and you know what it's like on home-game days at the restaurant."

As she drove past the high school, she read the reader board "Go Mountaineers! Thump the Wolverines!" They were playing their rivals from Alsea. It was one of the biggest games of the year. She knew the kids would all be in a festive mood...there would be a continuous buzz throughout the day. For the first time she felt jealous. She knew she wouldn't be in the center of it all.

As her new Jetta made its way out of town, she realized that she was heading for a tough day. There was a bus ride with Alix and a team without two of its best players, and she was going to be sitting on the bench. The season was still young, but now that she had had a taste of the competition, she wasn't satisfied with just being on the Varsity team.

Just as she pulled into the parking lot at school, her phone rang. It was Ashley. "Hey, I'm on my way to school right now. I want to play. It's up to Lindsay if I play, but I am coming for sure."

Keli's spirits immediately picked up. "That's awesome! Can you tell me what is going on with Greta?"

Ashley answered, "Wait for me in the parking lot. I will be there in two minutes."

The two friends met up and headed slowly towards the school. Ashley was sad. "Greta is in Portland at a teen recovery place. I still can't believe it...when she came home on Sunday, she was acting really weird. Dad sat her down right away; he knew something was wrong. It took about three hours of prying, and then all at once she just broke down and told us everything. For the past six months or so, she has been fooling around and drinking a little at parties and then when she started hanging out with Austin and his friends, it just got worse."

"Get this. For the past few weeks, she has been getting high almost every day. That is why she hasn't played very good lately. It all makes some sense. She even told us how much she was acting like her mom. She couldn't stop crying. Dad told her she had to go to treatment, and she kept saying she could stop on her own, but after another hour of him telling her stories about her mom and dad, she finally gave in. I just sat there in shock...I knew there were a couple of times she had a few sips off a beer, but I never saw it. She never asked me to go with her. She hid it all the way."

Keli put her arm around her. "I'm so sorry. Whatever I can do, you just let me know. How do you want me to handle it when kids ask about her?"

Ashley shrugged her shoulders and her eyes welled up. "I don't know. For the past day now, I've thought about it. Dad says to be up front about it. I don't know if I can. I don't want our family to be labeled like that."

Keli squeezed her shoulder a little closer. "My grandpa always tells me to just be me. Sometimes it's the only thing I can rely on..." she paused for a second..."I think your dad is right. We need to be straight up. No use in hiding or lying about something and having it come back at you later. We need to be ourselves. Greta is in this and her family needs to be there with their heads up."

The morning went quickly. Keli escaped running into anyone who would have asked about Greta. As the lunch period drew closer, she got anxious to see Ashley and find out how her morning had gone. When the lunch bell rang, Keli raced to Ashley's locker hoping to catch her there, but she didn't show up. Finally she headed for the team table for lunch. Ashley was there and most of the team was grouped around her. She could see Ashley was talking, and by the look on her face, she knew it had to be about Greta.

Jesse was just taking over the conversation. "So, ladies, it looks like we have a wounded teammate, and we need to pick her up with a win today." She put her lunch sack in the middle of the table, then dropped in an apple. She stepped back, and one by one each girl put something in the bag. When it came to Keli's turn, her faced turned a little red. "So what is this?"

Libby answered. "It's a sacrifice bag. When something bad happens to the team or a teammate, we make a sacrifice bag. We carry the bag with us wherever the team goes until the bad goes away."

Keli dropped her baggie of chocolate chip cookies in the sack. Jesse grabbed the bag and folded the top. Then she scribbled something on it, and each girl did the same, writing something special on the bag. When it was Keli's turn, she thought for a moment and then wrote "God, please return Greta to us."

The bus ride was a new experience for Keli. During her years at Falls City, one bus carried both the football and volleyball teams. The bus would be crowded and the boys generally dominated the ride. There was a rally bus with kids and parents who didn't want to drive themselves that followed. Behind the two buses, depending on the quality of the opponent, would be as many as two dozen cars of families.

Keli looked around the Dragon Wagon, which was filled with three dozen girls from the Varsity, JV, and C-team, but there was no rally bus, nor a parade of cars. The girls segregated themselves by team, with the Varsity in the back followed by the JV and the freshmen up front.

Ashley was quiet most of the ride. Keli finally asked, "What's on your mind?"

She looked around to see who might be focused on their conversation. "Greta mainly...I know she is sitting in that place knowing we are on this bus." She looked around again. "Do you think Lindsay will let me play today?"

"If she wants to win, she will," answered Keli. "Yesterday was a horrible practice without you and Greta. With Greta out completely and if you don't play, well, I don't want to think about it. You'll play. Lindsay wants to win and she isn't stupid."

Ashley nervously laughed. She needed to hear some positive reinforcement.

Finally an hour later the bus pulled into the Tiger parking lot. The noise in the bus picked up as the girls became anxious about the game.

CHAPTER 45

THE SPEECH

The night didn't start off well. Both the freshmen and JV teams got crushed. When the Varsity met for their pre-game meeting, the coach was tense. "Anyone see what I saw out there?" She didn't wait for an answer. "I see a bunch of girls who got off a bus and weren't ready to play and now they are getting their rears kicked."

The coach turned away for a second, then back towards them. "Losing is tough enough, but to lose because you weren't ready to play is disgusting. You want to go out there and put it all on the table, and if it's not good enough, then okay, we get humble and accept defeat." She slapped her hands together. "I will not accept you ladies not being ready to play. Do you understand me? I will not accept it."

She pointed at the clock. "You have 30 minutes to make sure you're ready. This is a good team we are playing today...there is no room for error. They are not going to hand this to you. They are looking for respect today and we are primed to be upset. Champions find a way to win matches like this...that is my question to you." The coach stood there with her hands on her hips. "Are we champions?"

Keli had never heard a speech like that before. Her instincts overtook her and she stood up, accepting the coach's challenge. "Yes, we are champions. I came here to play on a team like this." She didn't even know what she was saying. The coach had inspired her and at this moment she was running completely on her competitive heart. "We need to be ready for all our roles whatever they are today. I for one do not want to lose today...not with Greta..."

She paused, realizing this wasn't about Greta. "It not about her, it's about the team. It's about a team that is still trying to come together. Where I come from, it isn't about coming together because that is a given. Today it's time we come together. I gave up a championship to come and play with quality players like you. Today I want both...we can be champions if we are willing to work together, no matter what."

All of a sudden Keli realized that she was the center of attention. She looked around the room at each of her teammates, feeling like she had just came out from under a hypnotic spell, not knowing exactly what had happened.

The coach looked at her and then back at the rest of the players waiting for their response. The room stopped for a split second and then erupted into a cheer of, "Dragons, Dragons, Dragons!"

It worked. The team headed for the floor, and Lindsay knew they were ready to play. She followed them towards the court and stopped by the edge of the bleachers and watched Keli run onto the court.

Lindsay had never been more proud of a player than at that moment. It was a gift that a coach only gets once in a great while. Today she earned something much more important than a paycheck or a trophy. Today she knew she could change a young person's life, by setting the stage and allowing the student to teach.

Newberg was also ready to play. They were nearly all seniors, and their experience made up for their lack of size and speed. Their goal was the same as the Dragons...they were after a championship. It hadn't happened at their school in almost three decades.

Lindsay didn't start Ashley. Her excuse for not being at practice the day before was understandable, but she wasn't going to bend her rules either.

Ashley did a good job hiding her shock and disappointment. She stood next to Keli on the sidelines when the starters took the floor.

The first game seesawed back and forth...neither team was giving in. Both benches were up standing the whole game, yelling at each hit of the ball. The crowd was smaller than the ones in the Dragon Den, but they seemed louder. The winning point came on a service error by Ashley's replacement Teresa. It took the breath and heart out of the whole team.

It was the first time all season that they lost the first game of a match. Panic filled the huddle between games. The whole team was waiting for Lindsay to call Ashley's number, but as in game one she left her sitting on the bench.

Game two was a nightmare. The Dragons not only didn't start fast but were down 9-0 before they knew what had hit them. Lindsay's timeout didn't do any good, and by the time she called her second timeout, the Tigers had built up a 16-5 lead.

The timeout didn't change any thing. Newberg was too much for the weakened Dragons, with Ashley and Greta out of the lineup. The game ended without much fight from the Dragons, 25-12.

Game three wasn't much better at the start. The Dragons were able to keep it a little closer but were still behind 14-11. Lindsay could see she needed to do something drastic or the match was going to be over.

She stood up and called timeout. The coach was looking for anything to spark the team. Greta's absence was proving to be more of a loss than she expected. Newberg had scouted the Dragons and made adjustments in the second game. They were really taking advantage when Allison was up front. There was nothing left to do but gamble. Lindsay called Jesse over for a quick one-on-one meeting. "I need you to play middle...that will bring their focus to you."

Lindsay looked over at Keli. "You take Jesse's spot outside." The team seemed a little confused by the move. Keli's heart skipped a beat. Again she was changing positions after starting to feel comfortable on the right side.

Ashley put her arm around her and whispered so only Keli could hear, "This is a good lineup. If I were playing, we'd kill people with this."

The lineup worked, and the Dragons fought back, winning game three, 25-21. Lindsay and the Dragons had found a lineup that worked. Putting Jesse in the middle seemed to really confuse them.

It was now clear to everyone that Ashley wasn't going to play today. Lindsay again left her on the bench and went back with Keli at the four and Jesse in the middle.

Game four went back and forth. Lindsay didn't like the score, but she knew she had found a lineup that might work down the road against the bigger, better teams they would face in the playoffs. It was easy to see that this was maybe their best blocking lineup. Greta was tall but not nearly as aggressive as Jesse.

The game was tight, very tight, 22 all, when the Tiger coach called timeout.

Lindsay waved them over. She had the serve and looked at Ashley, and for a second everyone thought she might let her serve in this critical situation. But no, she stayed with Teresa. It was a costly error. Teresa's serve buried right into the net.

Newberg had the lead and the serve. Lindsay wanted a timeout but she didn't have any left. Newberg's best player grabbed the ball and headed for the service line. A minute later after two straight aces, the game and match were over. The Dragons had lost.

CHAPTER 46

THE VOICE IN THE DARK

The bus was dark, and Keli was slouched down in the seat. After a few minutes thinking about what had just happened, the reality of everything began to hit her. She looked over at Ashley, who had her eyes closed either asleep or trying to be. All of the thoughts came rushing in. She looked around the quiet bus. Where was she? she wondered. The world she was in was so different from the one she had left.

The old world had been easy, secure, safe, and most of all predicable. She looked up at the shadows of car lights racing by on the roof of the bus. Her mind went back home; it was the first time in her life that she missed the rivalry with Alsea. She could smell the wet grass and see the whole town lining the lighted football field hoping that this year they would have bragging rights to the rivalry.

She looked back at Ashley, hoping to see her eyes open. Keli desperately needed some companionship, but her eyes were closed. A cold chill ran down her back. Her mind yelled, "You made a mistake. This is a mistake."

Everything but Ashley seemed like a nightmare. Her relationship with Alix, Greta's problems, and most of all no longer being a star. She started to convince herself that the best thing to do was go back home. Sticky and Charlee would take her back, and she could pick back up and play basketball in a couple of months. She could stay friends with Ashley. A twinge of euphoria had come over her. That is what I....

A voice inside her head blunted out the rest of the thought. The voice seemed deep and powerful. *Grow from this, don't run... please don't run.* It wasn't her voice, though it was vaguely familiar. Her eyes were shut, but she squinted anyway trying to hear more. The voice was gone as quickly as it came. She opened her eyes, wondering if it had all been a dream. She scanned the bus. Only a few heads were visible; it seemed almost deserted.

She stared out the window for the rest of the ride, wondering how she knew the voice. The words continued to ring in her head...*Grow from this, don't run... please don't run.*

She was exhausted when she got into her car at the parking lot, and she drove slowly into Falls City. It was nearly midnight, and the town was asleep. As she drove into the driveway, she could see the light was on in the living room. She grabbed her bags and raced for the house. Her mom was asleep on the couch when she opened the front door.

"I was hoping you would call. How did it go, sweetie?"

Keli went straight for the couch and sat down her feet. "Sorry, Mom. I would have but things were tough and I just forgot. How did Falls City do tonight?"

Cindy frowned, "We got beat. Alsea won the tie-breaker." Cindy sat up a little straighter and crossed her legs. "We played pretty good from what I hear. I only got to see the last few minutes of the last game. They could have won if..." Cindy paused and changed the subject. "So how did you do tonight?"

"They could have what, Mom?" Keli wasn't going to leave that half-sentence alone.

Cindy smiled sadly. "What I was going to say was they could have used you tonight. Now tell me how things went. Did you win? Did you get to play?"

"We lost too. Lindsay didn't play Ashley the whole match. We would have won if she played. The coach put Jesse into her spot and I got to play outside for Jesse."

"Wow... that's awesome! That is where you want to play. How did you do?"

Keli leaned against the back of the couch. "I played okay but it was tough losing. I still don't feel like I belong out there. It's weird..." Her mind went to the bus ride home.

Cindy started to ask but she knew it was late. "I think it's time for bed. Tomorrow after practice I want the whole story."

Keli grabbed her bag and headed up the stairs. On her way up, she looked at Cindy, who was watching her. "It's my fault they lost tonight."

Cindy looked confused for a second, then realized Keli was talking about Falls City. She stood up quickly, "Oh no, don't think that way. It's their game to win or to lose. Just as it is for your team. No more talk like that...I'm not kidding. You're just tired. Get some sleep. And just so you know, my favorite team now is the Dragons!"

Keli looked down at her and couldn't help but smile. "Thanks, Mom, I needed to hear that."

CHAPTER 47

THE PAPER

The next morning the sun was bright and so was Keli. She woke thinking about her play from the night before. In less than 12 hours, she had gone from a self-doubting depression and guilt to feeling as strong as she had since she first made her decision to change schools.

She jumped out of bed and raced down to the kitchen. Cindy was sipping her coffee and reading the paper. Keli could tell it was the sports page. "Does it say anything about our game?"

Cindy looked around the paper. "It sounds like Alix played pretty good even though you lost."

Keli smirked. "Well if you owned that paper, I would have a great game every time too. Mom, I really can't stand her, but I know I need to figure out how to make it work between us." She rethought her answer. "Actually, she did play pretty good. We all played good. If we had had Ashley, we would have crushed them."

Cindy handed her the paper. The headline read "Lady Dragons Retool But Lose to the Tigers." Under the headlines as big as life was a picture of her stuffing the ball back down on the Tiger captain. She stared at it in amazement. Her arms were high above the net, her eyes zeroed right on the ball. She looked over the top of the paper.

Cindy was looking back, eyes full of tears. "You did have a good game, didn't you? I think you owe some paper family an apology."

Keli lowered her eyes back to the article. It was even better than the picture. When she put the paper down, her heart was pounding with excitement. For the first time since she made her decision, she felt important.

Cindy was beaming. "Why don't you go put that upstairs?" She nodded at the paper. The phone rang. Her mom laughed. "I think it might be for you, but you'd better hurry or you'll be late for school."

Sure enough, it was Ashley. "Well, the small town kid has made it big time."

Keli couldn't do anything but grin. Ashley didn't wait for Keli to respond. "Hurry up and get in here!"

As soon as she hung up the phone, it rang again. Keli looked at her mom. "Please answer it. I need to get in the shower or I really will be late." She headed for the shower, but a few seconds later she heard a knock on the door.

Cindy shouted through the door. "It's for you. It's Sticky."

The bathroom door immediately opened up. Keli stood there mouthing, "What should I say?"

Cindy had the phone covered. "Just talk to him. Don't forget he is your best friend."

Keli took the phone and slowly closed the bathroom door. "Hello?"

"Hi, I just wanted to call and say congratulations on your game last night. The picture is amazing. It sounds like you really played great even though you lost too."

Just hearing his voice brought tears flowing down her cheeks. She knew he was going to know she was crying."

"Keli, are you there?"

"Yeah, sorry...I guess you caught me a little off-guard."

Sticky could tell she was emotional. "Hey, sorry if I caught you at a bad time. I just wanted you to know it was awesome seeing your picture in the paper this morning."

Keli quickly wiped her nose on her towel. "Thanks, Sticky, you made my day!" Her mind raced for what to say next and then the words just came out. "Do you think one of these days we can go for a hike or something. I miss you."

She could feel her face turn red hot with embarrassment. A part of her didn't want to hear the possible rejection.

"Sure, that would be cool," answered Sticky.

The tears started to well up again. "Well, I need to get in the shower or I'm going to be late for school. Thanks for calling." She didn't want to say goodbye but it came out anyway.

She heard the same from the other end. "Bye, Keli."

CHAPTER 48

ALIX

The day was filled with acknowledgements from students she didn't know. When 4th period came, she walked into class and made eye contact with Alix. Neither made any more of it than that. One of Alix's football friends shot a comment across the room. "So when did they start putting pictures of JV players on the front page of the sports section?"

Keli didn't even look in his direction, and no one in the class responded to his lame try to hurt her feelings. For the first time, maybe the tides had turned, maybe she was winning respect from the others. She desperately wanted to look at Alix to see what her response was, but she forced herself not to.

The bell rang. Steen was waiting for her right outside the classroom. "Well, looks like you've arrived."

Keli shyly grinned. She wasn't sure how to handle this bit of fame. "Thank you, I got a little lucky last night."

"Right, that's it. You got lucky and jumped two feet above the net. So what are you doing this weekend? How 'bout we try to hook up and study or catch a movie?"

Her mind went to her conversation with Sticky earlier. "Uh, I'm not sure. Let's talk tomorrow."

Steen didn't seem to sense that he was getting the brush-off, and Keli wasn't sure if that was what she was doing. She was growing closer to Steen as each week passed. He and Sticky were a lot alike.

They parted ways at the same place every day. Steen knew he would catch the wrath of the other volleyball players if he got too close to their table. Keli started to laugh as she approached the table. All of the players had a newspaper in front of them. They were all staring at her picture; it was their way of congratulating her. She scanned the table to see if Alix was doing the same thing, but she wasn't there today.

When school was done, Keli made her way to the coach's office. It seemed like it had been a long time since she had been in for one of their sessions. When she walked in, Coach Lindsay and Coach Jim were both there. "So, Jim, have you seen today's paper?" asked Lindsay.

Keli could tell they were playing a skit on her behalf. "No, Coach, I haven't. Let me take a look at it."

Jim opened it up and, trying to win an Oscar, said, "Hey! Isn't that you, Keli?"

Keli grinned. "Yeah, I think it might be." She played into their little game. "So what words of wisdom can you two share with me today?"

Lindsay looked at her, more serious now. "Learning the rotations from every position and passing. Rotation should become second nature. You need to study it every chance you get. It's extremely important. Nothing panics a team more than worrying if everyone is in their right spot. Just as important is looking across the net and being able to see the back row players from front row hitters, and whether the setter is front row or back. It's not just Ashley or Jesse's job to call that out for you."

"When you are playing left outside and you back up for serve receive, you need to make a higher pass to the setter and keep the ball in front of her. That gives you both more time to set back up for a good attack at the net. Your passes are coming too flat or too far off the net. The farther you pass off the net, the more limited you make your setter and it allows the defense to cheat. Work at really getting the ball in the air and split the 10-foot line and the net."

Keli wasn't prepared for this barrage of commentary. She felt a little deflated.

Jim grabbed a piece of chalk and diagrammed the area between the middle and Ashley. "That is where you want the ball. You need to pass the ball with a spot in mind, not just pass and wonder where it's going to go." He tapped the chalk on the board. "Have a clear vision in your head of exactly where you want the ball to go."

Lindsay looked at Jim. "Can you give me a minute with Keli?"

He nodded. On his way out he gave Keli a high five. "Good job yesterday!"

When the door shut, Lindsay didn't waste any time. "So let's talk about chemistry. How do you feel things are on this team?" She put her elbows on the desk and her chin in her hands and looked right at Keli.

Keli's eyes went to the floor. She knew she was going to have to address the Alix issue. She took a deep breath. "Well, it's mostly good, except for..." She paused again, then answered straight to the point, picking her eyes back up to look at the coach, "except for me and Alix. We can't seem to get along. Coach, honest, I have tried many times and nothing is working. It's not all her fault...lately I have challenged her. I got tired of her constantly teasing..."

Lindsay broke in. "Let's take the individuals out of this. Believe me, this is affecting more than just you two. Don't kid yourself. Your teammates know what is going on. It's probably as tough or maybe even tougher on them. More good teams have been destroyed by this kind of thing than anything else. Dreams, expectations, and even careers have been shattered because a couple of players couldn't leave their differences at the door."

Lindsay leaned back in her chair and folded her hands on top of her head. "Where do we go from here? How does a team recover from a loss like yesterday? How do we get back on track? Losing Greta maybe for the rest of the year and this chemistry challenge might be too much to overcome. And if we can't overcome these things, I'm pretty sure this team will fall short of its goal."

Keli opened her mouth but nothing came out. She just shook her head and looked back down at the floor. Lindsay waited her out. Finally Keli said, "I'm sorry, Coach. I will do everything I can to make things better. I promise you I will not start anything."

The coach smiled. "Can I give you some advice?"

Keli swiftly nodded.

"This isn't about trying to win someone over. Sometimes that will make it worse. This is all about the team and the moment. There are times in a practice and in a game when the next play is the only thing that matters. Regardless of how you might feel about another player, you must take the position that nothing gets in the way of the team and its intention. You must prepare yourself and the rest of your teammates to be ready to win the next point."

Lindsay leaned forward. "Let me tell you a secret. When there is only one person perpetuating a problem, generally their teammates or the coach will find a solution to the problem. Keli, I am really proud of your growth on the court. To be honest, I thought it would take you much longer to work your way to this level. Some of your potential lies in how you handle all your teammates. Believe me, the higher the level, the more competitive, and in a lot of cases, the thicker your skin needs to be to handle it. I have seen the potential of a lot of very talented people get stunted by this type of situation. Some of them stood to make millions; others saw their Olympic hopes disappear. And every year or so, I see someone similar to you who has a chance to be something special and they get caught up in something that destroys them."

Lindsay leaned forward, slapping the table so hard that Keli jumped. Then quietly she said, "I don't want that to be you! I am a Keli Stennes fan and I plan on being in your cheering sections for many years to come." A gentle smile crossed Lindsay's face. "You'd better get out there and warm up."

Keli didn't move. She just stared at the coach. Slowly the words came to her. "Thanks, Coach, I needed to hear that." She stood up and headed for the door.

The coach called out her name. Keli turned around. "My parents and brothers were at the game last night. After the game, my little brother came up to me and said you reminded him of your father. He said your dad was the best player he ever played against."

Keli's shoulders drooped and her lips quivered. The coach again gave Keli a gentle smile. "I just thought you should know what he said. Have a good practice today, and I will see you tomorrow."

The rest of the week Keli worked on what the coach had talked to her about. She took care of her business on the court. She let her playing and leadership do all the talking. Alix tried a couple more zingers, but Keli let them go.

The rest of the team took care of business too. Over the next two weeks, the Dragons ran off four impressive wins. Keli got stronger and more confident in each game. Lindsay's new line was the key. Jesse had her way in the middle, and when teams tried to shut her down, Ashley used her other weapons. Keli was quickly becoming a key player.

CHAPTER 49

IT'S NOT YOUR FAULT

The next morning went quickly and at mid-afternoon, Ashley and Frank walked into the store. Ashley's bag was hanging on her shoulder. She gave Keli a wicked grin, then announced to the other staff and a couple of customers that she was going camping in the woods with Keli.

Frank was carrying the morning paper and waved it at Keli. "Your name is all over the article again."

She smiled, "I pay ten bucks for each time and figure it's good marketing. Can I get an advance on my paycheck?"

Everyone got a good laugh out of that.

Frank looked at both of them. "Get out of here before you scare away business. I'll try to make it to the football game, so save me a seat."

Keli laughed. "Bring some good shoes...we don't sit at Mountaineer games."

The car ride to Falls City was all about Greta. Ashley didn't wait for Keli to ask questions. As soon as the car started to move, she unloaded. "I talked with Dad last night about Greta, and it is not going all that good. I guess she has called him a few times and said she wanted to leave. She doesn't like the counselors."

Ashley paused. "The reason my dad went yesterday was that Austin was up there trying to see her and I guess all hell broke loose. So he raced up and got Austin out of there." Ashley banged her head against the headrest in frustration. "This is so stupid. I just don't understand it. Why did Greta just freak out and give up everything like this?"

Keli just listened to her; there wasn't anything she could say. Finally they crested the gentle hill that led into Falls City. The Perrydale buses were unloading in front of the gym. She slowed down hoping to recognize some of the players.

Ashley giggled. "Look! Most of them are so small. You must have been a giant in this league."

As they drove past the restaurant, Ashley strained to see if Cindy was working. "So, is your mom there?"

"Yep, she will work until about 6:30. Then they will close."

"Why do they close so early on a Saturday night?" Ashley asked.

It was Keli's turn to giggle. "'Cuz everyone will be at the game."

Once at Keli's, Ashley followed her up to her room and zeroed in on the picture. "Wow...that picture is amazing! Did Sticky really draw that?"

Keli answered "Yep" from the bathroom.

"I can't believe it. It is so good! He is a hottie and an artist? You'd better snatch him up. One of these days he is going to be a superstar."

Keli came out of the bathroom. "I hope so. A lot of kids seem to get trapped here." She reached into her closet and pulled out a couple of sweatshirts and tossed one to Ashley. "Here, wear this."

"You're kidding, right?" Ashley held it up towards Keli to point out the "Mountaineers" across the front.

"Nope, tonight we are Mountaineer fans." Ashley laughed and put on the sweatshirt with no further argument.

On the way back to the gym, Keli laid down the rules on how to be a Mountaineer fan. Ashley could do nothing but giggle and nod.

They stopped at the restaurant, which was packed with parents from both schools. Cindy didn't have any time other than a quick wave and a wink at Ashley, who was pointing at her sweatshirt. A group from Perrydale was seated at a table in the corner. One called out, "Hey, Stennes, aren't you playing today?"

Keli froze for a second, not wanting to look around the restaurant. Ashley blurted out, "She transferred to Dallas."

The people at the table looked at each other. One mother said, "Good, sounds like we have a chance then."

Keli grinned and said, "Well, I hope not," as she and Ashley headed out the door.

On the way to the gym, Keli got even more serious. "When some of my old friends see us in the stands, they might get a little nervous thinking we are criticizing or mocking them. We really need to be low key...the last thing I want is to make things worse than they are between me and some of them."

When they pulled up in front of the small, old gym, Ashley looked around, trying to keep a straight face. "So where is the gym anyways?"

"That is exactly what I am talking about...you are going to get me into trouble." Keli frowned.

"Don't worry. Once I walk through that door and into that closet, I will be a perfect angel." Ashley busted up laughing when she saw the look on Keli's face.

Keli entered first with Ashley right behind her, Ashley whispered in her ear, "It's so small."

Two junior boys were manning the admission table. They had known Keli since grade school. One whispered to the other, "We can't charge her, can we?"

The other boy shook his head and motioned the girls to just go on in.

Ashley whispered. "You *are* a star here, aren't you?" but Keli didn't answer.

They found a seat on the Mountaineer side of the gym. All the seats were on one side of the gym, and the team benches were up against the wall on the other side. Both teams were sharing the court, warming up.

Keli didn't realize how nervous she was going to be walking in and seeing her old team, their parents, and her old schoolmates.

Ashley saw the football team sitting up on the top rows. She waved at Sticky and then looked back at Keli, who was almost white with tension. "Dang, girl, you're psyched out right now, aren't you?"

Keli nodded and quickly sat down and stared out onto the court.

They watched both teams warm up. Ashley said, "You know, Perrydale looks pretty strong."

Keli saw the same thing. The last thing she wanted was for the Mountaineers to lose this game. Not this one, she thought.

Coach Edwards made eye contact with her and waved. Keli smiled and cautiously waved back. She tried not to be too obvious as she watched Charlee warm up. Charlee didn't acknowledge her though some of the other girls on the Mountaineer team did.

Just as they thought, Perrydale started out strong and won the first game 25-19. Charlee didn't play very well. Ashley could now see how important Keli was to this team. They would have won the game if she had played, she thought to herself. She peeked over at Keli. Her face said it all...she was devastated.

"Is this seat taken?" The girls looked up to see Tom standing there. Keli patted the spot right next to her. When he sat down, she grabbed his arm and leaned up against him looking for a little comfort.

"It's harder than you thought, isn't it?" he said. Keli looked at him; she didn't have to say anything. He knew the answer.

The rest of the match wasn't much different. Perrydale won three straight games. When the match was over, Keli didn't know what to do. She couldn't just go up to Charlee and the rest of the players. She looked at her grandpa and whispered, "What should I do now?"

Tom took off his glasses and started to clean them. "Well, what do you think you should do?" He looked at her and could tell she had no clue. "I would leave the players to handle the loss between themselves for now. There will be time at the football game to talk with them if you or they choose for that to happen. If I were you, I would just talk to some of your friends here in the stands."

Instant relief came over her. She turned around and started looking for someone to talk with. Then Tom leaned over and quietly said to Ashley, "Maybe you should get her out of here as soon as you can." Ashley winked at him.

A few minutes later they were back outside and walking towards the car. Keli looked at Ashley. "There is no way they will win the state championship."

Ashley gave her a tight smile, agreeing with her.

When they got into the car, Ashley calmly said, "You know it's not your fault they lost."

Keli looked at her as if Ashley could read her mind.

Again Ashley said, "It's not your fault. You're not on their team. Last night I was talking with my dad about coming out here. He predicted they might lose the volleyball game and knew you would really be down. He told me to tell you that you outgrew that team, kind of like going from JV to Varsity. He said it's them who should be proud of their star moving on."

Ashley pounded her fist into her other hand. "I agree with him. They should be huge fans of yours. It isn't your job to give up your dreams just so they can win a few more games."

"You watched that match," she continued. "Be honest. Our JV team would beat either one of those two teams. No one should fault you for trying to become a better player. Dad told me to tell you to be available for those who are available to you. Some of your friends and the community deep down are very proud of you and really would like to find out more about how things are going for you. Tonight when we are down there watching the football game, be the star that you are. Don't apologize for your success.

"You want to know a secret? My dad talks about you all the time. He keeps telling me..." Ashley stopped mid-sentence.

Keli turned to her. "He keeps telling you what?"

"I'm not really sure if I should say." Ashley looked away realizing that she opened up a can of worms. She looked back at Keli and blurted out, "He thinks you're fulfilling your dad's dream at the same time that you're chasing your own. It's destiny, he keeps telling me. He said your dad had more potential then any player he had ever seen, but in the end he couldn't do what you are doing and that is moving on and becoming the Keli that we all see now. He told me last night that if your dad had come to Dallas when he was your age, it would have been differ- ent. I never realized that they were friends way back then. He said when they were sophomores, they played in an all-star baseball thing together and stayed in touch and talked a lot about stuff. He told me your dad really wanted to play at a bigger school but could never do it because of his buddies. Isn't it freaky weird that they were friends and now we are friends? Do you realize how amazing this is?" Ashley rubbed her arm. "It gives me goose bumps just thinking about it."

Keli smiled and thought about the goals she had found behind the picture. "It is weird." Her face saddened. "I wish I could have learned all this from him."

They got out of the car and walked down the dirt road towards the football field, which was lined by the river on one side and a fairly steep little hill around the rest of the field. The lights lit up the whole bowl. The same two boys were now manning the ticket booth. Again they looked at each other and without saying a word pointed towards the field.

Ashley bumped up against Keli. "They're some of the ones who accept what you have done." Keli smiled and kicked a rock in her path.

At the bottom of the hill were small groups of people talking and laughing. Ashley couldn't help but snicker at the bleachers that held maybe 40 people. "So where does everyone else sit?"

Keli pointed to the yellow, staked area around the field. "We stand around the field. Only the older people actually sit on the bleachers. Most people move with the ball as it goes up and down the field. So does the visiting team."

Ashley's snicker turned into a full-fledged teasing laugh. "You have to be kidding."

"Yes, I'm kidding," Keli said sarcastically. "In a few minutes someone will flip the switch and the domed stadium will cover this whole area." She pushed Ashley. "I told you up at the gym to watch that kind of talk. Someone might hear you. This is what we have."

Coming down the hill was the volleyball team. Charlee and Rachel and some of the others were dressed in their cheerleading outfits. The rest were in their vol- leyball sweats.

Rachel was the first to speak. "We sucked today," she said, looking right at Keli. A couple of other girls slowed down wanting to talk.

Keli smiled, then frowned back at Rachel. "Yeah, it was a tough game. I wish you'd won." Then most of the volleyball team in sweats stopped to talk as the cheerleaders headed towards the field.

Tracie looked towards the cheerleaders to make sure they were a safe distance away. "So we've been keeping up on how good you're doing. That picture in the paper was so awesome. It made you look like your shoulders were above the net."

Ashley quickly answered for her. "They were. She jumps higher than anyone I have ever seen."

Keli gently bumped Ashley to shut her up. "Actually I paid her to say that."

This made all her old teammates laugh. She looked at Ashley. "If you think I can jump, you should see Tracie... she is really the Queen of Jumps!"

Tracie beamed.

Keli stuck out her hand to give Tracie a high five. "Sorry you ladies lost today. Perrydale was pretty tough."

Tracie started walking towards the field. "We need to get over there. The team will be out in a minute, and we need to be there to cheer them onto the field." She had a sincere smile on her face. "Keli, it was good to see you again. Good luck with the rest of your season."

"It was good seeing all of you!" Keli scanned the group trying to make eye contact with each one. "You all made my day by stopping and talking for a minute!"

At halftime, Ashley elbowed Keli, "Look! It's Charlee standing in line at the concession stand. You should go over there and talk with her while she is by herself."

Keli looked at her as though she was crazy. "Why should I go over there and get rejected?"

"Cuz she's been your good friend your whole life and it never hurts to try one more time."

"Okay, wait here. I'll be back in a minute." Keli took a deep breath and walked over to Charlee.

As she approached her, she started to freeze. She didn't know what to say. Charlee realized that someone had just walked up behind her and she turned around to see Keli.

Charlee quickly started to turn back around, but Keli blurted out, "I just wanted to say I'm sorry you lost tonight, and I hope one of these days we can find a way to be friends again."

Charlee turned back towards her. This time she didn't have anything harsh to say. She shrugged her shoulders and mustered a small smile. "Yeah, it's too bad we lost tonight. Hopefully we will win the football game." She ignored Keli's comment about rekindling their friendship.

They both heard "Next?" and "Come on, Charlee, you're holding up the line."

Keli frowned and then smiled. "Hey, you'd better order. I'll talk with you later." Keli could tell Charlee wanted to say something else but it didn't come out. She walked back towards Ashley.

Ashley was beaming. "So that didn't look too bad."

"It went okay, I guess," answered Keli. "I told her I was sorry they lost the game and that I hoped one of these days we could figure out how to be friends again."

"Damn, chick, sometimes you are the gutsiest person I know." Ashley smiled. "Hey, look, it's my dad." The girls waved to him and he waved back. Then he waved in another direction. When he got to the bottom of the hill, he took a left instead of a right towards them and headed right towards Cindy, who was standing by the bleachers.

The girls smiled and gave each other a high five. Ashley grabbed Keli's arm and they jogged over to bleachers. "Hey parents, it's funny that neither of you decided to come and talk to your kids. Yet you find each other to chat. So which one of you wants to explain this to your fragile children?"

Keli smiled, "Mom, when did you get here?"

"About 20 minutes ago. I went home and changed before I came down."

Keli wanted to say "Mom, you never go home and change," but she knew that might be too much of an embarrassment so she passed on the thought.

Ashley got all excited and said, "You won't believe it but most of the girls stopped by and chatted with us, and Keli even talked with Charlee just a few minutes ago. It was awesome."

Cindy looked back to Keli, "So how did it go?"

"It went okay," said Keli, "It wasn't warm and fuzzy with Charlee, but we didn't fight either so I guess that is progress."

The second half began and so did a misty rain while they were all chatting. A loud cheer interrupted the conversation from the far side of the field; they all turned to see a Perrydale player crossing the goal line with the ball. Keli kicked the ground. "They can't lose both games when I come. I must be a jinx."

Frank put his arm on her shoulder. "Don't panic. There is a lot of game left to play." They all walked over towards the field to get a closer view. It didn't take long for Keli to get into her old world, yelling encouragement to the team.

By the end of the third quarter, the Mountaineers had closed the gap to 27-21 and the girls had split up from their parents. Keli grabbed Ashley's sweatshirt and shook her up and down. "They have to win this game...they just have to!"

The rain started to fall hard. Both teams struggled to make anything happen on the muddy field, and everyone was drenched from the cold rain. Keli was the loudest person on the sidelines. Finally with a minute and a half to go, Perrydale fumbled the ball. Sticky raced over and scooped the ball up and ran it back all the way for the winning touchdown.

Keli started to race towards Sticky. Ashley was barely able to grab her arm and save her from being the only fan on the field. "There is a minute to go...you can't go out there!"

When the horn finally sounded the end of the game, Keli was the first one to race out. She headed straight to Sticky, nearly tackling him. "That was awesome, you guys did it...you did it!"

The rain was really coming hard and was dripping straight down off of his face-mask; it was the only part of his uniform that wasn't caked with mud. "Thanks, we got lucky when they fumbled the ball." That was the end of the conversation; half the team and fans swarmed Sticky. Keli stood and watched, smiling.

CHAPTER 50

WE ARE GOING TOO!

By the time Keli finished her shower, Ashley was curled up on the bed looking through the old scrapbooks. "Your dad was a stud," she said, pointing to the book. "I hope you don't mind me looking at them."

Keli shrugged. "I don't care...look all you want. I have looked at them a dozen times since Gramps gave them to me. Did my mom get home?"

"Yeah, a couple of minutes ago."

Keli stopped toweling her hair. "She just got home?"

Ashley jumped off the bed. "Do you know what that means? They were to-gether again, in the rain no less!" Ashley was beaming. "I'm telling you, Keli, I think they are falling for each other."

The girls were making hot chocolate and toast when Cindy came into the kitchen. "Mom, do you want some hot chocolate?"

"Sure, that sounds good. So the boys pulled it out in the end. Did you get a chance to talk to Sticky after the game? Why didn't you girls go to the dance? I was surprised to see you here when I got home."

Keli threw a few marshmallows on the top of the steaming cups. "Well, actually, Mom, I am a little surprised by how long it took you to get home."

Ashley chimed in. "Did you get lost or something?"

Cindy caught on and laughed. "The last time I checked, adults don't have to be home at a certain time. If you must know, I was talking with your dad, Ashley."

"And?" came from both girls.

Cindy sipped the chocolate. "And nothing. We just talked for a few minutes and then I came home."

Keli smirked. "Right, Mom, in the pouring down rain. You two just talked for a few minutes like it was a summer day in the park, huh?"

Ashley giggled. "So come on, you can tell us. Did you two go park some-where?" All three laughed.

"Well, if you must know," said Cindy, setting down her cup, "we talked about Greta. We did sit in the car for a few minutes, but it's not what your silly minds are thinking."

Cindy looked right at Ashley. "Your dad is very worried about her. He thinks she is going to leave the treatment center before it's time. He is very confused about what to do if that happens."

The girls' giddiness faded with the news. The room was quiet for a minute while they all sipped the chocolate. Keli broke the silence. "What can we do, Mom? What do you think about Ashley and me talking to her?"

Cindy shook her head. "I don't know if there is anything anyone can do right now. Frank is going back up there tomorrow. Hopefully things will be better."

Ashley stood up. "I am going with him."

Keli stood up too. "So am I!"

"Whoa, girls!" said Cindy. "Before anyone goes, you should talk with Frank."

The girls both headed for the phone. Keli was coaching Ashley as she dialed. "Tell him we will meet him in town first thing in the morning."

As soon as Frank answered the phone, Ashley blurted out, "We are going with you tomorrow." There was silence from the other end. "Dad, did you hear me?"

"Yes, Ash, I heard you, but no one is going tomorrow. There was a phone message when I got home. Greta left sometime this evening. No one knows where she went."

Ashley's eyes filled with tears. "Dad, what are we going to do?"

Keli waved her mom over to the phone. Cindy reached for the phone and said, "Can I talk with him?"

Ashley nodded and handed her the phone, then headed back towards the kitchen table, crying. Keli followed her and Ashley repeated what Frank had told her. Keli looked grim.

Cindy hung up the phone and came back to the table. "Ashley, I'm so sorry. Your dad says he will call as soon as he hears anything. He is pretty sure she left with Austin. He called Austin's parents, who said they hadn't seen him all day and he wasn't answering his cell phone. So for right now we have to wait. Girls, why don't you get dressed and go to the dance? It might take your mind off all this."

Both shook their heads. Keli answered, "That is the last place I want to be right now. I think we are just going to head for bed."

The comfort of the bed won out and they fell asleep, but the phone rang early the next morning. Cindy got to it first, and the girls raced downstairs hoping it was news from Greta.

They watched Cindy nod a couple times and finally say, "Well, thanks for the update. Good luck and call us when you can. Here she is," and she handed the phone to Ashley.

Ashley answered anxiously. "Dad, what is going on?"

"Hi, sweetie. I heard from Greta, and she is up in Seattle with her mom."

Ashley felt like she was going to throw up.

"I am going up there right now to talk with them. I might not be back to-night...so I want you to stay there, okay?"

Ashley said sadly, "Okay," and hung up.

Cindy grabbed both girls and hugged them. "Let's let Frank deal with this right now. None of us can do anything, so we need to do what we need to do today. Homework and get ready for tomorrow."

The day dragged by. They all found themselves done with everything they needed to get done. The phone became the focus of the evening waiting for it to ring, but it never did...Finally Cindy had to end it, "Okay, you two. Go get some rest."

After a couple of futile attempts to change her mind, they headed for Keli's bedroom.

As they lay in the dark room, Ashley said, "I can't wait to play tomorrow. I need it to take my mind off all this. This weekend has seemed to last forever. You know the playoffs are coming in two weeks, and we still have to face Woodburn. They haven't lost this year. We really need to go into the state tourney a number-one seed. We don't want to start off against the bigger programs in the pool play."

Keli sat up in the bed. "What do you mean bigger programs? We have a big program, don't we?"

A small giggle lightened the air. "Not like some of the schools from the Mt Hood conference or down in Eugene. Their club programs are huge. The past couple of years we have been able to compete with them but we lost."

Keli's head swam. "Dang, I thought Dallas was as big as any of them. So do you play club?"

"Yeah, I play for a club called Digits out of Salem. We're pretty good. You need to play with us this winter."

"I looked into it once, but there's no way we could afford it," answered Keli.

"Working for my dad, you'll be able to pay for it, right?"

The room was quiet for a moment. "I don't think so. Between my car payment, insurance, and gas, there isn't much left over." Keli sighed loud enough for Ashley to hear, then lay there depressed, her mind racing with the thought that there was another group of players who were ahead of her and her goal.

Ashley answered, "Well, don't worry about it tonight. We'll figure something out."

Again the phone woke them up. Cindy answered it. The girls were slower to get downstairs and by the time they did, Cindy was already off the phone.

"Was that my dad?" asked Ashley.

Cindy answered slowly. "Yes, it was...Greta isn't coming back. She has decided to stay with her mom up north. Austin is staying there too." Cindy looked at them trying to read their emotions. The girls looked at each other wanting the other one to respond, but neither spoke.

"Okay, you two. You'd better get going or you'll be late to school."

Up in the bedroom, Keli spoke first, "I'm sorry all this has happened, but I think until she gets her head on straight it's better for her not to be home. I hope that doesn't make you mad, but it's how I feel. She is messed up and it will only mess you up trying to fix her."

Ashley was quiet all the way to school. As they started to enter the building, Ashley finally spoke up. "You're right, I think. I would try to fix it and she would probably drag me down too. It doesn't help the hurt feeling I have on the inside. She has really become my sister. It's the first time I ever had anyone to really talk to and share stuff with. Now she's gone and I might not ever see her again."

Keli could see Ashley was on the verge of tears. "Hey, you can adopt me as your sister."

Ashley smiled, "I still think one of these days we are going to be sisters." The first bell ended the conversation.

It was a relief to be back in classes. The morning zoomed by and at lunch most of the team was doing their own thing today. Keli looked for Ashley but she wasn't there. She scanned the commons eating area and noticed that Steen was sitting by himself. After one more quick scan, she made her way over and sat down across from him. "So how was your weekend?"

Steen looked around him to see if he was getting set up by the volleyball team for eating lunch with one of their players.

Keli laughed. "It's okay. I'm by myself," which made Steen laugh too.

They chatted about their weekends, Keli revealing a little about Greta.

Steen said, "I've already heard about her and Austin running away to Seattle or something like that. How weird is that anyways?" He looked at Keli's lunch. "Are you going to eat those carrots?"

Keli laughed, "Yes, I am going to eat them, but you can have my apple if you want." Her next comment surprised both of them. "So the season is going to end in a few weeks. Don't forget you still owe me a movie."

Almost choking on the apple, Steen said, "I haven't forgotten. Let me get this right. When our seasons are over, you and I are going to a movie together," pointing at her, then himself. "Hmmm, maybe I should get this in writing," searching his backpack for a piece of paper.

"Come on, goof, we need to get to class." Keli stuffed her trash into her lunch bag and waited for Steen. On the way to class they ran into Ashley. "I missed you at lunch. What's up?"

Ashley looked at her and smiled, then looked at Steen, who was still standing there waiting for the scoop. Keli realized that Steen was holding up the news. She gently shoved him towards class. "I'll catch up in a few minutes."

"Fine," he said, "I can take a hint," and headed for class.

Ashley said, "I went home after third period and talked to my dad. He said that Greta looked good and actually so did his sister. He said it was the best she had looked in more than 10 years. She was getting married again. Dad says the new guy seems to be really good for her. He tried to act upbeat and happy about the possibility of things being good up there, but I know he is devastated. Greta had become his other daughter, and I think he feels a lot of rejection right now."

The bell rang. Keli scrambled to find something positive to say. "Hey, just think, in a couple of hours we can play some ball. I am excited. Are you going to be there?"

Ashley's eyes lit up a bit, "Of course."

CHAPTER 51

CLUB VOLLEYBALL

Classes were finally over. Keli found herself jogging towards the gym...she couldn't wait for practice. Even the smell fired her up. She dressed quickly and then bolted through the coach's door. Generally she gave an announcing knock as she opened the door, but today she just came right through.

Sitting across from Coach Lindsay were two men. Lindsay frowned at her entrance. The men turned towards her and smiled. One said, "Well, I guess we should get going and let you get to your players."

Lindsay quickly said, "Keli, can you give me a couple of minutes?"

"Sure, Coach. Sorry to interrupt...I didn't know."

Keli waited outside the door wondering who they were. They weren't parents that she had ever seen. Just then they walked out and both of them smiled. The talkative one said, "She's all yours." Keli smiled back and noticed MSU written on their golf shirts.

Keli headed through the door, still thinking about where the men were from. "So, Coach, who are those guys? What does MSU stand for?" Then it hit her, "Montana State?"

Lindsay smiled and nodded. "It's my old college."

"So what are they here for, recruiting? I thought Jesse and Libby had already accepted scholarships." Keli smiled and said, "Tell them I am not ready to commit to any school yet."

They both laughed, and Lindsay said they were just checking a few things out. "So let's get to volleyball. The playoffs are coming, and Woodburn is still in our way and we really need to go into the tournament the number-one seed."

Keli felt a bit of *déjà vu* having had the same conversation with Ashley the night before.

"Well, now that we know for sure that Greta is not coming back—yes, I did have a conversation with Frank Webb this morning. I am very sad about it all, but in our world of volleyball, we need to work through this and move on. I know that doesn't sound real personal, but there are 11 other girls who have worked really hard this year, including you, and we need to focus on what we have, not on what we don't. Do you understand what I'm trying to say?"

Keli nodded.

"Good. So I am going to talk with Jesse and let her know she will be staying in the middle, and you really need to come through for us on the outside. One thing we need to go over is making the right decisions. It's especially important when we play Woodburn. This could be a five-game match very easily. Every point is critical. When a young player's adrenaline starts to take over, they think they can do the impossible sometimes. That isn't what we need. Not all sets are created equal."

"What I mean by that is being very sure of the right hit for the set that you have. Not all sets are kill sets. You jump so well that sometimes when you're out there, I sense you think you can handle all of them with a kill mentality, but mature players realize that there is a time for holding back. This does two things. First, instead of hitting the ball out and losing the point, you let up and keep the ball in play. Now we have a chance to still win the point. Second, you keep their defense guessing. If they know you are going to rip it every time, they will set their defense to handle it. You need to dump a few balls now and then to get them wondering if it's going to be short. Once you do that, then your kill shot will be even more effective."

The coach looked up at the clock. "You'd better get out there and get warmed up. We have a lot to go over today. Oh, I almost forgot. Have you ever played on a club team?"

Keli's first thought was the coach had been talking with Ashley. "No, Coach, your summer camp this summer is all. Ashley was telling me about it, but I don't think I can afford to play."

Lindsay smiled and handed her a piece of paper. "Here are a couple of clubs. I have already talked to the coaches about you. Both would love to have you play for them this winter. Somehow you need to figure out the money end of it. You need to play club this year." Lindsay leaned forward a bit and repeated slowly, "You need to play club this year."

"Coach, really I don't..."

Lindsay cut her off. "For a kid who in six months has fought her way to where you are today, I think you can figure this one out, too."

Keli looked at Lindsay, who was smiling broadly at her.

The whole practice was loud and focused, and the two and a half hours were over in a flash. Keli and a few others stayed for a while with Coach Jim and hit off the machine until Lindsay kicked them out of the gym.

In the parking lot before she headed home, Keli looked at the paper the coach had given her about the clubs. Her mouth dropped open when she saw that one club charged $2,000, but the shock was even greater when she looked at the next one, which was circled and starred by the coach. It read $4,500.

All the way home she kept glancing at the piece of paper lying in the seat beside her. She kept telling herself there was no way she could pay for it. By the time she pulled up in front of the restaurant, she had convinced herself that even the first club wasn't possible, that $2,000 was too much.

As she walked into the restaurant, she called Ashley, "Hey, what is the name of the club you play for again?"

"Digits. Why?"

Keli looked at the paper and sure enough it was the $4,500 club. "Do you know how much it costs to play on that club?"

Ashley answered. "Yeah, it's a lot. But it goes for like six months and we play all over." She was trying to convince Keli that it was a good deal. "Remember what I said. Don't worry about it right now. When the season is over, we will think of something."

"Well, I am worried about it right now. Because there is no way I can figure out how to pay that much money...it might as well be a million dollars." Keli realized that by now the whole restaurant was listening to her conversation, which included Sticky and the gang. "Hey, Ash, I gotta go. We can talk about this later."

"No worries, chick. See you tomorrow. Hey, bring your A game tomorrow. We are going to need it."

The restaurant was pretty full for a Monday night. Cindy was busy working on the large table filled with her old classmates. Her first instinct was to go sit with them, but fearing rejection, she sat on her usual stool by the cash register.

Her heart skipped a beat when Sticky said, "Hey, Keli, there's enough room here."

The rest of the kids started to make space for her. Keli smiled and looked at her mom, who winked back at her.

Grunts asked the first question. "So why didn't you come to the dance on Saturday...and bring your friend with you? I was psyched to dance with her." The rest of the kids laughed and threw shots at him.

Before she could answer, Sticky grabbed the piece of paper still in her hand. "So, what's this all about?"

Keli immediately felt embarrassed like it was some kind of middle-school love note. "Give it back," she said, and tried to wrestle it from him.

"Wow! It costs over four grand to play volleyball?" He looked at her. "Are you going to do this? It sounds like a rip off to me." He showed the paper and the cost to everyone around the table.

Keli finally grabbed it back. "It's not going to happen. It costs too much. My coach wants me to play this winter for the team that Ashley plays for, but there is no way I can do it." Trying to change the subject, she asked, "Who's up this week for you guys?"

Don answered. "Well, we have Valsetz this week and finish with Detroit next week. We have to win them both to have a chance at the playoffs."

Grunts added, "The girls are out of it."

The table got quiet for a second, everyone thinking the same thing: If you played for us, they would be headed for the tournament.

Sticky went back to the club topic. "Is this club thing a big deal?"

Keli nodded. "I guess so. It's where all the college recruiters go to watch kids play. Ashley said that is where most of the recruiting is done, since their season is the same time as ours. I guess most of the girls on my team play for one club or another. I didn't even know this stuff existed."

She stood up. "I gotta run. I have tons of homework and we have a big game tomorrow." She stared right at Sticky and said, "It was great seeing all of you."

Grunts tried to pull her back down, hoping to get her to stay, but Keli headed for the car. She glanced back through the big window one more time at the table and Sticky was staring at her. Again her heart skipped a beat. She thought to herself on the way up to the house that things were finally getting better.

CHAPTER 52

SORRY, COACH

Keli could smell pancakes as she walked towards the kitchen. Cindy had a small pile of them on the table waiting for her. "Big game today, huh?"

"Yep, we need to win this one for sure today. Are you going to be able to come?"

"I don't think so. Falls City has a volleyball game today too, and I need to be there for the dinner rush. I might be able to make it for the last part, but no guarantees."

Keli flopped a couple of pancakes on her plate. "From the way it sounds, it might be a long one, so if you do get out early, call Frank and see if it's still going on."

Cindy sat down. "So what is this flyer about club volleyball? Does it really cost that much to play during the winter?" She looked discouraged.

"I guess so," said Keli through a mouthful of pancake. "Right now I am not going to think about any of it. Woodburn is all the matters."

"It was nice to see the gang invited you to their table last night. It looks like they are all finally coming around." Cindy had a little grin on her face. "I told you they would."

Keli grabbed her bags. "Yeah, yeah, you're always right." She smiled. "I'll see you later. Wish me luck, but I hope we don't need it."

The day dragged by. Game time finally arrived. Woodburn's freshmen and JV teams were impressive, sweeping all the games in both matches. During the pregame meeting, Lindsay was quick with her motivational speeches. She got straight to the X's and O's, going over each Woodburn player and where they liked to hit. The film she showed was also impressive. Their outsides, both left and right, could really jump. Keli looked around the room and felt a little like she had watching Perrydale warm up against Falls City.

Everyone was focused on the film. Keli was staring at Jesse, when the coach stopped the film and yelled across the room, "Stennes, what is so interesting with Jesse that you're not watching the film?"

The room was silent. Keli could feel her face burn hot with embarrassment.

"Sorry, Coach, it won't happen again." It was the first time she could remember ever being singled out in a negative way like that. There was no way she was going to take her eyes off the monitor even when it was off. Now her worry was making eye contact and being embarrassed again in front of her teammates.

When the film ended, the coach asked for questions, but there weren't any. Keli tried to be the first one out the door, but her worst nightmare happened. Lindsay spoke, "Keli, can you wait back a minute please?"

As the girls passed her, a few said under their breaths, "Hang in there. It will be okay." And Ashley gave her a high five as she passed. Finally the room was empty except for Keli and the coach.

Lindsay leaned up against the desk in the front of the room and stared right at Keli. The look was enough, but Keli knew there were words coming. Finally Lindsay said, "Keli, you and I have spent hours talking about focus and concentration and while it's impossible to do it perfectly, it needs to always be the goal. This team we are playing today, I guarantee you, will be focused, and it might come down to who blinks first and makes a mental mistake. I don't want that to be us. I am going to expect that you have already had your mental mistake for the day." Lindsay broke a very small grin on her face, trying to soften the moment just a bit.

All Keli could do was nod and apologize again. "Sorry, Coach, I will..."

Lindsay interrupted her. "It's not me who needs the apology, it's your team-mates...they count on you as you count on them. When you check out like that, you're letting them down. The best way to make it up is through your actions and playing even harder. Championships are won by the little things, simple details that average teams overlook. What happened earlier was a good example of skipping over the details. You can't allow yourself to fall into that trap of minimizing the details."

Lindsay could tell her points were being received and motioned towards the door. "Go get warmed up."

The gym was packed. Woodburn had a couple hundred of their own fans trying to cheer as loud as the Dragons. Keli struggled with how to get past the last 15 minutes. Her first few passes were off the mark and so was her hitting. She could feel herself winding up and getting tighter. Panic started to set in. She knew that she was really messing up and that she could be back on the bench.

"Hey, Keli," came from behind her...Keli turned around to see Alix staring right at her. The last thing she needed was Alix to have a zinger for her. But it was just the opposite.

"Settle down. Most of us have had that speech at one time or another. It was your turn. We need a big game out of you today." Alix stuck up both of her hands in the air; Keli could feel her nerves settle a bit and gave Alix a huge high five.

For the first time all season, Keli didn't look in the stands during warm ups to see who might be watching. Her entire focus was on the floor. The only sounds she could hear were her teammates and coaches. It was strange; everything seemed to slow down after her quick chat with Alix.

The first game was all Dragons; the crowd and band kept the place rocking. When it was over, the Dragons had cruised to a 25-16 win. Keli was everywhere making plays, but most of all she dominated the front line with both kills and blocks.

In the huddle between games one and two, Keli's eyes never left the coaches. Ashley was across the huddle staring at her and never once did Keli look back.

In game two, Woodburn's serving got the best of them. With the score tied at 24, Jesse had the serve and missed. Giving the ball back to Woodburn with the lead, the game ended on the very next play with an ace by their all-state setter.

But that was the only game Woodburn took. Dallas played flawlessly in games three and four. Ashley knew Keli's timing was really on, and she fed her the ball every chance she could, with the same results...kill after kill. Woodburn was unable to stop her. When they took away the cross-shot, Keli would take it down the line.

When it was all over, everyone crowded around Keli, slapping on her head, pushing her with excitement. Right then the noise of the gym flicked back on. It was like taking out earplugs. Keli looked around half-wondering why it was so loud now and not during the game. Ashley got right in her face yelling "Wow! You were completely amazing!"

The Dragon coaches yelled for a team cheer for the Bulldogs. Keli and the Dragons went down the line congratulating them on a well-played game. When Keli got to their coach, she grabbed Keli's hand and shook it firmly. "Great game, young lady. You dominated us."

Keli almost felt embarrassed by the comment but answered "Thank you" with a big smile.

Waiting for Keli as she turned around was Coach Lindsay, who had her hand out. "Keli Stennes, we will have to put out a new set of expectations for you. That was a great performance tonight."

Keli grinned broadly and shook her hand. "Thanks, Coach. After what happened earlier, I was really worried that I was going to mess up tonight."

Finally Keli and Ashley made their way over to the stands. Cindy was standing by Frank, both of them clapping in their direction.

"Mom, when did you get here?"

Cindy clapped a little harder. She looked over to Frank, who answered for her. "Your mom got here just before the start of the fourth game. I told her she missed one of the best performances I have ever seen by an outside hitter."

Keli smiled at both of them. She was embarrassed by all the attention she had been getting after the game.

"Tom, are you up for some dinner?" said Frank.

Keli turned around to see her gramps and the lady from the volleyball game she had met a few weeks before in Corvallis.

Judy frowned at Tom. "Sorry, I need to get going." She turned her attention to Keli and smiled, "Hello again, Keli. Great game tonight! Very, very impressive."

Tom introduced Judy around, including her past association with the Ducks.

Ashley smiled and said, "Wow! What are you doing up here? Do you still coach?"

Judy shook her head. "No, I've been retired now for a few years. Tom here was my assistant for nearly half of those years and I wanted a chance to come up and see what he is so proud of. And now I know. The university could use a couple of players like you two."

The girls both blushed with pride at the thought.

Keli reached her hand out to the coach. "Thank you for coming up and watching the game. It was an honor having you here."

As Judy and Tom started for the exit, Judy looked back at them and said, "I look forward to seeing you all again."

Cindy answered, "Be careful driving home and we hope to see you soon too."

Keli grabbed her backpack. "Actually, I can't have dinner either. I have so much homework I'll be up 'til midnight." She motioned towards her mom. "You go and I'll see you when you get home." Ashley didn't have any homework but used the same excuse to get out of the dinner.

Can I Play...

Cindy looked at the girls, then back at Frank, "Well, I'm starved."

Frank smiled and said, "Let's fix that."

They were barely out of the parking lot before her phone rang. Keli knew it was Ashley "Hey, Kels, great bluff on the homework. That was genius. They are on a date.

Keli started to laugh. "You have this all planned out, don't you?"

"Of course, Sis, I got it all planned out," giggled Ashley.

CHAPTER 53

WHERE IS SHE?

Keli walked into Lindsay's office for their daily chat only to find Coach Jim sitting at her desk. "Well, Breanne, how are you today?" teased Keli.

Coach Jim laughed. "So you and the coach are now on a first-name basis, huh?"

"Well, I guess one of us is." Keli was laughing too. "So where is she today? She'd better not be standing me up. I have some really big questions for her."

Jim leaned back in the chair. "Hmmm. I guess your really big questions are going to have to wait till next week. Coach Lindsay won't be back until Monday. You are going to have put up with me today and tomorrow night at the game."

Keli looked at him quizzically.

"The coach is out of town on an unexpected trip 'til Monday. I will run practice today and coach the team tomorrow night." He leaned back, waiting for Keli's reaction to the news.

Keli leaned back in her chair too. "What happened? Did someone die or something? The coach wouldn't just up and leave unless it was really, really bad."

Jim stood up. "The good news is no one died...when she comes back Monday, I'm sure she will fill everyone in on her trip. Maybe we should get out there and start warming up. Don't forget. Tomorrow we have a chance to win the league championship. Sherwood isn't going to care whether Coach Lindsay is there or not. We win this game and we are the number-one seed from our league. That's what's important." Jim walked out the door, leaving it open for Keli to follow.

Keli stood there looking around the empty office with a strange feeling in her stomach. She realized how important the coach had become to her. Their before-practice meetings had been a huge source of her growth. She looked at the blackboard, which still had the drawings the coach had diagramed about angles from the day before.

A loud whistle brought her back to the moment. She closed the door behind her and ran to the court. Coach Jim called all the girls in and gave them the same story. Then he didn't wait for any questions and put the girls into their normal station drills. Keli grouped up with the other hitters on the setting machine, while the middles worked on blocking. The rest of the team worked on serving.

By the time all the girls met back after the sub drills for the team practice, each group had their own theories about why Lindsay was gone. Jim quickly got them refocused on the scrimmage drills. Keli successfully put Lindsay out of her mind through practice, but as soon as the final whistle blew, she went straight for Ashley and Jesse.

"So what do you think is up with Lindsay? It must be pretty bad if she would miss a game like this." The other two both looked at each other knowing their theory would send Keli into orbit.

"So, do you guys know something I don't? Am I the only one freaking out about this?"

Jesse bounced the volleyball she was holding a couple of times. "Okay. Most of us think she is going to leave Dallas after this year and..."

Keli exploded. "Leave here? Why?"

Ashley said. "Let Jesse finish what she was saying!"

Jesse hugged the ball. "For the past couple of years, colleges have been trying to get her to come to their schools, and we think this time she is going to take one. Rumors say she is interviewing right now. Lindsay is too good to stay here forever."

Keli looked at Ashley, who gave her a sad grin and shrugged her shoulders at the thought and then answered, "None of us really want it to happen, but we have been preparing ourselves for a couple of years now."

Keli grabbed the ball from Jesse and threw it against the wall in anger. "Why didn't anyone ever tell me that this was happening? Now what? We get a new coach next year?"

Ashley fired back. "Jesse and Libby are leaving this year too. The rest of us pick it up and go on." For the first time Ashley was sarcastic with Keli, "So are you telling me out in Falls City you never changed coaches, that it's someone's dream job out there? Come on, Keli, grow up. It's her job and if someone is willing to offer her a great job, why should she stay here?"

Jesse put her hand on Keli's arm. "I know it's tough. Lindsay is awesome, but it's part of sports. You'd better get used to it. Each time you get tight with a coach or a player, it's always hard when it ends, but hopefully the love for the game will override the negative parts." She headed towards the locker room, leaving Ashley and Keli standing there, both wondering how they should handle the awkwardness of Ashley's last comment.

Keli looked back towards Lindsay's office, sighed heavily, and started towards the door without saying anything to Ashley. After a couple of steps, she turned around and said, "Sorry for popping off earlier. I just really like Coach. I don't want to play for anyone else. I know that sounds childish and I know I have to deal with it, but right now I am just shocked. It's the last thing I would ever dream would happen." She walked back towards Ashley. "Do you think Jim will become the Varsity coach?"

Ashley shook her head. "My guess is he will go with Lindsay. You know just because she is interviewing doesn't mean she will take the job. She has done this before, and she hasn't left. The best thing we can do is beat Sherwood and wait for Monday to find out for sure what is going on."

Keli silently nodded and bent down to retie a shoelace. "Okay, okay, you're right. So Mom told me that she and Frank are going out after the game. Which means you should invite me to stay the night. We could celebrate or something. You know, they're both acting like teenagers. It's weird thinking of my mom dating. Do you think they have kissed yet?"

Ashley dropped her backpack, laughing at such a naïve question. "YES! I have seen them!"

Keli screamed, "NO WAY! When were you going to tell me? Where did you see them?"

"Your mom stopped by the store a couple of days ago and when Dad walked her out, I spied on them." Ashley laughed. "You should have seen Dad's face when I asked him about it. When you get home, ask your mom about it."

The drive back to Falls City seemed to go slowly. Keli's mind raced back and forth between Coach Lindsay and her mom's relationship. Finally her car came to a stop in the driveway. She glanced over at Sticky's window out of habit and then raced into the house yelling, "Mom, we need to talk!"

Cindy came out of the kitchen smiling. "So what do you want to talk about?"

Keli knew her mom had been tipped off about the conversation. She pointed to the couch and acted like the roles were reversed.

"Okay, Mom, let's have it. So are you and Frank officially dating or whatever old people call it? Do you know how weird this is?"

"I guess we are kind of dating. We haven't really defined it. But it is nice. Frank is a wonderful man, and we have a lot in common."

The room was quiet as they looked at each other, each waiting for the other to speak first. Keli finally broke the silence. "So do you think you would ever marry him?" The question surprised them both.

Cindy folded her arms and took back her role as the parent. "I think that question is a really premature. We have only known each other for a couple of months. Maybe we should change the subject to Coach Lindsay. Frank told me that she might be leaving to take a job at Montana State or something."

Keli's mind wandered back to a few weeks ago when she walked into Lindsay's office and the two men who were in there from MSU. It all was making sense now. She knew that had to be it. Finally she answered her mom. "Yeah, I heard today. I didn't think about it at the time, but there were a couple of men from there in her office a few weeks ago. Did you know that's where she went to college?"

"Well, it would be a pretty good deal for her to be able to go back and coach at her alma mater."

"I don't want her to leave, Mom. She is amazing. She really understands me, and I am afraid that if she leaves, I won't get any better. Every day she tells me what I need to hear. When I am in her office talking about stuff, I feel confident. I am really afraid of losing that feeling."

Cindy scooted across the couch and put her arm around her. "I don't know much about volleyball, but I know you and you have always been confident. You're right, Coach Lindsay has really helped your game, but I think you need to give yourself more credit. A coach can only give you the answers. You or any player needs to have the desire to follow through with the answers."

"Frank has told me many times this past couple of months that he has never seen any athlete improve like you have this season. I think most of it comes from your desire. Whoever your coach is next year will be the lucky one, and I'm sure whoever it is will have more answers on how to improve your game."

Keli sighed. "Mom, can you believe how much has changed in our life these past few months? It seems a little like a dream at times. I still wonder if it is all worth it sometimes or how things would be if I had stayed in Falls City."

Cindy kissed her on the cheek and then said, "Well, things are different for sure, and I know it's all worth it. When I see you play now, I can't believe it. You have expanded your world and that is worth it too. Falls City is a nice little town, but there is a whole world out there, and I think you are starting to understand that. I am so thankful that you're getting a taste of it. I used to worry that you might never get the chance, but now I am confident that you're on your way. I am very proud of your risking everything you knew to take a chance. Be proud of yourself!"

She stood up and pulled Keli off the couch. "Now you'd better go get your homework done. And by the way, you had a couple of calls before you got home."

"Who?"

"Sticky and Steen."

Keli came back to the doorway. "What did they want?"

Cindy laughed. "Last time I checked I wasn't your personal assistant. Why don't you call them yourself and find out?"

Keli sat at her desk and dug out her homework and cell phone. She dialed Ashley's number instead of either of the boys.

"So guess who I got messages from today when I got home. Sticky and Steen."

Ashley laughed. "That's a good thing, right? I wish I could get a couple of stone-cold studs to call me. I would pay! So who did you call first?"

"You!" answered Keli.

"That's so wrong! Call me when you have details." Then she hung up the phone.

Keli laughed to herself and started to dial but then she hung it up. "I can't deal with this," she thought and dug into her homework.

Later, Keli lay in bed thinking about Sticky and Steen. One had been her best friend her whole life and the other had become a true friend. She stared up at the luminous stars on her ceiling wondering what it would be like to have one as a real boyfriend. Thoughts ran through her head: Would she lose the other's friendship? Would it mess with her volleyball?

Just before she fell asleep, the thought of her dad came into her head. She rolled over onto her side and squinted through the dark room at his picture on her nightstand. She could barely make out his smiling face. Keli smiled back and said, "Well, Dad, what do you think of all this?"

CHAPTER 54

THE LAME NOTE

Steen met Keli at the front door of the school. "So did you get my messages? I left one on your phone, and I talked to your mom on your home phone and asked her to have you call me." The crowd of kids coming in the door pushed them in the direction of their first periods.

"Yeah, I'm sorry. My mom told me. Actually I did start to call you, but I hung it up before it rang last night. To be honest, I'm just overwhelmed with stuff right now." She paused. She knew if she said any more, it would open the door to the subject of relationships.

Ashley came down the hall, and Keli smiled at him. "I'll see you after lunch, okay?"

He took the hint and headed towards 1st period. As soon as he had his back turned, Keli sighed heavily, "I've got to find a way to finish out the season and then worry about Sticky and Steen."

Ashley nodded her head. "I don't think either one of them are going to wait a couple more weeks. Have you forgotten winter formal is coming up at the end of the month?"

She could see by the look on Keli's face that she had forgotten. "Dang, girl, you have probably the two best studs chasing you for the biggest dance of the year and you're clueless."

After lunch, Steen was waiting for Keli in their usual place. She could tell he was nervous as she approached him. She quickly figured he was about to pop the question about the dance. She needed a diversion to avoid the subject. She slowed and purposely looked at the clock above the door, hoping Steen would think they were running out of time.

Keli quickly asked, "Are you going to the game tonight?"

Steen answered, "Of course. What are you doing afterwards?"

"I'm going to Ashley's. Our parents are going out on a date." She looked at Steen for his response.

A smile came across his face. "So your mom is dating Ashley's dad? Wow, wouldn't that be way weird if they hooked up. You two would be sisters!"

Later, halfway through the class while Mr. Lippon was writing on the board, Steen slipped Keli a note. She looked at him and then back at the folded piece of paper. There was little doubt in her mind what was written on it. Keli looked back to make sure Lippon was still writing. She slowly unfolded the paper.

Can I Play...

Keli, I know this is a little goofy doing it this way. But it seems like I can't find the right time to ask. So please check one of the boxes below.

Keli, will you be my date at winter formal on November 22nd?

Yes   ☐

No   ☐

P.S. Don't tell anyone about this lame note.

She could feel her face getting hot and wondered if anyone was looking at her. She quickly folded the paper in half so no one could read over her shoulder. Slowly she opened up the note again and hovered over it with her pencil. Then she scribbled something on the note.

Steen could see that she was writing more than just checking one of the boxes. Just then Lippon turned back towards the students and Keli quickly hid the note under the desk.

As soon as Lippon turned back towards the blackboard, Steen stuck out his hand and Keli quickly slipped it back to him. Again she could feel her face heating up as she glanced out of the corner of her eye to see if Steen was reading the note.

When class finally ended, Steen was laughing at her. "I can't believe what you wrote."

Keli put her hands in the air, "What? I can't believe you ask me with a 6th-grade note either!"

He pulled out the note and read it quietly back to her. "Dating is a winter sport and as soon as volleyball season is over, the answer is yes."

She was grinning at him "Well, you know me...I like to follow the rules."

Steen waved the paper in front of her. "So as soon as the season is over, this becomes official. It's like an iron-clad contract."

Keli tried to grab it from him teasingly. "Well, then you'd better hold on to your proof!"

After school, the whole pre-game ritual was turned upside down. There was a note on the locker room door announcing the Varsity pre-game meeting would be run by the captains. Keli realized that Coach Jim had to coach both the JV game and then go right into the Varsity game.

When the whole team finally finished straggling in, Jesse started the meeting.

"Okay, listen up, ladies. Everyone knows Lindsay is gone and Jim is out there. So here is what she wrote for today's game. Sherwood's record is 6-7 in matches and fourth in the league standings. They are a very fast team and excellent defensive players. They dig everything."

She looked up and said that Lindsay had underlined this last part. Then she went on, "Good serve receive and the setter is very tricky and will dump a lot, so be ready. They are weak blockers, and we need to really find the lanes in between their defense."

"Ashley?" Jesse quickly looked at her. "Here's what it says to you. 'Their middle is very weak, read it and set Jesse early, and then see what they give you after that.'"

Again Jesse looked up at the group and handed the paper to Libby to finish reading.

Libby looked at the paper and then back to the team. "Okay, here is her speech part. 'Ladies, this is our last home game and regular season game. We have come a long ways this year. This game is very important to our seeding in the upcoming State tournament. I expect all of you to perform just as if I were there. I am counting on it. Watch the film, be focused, and finish our first goal.'"

Jesse started the video of Sherwood's game with Newberg. Most of the girls watched, but the focus wasn't like it would have been if Lindsay had been in the room. Keli caught herself looking around the room judging everyone's behavior instead of sharpening her mind for the game.

Jim opened the door, startling the girls. "Come on, let's get out here."

On the way out the door, Ashley grabbed Keli. "Hey, you've heard it before, but I'm just reminding you that coaches don't win games, players do. Just play the way you've been playing."

The game was delayed at the start to honor the graduating seniors. As each one was announced, Keli cheered and thought about how different next season was going to be without them. Especially Jesse and Libby, they truly were the heart of the team.

The first game of the match was too easy. Ashley followed the coach's instructions and fed Jesse the ball in the middle and Sherwood didn't have an answer. Ashley's sets were flawless. Keli and the rest of the team were merely window-dressing as Jesse and Ashley dominated the first game 25-17.

However, in the second game, Sherwood came out and on the first two attempts, Jesse had blocked back for kills. Ashley quickly went around the court telling Keli, Alix, and Libby to be ready. On the next play, Ashley set a nice low ball exactly where Keli liked it, but to the Dragons' dismay, the ball sailed way out even though she had no pressure on the attack.

Ashley quickly came over and slapped hands with her. "No worries. You'll get the next one. There is no one there to stop you. They are packing it in on the middle so make them pay."

Keli could feel herself tightening up, realizing that she was on the spot to perform. She looked over at the bench and Jim pointed at her and nodded his head to tell her it was coming and to be ready.

Libby made a great pass on serve receive, and Ashley put the ball back in the same spot for Keli. She exploded off the floor and did the same thing with the ball. It didn't help that the Knights all yelled out almost the second she made contact.

Jim called a timeout and tried to calm the team down, but it didn't work. What happened to Keli was contagious, and the rest of her teammates started pressing too hard. By the time the game was over, the Dragons had made 12 unforced errors hitting. The match was tied up one game each.

Before the start of game three, Jim had the starters take a seat. Jesse and Libby were shooting off instructions and words of encouragement. But it didn't do any good. Game three was a carbon copy of game two. This time the Dragons had 14 unforced hitting errors. Keli was in shock. She whispered in Jesse's ear as they walked towards the huddle after being beaten 25-15 in game three. "I can't do anything right. What's going on?"

Jim had a grease board in his hand, again setting down the starters. "Okay, we are going to shake some things up this game. Jesse, you're in for Keli, and Alison, you play in Jesse's spot. Ashley, get the ball to Jesse on the outside, and if they adjust, bring the ball back to the middle."

Keli couldn't believe what she was hearing. After half a dozen matches where she had been a central part of the team, she was out. But Jesse looked at her and winked. "It's going to be okay."

The new Lady Dragon group walked back onto the floor with Keli left on the sidelines. Jim's adjustments were just what the Dragons needed. Jesse was back in her old position and made the Knights pay. Ashley was perfect at reading the blocking schemes and put the ball where she needed to, and the Dragons tied up the match with a 25-20 win.

Keli quickly told Jim as the game ended that she was really ready to play. Jim didn't respond to her statement and focused on the players coming off the floor. He had made up his mind to finish with this group.

Jim's roster changes turned out to be the right decision. The Knights didn't have enough strength up front to stop the Dragons now that everyone was clicking again. Match point came on a perfect back set to Alix, who hammered home the final point.

The Dragons had completed step one—a league championship and the number-one seed from the league going into the state tourney. On the inside Keli was filled with jealousy and envy, but she forced a smile and congratulated her teammates.

By the time the girls had spread out finding their friends and family, Keli was ready to cry. She didn't know what to say when Ashley walked up to her and gave her a hug. Ashley pulled back from the hug and looked right at her. "So you played like crap today," and then she started to laugh. "We have all had games like that. Go ask any of them," as she twirled around pointing. "The point is we won; we're a team. God knows you have picked up others when they had their crap games. It was someone else's turn to pick you up today." Ashley looked back into Keli's eyes for an answer.

Keli's eyes were welled up with tears as she nodded. "I know you're right. I'm just mad at myself, that's all. I can't believe how bad I played."

Keli wiped away the tears when she saw Cindy and Frank walking towards them. "Congratulations, ladies" came from both parents. "Sherwood almost had you," chuckled Frank as he gave Ashley, then Keli a quick hug.

Frank grabbed Keli's shoulder and gave her the same analysis that she just received from Ashley. "So, you sure didn't have your A game today, did ya?" Frank laughed again, trying to loosen it up. "Heck, I was wondering when you were going to have one. Most kids can't go more than four or five in a row without stubbing their toe." He shook her shoulder gently and said, "Shake it off. It happens to the best of us."

Cindy gave Keli a simple frown. "Don't worry about it, sweetie. It's just a game, and besides, you still won."

Frank looked down at his watch. "Hey, we'd better go. Our reservations are at 9:00."

He glanced at each of the girls and said, "You two are staying at the house tonight, right? No big parties either!"

CHAPTER 55

AN ENCOUNTER WITH GRETA

When the two girls pulled into the driveway at Ashley's, Austin's car was parked there with the hatchback open.

Keli jumped out of the car and motioned for Ashley to do the same. "Come on, Ashley, let's go inside and see what's going on."

Just then Greta and Austin came around the corner with their arms filled. All of them stopped dead in their tracks for a second. Keli was the first to speak. "Hi Greta. You kind of freaked us out when we pulled in. How've you been?"

Her comments somehow unfroze everyone. Greta headed towards the back of Austin's car with Austin following her. As she put the bag in the back, she smiled and said, "I really wasn't expecting you to be back yet from the game. Who won anyways?" Then she quickly went on. "Austin and I are just here picking up some of my stuff before we head back up towards Seattle."

Even if it was just for a split second, Greta seemed like her old self. Greta smiled and headed back towards the house, with the rest of them trailing her. Ashley had yet to speak.

At the bottom of the stairs were another bag and a smallish box. Greta grabbed the bag and Austin picked up the box. Again everyone stood frozen wondering what to say.

Keli approached Greta to give her a hug, but she could tell Greta wasn't open to it as she moved a half step back.

Greta looked back towards Ashley and said, "Take care of yourself, okay? Tell Frank hi for me too." Then she walked out the door without saying another word. Austin looked at both of them and left without ever speaking.

Ashley and Keli stood there watching as the two disappeared around the corner. Keli slowly started to close the door as they heard the low growl of Austin's car pulling out of the driveway. When Keli turned around, she found Ashley sitting on the second stair leaning over with her face in her hands.

Keli sat down beside her. "I know that was amazingly hard. Do you want to talk about what just happened? How are you feeling about seeing Greta? She looked a little skinnier to me."

Ashley answered, "I really don't want to talk about her. I am very angry about the whole thing. This past month or so I have tried to block it all out of my mind. Maybe it isn't the best way to handle it, but I am tired of thinking about her and her choices."

CHAPTER 56

LINDSAY'S DECISION

The final bell rang. Keli wandered towards the gym. Actually she was dragging herself there today. It was the first day since she had made the Varsity that she didn't want to go to practice. There was no way she wanted to face Coach Lindsay. She was sure Jim had told her about the game on Friday, and she surely didn't want to find out about her decision.

As Lindsay's office came into view, Keli could see the light was on but she couldn't force herself to stop, and so she went right on by and into the locker room. She slowly dressed and was thinking about how practice might go when Jesse poked her head around the corner and yelled in. "We have a meeting in the prep room before practice today. Hurry up, ladies! Coach said 10 minutes!"

Ashley was waiting for Keli by the prep room. She had a big grin on her face and said, "You know the coach just wants to hammer you 'cuz you played so crappy last Friday."

"Very funny. I probably won't play again the rest of the year," answered Keli.

"Right. Sure you won't..." Ashley held the door open for Keli. As she passed, Ashley whispered in her ear, "Sometimes you whine too much. Has anyone ever told you that?"

The rest of the team was already there. Keli was relieved that the coaches weren't. Everyone was talking softly in small groups, and Keli sat down and took a deep breath.

The door opened and everyone turned around to see Coach Lindsay and Coach Jim walk in and shut the door behind them. They made their way to the front of the room with their clipboards in hand. Lindsay asked for everyone's attention. Jim stood a few feet away looking around the room as if he were analyzing the mood of the team.

Lindsay looked down at her clipboard and started to speak. "Okay, ladies, we have a lot to go over today before practice. First, I am very proud of you. It was very important to win the league. Now we get to take another step."

She looked back up. "That season is now over as of today!" She scanned the room trying to make eye contact with each player, making sure she had their attention.

"Today we start the second season and, for some of you, your last season as a Dragon." She looked at Jesse and some of the other seniors.

Lindsay walked over to the podium and set the clipboard down, then stepped closer to the players. "I believe is this the best team I have ever coached, for talent, attitude, and most of all desire. The state tournament begins Thursday, so we don't have much time to prepare. Winning our league helped. We don't have any playoff games to go through and that allows us to focus on our strategy."

She walked back over by the podium and looked over at Jim. "We believe this team can really make a run at the championship. It's been our goal all year. Sometimes goals can be more wishful than others. I..." She looked at Jim, then said, "We believe it's not wishful thinking but very attainable if we all work together and you believe in yourselves and your teammates."

Again she looked back at Jim, who gave her a slight nod. Lindsay looked back and fidgeted with her clipboard for a second, then said, "I have some news for you all. I wanted you to hear it from me first."

All the players seemed to straighten up a bit in their chairs, bracing for news that in their hearts they already knew.

The coach seemed to freeze for a few seconds; tears welled up in her eyes. With one more quick glance at her clipboard, she raised her head and spoke, her voice cracking, "I want you all to know that it was an extremely hard decision. I have enjoyed these past eight years so much. But this past weekend I was offered the head coaching position back at my alma mater Montana State. After talking it over with my family and friends, I have decided to accept the position. I will finish out this season of course..." She slowly looked at the room smiling at each girl. Keli and some of the others also had tears in their eyes.

Lindsay turned away for a second to regain her composure. Jim jumped right in and said, "Practices for the next three days will start at 4:00 instead of 3:15." He pointed to the video machine. "Right after school we will watch film and discuss strategies on how we are going to approach the tournament. Make sure your parents and any other commitments you have are cleared until after State." He looked around the room and asked if there were any questions. Lindsay was turned back towards the conversation and looked for questions too.

Jesse stood up, tears running down both cheeks. "Coach, I think I can speak for the whole team...we are excited for you. You have been amazing and we know you have had other chances to leave." She started to clap and looked around at the rest of the players, who all stood and started to clap.

Keli stood there clapping with tears flowing freely down her cheeks. She felt an arm give her a hug; she looked to her left to see Ashley standing there with her arm around her. Ashley was crying too.

Lindsay's lips trembled and the tears came back again. Jim handed her a few tissues and took over the conversation again. "Ok, let's have a seat and watch some film."

By the end of practice, it felt like the first day of the season. Everyone was sweaty and exhausted. The sad emotions that had started the day were now dominated by moans and groans from teammates making their way out of the gym.

Jesse walked by on her way out and said, "Great practice today," looking at both Keli and Ashley.

Ashley confirmed to Keli that she was back. "You really hit the ball great today." She slapped Keli gently on her back, propelling her towards the exit, and said, "Actually, I was a little worried that your funk from the game last week and the news today was going to affect you, but you sure played your way out of it."

As they veered towards their own cars, Ashley continued her lecture. "I expect you to go see Coach tomorrow even though you didn't go today. You two have this thing and you need to talk. Big Frank says it's never good to burn bridges. Coach has been there for you all year! You'd better go see her tomorrow!"

Keli didn't respond, but she heard every word.

The drive back to Falls City was filled with Ashley's comments ringing loud through her thoughts. It was already dark and raining lightly by the time she got back into town. She could see the restaurant was busy with all the cars around it. She threw on her Dragon warm-up jacket as she walked across the street towards the restaurant. Today she proudly walked into the restaurant wearing it.

The door clanged as she entered and as usual, it brought most of the eyes in the building to see who had entered. Cindy saw her right away and smiled. Keli busted up laughing seeing Frank sitting on her favorite stool by the cash register.

Over in the big corner booth were Charlee and her family. Kay waved at her to come over. Keli smiled and looked at Charlee to see if she was also welcoming her over. Charlee gave her a blank stare.

Keli headed towards their booth past Frank, who was sipping his coffee. "Hello there, boss, what brings you out this way?" Keli giggled and patted him on the shoulder as she headed towards Charlee and her family.

Kay slid over to make room for her. "Come sit down. Do you want to eat with us? We are just getting ready to order."

Keli glanced at Charlee, who frowned, then back to Kay. "Sorry I can't. I have a ton of homework. I just stopped here on the way home to say hi to Mom real quick. How are you guys doing?" Keli looked directly at Charlee.

Charlee shrugged her shoulders, then answered. "Things are pretty good, I guess."

Bill interrupted the awkward conversation. "Congratulations on the season. You and your team have really done well. It sounds like this has really worked out for you." He looked at Kay and Charlee, then continued. "We have been following you through the paper. So when does the tournament begin?

Keli's face blossomed into a huge smile. "It starts Thursday in Portland. It's a long ways but if you could come up, it would be great. The finals are on Saturday."

"It would be a fun thing to do," answered Kay, "but my parents are in town this weekend. Are you sure you can't stay for dinner? It's our treat." She tried handing Keli a menu.

"Really thanks, but practice went long tonight and as it is, I'll be up 'til midnight. Maybe after the season is over and things calm down, we can all get together for dinner." Keli looked at her mom. "Has she introduced you to her new friend?"

Glenn laughed, "We all know Frank."

Frank stopped her on the way. "So how did practice go today? Ashley just called me and told me Lindsay did take the job. How are you doing with the news?"

Cindy stopped by the cash register to listen to Keli's answer.

She stammered for a couple of seconds trying to find the right words; then she threw up her arms. "I am all over the place actually. I get mad, then sad, then happy for her." She looked at her mom. "I guess I am mainly sad. She has taught me a lot about the game, and I am sad she won't be there to teach me next year," Keli folded her arms against her chest, "but right now I am really not going to think about it."

She headed for the door. Cindy called after her. "You need to call Sticky. He was in here at lunch telling me you never returned his call."

Keli nodded and headed for her car. On the way up the hill towards her house, she dialed Sticky's number. When he answered, she got right into her apology.

"Hey, don't worry about it," he said. "Your mom told me that things are pretty crazy for you right now. Did your coach decide to take the job?"

"Yeah, she did take it. I am pretty bummed. So what's new with you?"

There was a long pause. "Well, the reason I called a few days ago...I was wondering if you want to go with me to the winter formal."

It was Keli's turn to pause. "Sure, I guess, as long as it doesn't interfere with volleyball." Keli knew in the back of her mind that it might conflict with her commitment with Steen. "Do you know what day?"

Sticky's voice became very excited. "It's two weeks from this Saturday. I think you're done with State after this weekend, right?"

Keli's heart leapt with relief. "So it's two weeks after this weekend, right?"

Sticky confidently confirmed it.

She pulled into the driveway and looked across to see if she could see him in his window but his room was dark. "Well, it sounds like fun. Let's talk next week about the details. Until then I am buried with homework and volleyball."

"Perfect," answered Sticky, "call me when you get caught up and maybe we can go for a hike or something too. Hey, good luck this weekend. Do you think you have a chance to win?"

"I'm not sure. The film I saw today tells me we have our work cut out for us. Some of the teams in the tourney are really good. I think we are pretty good too...so we'll see."

Sticky almost choked. "You guys watch film on other teams? Wow, you really are big time. Well, hey, anyways, good luck. I would try to get up there, but we have our banquet this weekend."

The call ended and Keli sent one more glance over to Sticky's house to see if he was watching for her as she watched for him, but his room was still dark.

CHAPTER 57

COACH, DO YOU HAVE A MINUTE?

Libby and Jesse were waiting for Keli outside her last class. As she walked out of the classroom, she shot them a quizzical look. "Are you two lost?"

Jesse quickly answered. "Nope, we're here to escort you to Lindsay's office." Libby moved to the other side of Keli and they led her towards the gym and a meeting with the coach.

She started to laugh. "Let me guess. Ashley put you two up to this, didn't she?"

Neither answered; instead, they led her straight to Lindsay's open door and pushed her in. Lindsay smiled and leaned back in her chair. "I was wondering if you were going to stop by today. Have a seat for a minute."

Keli sat down in her usual chair and looked around the room.

The coach leaned forward. "Jim tells me you had a pretty tough go of it last Friday."

Keli looked down at the floor. "I sucked actually."

"Well, you looked pretty good yesterday, so whatever it was, it looks like you got it out of your system."

Finally Keli said, "Coach, I need to apologize to you."

Lindsay looked serious. "What for?"

"Last week when you left for your job interview and I heard rumors why you were gone, I got very angry and blamed you for deserting us. The whole team was on your side except me. It affected the way I played on Friday and almost cost the team. Jim had to pull me or I might have dragged everyone down with me. My grandpa and I talked last night for quite a while." Keli sighed. "Actually, he talked for most of it and I just listened."

"You taking the job at your old school was like me leaving Falls City to come here. I made a lot of people mad and for my two best friends it was like I was rejecting them. Even now, one of them still really hasn't accepted my decision. Gramps said what you and I have done is very similar. I didn't realize it until he explained it."

Keli leaned forward, looking at the floor. "Gramps told me that it's part of life to move on when the calling is right. He reminded me of our conversation last summer about my motives...it's all about motives and if they are right, then we should follow the calling. I did it and so did you."

She looked back up from the floor and right at Lindsay, who was looking at her. "Coach, I'm proud of what I have done and I'm proud of you for what you're doing. I'm not sure if I can put into words what you have done for me this season. I came here scared and struggling to keep up."

Keli stood up. "You figured me out and walked me through it. I know I have a long ways to go to become the player I want to be, but if it weren't for what you did for me this year, I would have never had the chance." She walked over to the front of Lindsay's desk and stuck out her hand. The coach stood up and walked around the desk and instead of the handshake she gave Keli a hug.

"Okay, it's my turn to talk," said Lindsay. She motioned for Keli to sit down again. Lindsay leaned up against the front of her desk and folded her arms across her chest. "First, thank you for coming in here and telling me all this. That was one of the first things that really caught my eye about you last summer. Regardless of your fears, you have had the ability to share them and ask for help. The day you came in here after I put you on the JV team was one of the most meaningful days I've ever had as a coach."

Lindsay looked at the clock to see how much time she had. "I want you to know that the past couple of years when I have had offers to leave for some pretty good jobs, I have turned them down. When my old alma mater came to me about going there, my first reaction was I can't, I'm not good enough, what if I fail, what will people think of me? They were the same old tapes that kept me from taking the jobs before. It was you who changed it for me. I watched you walk through all the challenges back in your hometown and struggle to fit in and make it here. A few months ago you sat in the same chair and said, 'When the student is ready, the teacher will appear.' You told me you were ready. Do you remember that?"

Lindsay smiled at her and repeated, "Do you remember?"

Keli smiled back and nodded. "Yes, I do remember."

"At that point, I was ready to tell my old school I wasn't going to take the job. My father called me and we had a long phone call where I just listened, and he reminded me of the story I had told him a few months about what you said. When he was finished, I knew I was going to take the job. Those were all the things that I watched you walk through. So, Keli Stennes, I want to thank you for being my teacher. I will never forget it."

The coach stood up before the tears started coming down. "We have a tournament to prepare for and it's time we get started."

They walked out together. Most of the girls were stretching or playing pepper. Lindsay waved at Jim, and he opened the door to the strategy room and blew his whistle.

Watching the film put a fresh fear into the team. Libby and Jesse interjected at various times when they recognized players from the club seasons. Lindsay did most of the talking, stopping the film at random and explaining how to attack weaknesses and to counter strengths.

Half an hour later, Jim turned off the monitor. "Tomorrow we will watch some of our own film. What you have seen for the past couple of days hopefully helps you understand what we're going up against."

Lindsay interrupted. "There are as many as eight teams talented enough to win this tournament." She looked around the room. "We are one of those teams. Great teams that should win championships sometimes don't." She put her hands together. "Why do teams that are heavy favorites to win get upset?"

Ashley spoke up first. "Sometimes it's overconfidence and other times the underdog just outplays them. They are the better team on that day." She shrugged her shoulders. "Upsets are just a part of sports."

The coach nodded. "Yes, they are, but if you ask any heavily favored team that'll give you an honest answer, they'll tell you that they weren't able to play through adversity. Champions must be able to recognize when things aren't going their way and figure out a way to overcome whatever is thrown at them."

Lindsay walked around the room. "Who can give me examples of adversity we might face this weekend?"

Jesse quickly said. "Bad calls by the refs."

Libby looked around the room. "Unforced errors...like missed serves."

"How about injuries?" added Keli.

Lindsay was nodding the whole time. Her voice was excited. "Exactly. Those are the things that can really drag a team down." She stopped in the middle of the room. "What else?"

The room was quiet. Lindsay spun around in the room. "Come on, ladies, what are other adversities we might run into this weekend? Think about games we have lost over the years or almost lost. What kinds of things were we faced with?"

Jim assisted the conversation. "How about the good play of the other team?"

Lindsay picked up the topic. "Exactly. What happens when a player or two or for that matter the team you're playing just goes off. Everything they are hitting or digging is working."

The coach wandered back to the front of the room. "All these things can cause a team to get frustrated, lose focus, lose confidence. We must be as tight a team as we have ever been. Nothing should get to the team's focus. The bench, the coaches, and most of all the ladies on the court must be completely together. None of these things we've talked about should be able to break our team. The state champion will be the team that can play through the most adversity."

She paused for a few seconds. "Ladies, if you play your game and stay in your zone, we can be champions! We have two more practices to tune ourselves. I expect these to be our best practices of the year. Jim handed you all an itinerary that we need to follow when we're up in Portland. Make sure your parents review everything."

Jim knew she was done. "Okay, ladies, let's get to the court and warm up. After that, I want the hitters on court 2 with me, and everyone else with Coach Lindsay on court 1."

CHAPTER 58

STATE TOURNAMENT, HERE WE COME!

"Hurry up, Keli, your grandpa is here."

"I'm coming," yelled Keli, as she struggled down the stairs with two full bags and her backpack.

Tom walked in the front door just as Keli hit the last stair and dropped the bags on the floor. "Just a minute, Gramps," she huffed as she headed towards the kitchen. "I need to say goodbye to Mom."

Cindy met her halfway. "Good luck, sweetie. I wish I could come up tonight but I just can't get away from work. Frank and I will drive up first thing in the morning. Make sure to call me tonight after your game."

Tom picked up Keli's bags. "If we don't get going, Keli, you might as well drive up with your mom tomorrow 'cuz you're going to miss your bus."

Just as they got into the car, Keli's phone rang. She looked at the caller ID. It was Sticky. Before she answered, she looked over at his window. He was standing there waving at her.

Sticky said, "Looks like you're off. I just wanted to wish you good luck. I hope you go all the way!" The excitement in his voice calmed a bit. "One more thing, I also want you to know I'm sorry for these past few months. I really haven't acted much like a friend. What you have done is great, and I've been pretty selfish in the way I acted."

Keli smiled and waved at him. "Thank you. It means a lot to me that you called. I should have been more up front in the beginning. I know it taught me a lesson."

The beeping sound of another call interrupted theirs. Sticky heard it too. "Well, sounds like you need to go. Kick butt up there, okay?"

"Thanks for the call, Sticky. I'll talk to you later." Keli quickly flashed over to the other call.

"So where are you? The bus leaves in 20 minutes!"

Keli laughed. "Well, good morning to you too, Ash. I'll be there on time. Save me a seat, okay?" She glanced over towards her old high school as they drove by and waved at Dan and Tracie as they walked up the sidewalk.

"Okay, fine. Just hurry up," answered Ashley nervously. "You know the coach. Being late is never a good thing."

As Keli put her phone in her backpack, Tom asked, "So do you think you can win it?"

She looked at him as he stared at the road. "I hope we can. We practiced pretty well all week. Coach says we can if we play hard and don't let anything get in our way."

Keli could see Tom frown. "Well, I was hoping for a little more conviction from you, I guess. Belief is power. If I were you, I'd start addressing the issues where you have doubt. I hope tonight when you walk out onto the court, you know in your heart that you're going to win the match."

He looked at her quickly. "Believing in something allows for a certain type of calmness. It's that calmness that allows a champion or a leader to overcome whatever challenge comes their way. Without that inner calmness, even the very best will eventually succumb to pressures brought on by adversity."

Keli looked at him in awe. Her first thought was "Wow, did you rehearse that before today?" Strangely enough, it made sense. She laid her head against the headrest and thought back to the game a few weeks ago when she had gone into her own world. Everything had slowed down, her emotions had stayed calm, and she had played in a way that she didn't think possible.

She rolled her head towards her grandfather. "Thanks, Gramps. I'm not sure why all that made sense, but it did."

A couple minutes later the old Jeep pulled into the school parking lot. Around back by the gym was the Dragon Wagon all decorated with slogans made from shaving cream. Half the team was standing around waiting to board the bus and talking with a few parents and friends.

The Jeep came to a stop near the bus. Ashley jumped off and raced over to her. She yelled loud enough that everyone around the bus could hear. "We're heading for Portland for three days and bringing home the hardware."

Tom looked at Keli and winked. Then he pointed at both of them. "I hope to see you Saturday. It's way too far for an old man like me to drive unless you plan on winning." He hesitated, then asked, "You do plan on winning, don't you?"

Both girls put huge grins on their faces and gave each other a high five, then got on the bus.

Keli looked around the bus and made eye contact with Alix, who seemed to be staring at her. Their eyes locked for a couple of seconds. To Keli's surprise, Alix mouthed, "Good luck," and then smiled. Keli stood up and reached her hand as far as she could across a couple of seats to Alix, who reached back and slapped it.

The event triggered euphoria throughout the bus; everyone started giving each other high fives. The coach finally had to settle them down after the bus driver told Lindsay everyone needed to stay seated.

A couple of hours later the bus pulled in front of their hotel in Portland. They could see the stadiums, the old Memorial Coliseum and the newer Rose Garden, right across the street.

"Wow...is that where we're playing?" Keli asked.

Jesse chuckled as she walked by. "Welcome to the big time, country girl."

It finally hit Keli. This was as far away from her old world as she had ever been. The team was checking into an amazing hotel. All of the very best teams and players were assembled to crown the best team in the state.

Ashley and Keli walked into their room, both racing to a bed, calling dibs. Keli was in a daze, "Ash, I can't believe this. We're staying in this hotel for the next three days. It's like we're celebrities or something."

Ashley laughed. "Dang, girl, we need to get you out more." She did a belly flop on her bed. "Wait 'til club season. We do this a lot."

As they came out of the elevator to meet with the coaches, Jesse pointed discretely towards the lobby entrance. They weren't alone; standing by the entrance of the lobby was the team from Shelton High, one of the teams in their pool. Both teams were trying to check each other out, but neither wanted to show it.

Coach Jim handed each girl her tournament pass and they headed for the Rose Garden for their scheduled 30-minute practice. As they passed some of the Shelton players, Keli made eye contact with a couple of them. The Shelton players looked away immediately.

Keli whispered to Ashley, "We are going to blow them out."

"Really?" answered Ashley. "How do you know this?"

"I just know," she replied. "I just know."

Keli was in awe when she walked into the Rose Garden. She was in the finest athletic building in the state. Jesse put her hand on her shoulder. "There aren't many things better than this."

Keli touched her player's pass, then looked at Jesse. "I am pretty sure this is heaven. It's better than I imagined."

Their practice was the last of the day. By the time they finished, there were already a few hundred people watching. The teams from the first match were standing by the court ready to take over as soon as the Dragons' time was up. Coach Lindsay pointed to a group of seats about halfway up. "Let's all take a seat up there and watch the first game or two."

The first game went back and forth between Medford and Beaverton. Ashley sat there calling out hitters and challenging Keli to keep up with recognizing front row players from back row. She was calling out exactly where the ball was going to go even before the setter set it. Keli was always impressed at Ashley's ability to see the game from one step ahead.

At the start of the second game, Lindsay came over and sat down beside them. "You two really need to watch this match closely." She pointed as the two teams walked back onto the court for the start of game two. "I think Beaverton will win. Remember we saw a little film on them a couple of days ago. They do a good job on slides and dumping. You really need to recognize and be ready to call it out when you see it coming."

Keli watched Lindsay and Ashley go back and forth discussing the game. Just as Lindsay predicted, Beaverton made it two straight, easily winning the game. When Lindsay had moved back to her own seat, Keli leaned over. "I have a lot to learn. You two were in a different world. I couldn't keep up."

"Don't worry about it." Ashley turned and looked at her. Keli had just seen a side of Ashley she hadn't seen before. "Make no mistake. I really know my position. You just follow my signals and we will have no problem with this team." Ashley was in a different zone; even the tone of her voice was different.

Beaverton made short work by winning three straight. The Dragons then all headed for the exit, and Keli honed in on the body language of her teammates. They all seemed so businesslike. Most of the normal playful behavior had disappeared.

After dinner, Keli and Ashley rode the elevator to their floor in silence. Keli spoke first when they got back to their room. "Ash, what was it like last year when you guys were here? Where you nervous?"

Ashley thought for a few seconds. "Maybe a little more than I am right now."

Keli was surprised by her answer. "You're nervous? Like right now?"

Ashley lifted her head up off the pillow. "Sure. Why does that surprise you?"

"Well, you seem so calm. So do all the other players. And I'm freaking out on the inside. I really want to play well, but our last game is all I can think about. What if..."

Ashley sat up and responded sharply. "What if what?" She pointed at Keli. "Start thinking about good passes and being ready to hit. We are here to win this thing. Get out of yesterday; none of that matters anymore. Tonight is all there is, Keli, I'm not kidding. We need you to play solid. I'm counting on it."

CHAPTER 59

A STOMACHACHE OF NERVES

The walk back to the Rose Garden was brisk, the air cold. Keli looked around at all the lights and noises of the city. It seemed so different, foreign almost, to her world back in Falls City.

This time they entered through the players-only entrance and waited at the end of the tunnel that led to the court. The first game of the evening had just ended and the losing team was walking towards them, most of their heads hanging down. As they passed, Ashley whispered in Keli's ear, "That is not going to be us!"

Finally the time had come. Jesse was in front of the team, and she turned and walked towards the floor. The rest of the Dragons followed behind her single file. The sound system was playing music loud.

As they stretched, Keli glanced around the arena. She was amazed at how big it was. The warm ups flew by, and her mind immediately began to race when the final whistle blew. A cold shiver came over her as she walked towards the bench. The first thing that hit her was that she wasn't good enough to be here. Then her mind went into a free fall of negative thoughts: What if she couldn't do it? What if she made a fool of herself? What if she let her teammates down? By the time she got to the bench, her stomach ached from nerves, and she thought she was going to throw up. Her eyes darted, looking for escape routes.

Suddenly she felt a tight squeeze on her left hand. She looked over to see Libby pulling her towards the huddle. Libby brought her in tight by the coach.

Keli stood there frozen on Lindsay and her every word just hoping and praying for the feelings to go away. Libby squeezed a little tighter and didn't let go until the coach was finished talking.

Shelton's starters were introduced first as the visiting team. Keli and the rest of the Dragons clapped politely for their opponents each time one was introduced.

Keli couldn't stand still; the nerves in her stomach were starting to build again. She looked up in the stands hoping to see her grandpa, but there were too many people to scan. So she looked back at the coach, who was giving last-minute in-structions to Ashley.

The PA announcer finished with the Fighting Irish. It was the Dragons' turn. One by one the announcer called the substitutes onto the floor. Finally it was time for the starters. Keli felt her hands start to shake; she quickly folded them on top of her head. Finally she heard the words. "Starting at outside hitter, a junior, 5'11", number 21, Keli Stennes." Cheers came from her teammates as she headed for the court to greet Ashley, Alix, and Jesse, who had been called before her.

Ashley put her arm around her. "This is what it's all about, Sis...this is it!"

Keli started to feel strength come back to her wobbly legs. She looked through the net at the Shelton team. She sensed their nervousness too. Libby was the last Dragon called. She ran onto the court with her fist raised to the middle of the huddle. "It's time, ladies, right now! Come on right now."

The Lady Dragons all stuck their arms in the air and on Jesse's count of 1-2-3, they all yelled "RIGHT NOW!"

Shelton had first serve. Keli backed up from her left outside position to pass. Her hands were sweaty and her only thought was please hit it to someone else. She made a quick glance at Lindsay, who looked right back at her.

Keli's eyes picked back up on the server, who went right after her. The serve was a fast topspin ball diving in front of her. She made a quick move forward and dug the ball up. Ashley had to chase it a bit towards the 10-foot line, but she made a perfect backset to Alix, who calmly slammed a perfect kill cross-court from the right side.

The Dragons met at the 10-foot line. Ashley was now in charge. "Okay, we are on our way!"

Alix prepared to serve, Ashley called out the hitters, and the Dragons were ready. It was a complete game, nearly flawless. Shelton had no answers for all the Dragon weapons. Ashley moved the ball around the court, always seeming to pick the best hitter to attack with. The game ended quickly, 25-10.

The nerves were gone, and Keli was anxious for game two to start as the Dragons grouped around the coach, who wasn't ready to offer any praise. She kept tapping her clipboard. "We have to be more aggressive on the net. We are late to the blocks."

Game two was the same as the first. Shelton was just overmatched. Jesse completely dominated the second game. Keli got very little action until game point. Shelton's best outside hitter hammered the ball hard to the right of her. All she had time to do was stick her arm out; the ball hit perfectly on the inside of her forearm and floated softly straight to Ashley. Keli raced to get out-side; the set came right where she wanted it. She flew off the floor and crushed the ball right beyond the 10-foot line for game point.

Keli made eye contact with the Shelton middle, who was late to get over to block the ball. It was easy for Keli to see she was completely defeated.

Lindsay knew the match was over and played her bench in game three. She knew she might not have another chance to give them the opportunity. The bench took full advantage of the opportunity by downing the Irish 25-20, giving the Dragons an easy opening win.

Ashley caught up to Keli as they made their way to the tunnel. "Hey, you feel better now that you have one of these past us?"

Keli took a deep breath and smiled. "Oh, yeah. You have no idea how freaked out I was before the game. I almost hurled twice. I have never been so nervous in my entire life."

As they walked into the tunnel, last year's State champs started for the court. The star of the team wasn't paying attention and ran straight into Keli. Both girls toppled to the floor. It happened so fast that no one really knew what happened. Jesse was there first to help them up.

"Angie, you're still as clumsy as ever," laughed Jesse, but Angie wasn't in a joking mood.

She stared right at Jesse. "You just keep your cast of nobodies out of my way."

Jesse stared back and put her hands in the air. "I guess we will see you on Saturday."

The Beavers took the floor as the Dragons watched from the edge of the floor. Libby wiped her face with her towel. "You know, Angie has always been a bit..."

The coach interrupted her. "I think we should conduct ourselves maturely." She looked at her team. "You can stay and watch the first two games; then I want you back to the hotel and in bed by 10:30. We will meet for breakfast at 8:30. We play our first game tomorrow at 11:00." She looked around at each one of them. "Break the rules and you will go home immediately."

Keli grabbed Ashley. "Let's watch for a while," she said, but Ashley pulled away.

"No way. Dad taught me to never watch your real competition when you know they are going to dominate an opponent. Let's go. Dad says there are a couple of reasons...it can psyche you out thinking they are better than they really are or he says they never really play the same. Like substitutions are different or the sets aren't the same because they generally come off better passes. We'll watch them tomorrow. Besides, I'm tired and starving." Both girls grabbed for their cell phones at the same time to call home.

Keli couldn't wait for her mom to answer the phone. After the phone rang the fourth time, Ashley yelled over to her. "Your mom is with my dad. Do you want to talk to her?"

Ashley handed her the phone. "They are driving up here right now!"

Keli reached for the phone as they entered the hotel and began talking immediately, but it was still Frank on the other end. "Do you ladies want to have dinner with us?"

"Uh, thanks for the offer, but I think we are going to eat now." Keli could hear her mom yell, "Congratulations, sweetie!" A huge smile came across her face. "Tell her thanks for me."

"Sure," answered Frank. "Ashley said you guys really dominated them tonight."

"Yeah, Lindsay said we had our freebie. From here on out, it's going to take a lot more to win." Keli started to laugh mid-sentence. "Well, I think I need to feed Ashley. She's eating a paper cup."

The evening slowed when they finished the pizza and showered. Just before 10:30, there was a loud knock. Libby yelled through the door, "Lights out, ladies."

The room got quiet as they both started to fall asleep. Keli sat straight up in bed. "Do you realize our parents are driving to Portland, you know...like together! Do you think they are going to have separate rooms?"

A giggle came from Ashley's bed. "Oh, I am sure they will have separate rooms. Go to sleep. We have to play in the morning."

Keli lay back down. The reality had just sunk in. Her mom was starting to get serious. After all these years of having exclusive rights to Cindy's time and heart, Keli realized things would never be the same. Jealousy began to heat her bed until she finally had to kick off her covers to cool off. She looked back over at Ashley, who was asleep. She lay there and thought again about how things were changing in her life.

The tiny red light from the smoke detector caught her attention. She smiled to herself. I wouldn't be here right now and my mom wouldn't be on her way up here with Frank. After a few more seconds of staring at the light the jealousy dissipated and a calm happiness replaced it, she rolled over onto her side and said quietly but out loud, "Good night, Mom."

CHAPTER 60

DAY TWO

The team met for breakfast in a small banquet room. Coach Lindsay finished her last sip of her coffee, then stood up. "Okay, ladies. Last night was a good win, but I guarantee you all that today's matches will be like being on a whole new planet. Shelton is not an elite team, and on top of that, they played extremely poorly. We need to win both matches today to be assured of making the championship bracket. Both of these teams are very good, and if you don't play well, you could be just like Shelton..." she paused, "heading home at the end of the day."

"Our only focus right now should be on Gresham. The Gophers are very, very big!" Her eyes got intense. "Do not let their size intimidate you. Size is great in this game, but if that was all that mattered, then they could give them the trophy and we could all go home."

Jim interrupted the coach. "Nothing changes, ladies. You need to read the blocks and hit the ball accordingly. If you have to read blocks, don't just make up your mind where you are going to hit the ball as soon as you see your set."

Lindsay took back the conversation. "We just need to play our game. Ashley will run the offensive out there, so be ready at all times."

She looked at Ashley. "Make sure you cover your hitters. I don't want any balls hitting the floor inside the 10-foot line."

Ashley nodded as she took a bite of her muffin.

Lindsay looked over at Jim to see if he had anything else. She looked back at the team. "Okay, be in the tunnel by 10:35...no later!" She started to sit down and then added, "Ladies, all we need to do is play our game this morning and we will win this match." She stared at each of them sizing them up to see if they believed her.

It took a few seconds for the dining room to rid itself of the seriousness left by the coaches. Libby looked across the table at Keli and winked at her. "So I hear you almost chunked up the floor last night."

Her face immediately turned red. Ashley buried her head under her arm to protect herself. The whole table broke into laughter. Keli looked back at Libby, "So, I got a little nervous last night!"

Jesse came to her rescue. "Hey, we're just teasing you a bit." She pointed to Ashley. "Two years ago she made Varsity as a freshman...she was so nervous that she put her uniform on backwards. The referee had to come up to her before the game started and have her turn it around."

The whole room busted up laughing. Even the coaches joined in. Keli joined in laughing at the others and herself. It was just what she needed.

The walk to the arena was loose and a laugh fest for most of the players. Keli was right in the middle trying to get more details from Libby and Jesse about Ashley having her jersey on backwards. But the laughing ended when they all walked through the entrance and into the tunnel to wait for their second pool-play game.

There was a loud cheer, and then the announcer came over the PA system. "Beaverton wins, 3 games to 1. Gresham and Dallas, report to the court. Captains and coaches, to the scorers' table, please."

The Dragons walked onto the court. The stands were mostly empty during the morning session. Keli scanned the crowd and found her mom smiling and waving at her. She laughed out loud when Cindy stood up and proudly displayed her Dallas Dragon sweatshirt.

Jesse and the coaches returned from the meeting. Lindsay was dragging a ball cart. "Okay, our court. Let's go hitting lines."

A few minutes later the PA announcer read off the names of the starters. Today Keli had butterflies but it wasn't anything like the night before.

Dallas had first serve and like every game this year, Ashley stood behind the line waiting for the whistle. Keli looked across the net at Gresham for the first time. She was a little stunned at their size. The whole front line players were all over 6'. Coach Jim's words rang in her head. "Just read the blocks." Just read the blocks, she told herself.

Finally the whistle blew and as in a lot of their games, Ashley hit a huge driving down ball that was shanked out by the right back. The Dragons met in the middle brimming with confidence. The first game was going all Dragons. With the score 18-13, Keli backed up from her front left position to take serve receive and just like the first rotation, they went after her again.

The serve perfectly split the seam between her and Libby. Keli called for it but at the last second hesitated and the ball hit the floor for an ace. Her teammates came quickly rallying around her. "No worries," yelled Jesse, "we'll get this one."

And then again, like the serve before, the ball split the same seam. Keli didn't hesitate this time, but the results were no better. The ball bounced off her arms and flew out of bounds. Point, Gresham.

Lindsay quickly called a timeout, sensing a meltdown. Keli jogged towards the huddle, fully expecting to be pulled. Jim met her before she got to the huddle.

"Now, listen, you've taken thousands of these in practice. It's all concentration; you have to watch the ball." His eyes were focused directly on hers. "I am not just saying this to say it. You need to zero in on the ball and nothing else. You know where to pass it...just make the play." He moved out of the way and let Keli go into the huddle.

Lindsay looked at her. "They are coming your way again. You have to make this play," she paused for a second staring at her. "You'll be fine. Just make a good pass and be ready to hit."

The Dragons walked back unto the court holding a slim 18-15 lead. They needed desperately to get service back and stop the bleeding.

Keli watched the Gresham player bounce the ball a couple of times. It was easy to see by the way she lined up that she was coming right back at her. She tossed the ball in the air and hammered it this time to Keli's left. Without any thought, Kei took one step and lifted the ball right to the center of the court.

Ashley ran under it. Keli knew she was going to put the ball out to her. The set was too far off the net to go to the middle. Ashley led her perfectly, Keli was locked on the ball, but she could feel the Gopher blockers setting up to take away the cross-court.

The quick set that Ashley gave her was perfect for the situation. She loved taking the lower quick sets down the line, and she met the ball perfectly with a full swing. Gresham's defense was set up with a player covering the line for a tip, but Keli hit it flush and the ball ricocheted off the defensive player's shoulder and out of bounds.

Keli jumped in the air and ran to the huddle. Ashley greeted her with "Great spot. If I get passes like that, I am going right back there. Be ready."

The Dragons held on to win game one, 25-21. Gresham came out flat in game two. They had put all their mental preparation into winning game one. Game two was all Dragons. With the score at 20-11, the Gophers called timeout, hoping to regroup and get back into the game.

Lindsay was uncommonly relaxed when they huddled up. "Okay, ladies, have a seat." It was the first time the coach had called for the players to sit during a timeout. Lindsay pulled a chair around and sat down herself to face the starters. The bench players huddled closely behind the coach to hear what she had to say.

"Ladies, before we came up here for the tournament, we had a long talk about playing through adversity. Guess what? You are playing a team right now that is struggling with figuring that out. I don't think they thought they were going to lose game one. But they did, and now they are all pressing too hard, not communicating, and looking for someone to make a play instead of doing it themselves."

She clapped her hands. "We need to finish them off before they figure it out." Then she pointed at each one of her players. She even looked over her shoulder to make sure the bench players were listening in. "We need to learn from their mistake. That could be us right now trying to figure out what to do. Remember this if we get ourselves in this situation."

The horn sounded ending the timeout. She stood and watched them walk back unto the floor. She hoped the example would stick with them if the need arose.

Ashley took over the huddle. "Okay, let's finish this game." The Dragons did just that running off five straight points, ending game two 25-11. The win was impressive and all the other coaches scouting the game took note.

Gresham was in the tank. This was easy to see when they stood there before the start of game three bickering as to what needed to be done. Lindsay yelled at the Dragon players and motioned at them to witness the breakdown that a very good team was going through.

Ashley started game three with six service aces in a row, and the Gophers were looking for a hole to climb in to hide from the embarrassment they were being dished.

Keli had her best game of the match with five kills. The last one was the match winner. Ashley had to chase down an ugly pass and made a perfect bump. Keli was completely charged when she left the floor, pounding a cross-court rocket that closed out the match with an exclamation point and a showdown with Pendleton for the right to go to the championship bracket.

Gresham, one of the pre-tourney favorites, was locked out of that bracket. Keli stood there and watched them exit the gym, Lindsay's speeches on adversity ringing in her ears. She was grabbed from behind by Libby and Jesse. "Come on, we have a meeting real quick."

CHAPTER 61

EVERY POINT IS ITS OWN GAME!

Jim was standing by the white diagram board scribbling some notes about Pendleton while Lindsay reviewed her notes on her clipboard. The players chatted quietly until Lindsay was ready to talk.

Lindsay raised her hand. "Okay, listen up. Ladies, that was a good win, but please realize we haven't done what we have come here to do yet. These wins are great, but there is a team across the way that is strategizing right now on how they can beat you. Don't forget they crushed Shelton this morning, and I am sure they believe they can beat you too."

She set her clipboard down and leaned against the desk. "Ladies, I am going to stress adversity again. Gresham was a team that could just as easily have been the State champions this year. They got rattled in that first game and couldn't adjust. Do you understand what I am trying to tell you? Think about it. Their season is over now. They had a chance and weren't able to stay together as players or as a team."

Lindsay moved to the middle of the room, and all the players' eyes followed her there. "We have had two fairly easy wins," she paused for a second, then finished her thought. "While that's great, we have to be ready for a team to come in and knock us on our butts for a game. Then we will be in the same situation as the Gophers. I'm telling you, champions are the teams that don't blink, that don't question, that don't expect someone else to do it. They continue to play within the game plan and their abilities."

She pounded her fist into her hand. "You must remember every point is its own game—you either win it or not. When it's over, it should have nothing to do with the next point. The only thing you should be thinking about, regardless of the outcome, is getting prepared for the next point. Great teams and great players find a way to move on and get ready to win the next point; it's the only thing that matters. If you can do that, the game and match will take care of themselves."

She looked at Keli. "Great job in the first game." She patted her on the shoulder as she walked by. "Anyone know why I gave her that compliment?"

Lindsay made a full circle looking for someone to answer, but none came.

"I gave her the compliment because she was faced with adversity. She boneheaded three plays in a row." Her description of Keli's play brought some giggles from the team. "What made it a great game for her is that she responded on the next play. She didn't pout or worse, give up. On the next play she made a good play...and guess what? Game over."

She raised her voice, "Ladies, that is what winning a championship is all about. Every game from here out will get much tougher, not to mention the pressure. We need to stay focused; we need to approach Pendleton as we have these first two matches. This is the match, ladies. We win this and we play for the championship tomorrow. We have worked for this all season." Lindsay took a towel from Alix and wiped her face and tossed the towel back to her.

Can I Play...

The coach looked over at Jim, who was standing by the board waiting to go over his notes. "Okay, ladies... Jim has diagramed Pendleton's strengths and weaknesses. After he's finished, everyone go back to the hotel for lunch and then everyone to their rooms for a little rest. We meet back here at 3 for our 3:30 game."

CHAPTER 62

THE GAME WITH PENDLETON

The lunch buffet was set up and ready when they walked into the banquet room. Most of the girls were quiet in their own thoughts. The coaches huddled up and talked in the corner of the small room. As they ate, Keli thought to herself how serious this had all become. She took a bite of turkey and scanned the room; it was nothing like a pre-game meal or lunch at school before other games. She wondered what everyone was thinking.

Finally her eyes caught Jesse's; she was sitting across the table staring back at her. Jesse doubled her fist and did a slight pump, then asked, "Are you ready for this afternoon?" The room was so quiet that her question caught the attention of everyone at the table. Now they were all staring at Keli for her answer.

Keli's lips tightened and she nodded her head confidently. She looked at Ashley and the rest of the team at her table and answered, "Yes, I am...I'm ready. To be honest, I was just sitting here looking at all of you, wondering what you were all thinking. The table is so quiet. We've never been this way all year."

Her eyes darted back and forth from Jesse to Ashley. "It just really hit me how serious everyone is taking all this." She leaned back and pulled the hood of her sweatshirt up over her head and continued. "When I came to Dallas to play for you, I never really thought about playing in all this. I really just wanted to see if I could make it on a good team. My real goal was to get good enough as a player so I could maybe get a scholarship and play in college."

She smiled as her eyes filled with tears. "Wow...I didn't think I would be getting emotional right now, but it has just dawned on me that I am playing with a team that is not only good, but on the verge of going to a level I never dreamed possible for someone like me and where I came from."

Keli reached for her napkin to wipe her eyes. "It's an honor to play with you all."

Ashley reached over and pulled the hood down off of Keli's head and said, "Dang, girl. All she asked was were you ready." The whole table erupted into laughter.

It was a perfect way to end the lunch break.

Three o'clock came quickly; it was time to go back to the arena. The Dragons grouped up in the lobby. As they waited for Alix and Morgan, the Beavers from Beaverton walked into the lobby. Keli's eyes met up with Angie, the girl who had knocked her over the first night of the tournament.

Angie walked straight up to Keli. They stood almost nose to nose. "Just so you understand how things will work tomorrow when we play you guys. When I hit the ball...you duck so you don't get hurt." A couple of the other Beaverton players laughed.

Keli just stared at her until Libby stepped in between the two players. Libby tried to disarm the situation, "Let's go, Keli. We can deal with her tomorrow."

But Keli stood there. Her face was red hot, and she desperately searched for something to say. Her teammates wanted her to step away and not make things worse.

Ashley was way on the other side of the group. She yelled out, stopping everyone in her tracks. "Keli, it's game point. What are you going to do? Come on. Right now." She said it a second time. "Right now, Keli, we have a game to play."

Finally Keli broke eye contact with the taunting player, and she walked out the exit. Her face was still on fire and her eyes were focused straight ahead as she walked quickly towards the arena.

The Dragons waited in the tunnel for the current match to end. Keli stood there with her arms folded looking off into space and ignoring every else. The usher waved them towards the floor, and Keli was the first to run out of the tunnel and onto the court. She quickly studied the team from Pendleton warming up.

Keli's anger retreated as she peppered with Alix and Libby. Ashley ran by, "Okay, we have serve and first on the court."

The team immediately went to hitting lines. Keli was first...Ashley set her high and tight, and Keli was off the floor, way off the floor, hitting a bullet almost straight down.

Jesse yelled at her, "Maybe we need to have Angie follow you around the rest of the tournament."

After their warm up, Keli looked around the arena for the first time; sitting in the same place was her mom, Frank, and Tom.

Ashley walked up and patted her on the back. "Well, I see our cheering gallery...all three of them are here."

Lindsay called for everyone to huddle up. Keli's eyes were still beady with focus as she listened to the coach give out the final instructions. Her mind started to drift back to the confrontation earlier, but she clapped her hands and jumped up and down a couple of times to shake it off. Lindsay looked at her as if to say, "Are you okay?"

The PA announcer took over, and the teams were introduced. Keli stood there waiting for her name. For the first time in the tournament at the start of a match, she was eager. A couple of games ago she'd wanted to run and hide. Today she was jumping up and down in anticipation. Finally she heard "at outside hitter, 5'11", junior..." Keli didn't wait for the rest before she bolted out to greet her teammates.

Keli noticed the Beaver team sitting a couple of rows off the floor opposite the Dragon bench and sitting right in the middle was Angie. She could feel the heat coming back to her face. Jesse noticed what Keli was looking at. "Hey, Kels, turn it into a positive. Give her something to think about."

She stared back at Jesse and nodded. She put both hands high in the air and Jesse gave her a double high five. They were ready.

Ashley took the ball from the line judge and waited for the referee's signal to service. Keli crouched down and slapped the floor. The whistle blew, and the match to determine their fate was on.

Pendleton handled Ashley's serve and made a play back at the Dragons. The first game was filled with long rallies; every point was hard fought. The Dragons found themselves deadlocked at 22 when Lindsay called a timeout.

Lindsay was calm in the huddle. "Okay, they have a back row setter right now. We can cheat off her...we need a side out right now."

She looked at Ashley. "You need to read their blocks quicker. They are cheating to the outside when our passes are off the net. I want the ball if at all possible to go to Jesse in the middle. We have worked on it...set her a 2 if the ball is off the net. She can handle it. And if it's tight to the net, run a slide. Jesse, if it's a 2, wait and make sure the ball gets in front of you. Don't leave early. Keli, you need to really yell out for the ball and try to pull them to you. Ladies, the pressure is on right now...this next point is huge. We need it."

The Lady Dragons walked back onto the floor. The play was set. But Pendleton had a play of their own. Their setter hit a perfect short ball serve for an ace and the lead, 23-22.

Ashley called them back into the huddle. "Nothing changes. We run the same play. No balls on the floor."

The Dragons lined up again for the serve. This time it was a crazy floater to the right side of the court, and Alix made a great save pass that headed for the middle of the court at the 10-foot line. Keli was screaming with her arm in the air for the ball, Ashley yelled Keli's name out and lofted a perfect set at the net. Jesse met the ball perfectly for the kill. The coach had called it right. The Pendleton front line bit on the read, thinking Ashley had to take the ball outside.

Alix took serve and finished it...the Dragons ran off the final two points, winning the first game, 25-23.

This time Lindsay wasn't nearly as calm, tapping her clipboard. "Ladies, we need to play smarter. Pendleton is a very good team. They are patient and will not force things. Their game plan is to keep the ball in play and wait for us to make mistakes. We need to play smart; they are overplaying us on defense."

She paused for a second. "Ashley, you have to read the overplay and put the ball in the opposite direction. We are very late getting into our spots on the block." She slapped her clipboard. "Bottom line, ladies, we are playing sloppily. This is not the time to take a team lightly. Okay, same team that was just on the floor, go back in. We will start in rotation six, so Ashley can serve first."

Ashley huddled them. "Lindsay is right. We are playing sloppy. Let's get this one!" She put her fist in the air and the other Dragons reached for it and yelled, "OUR GAME!"

The Dragons continued their tournament dominance with a balanced game. Everyone was on and did their part in game two, and in the end, the score was 25-17. They now had run off eight straight games in the tournament, but no one was talking about it. They were gathered around the coach looking for direction.

Keli wiped her sweaty face and took a drink of water while she watched the coach talk about Pendleton's weakness in serve lanes. Lindsay was one step ahead of the team, and being a great coach, she was one step ahead of the match.

For the second time in the tournament, she started a complete new line-up except for Ashley, who stayed to set. The second unit didn't miss a beat, and as with their first two opponents, Pendleton was no longer able to keep the intensity up to win. The Dragons finished them off 25-20 to cap a perfect pool play and a seed into the championship bracket.

When the final point hit the floor, Jesse ran out and hugged Ashley, then stood in the middle of the court with her fist pumped in the air. Libby ran to meet her for a hug. Keli watched the mini-celebration between the three. She realized that they had finally made it to the big dance. After three straight years of coming up here and being denied, the disappointment was finally over for them. A grin crept across her face as she ran out there to greet them.

The players from the Barlow-Aloha match were coming onto the floor as Lindsay yelled for everyone to meet by the tunnel. Keli watched Ashley give a Barlow player a high five as they crossed paths. Ashley took a quick drink of water and explained, "Two years ago we were roommates at the Duck volleyball camp. She's a great player. I'm guessing they will win and we will play them tomorrow in the semis."

Keli looked back over her shoulder at the girl to make sure she remembered her for the next day.

Lindsay was the first to greet them at tunnel. "Make sure to drink something, and then I want you in our team area in the stands to watch this match. We will be playing the winner tomorrow. Save the fun for after the match. It's important to watch this game and understand what we are up against tomorrow. I know they both have watched you and have a pretty good idea of our game. And it's a 10:00 curfew!"

CHAPTER 63

AN UNEXPECTED VISIT

Just before the introductions to the next game, the Dragons reappeared in their sweats and took their seats in the designated area that each team in the tournament was assigned. Keli immediately searched the Bruin team to find Ashley's friend. She felt a tap on her shoulder and turned around to find her mom, Frank, and Tom sitting down behind them.

"So when are you ladies excused so we can go to dinner?" asked Frank, looking at his watch.

Ashley answered. "Coach said we need to stay for the match and then we are free until 10:00."

The conversation was drowned out by the PA announcer voice introducing the teams. Ashley whispered in Keli's ear. "It looks like it will be us against Barlow, and Beaverton will play Redmond in the semis tomorrow. Barlow is awesome. They have made it to the semis every year we've been here, and they won it all my freshman year. It was the next summer that I met Heidi at camp."

Keli whispered back, "So, how much better of a player would I be if I had Heidi setting for me?"

Ashley jerked away. "You know that was cold!" She tried to act serious but the grin on her face was a dead giveaway.

The match took over the conversation. Barlow and Aloha battled back and forth splitting the first two games. In the third game, Aloha got on a run early in the game and opened a huge lead 18-8 before the coach from Barlow called a timeout.

Ashley slouched down in her seat. "The Bruins are playing the same way we played in the first game against Pendleton, except they're playing a much better team. Heidi isn't reading the blocks and their back row is dog-slow rotating. If they don't watch it, they are going to get their butts handed to them."

Keli also slouched down. "You know I saw the same thing. I think I am finally starting to understand it."

The Bruins lost game three by two points but did win game four and game five to get their ticket to Saturday's semis.

Keli looked at Ashley. "You know I'm really tired. I think I am going to pass on dinner."

Ashley nodded. Their parents overheard the conversation and realized it wasn't worth trying to change their minds.

As they walked back to the hotel, it looked like most of the Dragon players had the same idea.

As soon as they entered the room, Keli ran and skidded onto her bed, grabbing the remote. "It's your turn to order. How about Chinese or Thai?"

It didn't take long for Ashley to get the food ordered. "I'm taking a shower. The food will be here in 20 minutes or so."

Can I Play...

Keli didn't pay much attention to Ashley's comments. She was too busy channel-surfing. A few minutes later there was a loud knock at the door. "Wow," she thought to herself. "That was quick". She banged on the bathroom door as she walked by. "Hey, Ash, the food is here. Hurry up!"

"Okay, how much do we owe?" said Keli as she opened the door.

"I'm not the pizza guy," answered Greta. "Though it sounds like I'm just in time for dinner."

Keli stood there like a stone, motionless and speechless.

Greta raised her eyebrows. "By the look on your face, you're surprised to see me."

Still speechless, Keli stepped away from the entrance to let Greta in the room. With a slight hesitation, Greta accepted the gesture and sat down at the small table in the corner of the room. Just then Ashley came out of the bathroom, drying her hair.

"Hey, Ash, long time no see."

Ashley immediately stopped drying her hair. She knew that voice. She slowly pulled the towel away from her eyes.

Greta stood up and walked straight to her offering a hug.

Ashley took a step back stopping Greta in her tracks, while Keli was still holding onto the doorknob staring at the scene.

Greta put her hands on her hips in an almost combative way. "So no hugs? What is up with that?" she asked.

There was another knock. This time it was the delivery guy. Keli waved him in with her free hand. He looked at the receipt. "I need $24."

Ashley broke away from staring at Greta and handed him $30. "Thanks, keep the change," she said and took the food from him.

Greta looked at her. "If you aren't expecting anyone else, maybe you should close the door and come over and eat."

Ashley set the food down and walked over to Keli and pushed the door shut. Then she turned around and said, "What are you doing here? Why now? I don't care if you want to screw up your life, be my guest, but to walk in here like it's some freakin' holiday and mess with the most important day of our lives," pointing to Keli, "Greta, that is just wrong." She stood rubbing her forehead trying to figure out what to do.

"Hey, I'll leave if you feel that way," responded Greta, who headed for the door.

Keli stepped in front of Greta, stopping her a few feet from the door. "Wait! Everyone sit down. Let's figure this out."

She stood there until Greta turned around and headed back towards the table. She pointed at Ashley and motioned her towards the table too. "Okay, Greta, what are you doing here?" she asked. "You have to understand how we feel. You dropped off the earth a couple of months ago and you show up here now. Why today?"

Greta looked down at the table gathering her thoughts. Ashley couldn't sit still fidgeting in her chair and waiting for Greta to answer Keli's question. The room was tense with anticipation of what Greta had to say.

Finally Greta leaned back in her chair and folded her arms across her chest. "I know I shouldn't be here. I know it. I really do," she said. "The truth is I broke up with Austin and ran away from my mom's house. Things got so bad, I couldn't take it anymore. I know I have completely screwed up my life."

She stood up. "I shouldn't be here...I'm sorry." She bolted for the door.

Keli grabbed her by the arm. "Wait! You just can't leave like this now. Let us call Frank, and he can come get you."

Greta immediately said, "No, no way! Frank won't understand. He will..."

Ashley reached for the cell phone on the table and dialed. "Greta, sit your butt down until Dad gets here. Keli is right. You need to talk with him. What else can you do? Run the streets of Portland? Don't be stupid again. The only way to get back on track is to get back on track now."

Frank was already on the other end of the phone. "Ashley, what's going on?"

"Dad, Greta is here in our room. Can you come get her?"

Ashley sat there motionless for a few seconds listening to her dad. Then she hung up. She looked at Greta and Keli standing in the middle of the room. "Dad said he would be here in 10 minutes and he wants you to meet him outside the lobby. He is in the Hummer."

Greta started to cry, and the other girls stood there looking at her, as she slumped to the floor weeping. Ashley finally bent down and said, "Greta, you need to listen to Dad. He'll help you. It's not too late to get things figured out." She put her hand under Greta's arm and gently pulled her to her feet.

"We'll go down with you," offered Keli.

Greta shook her head as she opened the door. "No, you eat your dinner before it gets cold." The door shut behind her gently, and she was gone.

Ashley looked up at the ceiling with her hands folded on the top of her head fighting back the tears, "Wow... I can't believe what just happened. She is right; she should be here with us playing right now. I really miss her; I didn't know how much until just now."

CHAPTER 64

THANKS FOR COMING

The next morning, Coach Lindsay called Keli and Ashley early. "Your father called me last night and told me what happened. I would like to meet with you two after breakfast. I also got a call from Morgan. She and Alix ran into Greta in the lobby while she was waiting for your dad. So, don't be surprised if it's a topic at breakfast this morning. I need you to try and keep it to a minimum. The last thing we need is for everyone to get distracted today. How're you two doing? I am very concerned about all this."

Ashley told the coach they were okay, and she relayed the coach's words to Keli. "Coach wants us to try and keep everyone from talking about it so we don't obsess about it." Ashley pounded her fists into the mattress. "This sucks...Why now?"

Keli could see the anger building inside of Ashley. "Hey now, come on. Keep your head. It happened, so now it's up to you on how you're going to handle it." The coach's speech went through her head. "This is what the coach has been preaching for the past two weeks about adversity. The last thing we need is for you to blow up. I agree with you. It does suck...the timing could not have been any worse but it's in our hands as to how we're going to deal with it."

Ashley forced a smile, "You're right. I know you're right. I need you to keep telling me that today if I start to drift. My head is really messed up right now."

Breakfast came and went without the subject. Lindsay was waiting for them at her table. She stood up as they got to her table. "Why don't we take a walk?" she said, motioning them towards the door. Lindsay nudged her way in between the two as they walked down the hallway towards the lobby.

"I know last night must have really been tough for you two, especially you, Ashley. I'm not here to tell you not to think about it or worry about it, because family is surely more important than a volleyball game. I will say that Greta is in the best hands possible right now. Your dad has her. Today is your day...you have worked for this, you have dreamed for this. I know Greta wants you both to have your day. The last thing she wants is to think she was guilty of causing you to not play your best because of her."

They stopped just inside the lobby away from the other guests roaming around. "Ladies, you don't want this day to end with you second-guessing yourselves. We have a match in less than three hours. Get prepared for yourselves and your team. That is all you have to do, and it's all you can do. When today comes to an end, you can choose what is next."

She turned and faced them. "Do you understand what I am trying to say?" Her eyes went back and forth between the two. A slight smile appeared on her face. "Ladies, days like today rarely come for most athletes. I hope you make the most of it. I can promise you this...regardless of the outcome, you will carry today with you for the rest of your lives. You have a chance to make it very special." Lindsay winked at them and walked back down the hall towards the team banquet room.

"Hey, Keli!" came from across the lobby. There was Sticky, waving his hand.

Keli screamed, "Sticky," and ran straight to him and gave him a bear hug. Sticky stared at Ashley and rolled his eyes at Keli's behavior. He gently pulled back from her. "So you guys are in the finals...very cool."

Ashley corrected him. "Actually we are in the semis. We need to win that to play in the championship tonight."

Keli looked around the lobby, hoping to see others from Falls City. "So who did you come with?" she asked him.

He shrugged. "I came by myself. There is a lot going on back home and..."

Keli didn't care at that moment. "I'm just glad you're here. You have no idea how happy it makes me." Then she said, "We play at 3:00. What are you going to do until then?"

"I might just go over and watch some of the other matches, I guess."

"No, hang here with us for a while," pleaded Keli.

Ashley shook her head. "Kels, we can't have boys in our room. If Lindsay found out, we would be up a creek. Sorry, Sticky, I hope you understand."

Then she looked at Keli. "Hey, I'm going to go up to the room. I'll see you up there." She gently hit Sticky in the arm. "It's really awesome that you came up. You know, I might have an extra Dragon sweatshirt you can wear," flicking his Mountaineer sweatshirt on her way to the elevator.

Sticky answered, "Thanks for the offer but I am good with this one. Hey, good luck today!"

An immediate awkwardness settled between the two friends as Ashley walked towards the elevator. They looked at each other, then away, both trying to find something to fix their eyes on and hoping the other would start the conversation.

Keli's eyes found two open chairs by the fireplace that was the centerpiece of the lobby area. "Do you want to sit down for a few minutes? I can't be long."

"Sure, that sounds fine," he answered. "I don't want to get in the way."

The awkwardness didn't fade when they sat down.

Again Keli was the first to speak. "Stick, you can't even believe how nice it is to see you." She started to explain why she said what she said but stopped before the words came out.

Sticky slouched down in the overstuffed leather chair. "Do you think you guys can win it all?" he asked.

Keli thought about his question for a second and then looked around the room to see if anyone was listening. "I don't know, I hope so. Some of the girls I play with really, really want it and deserve it." Again, she scanned the room before continuing. "It's kind of weird, Sticky. The deeper we have gotten into all this, the harder it is for me to keep up with it all. It's like the girls on my team and the other teams seem stronger both physically and mentally. I kind of feel like I'm hiding or hanging out where I don't belong. It's hard to describe. Back home I knew how I fit in; here it's just different." She looked back at the fire.

Sticky looked around the room. "It's sure a whole different world we're in right now. I just want you to know," he paused for a second. "I want you to know I am really proud of you for trying. It took a lot for you to go for it. I'm sure you are not being fair to yourself when it comes to fitting in. I've read all the articles and seen a couple of games; I think you fit in pretty good." He looked at his watch. "You should get going."

Keli squinted at the clock across the room by the registration desk. "I have a couple more minutes. So how are things back home? Is everyone down for not making it to state and everything?"

Sticky had never been good at hiding things. His face sank, as did his voice. "Well, things are not as good as they could be, but like everything else it will all get figured out."

"Huh?" asked Keli. "I don't understand what you're talking about, Nicolas Rodewald."

Sticky choked and then laughed, "That's the first time you've called me that since like the first grade or something."

Keli was serious. She put her feet back on the floor and leaned forward. "What's up at home, Sticky? Tell me!"

He looked at his watch again. "Really, it's not important right now. What is important is that you get back with your teammates and prepare to win a State championship." Sticky stood up, his way of saying subject over. He grabbed Keli's hand and pulled her up. Keli sighed, then gave him a high five and a hug before heading for the elevator.

CHAPTER 65

THE SEMIFINALS

Lindsay was the last to walk into the meeting room by the tunnel. All the players were seated and ready for her instructions. Her face was stoical, and her posture was stiff from nerves. "Well, anyone ready to go home?" she asked.

For a second the girls thought she was serious. Jesse was the first to catch on. She stood up and starting walking out saying, "Bye" to add to the joke.

The whole room seemed to lighten up a bit; a few laughs and smiles crossed most of their faces. Still, as a team they were tight. Lindsay and Jim looked at each other, having seen this behavior with teams in the past. Lindsay stood in front of the room thinking for a moment, knowing the team was getting tighter by the second.

Then she went over to the chalkboard behind her and scribbled each girl's name on it. "When I call your name, stand up and close your eyes." She turned around quickly and said, "No peeking. Keep your eyes closed until the last girl's name is called."

She turned back to the names on the list. "Jesse," she called out.

Jesse stood up and closed her eyes. The rest of the team's eyes were darting all over the place from Lindsay to Jesse and back at each other. Lindsay didn't turn around. "Ashley." Ashley stood up and closed her eyes.

By now the girls were beginning to grin and look around with the same curiosity as before it all started. "Alix...Morgan."

Some of the players started to giggle and predict the next name.

Libby yelled out, "Ashley, you peeked." Libby pointed at her. "Hey, I just saw Ashley peek." Ashley clinched her eyes tightly shut but started laughing at the accusations.

Lindsay calmly called out Keli's name. By now, the whole room was laughing. All the girls left sitting were pointing at the standing girls, calling out about them peeking. Jesse finally broke down and opened her eyes. The room exploded.

Lindsay slowly turned around with a quick glance at Jim, who was smiling.

Lindsay climbed up on the desk and sat down cross-legged. The rest of the girls opened their eyes.

Lindsay raised both of her hands above her head. "Okay, okay, everyone have a seat. It's nice to see we are back playing and having a good time." The girls understood what she had just done.

Jesse stood up. "Okay, now I really am ready to go home." She paused for a second, then finished yelling, "With a championship trophy, that is!" She slapped the desktop like it was a drum. "Is everyone with me?"

The rest of the girls started slapping their desktops too. The whole room was euphoric, and Lindsay winked at Jim.

Can I Play...

Lindsay took back over the room. "The only thing that matters from here out, ladies, is that we go out there and play volleyball in the purest way...to have fun. Everyone here loves this game or you wouldn't have worked so darn hard to get here. I saw a team, a team that I love, just play together in here a few minutes ago, and if we carry that with us out that door, I know what the outcome will be."

She looked at the door, and a soft smile came across her face. "Ladies, no X's or O's. You know what to do. Go have fun."

Jesse walked up to the coach and held up her hand. Lindsay gave her a high five, and the rest of the team followed her by the coach and out the door.

Keli was anxious for the match to start and she wanted the ball. No more hiding, she thought to herself. She went up for her last warm-up hit and said it under her breath just as she smashed the ball down hard onto the floor. "No more hiding."

The whistle blew; it was time. The PA announcer took over and announced the first semi-final game of the day: the Dallas Dragons and the defending State champions Barlow Bruins.

Lindsay said only a few words before the team took the court. "Ladies, today is the last day of the fairly tale we started writing a few months ago. Go make it magical."

Barlow had first serve and, like most teams, went straight after Keli, who rotated back to cover serve receive. The difference was that today she wanted the ball. She already knew in her mind that she was going to make a perfect pass.

She did just that. The ball came high and fast, and she barely had time to get her hands up and set before she passed the ball to Ashley. It was perfect. Ashley raised her right hand early to let Keli know to lock and load—the ball was coming.

The whole match was a mirror of the first play. Ashley met the pass just inside the 10-foot line and lofted it across the court. Keli was ready and flew off the floor and met the ball two feet above the net and literally creamed it just to the right of the middle blocker and straight down on the 10-foot line.

No one on the Bruin team had a chance on that play or for the whole match.

The Dragons never let up. The match was over in less than hour. They had climbed the ladder. The championship was only one match away.

There was little celebrating after it was over, and they quickly shook hands with the defeated Bruins. On the way to the meeting room, they crossed paths with the Beavers from Beaverton.

Angie made a point of getting right in Keli's path. "Hey, little girl," she said. "It won't be that easy tonight. Tonight I am taking you to the school of volleyball, according to Trish."

Keli stood there staring at her. Then she smiled back and raised her arms in the air, as if to say, "Bring it on."

As each girl came back into the meeting room, their roaring got more and more deafening. Jim and Lindsay walked in and the girls all calmed down.

"Well, ladies, that was quite the performance out there. You just beat, no, you dominated a very, very good team." Lindsay clapped her hands in applause. "Okay,

235

we want to watch the match getting ready to start and then meet back for dinner. We play at 7:00 o'clock. I want everyone back in this room no later than 6:15."

A few minutes later the Dragons, dressed back in their black-and-red warm-ups, reentered the gym to a loud roar from the fans. Both teams warming up paused for a moment to see why. The crowd had taken on the Dragons as the Cinderella-underdog team and cheered their entrance. The Dragon players looked at each other and waved at the crowd.

Ashley slapped Keli's knee once they sat down. "Great game, chick. You were as good as I've ever seen out there."

Keli blushed. "Thanks. I felt different before the match." She toned her voice down a little so only Ashley could hear. "I think for the first time, I felt as strong and good as everyone else on the court. It's hard to explain..."

Ashley put her hand over Keli's mouth. "Shut up, girl. You belong here."

Beaverton won the first game in a battle 26-24. Keli looked across the court and up into the stands. She could see Sticky, her mom, and Frank. Sitting one row behind them were Tom and Judy, the retired coach. Her mind started to wander to what they were talking about. Finally she pulled herself back to the match. She was surprised when she looked at the scoreboard. Redmond was leading the second game 15-7.

She leaned forward and focused on Trish from the Beavers. She could see she was getting flustered being down. She decided to follow Trish's every move. By the end of the second game, Redmond had taken the Beavers completely out of their game and won the game easily.

Game three started the same way. Keli looked over at Ashley. "We are going to play Redmond in the finals."

"Nope," answered Ashley. "Beaverton will come back. They're too good."

Keli just shook her head but didn't argue. She knew Redmond's strategy now. Keep the ball in play and let the other team press the issue and make mistakes. It was working perfectly; by the end of the third game, Beaverton was mentally done. The harder they pressed, the worse it got.

Redmond won game three 25-18. Ashley leaned over and said, "We're going to play Redmond in the finals" and acted like it was her prediction.

Sure enough, Redmond finished off Beaverton in game 4. Even though she had predicted it, Keli was still surprised. Trish, probably the best player in the state, had fallen into the trap that the coach had been preaching the part two weeks.

The Dragons got to their feet when the match ended. Keli looked at Coach Lindsay, who was a couple of rows below her. "Hey, Coach, would that be a good lesson in adversity?"

Lindsay looked around to see how many players heard Keli's observation, but none had. Lindsay raised her eyebrows and answered, "Textbook."

CHAPTER 66

THE FINALS

The moment had come. The girls were in the tunnel waiting for the third place game to end. Keli leaned against the wall, watching her teammates mill around. She focused on Jesse for a moment and smiled with admiration, then she went from player to player thinking about the year that was ending. Her eyes met up with Coach Jim, who just nodded at her.

She found Lindsay looking at her clipboard, ever scheming and coaching. She stared at her, and as if the coach could sense Keli was looking at her, she looked up. Their eyes locked on each other for a few seconds. Lindsay mouthed five simple words that burned into Keli's heart, "I am proud of you."

Keli's eyes brightened and she mouthed back, "Thank you!"

The final horn blew. It was time.

Redmond and Dallas entered from their respective tunnels. Neither team had been expected to make the finals, but they both had.

Warm ups seemed to fly by. Then Keli stood bouncing up and down in place waiting for her name to be called. She looked up into the stands and found Tom grinning right at her. He reached up and slowly took off his baseball cap and looked upwards and then nodded at her.

Just then she heard it. "Starting at outside hitter, number 21, Keli Stennes."

She ran onto the court, hugging each of her teammates, then turned to face her bench. Without thinking, she too looked up and said quietly to herself, "This one is for both of us."

Lindsay's instructions were brief. "Ladies, we have already talked about this. Redmond is very patient. They will dig everything and keep putting the ball back on our side of the net. We have to be patient when we don't have a kill opportunity."

Redmond played just that way. Their defense always seemed to be right on the swing plane. Ball after ball, they dug it up and kept it in play. The first game was a battle, and neither team could muster more than a 2-point lead until Keli took a set from Ashley. She made her approach to take the ball cross-court, and as she jumped, she could see the defense was there and ready. At the last minute, she tried to take the ball down the line and took her eye off the ball. What resulted was a bad miss hit that was both wide and long.

Redmond now had the serve and a 23-20 lead. Lindsay called timeout. Keli and the rest of the team made their way into the huddle. Keli dropped her head. She didn't want to make eye contact with the coach or any of her teammates.

Lindsay recognized it and snapped at her, "Stennes, get your head up. Next time, do not take your eye off the ball on the line shot."

Keli lifted her head. Lindsay's eyes were lasered in on her. Keli nodded, "You're right, Coach. I got it next time."

They went back onto the court. Ashley huddled them up. "Okay, we need side out right now. Jesse, look for a slide. And Keli, you need to call hard for a four. Let's see if we can get them out of position."

It all worked perfectly, except this time Jesse hit the ball long.

They huddled up again. Ashley barked out, "Okay, we need to make a play. Come on, ladies, we can get this game. We need the serve back. Let's go!"

They didn't get the serve back. Redmond's setter hit a perfect short serve and caught the Dragons on their heels. Game one to the Panthers, 25-20. The Dragons had just lost their first game of the tournament and it couldn't have come at a worse time.

Lindsay tried to stay calm. She knew they needed game two. Redmond was sneaky good and she knew it. They had the best defense her players had faced all year. She looked at the girls huddled around her. "Okay, we're fine," she said. "We need to continue to pound away at them." She laughed. "They can't get them all."

Jesse shook her head and said, "They have so far."

Game two was a carbon copy of game one, both teams determined to win. Redmond again built a 2-point lead late, 21-19. In almost the same situation, Keli went up for a cross-court and at the last second changed her mind, taking her eye off the ball and hitting it into the net.

Lindsay was furious. She called a timeout and met Keli on the court. "We just talked about this last game. If you're going to change your shot, what do you need to do?"

Keli wanted to look away but she knew she couldn't. "I know, Coach, I know. Sorry."

Lindsay turned and walked back to the huddle. Keli followed her. Ashley moved over and whispered in Keli's ear, "Hang in there. You'll get the next one."

Keli's mind went to the Beaverton match; it was their turn to face it.

Lindsay was diagramming the Panther defense. Keli barged right in. "It's adversity, Coach. Textbook. We are right where Beaverton was this afternoon. It's adversity and to this point we haven't figured out how to come out on the other side." She realized that she had just cut off the coach and grimaced. "Hey, Coach, I'm sorry for interrupting. I..."

Lindsay lowered her clipboard to her side and looked at Keli. The whole team didn't know what was going to happen next.

"She's right," responded Lindsay. "I have to admit I got caught up in it too. We just need to close our eyes for a minute." Lindsay stood there with her eyes shut, and the team laughed when she peeked. She opened them back up. "Sometimes it's hard to see when the walls close in around you, no matter how prepared you think you are." She smiled and put her hand in the air...all the girls grabbed it.

Lindsay slowly looked around at each one of them. "I think we are ready to play now."

The Dragons walked back on the court. There was a sense of calm, a matter-of-factness about it all.

Can I Play...

Ashley called out the play, and they all found their spots for the serve. The serve came short again. Libby hit the floor and pancaked the ball straight up. Ashley made a perfect bump set out to Keli, who was ready. This time she smashed the ball down the line, hitting the Panther playing up for the tip in the shoulder, and the ball went out of bounds. Point Dragons.

Alix grabbed the ball to serve. She looked at Jim, who called for a two, trying to give the Panthers a little of their own medicine. The serve was perfect. For the first time in the match, the Panthers weren't sure who was going to take the ball, and in the end no one did. Point Dragons.

The Panthers moved in a step and got it straight as to who would take the serve if she went back there again. This time Jim called for a one, and Alix responded with a hard topspin that was too much for the Panther back right to handle. Point Dragons.

They were tied, and the Redmond coach called timeout. The Dragons raced over to Lindsay. She bent down a little and said, "I wonder if their coach has his eyes closed." It was all she needed to say. The Dragons went back out and finished game two with three straight points.

Game three was all Dragons. Keli and Jesse were too much for them; both girls added five kills to their totals. When it was over, it was Dragons 25 Panthers 18.

Lindsay was a lot more serious now. "Ladies, make no mistake. The Panthers are going to come out fired up. They know they have to win this game." She pounded her clipboard. We do not want to take this match to a tiebreaker. Let's finish this now!"

Like games one and two, game four seesawed back and forth. Redmond ran off three straight points to tie the game at 23. Lindsay yelled for a timeout. The huddle was tight. "Ladies, everyone who steps out there has to be ready to win the next point." She put the clipboard against her chest and raised her eyebrows. "It's the next point, ladies. You need to find a way to win it."

Both teams went back on the court, with everyone knowing how important the point was. The Panther server calmly tossed the ball in the air on the referee's whistle. The ball dove over the net, and Morgan and Alix both dove on the floor attempting to bring it back up, but neither did. The Panthers screamed in confidence.

Lindsay started to call another timeout, but Jim stopped her. "Let them play," he said quietly.

Again the Panther coach called for the same spot, and again she found it. But this time Alix had cheated a step and it was enough to get the ball up in the air. Ashley had to chase the ball out of bounds and set it back over her head, and the Dragons could do nothing but free ball it back over.

The Panthers were ready to even the match. The pass was tight to the net, and their setter jumped high and set it perfectly to their best player who hammered the ball right into Libby's arms. And Libby made the biggest block kill of her career.

That evened the score at 24-24. Ashley took the serve and looked over at the coach, asking to jump serve. But Jim shook his head no, and Ashley's eyes got big and said "I got it, Coach, I got it." He looked at Lindsay, who nodded and said, "It's their game. Let her do it."

Ashley backed up about 10 feet. The ref blew the whistle, and she tossed the ball high in the air and took off leaping just back of the line and hammered a wicked topspin ball. The libero was right there and passed the ball up, but the serve was so hard, she over-passed it straight to Keli, who smashed almost straight down. The Dragons had the lead for the championship.

Jim yelled to Ashley to make sure to put it into play. Ashley did just that; she didn't press her luck and so hit her normal serve. Redmond covered it and, like the whole tournament, played conservatively, not wanting to make a mistake.

Keli was right there for the weak kill shot. Her pass was tight to the net, and Ashley jump set it to the outside, passing up the one. Keli had to hurry to get there; she exploded off the floor and went cross-court as hard as she could swing. It was enough. The ball split the two Panther players for match point.

The Dragons had just won! Keli was mobbed by her teammates. Jesse and Libby were crying, and Ashley had Keli in a headlock. The glass slipper fit, and the fairytale was complete.

After the presentation of the trophy, Lindsay called all the girls over. Her face was red and her eyes were still filled with tears. "Thank you. It's been an honor to have been part of this with you." Her face softened a bit, "You committed to this a long time ago and faced every challenge like the champions that you are." She put her hand in the middle. "I am proud of each one of you. Never forget this moment. You all earned it."

There wasn't a dry eye on the team.

CHAPTER 67

GOODBYE COACH

Keli pulled out of her driveway and looked over at the Lady Dragon bag in the seat beside her. Her mind wandered through the past few months with a bit of ambivalence. The season was over. "Now what?" she thought.

The drive down Main Street in Falls City was quiet. As she passed the school, she couldn't help but rubberneck, hoping to see Sticky or any of her friends. The ride was different today and she could feel it.

As she pulled into the parking lot at Dallas High, a cold chill came over her. What if somehow Ashley was different? Who was she going to have lunch with? What was she going to do after school? The reality of the rest of the year was hitting her right between the eyes.

Yet she grinned when she saw a banner across the entrance of the school: *2005 State Volleyball Champions!*

Some of the students smiled at her as she entered, and Steen was standing in the same spot as the first day of school, holding a rose. He held it out to her, "I'm sorry I couldn't be there to watch."

Keli shrugged her shoulders and took the rose. "I understand. Don't worry about it."

Steen could sense she was down. "Is everything okay?"

She smelled the rose and smiled a bit sadly. "It's Monday and volleyball season is over."

The first bell rang. Steen picked up his backpack off the floor and said, "So you know we can have lunch together today."

Keli laughed. "You're right. We can. I'll see you then."

Ashley was waiting for her after first period. She too was down. "This sucks. What are we going do now? It's over." She pushed Morgan as she walked by and yelled it again. "It's over!" She grabbed Keli's arm. "You have to promise me that nothing changes between you and me."

It was just what Keli needed to hear. She smiled. "Come on, we need to get to class," and she threw her arm around Ashley's neck.

Steen was waiting for her after 4th period. "Wow, we really get to have lunch today with no threats against my life?"

They found a spot in the corner of the busy cafeteria and sat down. Steen pulled out the wrinkled note and waved it in front of her nose. "Let me see what this says," he slowly unfolded it, Keli was already giggling. He teasingly cleared his throat, "It says that after volleyball season, the answer is yes!" He peeked around the side of the note. "Is it still yes?"

Her mind went immediately to Sticky for a second; her heart was definitely split. She smiled, "Yes, my answer is still yes."

When the final bell rang, Keli walked into the gym. Most of the players were standing around waiting for JoJo to check in their uniforms. Jesse called for everyone's attention. "We're having an end-of-the-year party at Ashley's house on Friday night. It's a sleepover so bring what you need."

Keli looked around the gym and noticed Coach Lindsay's office light on. She handed her bag to Ashley. "Can you turn this in for me?"

Ashley nodded.

Keli sprinted across the floor. She stopped and paused for a second before entering. Today opening the door felt different. She poked her head around. "Coach, do you have a minute?"

Lindsay didn't even lift her head. "Sure, Keli, come in. I'll be right with you."

Keli could see that Lindsay had already packed everything. A deep sadness of the reality of it all sunk in. Keli knew today was the last time she would be in this office with her.

Lindsay looked up and leaned back in her chair. "Well, how are you doing today?"

Keli slumped down in her chair. "It's strange, Coach. It's all over. Two days ago everything was sky high and now it's empty..." She looked around the office again, "Kinda like your office."

Lindsay sadly smiled back at her. "It is kind of sad, isn't it? If you love the sport like we do, you never want any season to end, especially one like this year. Keli, I want you to know how much I enjoyed having you come and join us this year." She leaned as far forward as she could. "I knew you were a special athlete the moment I met you at the camp recruiting booth. So what's next for you? Are you going to play club ball this winter? I think it's important if at all possible to play. I think you will find the club season in some ways more fun than the school season." The coach laughed a little. "More games and less practice."

Keli grinned and then frowned, "I don't think it's going to be possible." She put her hands on top of her head. "There is no way Mom and me can afford it. But who knows, I never thought I would be here six months ago either."

That comment made them both smile. Lindsay softly finished the topic, "Well, Keli, whatever happens, you will always be in my thoughts and prayers."

"So how about you, Coach? When do you leave?"

"Tomorrow. I need to get settled in over there and see what I have to work with. The program has fallen on a few tough years. Jim and I have our work cut out for us."

Lindsay could see Keli cringe when she told her this last news. She scribbled down her phone number and email address and slid it across the desk. "If you ever need anything, you call me! I want emails weekly keeping me posted on how you're doing."

Keli forced a grin and nodded. "Coach, I want to thank you for believing in me and giving me a chance to play. When I walked into this office a few months ago, you gave me your time and knowledge. I will always be grateful."

Lindsay laughed. "We have spent a lot of time in here, haven't we? I think we wore out the blackboard over there. Keli, just so you know, coaches like me dream of having kids like you...some of us never get the opportunity. I'm the lucky one."

It was time. Keli stood up and folded the coach's phone number and then stuck out her hand.

"No way!" Lindsay stood up and came around the desk and gave Keli a hug. "You stay in touch, okay?"

Keli nodded as Lindsay opened the door for her. Walking out of the office was painful for both of them. She wondered when she heard the door shut behind her if she would ever see the coach again.

On the other side of the door, Lindsay was wiping tears from her own eyes.

CHAPTER 68

IT CAN'T BE TRUE

Ashley raced over to Keli. She still had her cell phone glued to her ear. "Just a second, Dad. Keli, you are not going to believe this..."

"What? What's going on?"

Ashley hung up her phone and took a deep breath. "My dad said he heard that tomorrow's paper is going to..." Ashley stopped and took another deep breath. "It's going to say that Falls City High School is closing after this year!"

Keli was in shock. "Oh my God! Is he sure?"

Ashley nodded.

Keli headed for the door. "I've got to go."

Ashley chased after her, "What are you going to do?"

"I don't know, but I need to go home. I'll call you later."

Ashley knew it was time to back off. "Okay, go do what you need to do. Call me later or I'll come out there to see you."

The phone at the restaurant was busy, and she tried Tom's house with no luck either. Her mind raced as she drove towards home. She dialed Sticky's house but again no answer. She slammed the steering wheel.

The next 10 minutes were a blur. All she could think about was getting to the restaurant as quickly as she could. As she drove down Main Street, she could see dozens of cars parked in front of the little restaurant. She knew everyone was there.

Keli left the phone on the seat beside her and ran over. The door clanged loudly. The restaurant was packed. She could see her mom by the cash register.

Cindy looked up and frowned at her sadly.

Keli pushed her way through the room to her mom. "What's going on?"

Frank was sitting on Keli's favorite stool answered, "It looks like they are going to have to shut the school."

Cindy nodded, "It looks like that's happening. The school board had an emergency meeting this morning, and there isn't enough money to keep it running after this year."

"Mom, this can't happen," she looked around the restaurant. "Do you know where Sticky and the rest of the gang are?"

Jack was calling out for Cindy to serve orders. "I gotta go, honey. We're going to have to talk about this tonight. If I had to guess, your friends are probably at the gym. Basketball practice starts today or tomorrow."

Keli was out the door and headed for the gym. Her mom was right. She pulled into the parking lot and walked into the gym. No one was playing; everyone was sitting around by the concession stand.

Charlee looked up at her and said, "Why don't you just turn around and leave? You're not welcome in our school!"

Her words weren't the biggest dagger. Keli's eyes were fixed on Tanya leaning up against Sticky. He had both of his arms wrapped around her.

She started to feel her face heat up, and yet she couldn't take her eyes off of them.

Charlee noticed and giggled. "Hey, Tanya, watch out. The city girl might pick a fight."

Keli regained her composure. She realized now what Sticky had wanted to talk to her about at the tournament, and she felt a twinge of sadness. Her eyes met up with Tanya's and she smiled a little at her. Then she looked over at Charlee.

There was an uncomfortable silence. Finally Sticky said, "Shut up, Charlee!"

Keli took over the conversation. "It's my town and school too." She was still looking right at Charlee. "It's time to stop this stupid fight, Charlee. If you don't want to be my friend anymore, that's fine, but there's no need to continue fighting."

Keli sat down next to Sticky and Tanya. "I just heard the news. We can't let this happen. What can I do to help?"

Sticky started to answer her when the gym door opened again. Ashley walked in; she could see all the kids sprawled on the floor. She looked at Sticky and Tanya, then at Keli.

Everyone was staring at her, but Ashley didn't take her eyes off of Keli. "Hey, I want to help. You guys shouldn't have to lose your school."

Charlee opened her mouth, but Sticky again interrupted her. "Charlee, either shut up or leave yourself."

He looked at Ashley and smiled. "Have a seat. We're just getting started."

J. Dillard

Can I Play...

Hey, sorry it's not Coach Lindsay here. She is off on her new adventure, and hopefully, we will catch up with her in the future.

I'm **Coach Dillard**. Yes, I too am a coach. I have been working with young athletes since, hmmm...let me see, since...wow, 1975! My coaching experience is both on the boys' and girls' sides of the gym and both basketball and volleyball. I also know the competitive world from the athlete's viewpoint. I too was an aspiring athlete with an abundance of God-graced talents.

I thought I would give you my views on being an athlete and playing on a team. In fact, I'd like to talk about **the difference between the Super Elite player and all the rest**.

Let's start with what I see when I travel around to tournaments and gyms coaching and watching a lot of you play. Most of you are all technically sound players, and that is a great start! So, what is that separates you from the super elite players out there?

Size? Nope. You may think they're all 6'2", but they're not!

Here is what I've seen. First, as the years of play pile on, players become desensitized to their coaches, especially in certain areas. The one I am talking about in particular is the mental side of the game. How many times have you heard the words "focus" and "concentrate"?

Do you recognize this from one of Coach Lindsay's talks with Keli? There's a good reason for that. This is a huge part of going to the next level. I believe it's the key. Why does the elite player always seem to be in the right spot to make the play?

By the time you're a sophomore, you're mostly done growing up physically, but you are usually just starting to grow up mentally and that includes your ability to really focus.

Most players I see can rarely hold on to the word "focus," when the coach says it, for more than a few seconds. Somewhere along the line we shut it out. I think we then begin to self-coach ourselves and start thinking we know as much as the coach. Me included.

In some ways, that can be corrected. No one knows more positively than you do if you're focused or not. No one knows better than you do if you're giving it your all. No one knows better than you do if you really want to be out there.

Here is the problem. We accept less of ourselves than we are capable of. We lie or minimize the importance of focus to ourselves. It's a part of practice that is easily faked, and we become experts at faking it. In the book, Coach Jim tells Keli that most kids only practice a fraction of the time they are actually on the court.

This is true. Every time your mind wanders, every time you stare off at someone walking through the gym instead of studying the game, you have left practice. Your body is there, of course, but the most important part of you, your brain, is gone and for some players, way gone. They hardly show up at all. You know the ones I'm talking about. They are constantly jabbering about this boy they met or work or music or some other topic that should be left at the door and picked back up on the way out.

So I think we can start to understand the difference between the super elite and the rest. The super elite are the ones who have found a way to discipline themselves to truly stay at practice or in a game. By doing so, they have taught themselves something that sets them apart. I will get to that in just a few seconds. I have a little more browbeating to do first!

Yes, we leave the game right in the middle of a play sometimes! Why? Most of us won't admit it but it's just you and me here right now, and you know I'm right! Dang, I've done it. Everyone has, but it's the elite player who has learned to keep it to the absolute minimum.

Some players will use the excuse that they will be focused when the game comes around. Sorry, that's not possible. Don't mistake being more serious with being focused. They aren't the same thing, in fact, not even close.

For those of you scratching your heads, let's make sure we understand the difference between acting serious and being focused.

Here's an example of acting serious (note the word "acting"). Coach yells, "Taylor, focus!" and Taylor stops laughing and telling her story about her date from the night before. Here's another. The coach stands up from her seat and looks down the bench and catches Taylor and Megan talking during the game. Megan sees the coach and stops talking and starts watching the game. This isn't focus, it's acting serious. In fact, it's faking, plain and simple.

Focus, on the other hand, is being completely in tune with what is going on around you. You can't just stop talking and all of a sudden be in tune with everyone and everything. It's not possible. Being focused takes a tremendous amount of hard work and is tiring for those who don't practice it.

That's the problem with it. It's tiring, just like running lines. We all understand running lines and hate it. Why? Because it's hard and tiring. So we whine and loaf when we think we can get away with it. Again, me included. And since focus is hard and tiring, we loaf at that too. We get good at faking it. How? We put on our serious face. It looks kinda the same, doesn't it?

The elite player has fought through this. She has mastered the ability to focus and stay in tune at practice and during the game. It has taken her a lot of hard hours of practice learning how to do it. These are the players who check everything else at the door like we talked about and go about practice working, watching, listening, asking questions, analyzing, and pushing themselves.

Desire is the main ingredient in mastering this part of your athletic talent. Don't kid yourself either. Learning to focus needs to be mastered the same as a jump serve, a 4-step approach, or a back set. It easy to see when a player hasn't mastered the 4-step approach; they look awkward or funny. Even the novice spectator can see it.

Focus is something that we can hide with our serious face, but for those who have mastered it, they can tell when someone isn't in tune just as even a novice can tell when a player is attempting their first jump serve.

The most evident flaw in our lack of focus is reaction time.

Here it is: The difference between the super elite and the rest of the players is reaction time. Your brain needs to be trained to tell your body what to do when it realizes what is going to happen. For those who don't practice it and fake it, they are a half step slower getting to a ball or leaving the ground to attack or block. They haven't mastered the transfer of information to action! Why? Because they haven't practiced staying focused enough.

How many times have your feet been glued to the floor and you watched a play, then all of sudden you're now involved, but it's too late? After it's over, you kick yourself and tell yourself and your teammates that you'll get the next one. It's the moment of transfer. Your brain sees it, but you haven't developed the ability to transfer it to action. The only way to accomplish it is by truly being focused, staying tuned in.

Another way to describe this is that the player has become a spectator on the court, no different than one in the stands. The non-elite player is constantly shifting from being a player to being a spectator while she is on the floor. When she becomes a spectator, her transfer-to-action ability relaxes and she can't get back to being a player quick enough.

The elite player, on the other hand, rarely becomes a spectator on the floor. That is why the elite player always seems to be in the right place making the play. That is why the super elite player seems to always be in front of the ball on a kill shot digging it up, versus a less focused player who makes a stab to her left or right. The elite player also seems to be able to do something with any kind of set. You know, when the rest of the players are yelling over at the setter telling them where they need the ball and the elite player just plays it.

The elite player has trained herself to read and react at a level that puts her into this category, a category that the rest look at in awe. The truth is that the next level is attainable for many more players if they would just practice the mental side of the game instead of faking it.

It's not easy, but if you truly have the desire, it is attainable. Some of you still reading might now being saying to yourselves, "Yeah but..." Stop right there.

The ability to learn to focus far exceeds the boundaries of being an athlete. It's one of the main things you can take with you when you leave the competitive volleyball court. It's something that will truly help you with many areas of your life. Whether it's your career or being a parent, being in tune, truly in tune, is a skill that can make you elite for life!

I challenge you to practice it. Don't get me wrong. It's hard. It really is. That's why most players don't. But if you dedicate a season to it, I promise you, the rewards will be worth it.

Please visit my website www.stickyrocks.com from time to time. I will post my thoughts on other subjects, like these:

- Being a teammate
- Handling adversity
- Is volleyball the right sport for me?
- How to handle a coach
- How to make everyone around you better
- Being a role player
- But Coach, I want to be a hitterr
- Priorities

Oh yeah, a couple of things about my next book, **WE CAN PLAY**. In this sequel, Keli's world is evolving so fast that something has to give. Find out what happens with Falls City High, the Sticky and Steen heart tug, and Keli and Ashley's chance to become sisters.

So much is going on that I wish I could tell you right now! Okay, here's one hint. Keli does get to play club, but you won't believe who she's playing with! And I'm a little concerned about whether Cindy and Frank are moving too fast. And oh yeah, what the heck is Ashley doing in the Falls City gym anyways?

I sincerely hope you enjoyed my first book.

My best wishes for you and your family always! And, hey, if we run into each other at a tournament, please say hi. It would be fun to watch you play!

J. Dillard

Can I Play...

Author J. Dillard

Read the whole series!

We Can Play!
Final Point... the conclusion

Future Book

Greta... the road back!

CAN I PLAY? T-Shirts are now available!

www.stickyrocks.com